HELL

UNDER THE
UNITED STATES

RICHARD REZENDES

First Stillwater River Publications Edition

ISBN: 978-1-955123-55-6

Library of Congress Control Number: 2021920717

1 2 3 4 5 6 7 8 9 10
Written by Richard Rezendes
Published by Stillwater River Publications,
Pawtucket, RI, USA.

Hell Under the United States

CONTENTS

1. Volcano Under New York City...1
2. The Blue Hills Mini Eruption 8
3. Volcano Under New York City Part Two 20
4. Major Volcano Eruption in Vermont 30
5. Volcanoes Waking Up in Washington State.......................... 58
6. The West Coast Blowjob!... 90
7. The Mount Shasta Warning 107
8. The Volcanic Weather Aftermath..117
9. The Evacuation Shelters...140
10. The Alaskan Blowjob 152
11. The East Coast Big Booms in Blackstone, Mass................. 168
12. The Mystery Volcanoes in New England.............................175
13. Volcano Under New York City Part Three 204
14. The Blue Hills Volcano Two...222
15. Blowjobs in Florida 255
16. Ground of the Devil: The Gates from Hell...........................271
17. Ground of the Devil: The Gates from Hell Part Two........278

About the Author... *290*

CHAPTER ONE

VOLCANO UNDER NEW YORK CITY

July 18, 2007

Early in the morning buses and yellow cabs were crowding the streets in Upper Manhattan on 41st Street and Lexington Avenue. People were walking in all directions as New York City was waking up, everyone going to work.

It was a peaceful morning and everyone was going through their normal routine, then at 6:40 a.m., *boom!!* a blast came out of nowhere! The streets exploded like a volcano, sending a geyser of scalding hot water from under 41st Street.

People thought a volcano had erupted under New York City—actually a steam pipe under the city streets burst. The blast blew buses, yellow cabs, cars and trucks, and people high into the sky and through glass windows. People were burned by the hot water and scalding hot steam blowing out of the huge sinkhole. People and cars were blown into storefront windows. The blast broke several windows and triggered a 3.5 earthquake.

Trains and subways were arriving at Grand Central Station when the blast blew windows out, sending screaming people running for cover. People were blown off their feet, running all over and falling on one another. Nobody expected what happened; it was *boom!*, then people, cars, and buses blown in the air! It was *boom!* then *crash!* just like that!

People ran down city streets fearing another terrorist attack! The streets began flooding and it looked like the Grand Rapids. People were running in all directions trying to get away as the NYPD and the fire department arrived to see the shocking eruption still pouring out of the blast site. Buildings and subways were flooded and trains and transportation came to a stop.

The NYPD thought it was 9/11 all over again! When the NYPD, fire trucks, and rescue crews got to the scene, yellow cabs, buses, and trucks were washing down city streets and screaming people were being burned alive!

"Oh, my fuckin' God! We have a volcano erupting on 41st Street! City streets are flooded and a geyser with hot water, steam, dirt, and rocks is blasting out of a crater in the middle of the intersection of 41st Street and Lexington Ave.! Please send help, we need rescue vehicles! Many people are hurt; we need helicopters, we need 911 assistance. Another terrorist attack may have happened, threatening to blow Manhattan off the map! Mayday, mayday, mayday! We need help in a hurry! Car #11, Officer John Johnson, over!"

Later the water was shut off, though steam was still blowing out of the crater it made, along with dirt and rocks. Then gas lines ruptured. Fire and steam came pouring out like lava from a volcano. City streets were flooded under six feet of water. When the water receded, the firemen moved in to put fires out. The city gas was shut off and the flooding waters went back where they came from: the crater beneath 41st.

Lexington Avenue rescue vehicles arrived to remove the injured and the dead from. People were blown through windows and cars landed on top of some of them. One man's head was blown off; others were cut by glass from being thrown through windows. Some victims had drowned and many others were seriously burned.

Dive teams went into the crater to find out the cause. It was a steam pipe disaster. Later the divers were done, now work had to be done to put in new steam pipes. Later in the day there was a *boom!*, then a louder **boom!** then a blast of rocks, dirt, and compressed air, smashing more windows in nearby buildings. Pressure valves needed to be turned off before more explosions happened.

The area was closed off with police tape: a crater about fifty feet deep. Giant rats blown out of the crater—as big as medium size dogs!—were running down city streets. Other rats were found dead in the streets from drowning. Subways were flooded and trains below were buried.

Then it was a search for survivors. The area looked like a bomb went off and glass, sand, dirt, and rocks littered city streets. The National Guard was called in to help with the disaster.

City workers started fixing the broken pipe and a volcano crew was called in to do an investigation to see if it was an underground volcano that caused the steam blast.

A meeting was held with city workers to determine if a volcano was the cause of the steam pipe blast.

"Good evening, my name is Edward Fay, head of NASA's volcano investigators. The steam pipe blast was caused by pressure in the ground that could be a sign of a volcanic eruption in the future. We found out pressure from sea water mixing with limestone, and heat from the pipes below the city streets, subways, and waterways had something to do with pressure from old pipes. Those things need to be replaced every forty to sixty years.

"We have not found any signs of a magma chamber or lava from an underground volcano but that doesn't mean there isn't one. We will monitor the situation because you do have a fault line directly under Manhattan.

"Here's a diagram of what we found: The fault line is far below the blast zone, but pressure from the fault line can build underground to cause problems like this. You can have so much pressure building from underground until there's an explosion because it has to go somewhere. You're lucky it didn't happen in the middle of the Hudson or Manhattan could be flooded right now."

"Sir, do we have a volcano here or not?!" asked a policeman.

"You do not have a volcano here but we need to take measurements! There's a seventy-three-foot wide blast hole and a sixty-four-foot crater from the blast zone; that's a lot of pressure from underground. A steam pipe blast is not going to blow a hole like this; the pressure is coming from somewhere! You have gas lines ruptured, you have layers of dirt and rocks blown out of the hole, and God only knows if you will have more explosions in the future. The next thing will be trying to find the breaks before you have more eruptions!" said Edward Fay.

"Ladies and gentlemen, we have to shut down all of Midtown to get this piping fixed and more areas will be dug up and closed off. All transportation will be stopped—the subway system in all of Manhattan will close down, and Grand Central Station will be closed until the steam pipe is fixed and the hole is filled in.

"This is not the first time we've had steam pipe blasts in New York City; it has happened before, but nothing like this. The NYPD thought we had another terrorist attack so we had to send a bomb squad in to investigate, but no bombs were found.

"The blast site resembles a bomb attack or a volcano eruption because this was the biggest explosion in New York since 9/11. Many people were seriously hurt, some died, and many people got seriously burned. People, autos, buses, and trucks were blown through buildings, and millions of windows were broken in mid-Manhattan.

"Many buildings will be closed until further notice, until the mess gets cleaned up and windows and damages can be repaired. We have a big mess out here and it's going to take some time to get back to normal. We have millions of dollars' worth of damage. A volcano crew will be here to monitor earthquakes or possible activity and their office will be located in the sub-basement of the Empire State Building. My name is Officer Rocky Cappuccino, NYPD, thank you."

"Good evening, my name is Eric Epicenter from the Environmental Steamfitter Company. We have a big pipe to fix below and it's more than one thousand feet long and twenty-seven feet wide. We have a hole more than sixty feet deep and it's going to be filled in with gravel and stone. We'll cement the area around the new piping to keep it in place. Stone and dirt will be dumped in this big hole and packed and graded off, followed by a black-top finish before the intersection can be rebuilt.

"All these plans will have to be finished within a month because the water will be turned off for a long time here in mid-Manhattan. Thank you."

The city workers were speedily getting their plan together because this was going to be a big job. Two days after the meeting the area of the blast site was dark and looters were getting into damaged buildings. The National Guard was on standby to catch these motherfuckers, shooting them.

One man smashed a jewelry case taking watches, pearls, diamond rings, etc. He was pistol-whipped across the side of the head and knocked unconscious by a guardsman before police arrested him. A man was stuffing clothes into a duffel bag in one of the stores and he was shot dead by police.

The next day reality set in. Buildings were so damaged it looked like a bomb hit and the National Guard was policing the damaged areas. Work crews went in the crater, getting ready to move old piping, and thirty-wheel trucks were bringing in new pipes to replace the old. Water, gas, and electricity were shut off for a while and stores, restaurants, and the workforce were shut down.

The city worked at cleanup and rebuilding 24/7 to get mid-Manhattan running again. Cruise ships were used as hotels, housing, and hospitals until 41st Street and Lexington Avenue recovered. Heavy rain and thunderstorms for three days didn't help. The workers worked under floodlights during the night. A volcano crew was setting up a post with monitoring equipment lining all the underground of Manhattan and Long Island. They settled in Room 007 in the sub-basement of the Empire State Building.

The crew flew in from Houston, Texas and bused to their destination on 34th Street.

"Welcome ladies and gentlemen, welcome to New York City. My name is Edward Fay, the head of NASA's volcanologists, and we are here to investigate a possible volcano under New York City. About a week ago there was a steam pipe explosion blasting a crater about sixty to seventy feet deep, and a sinkhole about eighty feet wide. The blast killed eleven people, injured about two hundred, and destroyed buildings.

"I believe we have a volcano underground somewhere in Manhattan. The pressure from that blast was so strong that it indicates that we may have an underground volcano, but we cannot tell the public here until we find out for sure. There is no magma chamber and no lava tubes, but we do have a major fault line under New York City.

"We have six people including me. Linda Brew and Katrina House will monitor computer screens, monitoring equipment, and TV screens throughout the process. I will give the instructions. Nathan Rivers and Paul Numbnutts, you two will be using equipment such as spudweb and getting news reports and going into volcanoes just like you did in Mexico. Any volcano that erupts in the United States, it's our job to track down, from earthquakes to eruptions! David Dunkin, you will be filing news reports and monitoring earthquakes.

"Remember, no information you find will go out to the public without checking with me first. If we find something, we do not tell anyone until we are sure the real thing is happening," said Edward Fay.

The crew started setting up monitoring equipment leading to all the subways, street sewers, underground treatment plants, and waterways, looking for lava tubes and steam vents. The crew worked with spudweb, a robot used to go inside volcanoes to check data and monitor earthquakes. NYPD and firemen were there listening and getting instructions from the NASA crew.

"Mr. Fay, my name is Lieutenant Bowa Bowser from the NYPD. Just suppose we have a volcano here, what do we do?"

"If you start getting multiple earthquakes and steam vent blasts, that's a sign that one may be brewing."

"Sir, we didn't have an earthquake; it was blast right out of the ground, a geyser. Dirt, rocks, mud, and whatever came out of a hole from city streets to hell!" said Lieutenant Bowser.

"This is why we are here. The steam pipe eruption caused a lot of damage. The reports we have showed strong energy pressure coming from deep underground caused such an explosion! We're here to find out why.

"First I said it is possible an underground volcano could have been the cause because of how severe the blast was, but we can't say it's a volcano until we find out why so much pressure caused these pipes to burst. These steam pipes are huge and it takes a lot to cause an eruption like this. A volcanic eruption could blow Manhattan off the face of the earth. This blast blew up an intersection, but why was it so wide and so deep? We have the equipment to find the cause. If we find out it was caused by an underground volcano, prepare for a massive evacuation because you might have a hell of a lot more damage in the future. In the meantime sit and wait until we find out what's going on," said Edward Fay.

No volcano was found. City workers filled in the crater and NASA stayed put in case something happened.

CHAPTER TWO

THE BLUE HILLS
MINI ERUPTION

January 11, 2011

Canton, Massachusetts started getting earthquakes and the problem went on for two months. Boston also felt the ground shake a few times. On that day, the ground shook in Milton. It was a cold icy day and a snowstorm was coming.

A police car was parked in the Blue Hills parking lot and the officer could feel his car shaking and moving. He heard the rocks rolling underground and the sounds of thunder. He started the car and he left the area. It was about seven thirty in the morning as he drove to a Starbucks coffee shop, and he met another police officer there drinking coffee and eating a blueberry muffin.

The cop said, "Hi Ralph, did you feel that earthquake?"

"No, I didn't feel anything!" he said.

"I was parked at the Blue Hills parking lot and I could feel my car moving and shaking. Then I heard the sounds of rocks falling and thunder! I got out of there quick!"

"Officer Kenmore, are you on drugs, because you fuckin' drink a lot!"

"No Ralph, if you don't believe me, let's take a ride there and you'll see for yourself!"

The policemen drove back to the main parking lot of the Blue Hills resort and waited—no more earthquakes!

"Maybe I'm still hungover from last night!" said Officer Kenmore. Officer Ralph laughed and he left to go on another call.

Later people were skiing and the mountain was shaking, rocking, and rolling for about a minute, then it stopped. Panicking skiers went to the ski lodge to report the shaking. One girl was screaming, "We're having an earthquake!"

"Yes, ma'am we felt it too!" People at the ski lodge called police.

"Milton Police, Officer Ralph Connors speaking."

"Hi, this is Carrol Page calling from the Blue Hills ski resort. We're getting reports of earthquakes. The mountain is shaking and people are falling in all the snow."

"Okay, you need to shut the resort down in case of an avalanche because we had reports of earthquakes earlier this morning," said Officer Ralph.

An announcement was made at the ski lifts: "Good afternoon skiers, we have to close down for the day because of earthquake and avalanche warnings. Please bring all equipment to the lodge and leave the area. Sorry for the inconvenience!"

People skied down the mountain and the rest arrived at the ski lodge on the ski lift and snowmobiles. The day was over, the snow machines were shut down.

Environmental police and park rangers were looking at the earthquake monitor and nothing was happening. Officer Ralph contacted Officer Kenmore. He said, "You're right Officer Kenmore, Blue Hills was reporting earthquakes and they just shut the resort down!"

The next day there was a snowstorm and it was a quiet day. A few days later was the Martin Luther King, Jr. holiday. A man was blowing snow in his driveway with a snow blower in Canton, a town not far from Blue Hills, when suddenly the ground shook violently. He thought his snow blower was acting up!

His wife was out shopping and she felt something while in the meat section. A woman said to her, "Mrs. Dunkin, did you feel that?!"

"Yes I did, was that an earthquake?!"

"It felt like it but I'm not sure; the store was moving and going up and down!" said the lady.

The man at home stopped what he was doing and he went in the house and his cell phone rang. "Dick, it's Jen. I think we had an earthquake! I was shopping and I felt the store moving and rolling and several people here experienced it as well."

"You too?! I was moving snow with the snow blower and I thought something was wrong with the machine at first! When I went in the house everything stopped. We have a cracked window but I don't see any more damages. Are you okay?" asked Dick Dunkin; he's a news reporter.

"Yes, I'm okay and I will be home in a few minutes. Has any company arrived yet?"

"Not yet Jen. Oh here's someone coming now; glad I just finished plowing the driveway."

"Hello!!!!!!!!!!!!!!!! It's Big Dick Dunkin, the WNAC Fox News reporter!

"Welcome Ben and Betty, happy holidays and happy new year 2011 in heaven! Come in and make yourselves comfortable. My wife Jen will be home shortly. I have to go on the air because we just had an earthquake!"

Jen came home and Dick went on the radio in his home while Jen was cooking dinner for the holiday. "Good afternoon, we have breaking news on WNAC radio. We had an earthquake in

Canton about a half hour ago; it was the third reported earthquake in the Blue Hills region since January 11, 2011. We do not know if there are any injuries or damage. On January 11, Milton Police reported an earthquake about seven thirty that morning. Six hours later a second tremor at the Blue Hills ski resort was reported, a 4.5, and that's pretty strong. It was felt in Boston and as far north as New Hampshire. Blue Hills was shut down. Dick Dunkin, WNAC NEWS."

Later, after Dick's news report, everyone sat down to have dinner. Dick said, "Excuse me, but I have to call in reports to the radio station when something like this happens. Did you feel the earthquake earlier?"

"No Dick, I didn't know we had one," said Ben.

"I heard rumors that Blue Hills was a volcano at one time; is that true?" asked Betty.

"Yes it was, it last erupted 440 million years ago according to history, but I heard it last erupted in the 1400s and it had several brief steam eruptions in the past. I don't know how true that is. A friend of mine, a much older man that worked for WNAC TV, got fired over an April Fool's joke claiming that Blue Hills erupted, sending lava down the side of the mountain and causing earthquakes. People were evacuating the area! He said it on the air as a joke, but it's not a joke because there have been several steam eruptions and sulfur deposits going off in this mountain every once in a while. We have not had any issues since the 1980 April Fool's joke, until now.

"We have been living in Canton since 1985 and today is the first time I felt an earthquake here. The one police reported and the one at the Blue Hills ski resort were unusually strong, but I didn't feel them. We have earthquakes all the time in Blue Hills, just not this strong. The one I felt today plowing snow, I thought something was wrong with the snow blower. When I shut it off I felt the ground shaking again and at that point I was thinking we were having an earthquake, and my wife called me and told me what happened," said Dick.

A few minutes after dinner Dick was putting wood in the fireplace to get a fire going and it was snowing again outside. The ground shook again, then again, and a pretty good jolt. The third time you could hear rocks rolling under the house. The house rose up and down and swayed back and forth, but it all stopped a minute later. There were no damages, but the lights went out at 3:02 p.m.

Jen and Betty screamed! Dick and Ben were shocked! Dick called the radio station to report the earthquake. Dick said to his company, "Get under a doorway to avoid falling debris."

Panicking people were out of their homes during the snowstorm. The police and the Canton fire department were out looking for damage. Mild damage was found, leaving some residences without power for a while. Ben and Betty left the Dunkin family home and went home after the shaking stopped.

News reported a series of small earthquakes in the area and power was restored once the shaking stopped. The next day was sunny and a foot of snow or more had fallen. The paper read: "Fifteen Inches of Snow Falls in the Boston Area, Followed by a Series of Mild Earthquakes Rocking the Blue Hills Region Again." There were no serious damages or injuries, according to the *Boston Globe*.

The next evening the Boston Celtics were playing the Indiana Pacers and the Celtics were winning 95 to 94 with a minute thirteen left to play. Fans were on their feet and the pacers were driving for the lead. Suddenly the TD Bank Garden shook and the lights blinked on and off, sending fans running for their lives—another earthquake!

The game was stopped and people were running in all directions trying to get out of the TD Garden. City lights were out, downtown Boston was in darkness. Subways were not operating, and people had to board buses. The trains were shut down. Many game fans had to walk in the darkness. The late night news came on and people watched at a Somerville bar.

"Good evening, we have breaking news on WBZ Channel 4 Boston. A freak earthquake struck downtown Boston, knocking out power and interrupting the Celtics basketball game at the TD Garden. It stopped ground transportation, trains, and subways, and plunged downtown into darkness. We do not know if there were any damages or injuries, but this was the third earthquake in the Boston area since January 11.

"The first was in the Blue Hills region followed by aftershocks closing the ski resort. Earthquakes struck in Canton a few days later, knocking out power during a snowstorm. There was mild damage but no injuries. WBZ 4 Boston News."

A few hours later power was restored in downtown Boston and the Celtics ended up winning. The Boston police were everywhere to make sure people were safe and there were no more aftershocks for the rest of the night. During the night environmental park rangers arrived at the Blue Hills ski resort to check the earthquake monitors and reported a 3.0 earthquake in Boston. Then the park rangers rode the ski lifts to the top of the mountain to find activity, and they found nothing.

The temperature was three degrees and freezing cold at the summit of Blue Hills. Park rangers were up there until daylight looking for a possible eruption. When nothing was found they went back to the monitors and waited.

A few hours later another tremor hit Canton. A woman was at home talking on the phone when the ground shook, knocking her off her feet, and she fell, dropping her phone. Then the ground shook again and she was lifted upright as she screamed hysterically, holding onto a bedpost in her bedroom!

She grabbed her phone and she cried, "Irene, I think we just had an earthquake! I was knocked off my feet and I had to hold on to the bed to avoid being thrown around in the house, and my bed and furniture shifted to one side of the room!"

"Sharon get under a doorway and when the shaking stops get out of the house. I felt it too but not as bad as you did. I heard *boom!, boom!,* and a little shaking, then it was over. There was no damage," said her friend Irene.

Sharon had damage in her house as she watched in shock trying to leave her house. Her kitchen floor had a big crack and her walls had cracks in them. Glass broke and light fixtures fell and smashed on the floor and some windows were destroyed. She went out the front door to go to the garage, carrying blankets with her, and the stairs leading outside had split, so she had to jump to the ground in the snow. She stayed in her car in the heated garage. The earth didn't shake again. Despite the damage she still had electricity in the house and garage. The time of the earthquake was 9:02 p.m. Sharon slept in the garage for the night.

A mini steam eruption occurred on top of Blue Hills, sending steam, rocks, and dirt out of a small hole underneath the ski lifts at the summit. The blast triggered an avalanche of heavy snow rolling down the mountain, which crashed into the ski lodge, smashing it into pieces, leaving a big pile of snow at the bottom of the hill. Milton residents heard a *boom!* with no shaking. Not to worry—we hear a lot of booms at night in the Boston area!

Dick and Jen were at a bowling league when the earthquake struck; they never knew what happened until they got home. They left Boston Bowl just after the earthquake. There were no problems in Boston. The blast backfired, causing earthquakes in Canton and on the Curry College campus. Dick and Jen arrived home to see their house was severely damaged from the earthquake and their cat was killed by falling debris.

At Curry College a basketball game had just finished and Curry lost to Endicott 86 to 58. The teams were going to the locker rooms when the ground shook, swaying back and forth.

The lights flickered, then they lost power, leaving players taking showers in the dark. Light fixtures fell, breaking on the gym floor just after fans left the game.

Some students were studying in a library when the earthquake struck. Kids were knocked off chairs and books were falling off bookshelves. A desk tipped over, full of computers, and some of them broke. The library building lifted up in the air and dropped before the lights went out! Lights fell on top of people.

A group of students were walking through campus when the earthquake struck, knocking them off their feet as the ground was rocking and rolling. It lasted less than a minute.

Two girls were in their dorm room when suddenly they were knocked off their feet and the lights went out. The whole Curry College campus was in the dark minutes after the earthquake!

A swim meet was going on when there was a big *boom!* then the building was shaking. The pool was a wave pool, washing swimmers out. The water smashed a window, washing swimmers out in the cold, causing a few injuries. The lights went out and it was darkness and it was a cold rainy night.

A bell from a church on campus fell and landed on the ground, just missing people walking by. The campus police came to get the injured. "We just had an earthquake!" said a group of kids.

A roof caved in in another building, sending students running for cover. Students were in a study room eating snacks when the earthquake happened. Windows broke and light fixtures fell and part of that building collapsed, forcing people out into the cold. Kids were sleeping in their dorms when suddenly they were thrown out of bed. All this damage plunging Curry College into darkness didn't last more than a minute!

Homes were damaged in Canton and police received several calls about the earthquake. The ground shook a number of times during the night afterward, causing mild damage.

One house lost a roof, another collapsed, windows broken

and power lost. A gas line rupture caused a fire and a house burned down as people were running in the streets looking for help. The police, fire trucks, and rescue crews were out all night long rescuing people.

Injured Curry College students were taken to area hospitals and park rangers went to the Blue Hills ski area. The parking lot was covered in piles of snow.

"We have a serious problem here. Police reported several earthquakes in Canton and also a lot of damage on the Curry College campus. These piles of snow must have been an avalanche on top of the mountain triggered by the strange earthquakes lately. Something may be going on in this mountain!" one park ranger said to the other.

The other park ranger said, "Roger, could it be a volcano eruption?"

"I don't know David but we have a lot of damage here. Let's wait until daylight and come back in the morning before we find out what went wrong."

The Milton police arrived to see all the snow. "What happened here?!" asked the police.

"I think the earthquakes triggered an avalanche on the resort, but we will find out in the morning," said Roger.

"The earthquake struck the Curry College campus where there was a lot of damage and injuries, and a few homes in Canton were damaged," said the Milton police.

People were left in the streets in the cold during the night, looking for places to keep warm. Tomorrow is Groundhog Day but who cares if we're going to get six more weeks of winter, we have a much bigger problem to worry about!

People were getting out of the Bruins game just after the earthquake and going to area bars to watch the Celtics playing on the West Coast, but the game was interrupted by the shocking news. The earthquake was very mild and unnoticeable in downtown Boston.

"Good evening, we have breaking news: a 6.6 earthquake struck Canton just after 9:00 p.m. this evening, damaging several homes and leaving residents homeless. The Curry College campus was heavily damaged by the earthquakes. Several students were injured and some buildings collapsed. More earthquakes occurred after 9:00 p.m. I live in Canton and my home was also damaged. Dick Dunkin reporting on WNAC Fox News." People in Boston bars watching the news were in shock.

The next day seismologists arrived to look at the damage from the Canton and Curry College earthquakes, then went to the Blue Hills resort to meet park rangers, Milton police, and Carrol Page the resort director. Tractors and snowplows arrived to move snow to get to the ski lodge, only to find it splintered to matchsticks and buried in mountains of snow. Carrol was in shock!

She said, "We had an avalanche triggered by the earthquake. We need to get reports regarding what caused this earthquake in Boston."

Later the crew went up on ski lifts to search the mountain and they found a pretty big crack at the summit. Steam was coming out along with the smell of sulfur.

"We have a volcanic eruption here! You need to get a volcano crew from NASA to see what's in this mountain. Don't worry; it's not a major crack that's going to blow Boston away. It appears to be a steam geyser, but the sulfur deposits are a concern. It should be looked at because you could have a magma chamber building up pressure in this mountain, causing these earthquakes!" said one of the earth seismologists.

A volcano crew was called in to investigate the steam eruption with a spudweb machine, coming in from New York the next day. A bus arrived with monitors and equipment, and a helicopter dropped off the spudweb machine at the summit of Blue Hills where the blast was.

Carrol Page, the resort manager, met with the crew in the Blue Hills parking lot. "Good morning, my name is Carrol Page, the Blue Hill resort manager."

"Edward Fay from the NASA volcanology department. My crew: Linda Brew; Katrina House; Paul Numbnutts and Nathan Rivers, who will be operating the spudweb machine; and this is David Dunkin who will be reporting the data from spudweb. The girls will be reporting earthquakes from the monitors on this bus."

"Pleased to meet you everyone and welcome to Blue Hills. We had a strong earthquake a couple of nights ago. An avalanche damaged the resort and we have no access to our earthquake monitoring equipment. We had to get information from Boston and all we are getting is earthquake warnings here at the Blue Hills resort, the town of Canton, and on the Curry College campus where there was quite a bit of damage. Students were injured and a few homes in Canton were damaged," said Carrol Page.

"Miss, will we find out when spudweb is set up?" said Edward Fay.

"What's spudweb?"

"Spudweb is a machine that looks for volcanic energy in the mountain. Have you ever seen the movie *Dante's Peak?*" asked Edward.

"No I can't say that I have, I don't remember," said Carroll.

"If you can run the ski lifts and get to the summit, you'll see what we saw," said Edward.

The NASA leader Edward Fay, along with Paul Numbnutts and David Dunkin, went up with spudweb, hooking it up and planting it down, screwing it into the bedrock inside the blast zone. Later spudweb was getting information.

Carrol Page arrived from the ski lift to find out what was going on. Later, the report! "Carrol, according to spudweb you had a serious steam eruption from built-up pressure in this mountain, caused by gases and sulfur deposits. Old steam pipes burst deep inside this mountain; they need to be repaired or removed. We had the same type of problem in New York City where a steam pipe burst in the middle of city streets and we found out that a volcano could be brewing there in the future. That happened in July of 2007.

"Here the pressure from built-up gases in this mountain has released. It triggered the earthquakes before the blast! There's no magma chamber or lava tubes, just like what happened in New York City. We cannot call this an active volcano because of the missing elements.

"You do have gases and sulfur deposits. It was a deep eruption that triggered several strong earthquakes and avalanches, and it released the gases. This mountain was full of methane gas and it could have blown the place into pieces if there was a magma chamber.

"Other readings I'm receiving from spudweb are that this mountain is an ancient volcano; it's inactive, dormant, and a dead zone! I also have reports that this is not the first time steam and gas eruptions happened here. But millions of years ago this was an active volcano. I have a report of an eruption in the 1400s but that was not confirmed.

"You see this spudweb machine is giving me all the history of this mountain and the land around it. You may get a few more mild earthquakes then it will stop. Once all the gases release it will be over. I don't see Blue Hills being a volcano but we will be watching it.

"The problem now is the steam pipes blew and they need to be fixed," said Edward Fay. Years passed and there were no more problems. The pipes were fixed and Blue Hills was quiet.

CHAPTER THREE

VOLCANO UNDER NEW YORK CITY PART TWO

People at bars and restaurants and at home in New York and Connecticut watched the news on national TV about the Groundhog Day earthquakes and eruption in Blue Hills.

"Good evening, we have breaking news on WNYC TV Channel 8. On February 2, 2011 a 6.6 earthquake rocked the Blue Hills region in greater Boston, Massachusetts, triggering a possible volcanic eruption and an avalanche, destroying a ski resort in Blue Hills. The earthquake damaged eleven homes and two collapsed. Several buildings on the Curry College campus were damaged and sixty-three students reported injuries but no deaths.

"The Blue Hills Mountain erupted, causing an avalanche that destroyed a ski resort there. There were no injuries because the resort was closed due to a series of earthquakes happening since January 11. Seismologists and the NASA volcano crew went there from New York, investigating a possible volcanic eruption. They reported a steam eruption caused by methane gas pressure in the mountain but found no signs of a volcano! Lisa Lippkiss reporting."

August 31, 2011, a 5.0 earthquake struck the northeast from the Virginias all the way to Canada, and New York City sure felt this one! At 2:11 p.m. it was a warm humid day and the city was all at work. It was a normal day; then New York City was rocking and rolling for a few minutes!

Manhattan was rising up and down swaying side to side like it was dancing the electric slide. Back and forth it went, then it stopped, sending Manhattan into a mad panic.

The lights flickered and people started running in all directions. They bolted out of buildings and ran in the streets up toward Harlem, getting away from the water. Some buildings had mild damage and some windows broke, landing on the running crowd below and causing serious injuries with people getting cut from the falling glass.

The NYPD, fire department, and rescue crews were out collecting the injured, trying to get through a panicking, running crowd. People were trampling over one another trying to get away from the tall buildings, causing more injuries. The injured were lying in the streets until help arrived and some were covered in blood from falling glass.

Most people thought it was another terrorist attack, fearing a bomb hit New York City. Others realized it was an earthquake!

FLASHBACK

At a police station, the NYPD was going over daily reports like all policemen do during a normal day. Then boom!, rocking and rolling and lights flickered at headquarters; then it stopped.

"Holy shit fellas, did you feel that?! We must have had an earthquake!" one policeman said.

"Maybe a volcano erupted at 41st Street and Lexington Avenue again. We better go check it out!" said another cop.

Buses and trains were arriving at and leaving Grand Central Station when the shaking started. At the Port Authority it was rocking and rolling and people running around like rats—even the rats were running to safety!

The Freedom Tower was rocking back and forth like a bowling pin waiting to fall down and panicking people ran down stairways trampling each other. Computer screens read: Earthquake! Some people ran to the rooftops and jumped off with parachutes and people at the Empire State Building followed suit. Manhattan was full of colorful parachuters jumping out of buildings!

Police were driving around warning people about the earthquake. Hospital boats arrived to get the injured and cruise ships came after the earthquake was over.

Then the evening news on CBS: "Good evening, we had a strong earthquake up and down the East Coast earlier today and the most serious damage was from Virginia to New York City. The Washington monument was damaged and there was some damage at the White House. President Obama was trapped but he's okay.

"New York City had damage to buildings. People were hurt and homes were damaged in New Jersey, Pennsylvania, Delaware, and Maryland. There was also some damage to homes in Connecticut and parts of Massachusetts and upstate New York.

"All transportation was stopped in New York City and bridges were closed. Connecticut casinos were used for shelters because many people lost power there. More than a million people on the East Coast from the Virginias to the Canadian Maritimes lost power. CBS News reporting."

Everyone on the East Coast was in a panic because they weren't used to earthquakes like the ones in California. The ground didn't shake again until one evening in July of 2018...

July 20, 2018, at 6:40 p.m. Office workers were all gone for the evening but shoppers and vacationers were hanging around in downtown Manhattan, then *boom!* a volcanic eruption on Fifth Avenue! Steam, hot water, dirt, rocks, big rats, fish, even sharks were being blasted from under Fifth Avenue onto city streets and inside buildings from 19th Street to 22nd Street. A geyser blasted up through Fifth Avenue, sucking up seawater and fish and exploding high into the air, blowing out windows in nearby buildings. Fish and all kinds of debris landed inside office buildings and upper-class apartment buildings on Fifth Avenue.

Asbestos was blown out of the new crater, gas lines ruptured, and fire was coming up from the crater. Fish were flopping around in city streets and the city rats were feasting on the fish. The rats were the size of big dogs. Some of them were dead from the blast! The blast looked like an underground volcano erupting.

FLASHBACK

A woman was cooking dinner before the blast and her husband was taking a shower, then boom!!!! *A big window in her living room blew in and a shark came flying in, flopping around.*

The woman screamed from the blast, and once she saw the shark that landed in the living room she was hysterical! "Larry, Larry, we have a shark in our living room!"

He came running out of the bathroom with a towel wrapped around him. He ran to the living room and the shark almost bit his leg and he jumped back in shock. He said, "Suzy, leave the house!"

The shark landed on the wood floor, flopping around in the broken glass. Larry, the naked husband, went to his bedroom, grabbed his shotgun, and fired forty rounds into this shark, killing it. Then he grabbed its tail to throw it out the broken window—it was the twenty-third floor—but the tail broke off from all the bullet holes from killing it! He had to get a chainsaw to cut the nine-foot shark in pieces and throw it out the window. "Watch out everyone below!"

Throwing the cut-up pieces out the window, he saw the eruption a few blocks away. "Oh my good God, do we have a volcano erupting on Fifth Avenue?!" he said to himself. He cut his feet trying to dispose of the shark, and he and his wife had a big mess to clean up before dinner. Then he called his landlord who lived in Connecticut.

"Hi Daniel, I have bad news. A volcano or something blew my living room window in and a shark about ten feet long came crashing in from the blast."

The landlord hung up! Of course this eruption happened on a Friday, ruining everyone's weekend!

The NYPD and hundreds of fire trucks and rescue vehicles arrived while the Fifth Avenue steam eruption was still going on, blasting everything that lived underground. A dead body was found on 21st Street, and apartments and a hotel had broken windows.

The gas and water were shut off and several residences and businesses were without power well into the evening. One person was dead and several people were hurt. People were burned by hot water, steam, and fire from broken gas lines.

The NYPD started evacuating people living in the area. Buses, taxies, and boats were waiting to evacuate the area for weeks until the mess was cleaned up.

People were picking up fish and sea life blown out of the crater and putting them in bags. They left the sharks, squid, and seaweed for the rats. The area from 19th to 22nd Street and Fifth Avenue was shut down.

The eruption finally stopped around midnight and the streets were flooded, with big rats swimming in it. About 3:00 a.m. the water went down and the floodwaters went back into the crater. The NYPD and the fire department were there all night long.

A steam fitting crew and the NASA volcano crew were there and the governor and mayor of New York City arrived around daybreak.

The crater was so deep you couldn't see the bottom. It was a massive hole in the middle of Fifth Avenue. The NASA volcano crew set up spudweb near the crater to get information on what happened; the machine was bolted to the ground to get readings. The fire department was there putting out fires and the police were keeping people away.

Flopping fish, sharks, crabs, and lobsters were washed back into the crater when the floods receded. The rats were washed down the hole as well! As was all the other wildlife.

Asbestos and all kinds of smoke, gas, and dirt were being blown into the atmosphere. People were choking in it and passing out. They were picked up in rescue vehicles and taken into area hospitals near the blast site.

The NYPD, firemen, the steamfitters, and the volcano crew were all wearing respirators and masks around the blast site. The volcano crew bolted a spudweb machine into the street and another was lowered inside the crater to sit by itself—it was out of sight the hole was so deep!—by cables from a helicopter.

Spudweb cams gave data about what happened. NASA gathered data from the spudweb cams and a meeting was held at Madison Square Garden. All New York City officials, the NYPD, the fire department, city workers, and the volcano crew and Edward Fay spoke.

"Good evening, we do have a volcano brewing under Manhattan according to spudwebs #1 and #2. On July 20, we had another steam geyser blow a hole about eighty to one hundred feet wide leaving a crater about three hundred feet deep at the intersections of Fifth Avenue and 21st and 22nd Street.

"It has happened a few times but not as bad as this one with the exception of the 2007 eruption on 41st Street and Lexington Avenue. We were called in from Houston for that explosion and I thought that may have been caused by a possible volcano because of pressure from deep under the ground.

"That blast was 73 feet wide and 64 feet deep. This one measured 106 by 82 feet and was 346 feet deep, pulling in sea water, sucking sea life out of the ocean, and exploding in the erupting geyser, crashing into buildings and landing in city streets. It's going to take weeks to clean up this mess!

"A couple had a ten-foot shark fly through their twenty-third-floor apartment window on Fifth Avenue! That's right, you heard right—a ten-foot shark blown that high in the sky!

"Two people died during the blast that occurred just before 7:00 p.m. A dozen people died in the 2007 41st Street blast. If this had happened in rush hour like the last one a lot more people would have died.

"There weren't a lot of people around for this blast but it's much worse than the last one. We can expect a lot more to come. Twenty-three buildings were damaged from 19th Street to 22nd Street. Two office buildings fell into the crater on Fifth Avenue. Asbestos pipes exploded from methane gas. Steam, hot water, dirt, rocks, seawater, sea life, and animals such as subway rats were blown out of this crater from deep in the earth.

"This blast was caused by a methane gas pressure explosion. It was another steam pipe disaster like the one in 2007 according to the spudweb data machines.

"We have a volcano brewing under Manhattan. There are no lava tubes or a magma chamber like the last blast, but we do have methane gas and sulfur deposits. Those are the signs we have a volcano brewing here.

"In 2011 Blue Hills had a steam eruption near Boston, Massachusetts and we found methane gas and sulfur deposits. It was identified as a weak volcanic eruption that caused several earthquakes in the Boston area before it exploded.

"We took the spudweb cam there and identified it as a weak volcano. But this blast was *boom!*—breaking Fifth Avenue out of Manhattan!

"We have several buildings we have to go through to check for bodies and a lot of repairs to make, including covering up the hole. City workers will need to replace all the old steam pipes under Manhattan to avoid more explosions like this. The eruption here had the energy to blow Manhattan apart—it was that bad!

"We have about ten thousand broken windows and spudweb recorded a 6.6 earthquake like the one in Blue Hills in 2011. The Fifth Avenue blast erupted more than one hundred feet high!" said Edward Fay, volcanologist.

Days later, city workers and the fire department went through damaged buildings removing dead rats, snakes, fish—even sharks had been blown into buildings!—and broken glass from busted windows. Large dead fish and sharks had to be cut up with chainsaws and thrown out of high-rise buildings.

After the steam pipes were fixed, the hole was covered up with big rocks brought in by thirty-wheeler dump trucks. The pipes were cemented in place in the hole—tons of it was dumped in by cement trucks—and the area was repaved before the damaged buildings were cleaned out and repaired.

The dead fish, sea life, rats, snakes, and broken glass were thrown out of the damaged buildings onto city streets. Earth mobiles with big plows moved the dead debris and the broken glass into piles in the streets that were torched with fire guns then scooped up into dump trucks to take to the city dump.

The National Guard was called in to help and the area was cleaned up. After damaged buildings were repaired it was back to business. Apartment buildings on Fifth Avenue were knocked down and destroyed. A meeting was held with the National Guard, the NASA volcano crew, and some New York City firemen and police officers at the blast site.

"Good evening, my name is Edward Fay, the head volcanologist for NASA. Welcome to the newly paved Fifth Avenue on this warm mid-August evening. We had a possible volcanic steam pipe eruption here, blasting asbestos out of a crater more than a hundred feet wide. An over-three-hundred-feet-deep sinkhole was caused by a methane sulfur pressure explosion according to this machine bolted on the sidewalk. It's called spudweb, a similar robot to the one NASA uses on Mars to get data from deep in the earth. We have another one inside the crater covered in a steel tank to keep it from being damaged that also gives us data to keep Manhattan safe.

"I said we have a possible volcano developing under Manhattan; that doesn't mean it is a volcano because there's no lava or magma chamber. But we do have methane gas and sulfur deposits developing pressure in tight tunnels where the steam and water pipes are installed, causing these eruptions. The pressure buildup is coming from under the seafloor, working its way to the surface.

"We could have had something worse than this! The subways had little damage from falling rocks, but some were severely flooded and we are lucky we didn't lose a lot of lives here. Methane gas is not going to make a volcano here but the sulfur deposits are a sign that something could be building. If a magma chamber builds, you better be evacuating because danger may not be far away.

"The spudweb cams will notify us of any warnings and it will be all over the news. The steam workers put new piping surrounded with insulation and cooling units to help stop anymore steam eruptions.

"More work is being done on repairs under all tunnels, subways, and steam pipe locations under all city streets in New York City and Long Island. The construction will be going on for the next five years.

"Meanwhile my crew will be monitoring the spudweb data machines 24/7 to keep Manhattan and all the boroughs of New York City safe. My crew: Linda Brew and Katrina House, monitoring equipment; Nathan Rivers and Paul Numbnutts, monitoring spudweb data; and David Dunkin, reporting news for NASA.

"We will be monitoring all earthquakes and volcanoes across the United States. The floor is open for questions for me and my crew. Thank you," said Edward Fay.

"Edward, I'm Lieutenant Bowa Bowser, NYPD. What happens if we get another blowjob like this in New York?"

"Spudweb will pick it up and the information will automatically be sent to the fire department and police department. You no longer have to play a waiting game for something to happen because you will know right away. As soon as the ground moves you will get a warning before another blast occurs thanks to spudweb data."

"Edward, my name is Allen Abbingtonconstantinopoliss from the New York Fire Department. Is it possible that an eruption like this can happen again at this very spot?"

"Yes it can. Chances are slim because the pressure was released, but it's possible it could happen again," said Edward Fay.

CHAPTER FOUR

MAJOR VOLCANO ERUPTION IN VERMONT

September 6, 2021, there was violent shaking in a hilly Vermont town.

Adamsville, Vermont is a small town overlooking Mount Ascutney which is 3,130 feet in elevation. It's a small resort town for summer vacationers and ski country during the winter. It has a lake, Lake Ascutney, the same name as the mountain, and there's a village with stores, shops, and restaurants overlooking the lake. There's hotels and bed and breakfast places, a steamboat gives rides on the lake, and a train goes through the village and up the mountain.

There are farmlands and residential areas. There's an all-religion church, a pretty big church, and a nice beach with a mountain view. The resort looks like a mini Lake Winnipesaukee, Overlooking Village is the name. There are campsites, and yes, black bears come in to visit once in a while here.

On Monday, September 6, Labor Day 2021, it was a cool morning, about fifty-six degrees at Allison's Bed & Breakfast. It was packed with people enjoying the Labor Day breakfast with a fire going in a big fireplace.

Then things started shaking, glasses and dishes rattled, and then a big *boom!* Windows cracked, but it was over in ten seconds! People in the restaurant started screaming.

"Ladies and gentlemen, we just had a brief earthquake. We get these once in a while but this one was a little strong, breaking some windows. Don't worry because they don't last long, you feel a little shaking and then it's over! The boom was scary, that's unusual but everyone will be alright," said the restaurant manager.

The rest of the day was okay. People leaving the restaurant said to a crowd, "Did you feel that earthquake?!"

"What earthquake?!" said the crowd.

"We just had an earthquake and windows broke in the restaurant we were at!" said one lady.

"Oh my God we didn't feel anything!" said someone in the crowd.

———

A week later a woman was moving into a house overlooking Lake Ascutney. "You must be Sarah Eli."

"Yes."

"Hi, my name is Suzanne McCarthy from Bennington Realtors. Welcome to Adamsville, Vermont overlooking Mount Ascutney. Scientists say that mountain is ready to erupt someday; it's a volcano!"

"Really! I didn't know we have volcanoes in Vermont," said Sarah.

"Come in and I'll show you the house. We have a two-floor small cottage home. Here is the living room/dining area and the kitchen and a small bath. Upstairs you have two bedrooms and a full bath with a jacuzzi tub and shower. Above the bathroom is a door leading to the attic.

"For a small house, it's bigger than you think. Down in the basement is a full cellar with washer and dryer hookups and a work bench. You have a big fireplace to keep you warm during the winter and it burns natural wood."

"Suzanne, is this house haunted? It's kind of spooky looking!"

Suzanne laughed. "Of course not! The only haunting you're going to get here is if that mountain erupts!"

"Thank goodness! By the way, Suzanne, this is Inc, my bull-dog," said Sarah.

Suzanne petted the dog and she showed Sarah the grounds outside the house. "In the front yard you have a shed and a horseshoe driveway. In the backyard you have a picnic table, a firepit, and a deck leading to the kitchen. Then you have a dock with hookups for a boat and a private little beach you will share with your neighbor. Is it just you?" asked Suzanne.

"Yes, just me and my dog," said Sarah.

Later Sarah and the realtor set the mortgage for the house. The next day a truck came to move in her furniture. She had a couch, recliner, two tables, two lamps, a fifty-inch flat-screen TV for the living room, and a closet to hang her sweaters and coats. The dining room had a table with six chairs, a hutch, and a side piece for the living room. She had a washer and dryer to hook up downstairs. In the kitchen was a refrigerator, electric stove, oven, a built-in microwave oven above the stove among plenty of cupboard space, and sliding glass doors leading to the outside deck. Then she had a queen bed with two nightstands, lamps, and two bureaus with closet space in her bedroom, and a spare bedroom with two twin beds, bureaus, nightstands, and lamps.

Sarah Eli was a news reporter for WWVT Channel 8. She had her family and friends move her in. The first night at her new home was quiet. Her dog slept in a doggy bed in her bedroom. The next day she met her neighbor after mowing the lawn.

"Hello neighbor!"

"Hi there! My name is Sarah Eli from WWVT News. I'm the new neighbor in town."

"Pleased to meet you. My name is Nick Jackson and this is my wife Nancy."

"Pleased to meet you," said Nancy.

"The realtor told me that mountain out across the lake is a volcano and it's ready to erupt soon," said Sarah.

"I heard that, but it has not erupted in thousands of years. We have been getting some earthquakes lately, nothing that's going to knock you off your feet but enough to make you feel them or jump out of your shoes. They come and shake and bake a little, then they're gone!

"The last earthquake we had was stronger than usual. On Labor Day we were having breakfast at Allison's Bed & Breakfast and suddenly the restaurant started shaking, and glasses and dishes started making noises; then a loud *boom!* and some of the windows cracked. We didn't even finish eating; I left a twenty dollar bill on the table and we got the hell out of there! It lasted five or ten seconds and we haven't had one since," said Nick.

"Sarah, I don't know if you heard the news or read the papers, but there's a super volcano brewing under Vermont, Massachusetts, and New Hampshire. An egg-shaped magma bubble that was found by scientists in 2017 is rising and there's no telling when this volcano will erupt.

"We have only one volcano in Vermont and it's right there! Mount Ascutney! If this mountain blows, the whole state of Vermont will go with it and it's only eight miles away!" said Nancy.

"Sarah, if you're not doing anything later why don't you come join us for a walk into town and we will get dinner at Jake's Restaurant and go on a boat tour, on us," said Nick.

"Okay!" she said.

Later the three of them went into town.

"Sarah we have been living here for eight years and we love it here! Once you get used to the small earthquakes once in a while you'll be fine living here," said Nick.

"We need a news lady here to make everyone feel safe," said Nancy.

"Sarah, welcome to Overlooking Village. We have all kinds of restaurants, amusements, gift shops, a train ride, boat rides. There's a nice beach here, nice parks, and here's the restaurant we're going to tonight.

"Welcome to Jake's Café," said Nick.

The three of them had fish and chips for dinner with red wine, then went off on a boat ride.

"Good evening. Welcome aboard Steamboat Ascutney. This is your captain speaking. My name is Captain Denny Canotch. It's a cool September evening and I hope you brought sweaters or a light jacket with you. Tonight's journey is a forty-five-minute ride on Ascutney Lake. The mountain straight ahead is Mount Ascutney, the only volcano in Vermont. It's 3,130 feet to the summit and it has a small crater about eight feet wide and two and a half feet deep. It's inactive and it has been dormant for more than a thousand years but scientists say that this sleeping beauty is ready to erupt soon.

"I don't mean to scare you ladies and gentlemen but a super volcano magma field is building right under this quiet volcano; it might be fifty years from now or it could erupt anytime soon—I hope that I'm wrong! It's a beautiful mountain and there are hiking trails and a train ride. You get tickets in the village and it will take us up the mountain around the village and through the town of Adamsville.

"In fact when you get off this boat your ticket will get you a free day-pass tomorrow to ride the train. Enjoy the ride and refreshments and coffee will be served. Thank you."

The captain was done talking and they enjoyed the dusk boat

ride, ending in the dark. Everyone got off the boat and visited the gift shops in the quiet village.

"Nick and Nancy, thank you for this wonderful evening. We'll meet in the morning for breakfast at Allison's Bed & Breakfast on me and go on the train ride tomorrow. How does that sound?"

"It sounds great, we will meet about nine thirty and we'll spend the day together," said Nick and Nancy Jackson.

The three walked up the hill from the village and went home. It was a clear chilly night, about forty-seven degrees. Sarah went home and she closed the door and locked it. She turned up the heat because the house was kind of chilly. She closed all the blinds and drapes in the house then she took a hot bath before she went to bed. She felt a brief shaking while she was in the tub sudsing up and then it stopped. Then she went to bed, fell asleep, and had a dream the volcano was erupting!

SARAH'S DREAM

She got off a city bus and walked up the mountain, a small hill in the dream, and it was smoking at the top. The smoke was spinning like a tornado and the ground opened up. She could see fire and smoke below and she got out of the way.

She was making her way back down and she was being chased by flowing lava, running down the mountainside. A pyroclastic flow was starting to overtake her, then she was panicking and running faster and faster down the mountain to get away from the eruption. Then the mountain blew up and she was blown sky-high into the clouds, into a thunderstorm, and a bolt of lightning struck her right between her legs!

She woke up screaming hysterically! "AAAHHH!!!" She jumped up out of bed out of a sound sleep. It was pouring rain, with thunder and lightning outside, and she was hysterical, thinking the dream was still happening before she came to her senses. Realizing that she was okay she turned on some lights and walked around the house for a while to walk off her nightmare.

She went to the kitchen to get a bottle of water to drink. She looked out a window overlooking the lake and she saw a bolt of lightning strike the water followed by a big *bang!* Then the storm was over a short time later.

Sarah was shocked! She checked herself before going back to sleep. At 5:00 a.m. another earthquake woke up Sarah, her bed was shaking and rocking and she was very frightened by it! The earthquake stopped a minute later. Then she went back to bed.

She got up about 8:00 a.m. and it was still raining hard outside, then she met with Nick and Nancy. Sarah drove them down to Allison's in her car because of the bad weather. "How was your first night in your new home?" asked Nancy.

"It was terrifying! First I had a dream about the volcano erupting and I was running into a smoky tornado. Then fire and lava came out of the mountain, chasing me and I ran down the mountain to get away. The smoke tried to trap me as I was running away then the mountain exploded and I was tossed into the air into a thunderstorm. A lightning bolt struck me between my legs and I woke up only to find out we were having a thunderstorm. I saw lightning strike the water outside my window! I thought I was still living my nightmare, I was terrified!

"Then I woke up around 5:00 a.m. and my bed was shaking and rocking, I swear we were having an earthquake! In my thirty-eight years of life I never was so terrified! I wonder if my house is haunted," said Sarah.

"We did have an earthquake early this morning, we felt it too. It didn't last long," said Nick.

"It doesn't look like much of a day for a train ride, it's pouring out there and I have to go into work at 5:00 p.m. this evening," said Sarah.

"We'll go tomorrow at 11:00 a.m. if the weather is better," said Nancy.

The three of them had breakfast and then went home after. Later in the day there was another mild earthquake but no damage. A little shaking then it was over.

Later Sarah was on the 11:00 p.m. news. "Good evening, this is WWVT Channel 8 News with Sarah Eli reporting. The town of Adamsville, Vermont has been experiencing a series of earthquakes since August 18, 2021. Footage has been recorded in Overlooking Village on Ascutney Lake. The August 18 quake was reported to cause ripples in the lake, stopping beachgoers that day. Allison's Bed & Breakfast reported a strong 4.0 earthquake, causing some damage to windows on Labor Day, then a few more mild earthquakes were felt in that town recently.

"Scientists discovered a super volcano brewing under Vermont, Massachusetts, and New Hampshire that may be causing these earthquakes. WWVT Channel 8 TV News reporting."

People living in the area watched the news about the earthquake warnings. The residents in Adamsville were living in fear and wondering what's next.

Sarah had a comfortable night's sleep after she came home from the TV station at 2:00 a.m. She met with her neighbors for breakfast and the 11:00 a.m. train ride. It was a beautiful sunny day.

"We heard you on the news last night Sarah," said Nancy.

"Did I sound good on TV?"

"You were great!" said Nancy.

"Good morning ladies and gentlemen, welcome to the Overlooking Village train tour. We have a wonderful couple with a guest today. Say hello to Nick and Nancy Jackson and their guest Sarah Eli: Welcome aboard!" said the tour guide, and the people on the train cheered, "Welcome!!!"

"Today we will take a tour around the lake and we will be

going up Mount Ascutney to the summit. We will go through the village at the end of this tour. Everyone kick back and enjoy our tour. My name is Jonathan Gold, your tour guide, and this is my assistant, Anne Cannabis.

"We are off! Look to the left and you'll see Overlooking Village Beach and Lake Ascutney. Over to the right is Allies Farm. Look at the cows, horses, pigs, chickens, goats, turkeys, deer, and all kinds of farm animals. The farmer has plenty of farmland and he lives on the hill. His name is Hank Grenadine.

"Again on the right is the Church of the Awakening, an all-religion church," said the tour guide.

"Does this church believe in Jesus Christ?" asked someone in the crowd on the train ride.

"Yes, this church believes in Jesus."

The train went *choo choo*! Then the tour guide continued. "Look to the left out on the lake and you can see the steamboat tour. Let's wave to them. The boat goes across the lake and back. You can go on the steamboat tour at the Overlooking Village near Allison's Bed & Breakfast, on the hour every hour until 10:00 p.m.

"On the right is the Adamsville ER and the next building is the animal hospital and shelter. Again on the right is a military base, helicopter port, and bunker huts in case this mountain erupts one of these days!

"Our next stop is the Ascutney Volcano Café, where we will get lunch before we go up the mountain. You have thirty minutes here; grab something to eat and drink before we visit Mount Ascutney. You have food vendors here, restrooms, gift shops, and a full bar."

Everyone got off the train to get a quick lunch and one couple decided to go to the bar for a quick Ascutney brewed beer.

The train went *choo choo*! Once everyone was aboard, the tour continued. "Ladies and gentlemen, over to the right is a residential area with condos, apartments, and homes. We're now crossing a rocky area. Look to the left and you will see a water-fall and a bridge. Once we cross this bridge we start going up the mountain.

"Welcome to Ascutney Village ski resort where you can get gondola rides up this mountain; you can get them with the steamboat lunch tour during the day. The gondolas do not run on stormy days.

"Here we go! *Choo choo*, up the mountain! Welcome to Mount Ascutney, the only volcano in Vermont. This mountain is 3,130 feet high! There are campsites during the summer months and it's a ski resort during the winter. Next month, if it's cold enough, we make snow for the skiers; otherwise the ski season starts in November and runs until mid-April.

"This mountain is a dormant volcano and you will visit the crater at the summit. It's eight feet wide and two and a half feet deep. You may have heard on the news about a super vol-cano brewing right under this mountain range and under New Hampshire and Massachusetts that could be causing the earth-quakes we've been having lately.

"But the last time Ascutney erupted was about eight thou-sand years ago and this volcano is inactive. Anne Cannabis will explain. Here's the crater and welcome to Ascutney's summit. Everyone will get out here and circle around the crater rim and Anne will tell you about the mountain," said Jonathan Gold, the train tour guide.

"Ladies and gentlemen, Mount Ascutney is part of the north-ern White Mountain range. We are 3,130 feet high and scientists proved that this mountain is indeed a volcano and it could erupt again.

"We have plutonic igneous rocks proving something is brew-ing down below. The plutonic series of volcanic rock expands into New Hampshire, north of Lake Winnipesaukee and south of the White Mountains. These areas are the skeleton of a massive volcanic solidified magma molten rock seismic Celsius underground making its way to the surface. Scientists and geologists say there are five reported dormant volcanoes in New Hampshire.

"Eight million years ago the Lake Ossipee mountain range was blown apart from a super volcano. The five listed volcanoes in New Hampshire are Mount Shaw in the Lake Ossipee mountain range, Mount Jefferson, in the White Mountains, then Mount Lafayette, Mount Lincoln, and Loon Mountain are three dormant volcanoes in Franconia Notch and Lincoln, New Hampshire.

"Mount Shaw, the tallest volcano in Ossipee, is the tallest volcano. Mount Jefferson at 5,712 feet last erupted five thousand years ago.

"A hot air balloon magma chamber has been recently found by scientists. In 2017 and 2018 they saw that these volcanoes are ready to wake up again and we are standing on top of what lies beneath. The Granite Mountain Range in New Hampshire is also a threat," said Anne Cannabis.

The tour was spooked listening to Anne's lecture standing over Ascutney's small crater. Suddenly the ground shook violently. People fell down and some were knocked off their feet trying to get back on the train, screaming hysterically!

The mountain kept shaking for a few minutes and you could hear rocks rolling underground.

"Ladies and gentlemen stay calm, board the trains slowly so we can get the hell out of here. Ascutney is still rocking and rolling." The mountain had a strong earthquake and shook for more than ten minutes!

There was thunder, rolling and roaring, and the sound of rocks falling. The tour was petrified as the train worked its way down the mountain until the train went off its tracks from another strong tremor. The rest of the way, the tour had to walk down the shaking mountain.

It became a rescue mission for handicapped people who couldn't get off the mountain without the train. Nobody was hurt. A little while later the shaking stopped and a helicopter arrived to rescue people who were handicapped. The train wreck was left there and buses arrived at the bottom of the mountain to pick up the passengers from the tour.

It started raining while the tour group was walking down the mountain in a state of shock and it was getting dark and cold. It wasn't until nighttime that everyone was off the mountain.

Park police and firemen rode the gondolas up the mountain during the night, making sure everyone was off the mountain. The buses got back to the resort by dark. Helicopters brought back the handicapped people just before dark.

It was a terrible ending for the train ride stuck on Mount Ascutney.

Flashback

The earthquakes started happening beginning at 1:30 p.m. and were on and off all day before quieting down around 4:30 p.m. Allison's Bed & Breakfast workers at the hotel were changing sheets and making beds in the rooms when suddenly the hotel was rocking back and forth, then a big boom! *and everything stopped.*

The time of that tremor was at 1:45 p.m. Dishes and glasses broke in the restaurant and windows cracked. Ten minutes later the ground shook again and a sinkhole formed in the middle of the main road in the Overlooking Resort and a parked car fell in it; the sinkhole was about eight to ten feet deep.

People were running and screaming, trying to get away from it. Ten minutes later the ground shook again and the rumbling ground damaged gift shops. There were six more small aftershocks before it stopped for a while, leaving mild damage to homes, businesses, and the Overlooking Resort.

Adamsville police drove around with loudspeakers. "Your attention, please: Everyone must evacuate the area due to several earthquakes! Get out of buildings and do not go into buildings. Please leave the area at this time. Buses will get you out of the resort. Get to higher ground in case a lake tsunami occurs." People were in a panic getting out. The boat tours made it in on time and all activities were cancelled for the day.

Earthquake victims: A man was mowing his lawn near the bottom of the mountain when he was knocked off his feet. Pastors were in the church when suddenly *boom!!!!!!* and windows blew in and light fixtures fell.

People were shopping in stores and eating in restaurants in Ascutney Village at the bottom of the mountain during the ten-minute earthquake. Windows broke, cracks formed in walls and opened up on floors, and the street cracked open, sending a crowd running in a panic outside in the pouring rain.

One man was cleaning the gutters on his house and the earthquake knocked him off the ladder and he fell to the ground. A dump truck full of gravel was on its way to a construction site and the ground shook violently, forcing the truck off the road until it tipped over, losing its load. Waves formed on the lake, causing a tsunami warning. People that ran out of buildings ran up to higher ground in case of a tsunami. The lake water just rippled then it was over with no danger.

A bus loaded with passengers riding through the Overlooking Village stopped and pulled over because the ground was rocking and rolling. Everyone on the bus was screaming and crying because the bus almost tipped over. A man was walking his dog when the ground shook and he fell down as the dog was barking.

A pontoon airplane landed safely on the lake and docked up in the village, but the police came over to the plane and the officer said to the pilot, "Hi there, sorry to bother you but everything is closed because we've been getting earthquakes all day and there's quite a bit of damage!"

"Holy shit! Is that right?!" said the pilot. Then the seaplane took off again.

———————

Later the bus with the train tour that got stuck on the mountain arrived in town at 7:00 p.m. Everyone made it off the mountain okay and boarded the buses. There was a headcount and the train tour guide said when the bus got back to Overlooking Village, "Ladies and gentlemen, the earthquake on top of Mount Ascutney was not the only one. There's been several aftershocks during the day and there's a lot of damage. Everything is closed; there's no bus or cab service and no ferry service. The only places open are the Overlooking Village Hotel and Allison's Bed & Breakfast for those who are staying there. Tomorrow you must make arrangements to evacuate in case we get more aftershocks," said Jonathan Gold.

The village lost power and everyone was in the dark. No streetlights and police and firemen had to direct the crowd with floodlights to get where they were going. Sarah Eli and Nick and Nancy Jackson walked up the hill in moonlight to get to their homes.

"This is great; I just moved here and a volcano is ready to erupt with all the earthquakes we've been having. Ha! Ha!" Sarah joked.

"Sarah, we have been living here for about eight years and we never went through anything like this! That mountain shook so bad I really thought it was going to blow and kill us all! It was that scary! I was knocked down by lightning in downtown Boston walking my dog when I was in college. The bolt struck my dog Chee Chee dead while I was knocked down to the ground and bounced back up and thrown up against a building. All I got was a couple of bruises, but by dog was fried to death like a marshmallow from the lightning bolt! I thought I was going to die—the strike lasted only a few seconds!—but today on top of that mountain I thought it was all over!

"I have gone through some scary things in my life but nothing like today. We have had many earthquakes since we've been living here but not as bad as we had today," said Nick Jackson.

Sarah got home and she looked at her watch and the time was 7:43 p.m. She was in the kitchen cooking dinner when she saw a big black thing on her deck as it ran off. She put the light on and nothing was there—maybe it was a bear? She locked all the doors, closed all the blinds and shades, ate dinner, and she went into work late. She went on the news.

"Good evening, we have breaking news on WWVT TV Channel 8. A series of violent earthquakes struck Mount Ascutney this afternoon. I was there and it was a scary scene. A tour train derailed forcing everyone to walk down the mountain to waiting buses. Rescue helicopters arrived to rescue handicapped people—there were only three of them—and there were no serious injuries.

"Several aftershocks above a 4.0 have been happening all afternoon causing some serious damage to stores and building structures. One man was hurt falling off a ladder and he was taken to a hospital. There were several mild injuries to people from falling debris in Ascutney village. Gas lines ruptured, burning a store and a barn, and two horses were hurt. Roads cracked open, causing a water main break in downtown Adamsville. Several aftershocks were felt in the northwest White Mountains region. The towns of Adamsville, Overlooking Village, and Ascutney Village suffered damage to buildings, roads, and power outages. This is Sarah Eli reporting."

Sarah came home after the news, just before 2:00 a.m. She went to bed and just when she fell asleep she heard a banging noise and the house was vibrating. She woke up and she looked at her alarm clock and the time was 3:02 a.m. *It was another tremor.*

She got up to check the house; power was restored. She turned the deck light on and nothing was out there. Then she went back to bed. When she woke up in the morning she heard banging outside her house like trash bins being tossed around. She went to investigate and she saw two black bears digging into her trash bins!

She went back in the house and she called the police. The animal rescue crew came to chase the bears away, spraying a substance to keep them out. One hour later it was *bang, bang, bang, bang, bang!!!!!* The bears were in the Jacksons' yard digging in the trash cans and Nick shot both bears with a shotgun. One bear was killed while the other got away. The animal rescue crew removed the dead bear and sprayed their trash bin area so no more bears would come to visit. Sarah went over to the Jacksons and she saw the dead bear and Nick standing there with a shotgun until animal rescue came. "The bears got you too, Nick, ha!" said Sarah.

"They sure did until I shot them, one dead and the second one got away! This is the time of year they come around to residential areas and get into everyone's trash before they go into hibernation in winter. It's the ninth bear I've shot dead since we've been living here!" said Nick.

Sarah and Nancy laughed. While the three of them were having fun with the roaming bears in the neighborhood the police, fire department, and the town mayor had a meeting. Sarah Eli was called to join them to report for the local news. The meeting was held at the Adamsville Middle School auditorium.

"Good evening. Welcome police, fire department personnel, and Sarah Eli from WWVT TV Channel 8 News. My name is Mayor Postal Fish from the town of Adamsville, Vermont. We're going to have a brief meeting tonight. We have been getting several earthquakes here in town causing injuries and some serious damage.

"Yesterday a strong earthquake on top of Mount Ascutney derailed a train, forcing passengers to walk down the mountain in a state of shock. The shaking was so bad people fell down, fearing the mountain was going to erupt. The earthquake knocked people off their feet and there were several mild injuries.

"I don't want to go into much detail about these earthquakes. We have been getting them for the last thirty-five years, but since August 2021 we have been getting some unusually strong ones; some of them were 5.0 or better. Yesterday's Mount Ascutney earthquake was a 6.3, raising concerns a possible volcano may be ready to erupt here.

"Scientists and geologists say there's a super volcano brewing under Vermont, New Hampshire, and Massachusetts, and the top of a magma bubble lies beneath our mountain. The first thing we're going to do is get the NASA volcano crew from New York City to examine this mountain. If they find out that we have a volcano here we need to have a town meeting and plan for a massive evacuation just like one seen on the movie *Dante's Peak*. Rent that movie on Netflix and you will have a pretty good idea on what to do. That movie is based on a true story.

"NASA reported deadly steam eruptions in New York City in 2007 and again in 2018. There was a small steam eruption at the Blue Hills region in the Boston area in Massachusetts, causing several earthquakes and damages on the Curry College campus and some injuries.

"What we have here is a bigger thing. If that mountain blows we will be in serious trouble. Starting tomorrow, October 1, 2021, the fire department and WWVT TV NEWS will be calling in NASA. I want the police department to be ready for a possible evacuation. Training will begin at 8:00 a.m. tomorrow morning. I want the fire department to call in NASA tonight after this meeting is adjourned. If NASA reports a volcano threatening we will have a town meeting immediately! This meeting is over. Thank you," said the mayor.

The next day training began with the police department and the NASA volcano crew arrived by helicopter with a spudweb machine. They landed on top of the mountain and the machine was bolted down into a big rock. Data was sent back to New York and the report was transferred back to the local spudweb. A report went into Mayor Postal Fish's office.

"Mayor Fish? This is Edward Fay, the head volcanologist of NASA. You do have a volcano here ready to erupt soon. You need to hold a town meeting and prepare for a massive evacuation. We need to set up a post to monitor this mountain." The crew set up computers, TVs, and monitoring equipment at the Adamsville middle school. Emails and news reports went out to residents and police drove around town, shouting on loudspeakers about a town meeting.

"Ladies and gentlemen, please report to the Adamsville Middle School auditorium for a volcano town meeting for your safety, tonight at 7:00 p.m." The police repeated the loudspeaker warnings all day!

The meeting: "Good evening ladies and gentlemen, welcome to Adamsville Middle School tonight for a town meeting evacuation plan due to a volcano eruption threat. My name is Mayor Postal Fish and Mr. Edward Fay will explain what is going on!"

"Good evening. I have Mr. Nathan Rivers and Mr. Paul Numbnutts, spudweb operators, David Dunkin writing up reports, and me, Mr. Edward Fay, the head volcanologist of NASA.

"We found out that Mount Ascutney is a volcano and it's a ticking time bomb ready to blow at any time. There is no telling when we will have an eruption; it could be tomorrow or take years. What we found is a full magma chamber that has no room to expand inside this mountain. We will be monitoring this mountain 24/7.

"The earthquakes you have been getting lately are a sign that this mountain is ready to go soon. You even had gas line ruptures and water main breaks and property damage due to stronger earthquakes.

"If the drinking water smells of sulfur the volcano is ready to blow! Everyone here must have an evacuation plan; if the drinking water goes bad, it's time to leave. Just because you have been getting a series of earthquakes lately doesn't mean this volcano is going to erupt. It might not for a long time, but because the lava chamber is at its capacity, we could have a major eruption with no warning!

"The magma bubble between all three western New England states sits right inside this dormant volcano. The magma bubble is rising, causing these earthquakes, and we need to take this very seriously. If you need to evacuate now go right ahead. If you want to stay and fix things up you may. We are not forcing you to leave but we will keep you posted. When we say leave, you better leave!

"We will have evacuating route signs posted, and we will be installing these signs right after this meeting. The evacuation route is very easy to follow:

1. Get as far away from the mountain as possible.
2. Get away from the water and get to higher ground away from the mountain.
3. Stay on paved roads getting out of town.
4. If we tell you to leave there's no second guessing, get out!! When you hear loudspeakers telling you to leave, leave your belongings and leave!

"Before we leave this meeting you can pick up evacuation route maps at the Adamsville police department and the fire department. The floor is open for questions," said Edward Fay, head of NASA.

The mayor spoke and suddenly everyone felt shaking and rocking for a few seconds, which stopped suddenly. People started screaming and running for the exits like in the movie *Dante's Peak*.

"Ladies and gentlemen, don't panic! Leave the building at a normal pace so people don't get trampled."

Everyone ran out of the school auditorium in a hurry, outside to their cars in the pouring rain, and left. Most of the tourists evacuated because nothing was open. They were checking out of hotels and getting out of Adamsville before they got a good blowjob—not the one they would like!

The residents went home and stayed put. The police, firemen, and the NASA volcano crew stayed close together in case something happened.

Sarah Eli went home and later she went on the air to report that night's town meeting about the volcano evacuation route.

Nick and Nancy packed what they could and they said to Sarah, "We're out of here before the shit hits the fan!" Then they left town.

Sarah decided to stay. The next day about 7:30 a.m. the earthquakes started again and the mountain was rocking and rolling! A loud *bang!* and shaking knocked Sarah out of bed onto the floor! She screamed hysterically! "AAAHHHH!!!!" She was bouncing around on the bedroom floor like a basketball! Then she got up and the shaking stopped. Then she left town.

The volcano crew was at the police station monitoring the earthquakes. The 7:30 a.m. jolt had the crew jumping.

"Wooooo!!!!!! Fellas, did you feel that?!" said Edward Fay.

"Yes we did!" said the workers, then it stopped.

"Nathan and Paul, go up the mountain to see if there's any damage. Look for cracks or leaks or any signs of a volcanic eruption; if there is we need to put this town on alert to evacuate," said Edward Fay.

David Dunkin was writing up reports of the 6.3 earthquake that had just happened. Nathan Rivers and Paul Numbnutts were on top of Mount Ascutney investigating spudweb's reports. It was just reporting earthquakes, no signs of an eruption.

2:22 p.m. there was a big *boom!* then *bang!* The volcano crew was at their post at the police station and everyone was knocked off their feet. The spudweb robot reported a 6.6 earthquake. Paul Numbnutts, Nathan Rivers, and David Dunkin went up in a helicopter, flying over the mountain, and there were no signs of an eruption.

"This fuckin' god damn mountain is playing games with us! If we get another earthquake of 6.0 or better we need to put this town on alert and set up an evacuation plan because this mountain might be ready to blow anytime," said Edward Fay.

3:00 p.m. there were more mild aftershocks. "I felt that; it's not a six, not even a three, but I still feel the ground shaking and moving. The magma chamber in the mountain is not changing, it's still over packed with molten rock and lava," said David Dunkin.

Then shake and *boom!* Then nothing! "I felt that! I have a 4.0 reading in the mountain," said Paul Numbnutts.

"This mountain is rocking and rolling, wanting to go very soon. There's too much pressure working its way to the summit! I feel it's going to blast off soon, according to the last 4.0 Richter report from spudweb," said Nathan Rivers.

"We need to set up bedding and food tables and stay close together 24/7 monitoring this mountain in case we get another six reading. If we do, just leave everything here, get on the helicopter and get the hell out of here!" said Edward Fay.

The NASA volcano crew contacted the mayor to hold another town meeting to evacuate at the Adamsville middle school. Most people had evacuated already and police were riding around with loudspeakers telling everyone to get out.

"Good evening, welcome to Adamsville Middle School for a second emergency town meeting tonight. There's not a lot of people here because most of the area evacuated after the first town meeting. We ask you to evacuate at this time because the NASA volcano crew reported a dangerous threat. Mount Ascutney is ready to erupt very soon because of the strong earthquakes.

"If you do not have a place to go tonight, shelters will be available at the Adamsville Fire Department after this meeting, but if you can, get out tonight. Leave as soon as you can before something happens!" said Mayor Postal Fish.

Everyone left town except for one person who slept at the fire station. 5:37 a.m. *Bang!!!!* The early morning sky lit up blue and green above Mount Ascutney as a small eruption occurred! The NASA volcano crew members were sleeping in a private room together at the police station and everyone was lifted and tossed out of their beds onto the floor. It was a loud *bang!* and the crew members were blown out of their beds. Computers, TVs, and motoring equipment got damaged!

Edward Fay said, "Hey fellas get what you can grab and get aboard the chopper, we're going back to New York right now! Well, do we have a reading now on spudweb? Nathan?"

"The blast was a 7.2 earthquake at Ascutney's summit and it looks like there was a weak eruption. We've got lightning flashing on top of the mountain!"

"We're fuckin' outta here! Put on your clothes and grab what you can and let's get out of here before we get killed!" said Edward Fay.

The crew got aboard the helicopter and David Dunkin was the pilot and Edward Fay was the navigator. There were lightning flashes across the lake still visible coming from Mount Ascutney, but it didn't appear there was an eruption because it's still too dark to notice!

6:16 a.m. the chopper left with the crew on board. The room they were in at the police station was locked. 7:45 a.m. smoke was seen rising above Mount Ascutney and there were more mild aftershocks. Sirens were blaring and police drove around on loudspeakers warning everyone to get out!

The town of Adamsville was a ghost town because all the residents and tourists evacuated earlier since there were so many earthquakes!

After every aftershock, lightning was seen coming out of the top of the mountain. Later military helicopters flew over Mount Ascutney and they saw the mountain had erupted, but no lava or fire was coming up yet. The NASA volcano crew was getting reports and pictures of the eruption from spudweb on their way to New York on board the helicopter.

The mountain continued to have small eruptions, mostly steam vent eruptions, for about a week before more, stronger, earthquakes started occurring, just before a big eruption!

October 14, 2021, a group of people were looking at the Mount Ascutney geysers through telescopes and binoculars, standing on a cliff and a bridge overlooking a brook with rapids. A hotel was in the background, and bald eagles flying over the brook. A sign at the hotel had an arrow pointing down at the flowing brook below and the name of the brook was Brooks Brook.

The geyser on top of Mount Ascutney was getting bigger, drawing a big crowd out of the hotel, joining the viewers already watching. Then a dark cloud rising followed by a loud noise, and the ground was shaking, rolling and rocking then a blast! The volcano erupted with rocks, fire and lava coming out! The volcano exploded with ash, rock and lava blowing out the top of Mount Ascutney!

A man said to a crowd of viewers, "Look at that! You can't get a better blowjob than this in Vermont!!!" A crowd of people had a good laugh.

Minutes later a violent eruption and a pyroclastic flow blew the mountain apart, sending ash and rocks like missiles miles away. Lightning was even coming out the top of the volcano! The blast was so violent that lava rocks flying out were striking the cliffs and the brook and bridge where people were taking pictures. The blast covered the sky and lava rock missiles struck homes and businesses, setting them on fire.

Then a pyroclastic flow erupted out of the volcano, setting brush afire and sending people running for cover at the hotel fifteen miles away! The Ascutney village below burned to the ground with residential areas around the mountain. Lava meteors blasting out of the volcano were landing in the lake and molten rock was pouring out of the crater at the summit.

Then the pyroclastic flow went over the lake and it burned more homes down. Boats and properties around the lake burned to the ground. A few buildings in the Overlooking Village survived with some structural damage, but it was almost destroyed.

The fire department shut off gas lines and water mains throughout the town of Adamsville during the eruptions. Later the eruptions calmed down and it was just smoking; then it stopped and the mountain was quiet a few hours later.

Sarah Eli the news reporter was on standby at the police station during the eruption, taking reports. She drove by her house and it was gone, burned to ashes. Her neighbors' house was gone too!

Later she went on the news with Fox. "Good evening this is Fox News Tonight, October 14, 2021. A major volcano erupted on Mount Ascutney in Adamsville, Vermont this morning with ash, fire, volcanic molten rock, and flowing lava. Later a second eruption with a pyroclastic blast spread a fifteen-mile ash cloud. Several homes and businesses burned to the ground.

"I recently moved to Adamsville and my house and my neighbors' burned to ashes. We do not know if anyone was injured or killed at this time. The NASA volcano crew, police, the fire department, and Mayor Postal Fish did a good job evacuating the town and villages after several strong earthquakes and aftershocks. Fearing a volcanic eruption, residents and tourists got out in time.

"The eruption caused millions of dollars in damages. The Ascutney Village and living community was completely destroyed. Pyroclastic flow and molten rock missiles caused severe damage to the Overlooking Village and destroyed several lakefront properties and boats. Just a few buildings remain in Adamsville tonight.

"The volcano is still active this evening and NASA will be back tomorrow for more updates from the volcano, and will fly over mountains in New Hampshire and western Massachusetts. It could have been worse because geologists and seismologists said that a super volcano is brewing under Vermont, New Hampshire, and Massachusetts, and the center of the core is inside Ascutney. More earthquakes and eruptions are possible. Sarah Eli reporting on Fox News Tonight."

During the night, the town of Adamsville was under a curfew—there was destruction everywhere! The volcano was quiet and dark and there were no more earthquakes. NASA was monitoring the volcano through the Adamsville Police Department webcam because the one on top of Mount Ascutney was destroyed by the violent eruptions. Ash missiles spared the hotel fifteen miles away, but the ash cloud spread far enough to set fire to the property's forests, setting the bridge, a dock, and trees on fire.

Hundreds of people ran for their lives, running into a cave and Limerock Village and the hotel where the ash cloud stopped. Fire trucks sprayed water and foam in Limerock Village and at the hotel. Airplanes flew over Mount Ascutney the next day, dropping water on the burning debris on top of the mountain. A cloudy rainy day helped finished the job, cooling this volcano down.

It looked like the fires in California, forests burning down the mountainside. Thank goodness the planes did a good job putting it out! Then NASA arrived with its crew and another spudweb data machine which they bolted to a rock inside the crater. The mountain crater was much bigger because part of the mountain was blown apart. The police and fire department and Mayor Postal Fish drove through town to view the destruction and the damage was so bad it was unrecognizable!

"Holy shit, we have been annihilated!" said a policeman. Before cleanup was done a meeting was held at the police station.

"Good evening. My name is David Dunkin covering for Edward Fay tonight. We have some serious damage from an eruption that could have been much worse! Cleanup may be next to impossible! Whoever did not evacuate when told to is probably dead! We will assess the destruction and damages tomorrow, October 16, 2021.

"Right now the mountain is quiet and I hope it stays that way! The lava chamber is much lower and very little pressure is building inside Ascutney at this time. We had quite a blast here; high into the sky instead of blowing the towns of Adamsville, Bronson, and Limerock off the face of the earth!!!!!! We have catastrophic damage here in Adamsville and part of Bronson, Vermont. We will be lucky to knock down and rebuild. We're still here. There's no electricity, the police station is running on generators.

"The mountain is safe, but if earthquakes start up again or this mountain acts up, don't even think of bringing tourists back because you could be in a volcanic dead zone. If that's the case don't even bother with cleanup!

"Tomorrow you may begin cleanup. Look for injured, trapped, or the dead, but if earthquakes begin to happen get out as soon as possible. We will still be here monitoring this volcano until earthquakes begin to happen. If they do, we're out of here!" said David Dunkin volcanologist news reporter.

The next day, October 17, 2021, police and rescue teams were searching through damaged areas and they found dead people, several dead animals under damaged debris, and volcanic ash. Dead humans and animals floated down Brooks Brook toward Limerock Hotel, and the bridge was gone. Most of the bodies were recovered in Bronson and the town of Limerock, which didn't take the volcano seriously until it was too late. Fifteen miles away the volcano still killed people.

Everything was shut down in Ascutney County, Adamsville, Bronson, and Limerock. The hotel was evacuated after the eruption, but some people got caught trying to run for safety and quite a few didn't make it! Dead people and animals lay ashore on both sides of the river, covered by volcanic ash! Early evening, the NASA volcano crew, the fire department, police, and rescue teams spent time eating dinner and counting the dead from the volcano eruption.

"Ladies and gentlemen, we did find a lot of dead people and animals under volcanic ash, and damaged property. The good news: We did a great job evacuating Adamsville because only one person and about five animals were found dead. Our neighboring towns Bronson and Limerock were not so lucky; we are still counting the dead.

"The blast was more severe in those areas because they did not have a good evacuation plan. I didn't think the volcano was going to erupt as bad as it did! I thought only our area would be affected and parts of Bronson, but I didn't think the eruption would travel as far as it did," said David Dunkin at the Adamsville police station.

Later people from all over Vermont were watching the news on TV about the Mount Ascutney eruption. "Good evening, this is Fox News Tonight. The Mount Ascutney eruption on October 14 has killed 278 people and at least 250 animals, mostly in Bronson and Limerock, sixteen miles away from the volcano. The death count may not be over yet! More than 450 homes and businesses burned to the ground and eighty percent of Ascutney County has been destroyed. The Ascutney Village is destroyed and the Overlooking Village and hotels and lakefront are uninhabitable and may never be rebuilt.

"Volcanic ash leveled all three towns. Several bodies floated down Brooks Brook and a bridge was destroyed in Limerock. Elaine Ezerins, reporting on Fox News Tonight."

The next day, bulldozers and military earth mobiles arrived to finish knocking down standing buildings and removing ash and volcano debris so rebuilding could begin. There were no more earthquakes and the mountain was quiet, but rescue workers were still rounding up the dead in Bronson and Limerock.

The residents burned out of their homes had to stay in hotels and makeshift shelters set up in school gyms, cafeterias, school buildings that closed and vacant buildings reopened to house evacuees, and at Vermont health centers.

The volcanic debris was scooped up into dump trucks by bulldozers and the dump trucks drove up a manmade makeshift dirt road up the mountain and dumped the debris to cover up the huge crater. Cement trucks arrived to cement the crater opening. A weather station was being built there with a heliport for helicopters to land on. The spudweb data machine was buried in the ash and cemented over, and it was still sending data from inside the volcano to the NASA team.

It was January, 2022 when the work was done and the Ascutney ski resort was open. New lifts and metal buildings were installed for the grand opening. The NASA volcano crew went back to New York. Ascutney kept quiet!

CHAPTER FIVE

VOLCANOES WAKING UP
IN WASHINGTON STATE

February, 2022

Mount St. Helens is ready to erupt again. Seismologists say that Mount St. Helens is safe but surrounding volcanoes Mount Baker and Mount Rainier are a threat. Earthquakes from Mount Adams raise concerns that this mountain is a threat to a maximum security prison that may have to be moved!

A major steel bunker is being built at the bottom of Mount St. Helens, big enough to house all the inmates on death row. The Tahoma prison is near Mount Rainier, on Glacier Peak, and the prisoners will have to be moved to a safe place because these volcanoes are getting ready to wake up: all five of them.

———

The NASA volcano crew in New York was called to this dangerous area and they will have their work cut out for them. The NASA group got together ready for a worldwide blowjob!

"May I have your attention ladies and gentlemen. We have a major job to contend with in the Cascade Range out west in

Washington State, a hell of a lot bigger than the blowjob in Vermont from the Mount Ascutney eruption.

"There are five big volcanoes out west all ready to go off at the same time. The magma molten rock levels are at their highest peak since the 1980 eruption of Mount St. Helens. We have to go there and set up camp because there's going to be a big blowjob there pretty soon!

"I'm getting readings of mild earthquakes in downtown Seattle. Mount Rainier is scheduled to go off first and if it does, say bye-bye to Seattle! We will meet other NASA crew there in a bunker underground near Mount St. Helens, the safest area of the Cascades, because she blew her load a few times already!

"Our camp will set up on top of Bear Mountain in California. If more volcanoes erupt across the United States we will have to go back and forth to monitor them. We will have more trouble out there because the Oregon volcanoes are a threat as well—Mount Hood, Three Sisters Range, South Sister Volcano, and Crater Lake Volcano. Mount Hood is the most active volcano in Oregon but the others need watching because all magma levels are high.

"Mount Shasta and Mount Whitney in East Central California are also dangerous; if these go off San Bernardino and Sierra Nevada will be gone! We have a lot of blowjobs ready to blow.

"They're loaded on the west coast of the United States. Alaska has several volcanoes. If eruptions start happening it's going to be a chain reaction of terror. Yellowstone super volcano could go off at any time and it's been a major threat for the last thirty-five years, but the good news is it has plenty of breathing holes to avoid a massive eruption. Yellowstone is very active.

"Kilauea Volcano in Hawaii has plenty of eruption sites for surface magma to flow without blowing up the big island. Kilauea feeds the Hawaiian Islands and delivers her little sisters in the western Pacific. Redoubt Volcano in Alaska is ready to blow very soon as well. When we get to Seattle we will have a meeting at the convention center with Eleanor Pepperjack-carmendonchamppinelli, the head of US Geology, and she will explain what's going on in these mountains and how to prepare us for what's to come.

"We have a series of very high and violent volcanoes to work with. The steam vent volcanoes here in New York City are okay. Blue Hills near Boston is okay and Mount Ascutney in Adamsville, Vermont is quiet. Let's be ready because we have a major task ahead of us out on the West Coast.

"Leave all equipment here at the Empire State Building sub-basement, Room 007, the main monitoring data room. We will be using our equipment on the chopper and when we get to Bear Mountain, Eleanor P. will have everything set up for us there and at Mount St. Helens.

"We will be followed by military helicopters and fighter jets to Washington State with a few stops in between. We will depart soon and our first destination when we arrive will be Mount St. Helens bunker. Thank you. Ready! Let's go!" said Edward Fay, head of the NASA volcano crew.

The helicopter took off from a closed off area and the crew was off. The NASA chopper had some stops on the way and it landed at a military base near Mount St. Helens. "Good afternoon NASA New York. Welcome to Washington State Cascade Region. My name is General Herby Hoxie."

"Pleased to meet you. My name is Edward Fay, head of volcanology from NASA, and my crew. Linda Brew works with monitoring equipment, and this is Katrina House, monitoring manager. This is Nathan Rivers who works with spudweb and data news reports. This is Paul Numbnutts who works with spudweb, and this is David Dunkin, news reporter for earthquake monitoring equipment data."

"It's quite a crew you have, Mr. Fay. Let's board the bus that will take us to the tram rail going up the mountain about three thousand feet and we will arrive at the southern face bunker at Mount St. Helens," said General Herby Hoxie, Washington State National Guard.

The bus took the crew to the tram rail and they went up the mountain in a snowstorm. "Welcome NASA New York, to Mount St. Helens. Set up here and we will go on a tour through the bunker and see a movie on the mountain's past eruptions," said the general.

Then he continued, "This door leads to the steel bunker of doom. It is thirty feet high and twenty feet wide and eight feet thick. A five-digit combination and an emailed code is used to enter the bunker. The space in here holds as many as 150,000 people, three times the size of any football stadium. The bunker is eight feet thick going through one side of the mountain to the other and its air is filtered and recycled, heated, and air conditioned. The heat is thermal heat from the molten rock below this volcano and it's a safe haven if Mount St. Helens erupts again.

"We have seventy-five thousand bathrooms, thirty thousand kitchens, 230,000 beds, thirty-five thousand living facilities, and 128,000 utility workers. We have no one here yet and we have not used these facilities in the last twelve years, but due to the threat of a super volcano eruption the prisons may have to be moved here, as well as some military bases. Mount St. Helens is the safest volcano in the Cascades because a series of eruptions in the past quieted this mountain and it's the only place a bunker like this can be built. It took fourteen years to build this.

"We will look at a few rooms then we will see the movie about Mount St. Helens's past because it will take more than twenty-four hours to walk through this place. There's a tram rail on both sides of the bunker for people to get where they are going. Here you have a bedroom that sleeps four people and a bath, kitchen, and living room area with a flat-screen TV.

"Each restroom has four toilets, sinks, and showers. All the underground bunker apartments are the same. You have mini malls and restaurants in these bunkers and people will come here for two reasons: nuclear fallout, or a volcano eruption.

"Let's see the movie. Mount St. Helens' last major eruption was May 18, 1980. It has erupted a few times since then. In 1983 it erupted again, then had some smaller eruptions in 1995, 2005, and 2008. This mountain is still active; the molten rock lava magma level is rising, and it may erupt again," said General Herby Hoxie.

After watching Mount St. Helens's blowjobs for an hour the general spoke again. "After you finish setting all your equipment up, you will board the bus to the Space Needle restaurant in Seattle for dinner and a view of Mount Rainier. Then you will stay at the Cascade Valley Hotel with beautiful mountain views.

"Tomorrow afternoon you will attend a national volcano learning session with Miss Eleanor Pepperjackcarmendon-champpinelli at the Seattle Convention Center, around 2:00 p.m. Pacific time. Thank you," said General Herby Hoxie.

Later the bus took the NASA crew and the Washington State National Guard to the Space Needle and dinner. It was raining and dark outside so you couldn't view the mountains. Dinner was served—steak, potatoes and fresh garden salads, red and white wine, and Seattle's best coffee with strawberry shortcake for dessert. There was thunder and lightning and it was very loud. The heavy rain was blowing sideways up against the windows in the revolving restaurant. The storm was a scary scene!

Katrina House drank a bottle of red Seattle wine by herself and she was starting to feel sick. She had a vision that Mount Rainier erupted! A fireball crashed into the restaurant breaking the windows, setting the Space Needle restaurant on fire. People were being sucked out and everyone died!

She choked up, then she threw up all over the table where she was seated! Then she fell down and passed out! The rest of the crew helped her up and Edward Fay said, "Are you okay Katrina, you have a little too much to drink? Let's go back to the bus; the elevators are on the left."

Katrina told the crew about her vision while riding down a glass elevator from the Space Needle revolving restaurant. "That can't happen Katrina, Mount Rainier is too far away!" said Edward Fay.

The bus arrived at the beautiful Cascade Valley Inn. "Ladies and gentlemen, welcome to the Cascade Valley Inn Bed & Breakfast. It's not the biggest place but it's nice, and you have fantastic views, nice rooms, and cabin style fireplaces," said General Herby Hoxie, military tour guide.

During the night, Katrina had a dream the Space Needle restaurant suffered an earthquake while everyone was on the glass elevator. The elevator broke loose and fell to the ground and a broken plate glass window chopped her in half and she woke up screaming!

She realized it was only a dream and she went back to bed. *It wasn't only a dream; she had a premonition! It could happen during an earthquake because if the mountains began erupting Seattle would suffer an earthquake!*

Katrina shared her dream with the crew and they were a little shaken up about her vision. "Katrina, what kind of drugs are you taking? You have some scary dreams and visions!" said David Dunkin.

"I feel that if the Cascade Mountains all erupt at the same time these premonitions could happen. God forbid! But I see these visions, how it'll be if things go wrong!" she said.

The crew looked at all the mountains from the Cascade Inn while having continental breakfast/brunch. Then the bus took them to the convention center in downtown Seattle for a 2:00 p.m. meeting.

"Good afternoon ladies and gentlemen. Welcome to the

Washington State Convention Center. My name is Eleanor Pep-perjackcarmendonchamppinelli, the head of volcanology on the West Coast, including Alaska and Hawaii. Most people call me Miss P. for short.

"We have a NASA crew here from Houston, Texas helping us out. Mr. Edward Fay, the head of NASA volcanology, and his crew: Linda Brew and Katrina House, volcano monitors; David Dunkin, NASA news reporter; and Nathan Rivers and Paul Numbnutts, spudweb robot readers.

"This team is new and stationed in New York City because of earthquakes and volcanic eruptions on the East Coast. On October 14, 2021, a violent volcano erupted in Vermont killing almost three hundred people in three titties—I mean three cities! And steam eruptions in New York City and a small eruption on Blue Hills near Boston, Massachusetts caused earthquakes in Boston and surrounding areas.

"There was damage on the Curry College campus injuring several students, and more than thirty homes were destroyed in the Boston area. Seismologists, geologists, and scientists say a super volcano is brewing under Vermont, New Hampshire, and Massachusetts, three of the New England states. Mount Ascutney in Vermont was the epicenter that erupted. Danger could be lurking in the future in New England.

"Then we have Yellowstone. The biggest super volcano in the world's magma chamber is building and due for an eruption soon, but we have issues here a lot like Yellowstone!

"Mount Rainier is 14,411 feet high. Mount Adams is 12,276 feet, our second tallest mountain. Mount Baker is third at 10,778 feet, Glacier Peak is 10,541 feet, and Mount St. Helens is our baby volcano standing at 8,363 feet high, but is also the most active volcano in the Cascade region.

"We have some very big volcanoes here in Washington State and all of them are becoming active because of high molten rock lava levels. We could be in serious danger very soon. If these big mountains go off like Mount St. Helens did in 1980 we will lose cities. We could be blown off the face of the earth if all five go off at the same time—it could happen!

"Mount St. Helens has erupted a few times since 1980. The mountain is quiet right now, but the magma chamber is building again. The area is safe for now and a military bunker was just finished going through Mount St. Helens from one end to the other. It took twelve years to build this bunker that holds as many as two hundred thousand people. This bunker is raised three thousand feet above ground level over the magma chamber. Nobody's had to use this facility except for storm evacuations, but that's about to change. The mayor of Seattle, Eric Condom, wants to move the prison in because of the threat of a mega volcanic eruption in Washington State.

"I want to introduce my crew to you before we talk about what we're going to do. The monitoring equipment, computers, TVs, monitoring screens, and spudweb—everybody works together. We have fifteen spudweb robots only to be used if there's a threat of an eruption. My crew is Steven Jennings; Gail Porter; Jill Santiago; Michael Kennedy; Dick Colon; Peter Oakland; David Vincent; Jessica Vincent; her brother, Aden Vincent; and myself, Eleanor W. Pepperjackcarmendonchamppinelli—just call me Miss P.!

"Peter Oakland is our news media personality and he will tell what is going on and why we're here."

"Thank you Miss P. Ladies and gentlemen, I am sorry to say but we are in serious danger here in Washington State and here in downtown Seattle is at the greatest risk. We have five major volcanoes, all ready to go off one at a time in a chain reaction, or all five could blow their lid within the next five months.

"The magma and molten rock levels are at their highest peak where there's nowhere to go but for them to blast off very soon!

The magma levels have been resting at the top of the rim for the last six months and time is not on our side! Mount Rainier at 14,411 feet is already rumbling with several earthquakes, five or better, and threatens the city of Tacoma and the Mount Rainier National Park.

"Mount Adams is at 12,276 feet, Mount Baker is at 10,788 feet, then we have Glacier Peak at 10,541 feet, not to mention Mount St. Helens at 8,363 feet. All are stratovolcanoes. A river caldera of molten lava following from one mountain to the next is at its max, and all of them could go off at the same time!

"A stratovolcano is a buildup of lava and molten rock pushing the mountain higher and higher. In other words, they're having an orgasm before they blow their load just like a woman having her time of the month. Volcanoes act the same way, it just takes longer before they come! If one of these volcanoes goes off, we need to have an evacuation plan!" said Peter Oakland.

Everyone started laughing at his comparison of sex to volcanoes. Then he continued, "Mount St. Helens's military emergency bunkers and barracks would be the safest place to go. Shuttle ferries will be leaving out of Seattle to Victoria, Canada, and Fairbanks, Alaska; not Vancouver, because if Mount Rainier blows, Seattle, Vancouver—heck the whole of Washington State and a chunk of Canada will be gone!

"If all five go off at the same time I can't imagine how bad it will be. Here is the mayor of Seattle to finish off this meeting, Mr. Eric Condom."

"Thank you Peter. Ladies and gentlemen, we are on the verge of a major volcanic eruption on Mount Rainier! Don't panic just yet because a major evacuation is not necessary. There have been some strong earthquakes in the mountain, threatening the areas around it. The only evacuations starting tomorrow will be the prisons, hospitals, and nursing homes in the Tacoma area. They will be moved to the military bunkers in Mount St. Helens.

"Please have an evacuation route planned just in case one or more of these mountains erupts. Please pick up an evacuation departure guide on your way out. There will not be a town meeting later. Use your own judgment if you hear a boom! If you need to leave, or a volcano is erupting, have your plan in place and keep your distance. Thank you, this meeting is over," said Eric Condom, the mayor of Seattle.

One man said to a lady leaving the convention center, "I'm out of here before the shit hits the fan! I'm not taking any chances!"

"Me too!" said the lady.

Many people boarded the ferry to go to Canada. Others boarded buses and trains for those who wanted to evacuate! The jails were let out and bused to the Mount St. Helens bunkers. With hospitals, and nursing homes, it was about 150,000 people in total.

The NASA volcano crew went back to Mount St. Helens to look at readings from the volcanoes. Mild earthquakes rocked them all with the exception of Mount St. Helens.

Is everyone safe here? We'll see!

The next day, the New York City NASA crew was flown by military aircraft to Bear Mountain in California, a possible safe haven in case Washington State was to be blown off the map!!!!!!!!!!!!

They set up in a lodge at the top of a snowy mountain about eight thousand feet. It was a very cold late February day near the summit of Big Bear Mountain in San Bernardino, California. Katrina was looking at one of the monitors and she said, "Edward, look at this! A Mars rover is sending back some kind of life; it looks like a giant fly or some kind of creature!"

"That's a bug stuck inside the lens. We don't have time to be looking for things on Mars or out in space! We have some serious volcanic activity in the Cascade Mountains we should be watching, Katrina.

"Ladies and gentlemen, welcome to Big Bear Mountain. We are located in San Bernardino, California. The reason why we're here is because we need to help Eleanor P.'s group in monitoring all the volcanoes on the West Coast and across the United States.

"Our job is called, US Mission Blowjob. No! It's not a sex thing! We have to watch more than fifty active volcanoes all along the West Coast. We don't need to leave here; we just need to do our job. We have a nice big fireplace to keep warm, nice bedrooms with jacuzzies, and great food here. We have some very dangerous volcanoes to watch here on the West Coast," said Edward Fay.

––––––––––

March 18, 2022. A tour was visiting Seattle and was boarding the ferry to go to Canada when suddenly a strong earthquake lasting about a minute triggered rippling waves in the water. Buildings started shaking in downtown Seattle. People started screaming and running in the streets. The ferry had just left the dock and had to turn back and redock in Seattle.

"Ladies and gentlemen, this is your captain speaking. We just had an earthquake and we have to return to Seattle. Sorry for the inconvenience. Please do not panic when we get off. All remaining scheduled ferry service to Canada has been cancelled for the day. Thank you."

In Canada: "Ladies and gentlemen, a 7.2 earthquake struck in Seattle. All remaining ferry service to the United States has been cancelled for the day. Repeat: there will be no ferry service leaving for the United States. Sorry for the inconvenience. Steamship Authority Canada." The warnings were translated in French at both US and Canadian ferry service docks.

A subway train was approaching the Corona Landing stop

when the earthquake struck, derailing the train and leaving it stuck in a tunnel. It was a packed subway train and people who were standing fell down, some becoming hurt.

People were shopping in the mall when the ground shook. Everyone was falling and holding on to poles and railings to avoid being swept away. Things were falling in the stores as the mall was rocking and rolling, swaying back and forth, and rising up and down, then it stopped!

Glass windows broke in storefronts and slid down the aisles in the big Seattle mall. Ceiling tiles fell on top of people who were trying to get out of the mall! The lights flickered and some stores lost their electricity. People were running everywhere, trampling over others while trying to get out of the mall, knocking people over, triggering a gang fight.

A PBA bowling tournament was going on when the earthquake struck and the bowling alley was rocking and rolling and shaking and rumbling. A bowler was up with 9 strikes in a row, determined to bowl his 300, and no earthquake, volcano, or gunshot was going to stop him! The bowling alley was shaking and people ran out of the bowling alley like bats out of hell!

The man going for his 300 score picked up his bowling ball and threw it down on the lane while ceiling tiles and wires were falling on his head and. The building was shaking so badly but he was determined to get his 300 game even if the earthquake was going to kill him!

He released the ball and the electricity went out. It was a pocket hit due to the earthquake and he got a 9, leaving a tenpin. He screamed *F-this!* and *F-that!* for twenty minutes! The tournament was over and he had to be satisfied with a 267 because the bowling alley was falling down; he's not able to pick up the spare.

Another man finished before him with a 268 game! He lost by one pin because he couldn't finish due to the earthquake! He was pissed! The bowling alley suffered severe damage and the screaming man was dragged out by other tournament members. He was covered with blood and taken to the hospital in a rescue vehicle.

People were golfing at a golf course when the earthquake struck. First it was the sound of thunder, a loud *roar!* Play was stopped, then the ground started shaking and swinging like a washing machine. Players went from putting on the greens and driving for the next hole, to *run for your life!*

People eating at the Space Needle restaurant never felt a thing. "Ladies and gentlemen, please head to the elevators and vacate the Space Needle, there was an earthquake in downtown Seattle. Please do not panic or crowd the elevators," said restaurant staff.

People ran for the elevators in shock but everyone got out of there okay. Panicking people ran under underpasses and others ran for the mountains to get to higher ground because tsunami warning sirens were going off. Downtown Seattle looked like a race against time with people running for their lives with or without clothes on!

The building swayed back and forth and some windows broke but most were cracked. It was a race to the end of the world, when all at once the shaking stopped after a minute. Everything was calm like nothing had happened, but people continued running for their lives! Movie theaters, office meetings, and the work-force were in a 9/11-like panic, racing downstairs in buildings to street level like a pack of rats running from a trash dump! Half of the city was without power!

Back at Big Bear Mountain: "Edward, a pretty good earthquake struck the center of downtown Seattle! I have a 6.9 to 7.2 reading, and I also have activity near the summit of Mount Rainier. The magma level has gone down and there has been a mild steam vent eruption. I'm not too concerned as the molten rock levels have dropped. That's good news, the mountain should be safe. The bad news is magma levels are rising at Mount St. Helens," said Katrina House.

"Okay, send the report over to Eleanor P.'s group at Mount St. Helens," said Edward Fay.

She got the report and the NASA crews continued monitoring all the mountains. Everything was quiet for a while after the earthquake.

Thursday March 24, 2022, about 5:30 p.m., the Space Needle restaurant was packed with people after a national convention meeting and tour. Most of the group was Asian. The tour guide spoke about the restaurant in English, Chinese, and Japanese before dinner was served.

"Welcome to the Sky City Restaurant. We have a view of Mount Rainier, Mount Baker, Mount St. Helens, the Cascade and Olympic Mountains, Elliott Bay, the islands of Puget Sound, and the skyline of downtown Seattle.

"The restaurant is a revolving disc that has 360-degree rotation with fantastic views below. The restaurant has three elevators and we are 550 feet above the ground. Enjoy your meal before we return to the Best Western Seattle Hotel," the tour guide said in English, Chinese, and Japanese.

Everyone was enjoying their meal until there was a *boom!* and the restaurant shook a little, then it was quiet. The disc continued revolving and people were taking pictures of the view from the Space Needle Skyline restaurant, overlooking downtown Seattle. A short time later, after the boom, somebody noticed a bright orange flash when Mount Rainier erupted! The Japanese tour guide said, "Look out there! Look out there! Look out there!!!!!!!!!!!!!!!!!! A volcano is erupting out there!!!!!!!!!!!!!!!!!!" They were speaking in Chinese and Japanese.

Back in California the volcano crew was monitoring the Mount Rainier eruption. "Edward, Mount Rainier just erupted with no warning. There is ash, molten rock, and a pyroclastic flow blowing out the top of the mountain! I don't know how bad it is but the mountain is erupting. It's not a steam blast, this mountain blew its top!" said Nathan Rivers.

Edward was looking at the monitors and he said, "Holy shit! We are just at the beginning; the magma chamber is heading for Mount Baker at a high rate of speed and its rising at Mount St. Helens! We might have a mega disaster on the way, just be prepared!"

Back at the Space Needle Skyline Restaurant, Mount Rainier really had erupted. People yelled! Everyone in the restaurant got up to get a good look when a mega eruption blew the mountain apart, sending volcanic rock missiles hundreds of miles away, striking buildings like asteroids coming from space!

Before the second blast, people hiking and skiing on the mountain and in Mount Rainier Park were killed instantly during the mega eruption because of the pyroclastic flow. Tons of snow raced down the mountain, burying everybody above and below!

A severe lahar buried cities and towns below! Tacoma was wiped out, buried in volcanic rock and mud!

Back at the Skyline Restaurant, people were watching the eruption until clouds formed, quickly blocking out the sight, and the sky turned a fiery orange color. Then the molten rock missiles blowing far out of the top of Mount Rainier started striking.

A giant rock on fire came out of nowhere, smashing into the Skyline Restaurant, setting the restaurant on fire in seconds! People were killed instantly! The scene went from people going to the windows to view the classic eruption, the clouds, to *crash!*—people were on fire and being sucked out the windows of the revolving restaurant. People running away from the fire went for the elevators and then the power went out!

The fire burned the cables on the elevators and they fell to the ground, killing hundreds of people! The Space Needle was hit by a second fiery molten rock missile, burning the structure to the ground! People burning in the restaurant jumped out of windows to their deaths. The sky was on fire from the pyroclastic flow, blowing out of Mount Rainier at the speed of a jet plane and its two thousand-degree heat!

The ash cloud set fire to some of the buildings in downtown Seattle before it stopped. The city was buried in a foot and a half of volcanic ash when it was over! Fiery molten rock missiles landed in the water and the burning villages below.

Some of the ash asteroids landed in neighboring Canada, killing thousands! People were watching the eruption from a hillside at a Canadian resort when suddenly a tsunami about fifty feet high came out of nowhere and drowned them all! The water was a tsunami of volcanic mud!

People in downtown Seattle were running for their lives when they saw the dark ash clouds and fiery rock missiles coming fast. They jumped into water, and some went into the subways but were burned to death by the pyroclastic ash cloud!

Tsunami sirens started sounding after the disaster! Fire sprinklers went off in all the buildings to save Seattle from burning to the ground, and in subways and waterways. The ash clouds and molten rock missiles stopped coming a little while after the second blast, but Mount Rainier was still erupting and lava was coming out of the top. Most of the mountain had been blasted away.

The NASA volcano crew were watching the disaster unfold, they could not believe what was happening! People and animals, towns and cities, were blown off the mountain. Thousands of people and uncountable animals were feared dead. The eruption was worse than Mount St. Helens when she blew her load in May of 1980!

———

Back at Mount St. Helens: The bunkers holding 150,000 prison inmates and hospital and nursing home residents shook violently when Mount Rainier was erupting. They were safe from the eruption, but some people were hurt from being thrown around during the earthquakes, and hundreds needed medical treatment.

"Good evening, this is National Fox News tonight with Elaine Ezerins. Mount Rainier erupted in Washington State and thousands of people are feared dead. Seattle is burning! The Space Needle was packed with people eating at the Skyline Restaurant when it was struck by the ash cloud. Molten rock strikes set the structure afire, burning it to the ground. People were forced to jump to their deaths while being burned alive from the ash cloud. Mount Rainier is still erupting this evening and more eruptions are possible! Fox News Tonight."

Police and the fire department worked through the night to try to save people and close roads and find bodies. Most areas were covered in ash and you couldn't drive through it. Heavy snow and icebergs lay in ruins, lahars blocked roads and bridges, not to mention the damaged buildings. The National Guard was called in to help.

Friday morning, March 25, 2022, it was dark because Mount Rainier's ash cloud was blocking out the sun. 6:37 a.m. Mount Adams erupted, blowing out ash lava then a large plume of pyroclastic flow high into the sky, followed by lightning and thunder! The blast looked like the 1980 eruption of Mount St. Helens.

Back at Big Bear Mountain where the New York NASA team was staying, "Edward, come look at this! Mount Adams just erupted," said Katrina House.

"Oh my fuckin' God!" he said.

Just before Mount Adams erupted a cop was riding on a snowy road during a snowstorm near the summit, and a grizzly bear appeared as the cop was driving around a corner. It was waving its paws over its head while standing in the road. The cop stopped in the road and the bear wouldn't get out of his way—the bear was giving the cop a warning because something was about to happen. The cop got out of his car, drew his gun, and fired a shot in the air. The bear waved its paw then it leaped into the snow and ran down the mountain!

The cop finished his journey then he drove to the summit to see if anyone was up there. He saw a portajohn up there and he said to himself, *Ah! Nice, I have to go for a shit!*

There was nobody up there, it was a ghost town. The cop checked the empty buildings before he went for his shit, then he heard a loud *boom!* followed by shaking while he was wiping his ass with frozen toilet paper in the portajohn. Then the mountain blew with no warning and his body was fried and blasted, getting stuck on a ski lift pole.

Bears and other animals were blown off Mount Adams. The eruption triggered a severe earthquake in Mount St. Helens and several evacuees staying in the bunkers inside were injured. *And she's about ready to blow her load again!*

Cornucopia, Washington was leveled. Teachers at Cornhole High School were arriving at 6:30 a.m., seven minutes before the eruption. Then *boom!*, the ground shook, earthquake sirens were sounding in the school, and the teachers ran outside to the courtyard and saw the eruption from nearby Mount Adams. "Oh my God!" they cried.

Then there was a *roar!* and a lahar was coming, so the teachers ran back in the school, running upstairs to higher ground, going on the roof. Suddenly a grizzly bear came crashing down where they were, smashing through the roof and landing in the cafeteria, dead. Every bone was broken in the bear's body and its head was smashed! The teachers were screaming hysterically then a few minutes later everything went quiet.

The lahar of volcanic mud, ice, and snow washed the school away, killing everyone in its wake! The city of Cornucopia was buried under twenty feet of mud. Lightning struck several homes and villages from the Mount Adams eruptions, and lahars washed cities and towns away, killing hundreds and thousands of people and farm animals.

The pyroclastic flow triggered violent thunderstorms which spawned tornadoes, dumping record rainfall and hail the size of duckpin bowling balls. Two hundred-mile-per-hour straight-line microburst winds came straight down from the ash cloud from the volcano! The sky was black as night all day and Mount Adams was still blowing her load, worse than the eruption of Mount Rainier. Lava was *still* coming out of Mount Rainier from *yesterday's* eruption.

The police, fire department, and the National Guard couldn't do anything until the eruptions calmed down. Military helicopters flew around the eruption sights taking pictures, keeping a safe distance to keep from getting caught in the ash clouds over both mountains.

The lightning strikes out of Mount Adams were apocalyptic, coming out of the crater in the pyroclastic ash clouds, strikes reaching all the way to the ground! The volcanoes were making their own thunderstorms and violent weather! Lightning was also seen coming from the crater of Mount Rainier. The helicopters flew by Mount St. Helens, Glacier Peak, and Mount Baker then flew around the damaged city of Seattle taking pictures for news reports. Seattle was covered in volcanic ash from the Mount Rainier eruption.

Eleanor P.'s NASA group stationed in the Mount St. Helens bunkers was preparing for the worst to come. "Ladies and gentlemen, this is Eleanor Pepperjackcarmendonchamppinelli, reporting that Mount Adams has just had a violent eruption! We're stuck here in the bunkers until these volcanic eruptions subside. The city of Cornucopia and all of the Mount Adams community have been buried alive. There will be no help for some time because the police and fire department can't get into the damaged areas, not even the National Guard.

"I understand that several people have been hurt because of the violent earthquakes from the eruption of Mount Adams. We will be experiencing several earthquakes. When you feel any shaking you have clamp straps coming out of the walls, on the rails of your beds, and on all chairs and couches. Buckle up when you feel shaking because we will be getting these earthquakes every time there's an eruption.

"Mount Rainier erupted yesterday, burning down the Space Needle, damaging downtown Seattle and dumping more than a foot of ash on city streets. Thousands of people are feared dead in Seattle.

"Mount Adams erupted early this morning, just before twenty of seven, leaving a trail of death and destruction. With Mount Adams's eruption it does not look good for Mount St. Helens.

"These bunkers have been here for twelve years and Mount St. Helens went through many earthquakes, including a mild volcanic eruption in 2018. We're safe here if Mount St. Helens erupts because we are living in a bunker with walls made of thirty foot thick fireproof steel. The only thing is you will be knocked on your ass during a violent eruption if you're not buckled up!"

Eleanor P. continued giving instructions, talking over an intercom loudspeaker throughout the bunker holding 150,000 people and preparing them from the coming disaster. Several people were hurt in the earthquakes inside the bunkers. About 1,500 people were killed from injuries caused by being knocked around from earthquakes and prison riots inside the bunker's jail.

The dead were packed up in body bags, thrown out of the bunkers and down the mountain, food for the bears and wildlife on Mount St. Helens. People who died in the nursing home section were also fed to the bears! The injured were cared for in the bunker's hospital. The families of the dead were contacted.

There was no electricity in Seattle. The evacuation bunkers luckily had generators for light, heat, air conditioning, and clean air. People around the world were watching news reports about a second volcano erupting in Washington State.

"Good afternoon, we have breaking news, KCMO Channel 10 News in Kansas City, Missouri. Mount Adams erupted early this morning just a day after Mount Rainier erupted, burning down the Space Needle and burying Seattle under ash. Thousands of people are feared dead. This morning Mount Adams had a bigger eruption, leaving a trail of destruction with lahars burying cities and parks under mud, ash, and lava. The death toll is unknown. Police and the National Guard have no access to recover or rescue trapped people because of the violent eruptions. All travel to Washington State from the United States and Canada is cancelled indefinitely!

"Seismologists say that all five volcanoes in Washington State and Mount Hood in Oregon are in danger of erupting. Three Sister South, Mount Shasta, Mount Whitney, and two major volcanoes in Alaska are in danger of possibly blowing up the West Coast. Lisa Livingstone reporting on KCMO Channel 10 News in Kansas City."

Nighttime and Mount Adams was still erupting. The orgasm was seen miles away, sending molten rock missiles into buildings and triggering forest fires during the night before quieting down the next day. A giant ash cloud blocked out the sun, causing permanent night that blocked rescuers from saving people and stopping buildings, homes, and forests from burning.

It looked like the end of the world! Lava levels were rising rapidly in Mount St. Helens, threatening another volcanic eruption. The molten rock was forming in a lava tube away from the bunkers working its way to Mount St. Helens's summit, sparing the bunkers inside the mountain. The Eleanor P. NASA volcano crew was watching the magma rise quickly. Eleanor made an announcement on the intercoms to buckle up and be ready for more earthquakes and a Mount St. Helens eruption.

Sirens sounded in the bunkers. Many people started evacuating Washington State due to the threat of more eruptions, and tents were set up in the Las Vegas desert to hold millions of people from the massive evacuation. Hotels and casinos were used for evacuation shelters. Closed casinos and storage compartments were also used for shelter in Las Vegas.

Nothing was being done to help the victims in the Cascade Region. Because of the eruptions, everyone was told to get out for their own safety! Police and firemen were driving around telling people to evacuate through loudspeakers.

In Crescent Village on the east side of Washington State on March 26, 2022, "Ladies and gentlemen, this is the Crescent Valley Police. You must evacuate your homes at this time due to volcanic eruptions. This is a life-threatening warning: you need to leave now! Please follow the volcano evacuation route on George Washington Highway to Idaho State or northeast British Columbia. Evacuation centers are also in California and Las Vegas."

Monday, March 28, 2022, Mount St. Helens erupted. There was a small to moderate explosion with ash and rock, not causing a whole lot of damage with the exception of just up around the summit where lava was flowing down the mountain, partly destroying trees and setting fires. The evacuees inside the bunkers just felt a *boom!* and it was over. Nobody in them knew Mount St. Helens just erupted. Almost.

"Miss P., Mount St. Helens has just erupted! It's not a large eruption but we might be in danger!"

"Steven, this is not good. Now we have three volcanoes erupting in Washington State. If Glacier Peak and Mount Baker go off, Vancouver and parts of Canada will be in trouble and Seattle might be gone. Mount Rainier is still erupting and Mount Adams is out of control! We cannot get out of here, we'd all burn alive! The sky is dark and full of volcanic ash and gases. If we open these doors we will choke to death! We cannot let that air into these bunkers until all warning signs are off.

"Glacier Peak, Mount Baker, Mount Hood, Three Sisters South in Oregon, Mount Shasta, Mount Whitney, and Mount Denali in Alaska are in great danger of erupting. Magma levels are at their peak in all these mountains, not to mention several smaller volcanoes in Alaska are about ready to blow their loads!

"What will happen if all these volcanoes erupt at the same time? The West Coast may fall into the Pacific Ocean and the western provinces of Canada and Alaska will break off and be gone! I hate to be negative but we're heading in that direction!

"Seattle, Vancouver, the state of Oregon, and northern California are in the greatest danger if these volcanoes keep erupting. Everyone has just two choices: Stay here with the 150,000-people family in these bunkers, or go outside and take a big breath of air and drop dead!" said Eleanor Pepperjackcarmendonchamppinelli.

People watching the news saw Mount St. Helens erupting, raising a worldwide panic! The evacuations were a mad rush to get as far away as possible from the volcanoes. Buses evacuated people in British Columbia, Canada to military shelters in Vancouver's underground bunkers. Military helicopters helped evacuate Washington State and borders and roadblocks were set up to keep anyone from going back, preventing volcanic eruptions from killing more people! Thunderstorms, heavy rain, life-threatening hail and tornado spin-ups from the eruptions roared for miles, sending people running for their lives.

Military helicopters were flying overhead calling over loudspeakers, telling everyone to leave. Helicopters picked up evacuees from rooftops in downtown Seattle and cruise ships and ferries arrived to take the evacuees out of state to Canada and California.

Students at universities were moved by air and by ships out of Washington State until the volcanoes stopped blowing their loads! Now Glacier Peak was smoking at the summit and this mountain was ready to erupt.

In Lancaster, Washington a few people remained in a small country town between Glacier Peak and Mount Baker. Volcano sirens were going off for hours. People just coming from a ski trip on Glacier Peak got aboard buses and were taken by ferry to Canada as the town was evacuated. Hikers on Mount Baker were picked up by military helicopters and taken to a shelter in Vancouver.

A mysterious gas got into the Mount St. Helens bunkers and choked everyone in their sleep; even all the West Coast NASA crew died. An estimated 150,000 people died due to sulfur gas exposure after a violent blast at Mount St. Helens. It was followed by several aftershocks, then a violent pyroclastic flow eruption with thunder, lightning, and volcanic poisonous rain, then another lahar joining neighboring Mount Adams.

Mount St. Fuckin' Helens lived up to her name again!! She blew a big load like the 1980 eruption, but she came straight up instead of blowing out her side this time! Tuesday, March 29, 2022, Mount St. Helens's second eruption split the mountain in two. NASA, New York located at Big Bear Mountain in California kept sending messages to the NASA crew at Mount St. Helens but there were not any answers.

"Ladies and gentlemen, let's get together. I think there was a terrible tragedy at Mount St. Helens. The mountain just had a catastrophic mega eruption blowing the mountain apart and

I fear that all two hundred thousand people in those bunkers may have died! We won't know if they are still there until the National Guard can go in!" said Edward Fay.

The military bunkers at Mount St. Helens were blown into pieces and everyone was killed instantly! Edward Fay was showing his crew the massive eruption from Mount St. Helens. Then he continued, "Look at these monitors, it shows the massive eruption. Now we have three mega volcanic eruptions in Washington State. The University of Washington in Bellingham has been blown off the face of the earth between Mount St. Helens and Mount Adams. I hope that college and Mason Junior College were evacuated.

"We have 8.2 million people in Washington State and we may have five million dead from all these blowjobs! We're now getting reports that three more volcanoes are ready to erupt! We have a catastrophic event going on, a life-threatening world-ending situation!

"Glacier Peak has a steam eruption going on at the summit and magma levels show that this mountain is next. Mount Baker is in danger of erupting as well, Mount Hood in Oregon is ready to blow, and Three Sisters South is being watched. God help us if these peaks blow because Vancouver, British Columbia will be completely destroyed. Doppler Spudweb shows that Glacier Peak is ready to be the state of Washington's fourth blowjob!" said Edward Fay.

Wednesday, March 30, 2022, at 7:18 a.m. Pacific time, Glacier Peak erupted, blowing ash and volcanic rock missiles high into the sky. The blast sent a dark ash cloud toward Seattle to join Mount Rainier, which was *still* erupting with lava coming out of its crater.

The molten rock missiles struck homes and villages around the mountain, setting them afire. Big flaming boulders came crashing into Crater Lake like asteroids from the heavens. A pyroclastic flow came roaring down Glacier Peak along with avalanches of snow, water, and mud, covering the lake below and setting the mountain afire.

The top of the mountain had a ring of lava coming out of the crater then Glacier Peak erupted. "Ladies and gentlemen, Glacier Peak just had a major eruption and the magma is racing toward Mount Baker. Vancouver, where most of the evacuees were sent, is in great danger right now. Mount Adams and Mount St. Helens stopped erupting but are still spewing steam, ash, and lava from the crater cone.

"The air needs to clear before military helicopters can fly in to get to the bunkers. According to Webcam #8 there are bodies lying on the side of Mount St. Helens. We could have a big mess on our hands when the dust clears.

"Mount Rainier is still erupting but magma levels are slowing down and that mountain should cool off soon. Now the molten rock levels have shifted to Glacier Peak blowing her load, and the lake and park may disappear under the ashes. We are dealing with a fourth mega eruption and Mount Baker may be next.

"Mount Hood just had a steam eruption so we need to get out of bed and monitor these eruptions and send data to news reporters, TV, radio stations, and the National Guard. Three Sisters South is now having steam vent eruptions and they're experiencing lightning at the summit. We have no reports out of Mount St. Helens because all data is out. If Mount Shasta or Mount Whitney goes off we're fuckin' out of here! We just leave everything here and go back to New York. Mount Shasta and Mount Whitney are both active but there is no serious activity right now," said Edward Fay.

Thursday, March 31, 2022, Mount Baker had a massive eruption! The next day, Mount Hood erupted! Mount Baker erupted and the city of Vancouver, Canada was in trouble! The next day, when Mount Hood erupted, Portland, Oregon was covered in a dark cloud of ash as black as night. The fallout blackened the state of Washington and part of Idaho. Lunchtime in the city of Vancouver in British Columbia, Canada was already under an ash cloud from the Glacier Peak eruption.

It was a dark, gray, cold, rainy day on March 31. Then at 12:02 p.m. the Vancouver sky turned orange! It looked like a nuclear explosion when Mount Baker erupted! Then thunderstorms with green and blue lightning bolts lit up the sky.

The Canadian Mounted Police called out on loudspeakers while driving through heavy rain, ash, and mud, telling everyone to get indoors because it wasn't safe outdoors. The police were wearing respirators to protect themselves from choking on the falling ash.

"Ladies and gentlemen, this is the Canadian Mounted Police. Please get indoors and keep windows and doors closed. Glacier Peak and Mount Baker in Washington State have erupted. A dangerous ash cloud and pyroclastic flows are heading our way with poisonous gases. If you breathe it in, it will burn you and kill you!"

Some people who were trapped outdoors choked to death and humans and animals lay dead from the ash from both volcanoes. Puget Sound was covered in volcanic ash, awash in a lahar of mud, burying the rivers from Seattle up into Canada and the Columbia River.

All five volcanic orgasms had killed every living thing from insects to animals to humans in Washington State and up into British Columbia. There was ash flow all the way to Alaska and parts of the Canadian provinces, depending on where the wind was blowing!

Back at Big Bear with the NASA crew from New York: "Ladies and gentlemen. Mount Baker erupted just after noon today and the ash and lahars are damaging Puget Sound, sparing Seattle and going up the Vancouver coastline into Alaska. With the eruptions of Glacier Peak and Mount Baker, anyone who did not evacuate from Washington State is presumed dead!

"Washington State University burned to the ground from the Glacier Peak eruption. We still have not heard from the Mount St. Helens eruption, if the evacuation bunkers are still there. If not, we have two hundred thousand more people dead. Four million people are already feared dead depending on the evacuation route in Washington State.

"The tectonic caldera could blow the state of Washington off the map. Oregon, British Columbia, parts of California, and Alaska too—we could all fall into the Pacific Ocean! Mount Hood is ready to blow as early as tomorrow. Three Sisters South, also in Oregon, is threatening to erupt. We have to pray because we're at the end of the world! All these volcanoes, all erupting, all lining up like this is unbelievable! The entire state of Washington will be destroyed when all this is over. Let's keep watching Mount Hood, it's ready to erupt at any time!" said Edward Fay.

April 1, 2022, Mount Hood erupted about 8:00 p.m. in the evening. People around the world watched the news on the apocalypse of multiple volcanoes erupting. "Good evening, this is KNWS Channel 10 TV News in Seattle, Washington, Isaiah Swallowhim reporting. Mount Hood has just erupted this evening at 8:02 p.m.. Here's a look at the violent eruption! It's the third volcano that has erupted this week, six volcanos altogether.

"Washington State was annihilated when Glacier Peak erupted on March 30. Mount Baker erupted yesterday, and now Mount Hood in Oregon. Millions of people are feared dead and the whole northwest of the United States continuing into Canada has been destroyed. There are warnings that more volcanoes are threatening to erupt. Hundreds of dead bodies were found in Vancouver, lying on city streets after being choked by the ash clouds and pyroclastic flows from the eruptions of Mount Baker and Glacier Peak.

"The Mount Hood eruption will affect the devastation in

Washington State and may not be a threat for Seattle, but the eruptions from Mount Adams and Mount St. Helens will be affected by the ash from Mount Hood. Portland and the Columbia River may be in serious trouble in the coming days. Rescue efforts in Washington State and British Columbia are next to impossible because of the thick ash from the six volcanoes erupting. It will take weeks to months before the National Guard can go in to rescue anybody and count the dead. The ash clouds are blocking out the sun and dumping serious acid rain and violent thunderstorms, and spawning several deadly tornadoes. This is not an April Fool's joke—Washington State has been completely destroyed! Isaiah Swallowhim reporting."

The next day was a massive evacuation in downtown Portland with people boarding buses and ferries at the Columbia River to go to Alaska or Canada. Three days later the military was able to get to Mount St. Helens to rescue the people in the bunkers, and there was nothing there! The National Guard rescue crew, wearing respirators, searched the opening where the evacuation bunkers once were and found piles of metal and burnt human bones! The mountain was blasted into pieces, split in two from a massive eruption!

Heavy rain, strong winds, thunder, and lightning made the rescue effort difficult. It was obvious that the mountain won and everyone was dead! The crew came in with pontoon vehicles because of the mud and ash. They had to hike 2,500 feet up the mountain; the rest was gone. Later the military contacted Edward Fay at Big Bear in California.

"Mr. Edward Fay, this is Lieutenant Gary Horsecaller from the Washington State National Guard. We were able to get to the Mount St. Helens evacuation bunkers with the Washington State Park Rangers to rescue the evacuees, but I'm sorry to say that they're not there anymore! We found nothing but pieces of metal and burnt human bones on the side of the mountain.

"The major eruption of Mount St. Helens blew the bunkers apart and half the mountain with it. The mountain is still active. I believe all 150,000 to 200,000 people are dead!"

"Thank you Lieutenant. Ladies and gentlemen, we have a report from Mount St. Helens. All the people in those bunkers were killed. The West Coast NASA crew is among the dead! We need to keep watching these volcanoes. Mount Hood erupted a few days ago and it's calming down, but magma levels are still high. There was a massive eruption, which has stopped, but it might not be over yet.

"Three Sisters South, also in Oregon, needs to be watched. Mount Baker and Glacier Peak are still very active. Mount Rainier is calming down and Mount Adams has quieted down, but Mount St. Helens is a very dangerous volcano and she might have more surprises!" said Edward Fay, of the New York NASA crew.

Days later a vision of the blessed Virgin Mary was seen over the city of Seattle! The dust settled and the military were ready to move into downtown Seattle and start there! Bulldozers and big military land moving mobiles started pushing and plowing a foot and a half of ash from the eruptions of Mount Rainier, Glacier Peak, and Mount Baker to clear the streets and begin counting the dead.

Two hundred thousand people were confirmed dead from the Mount St. Helens eruption. The seaway was full of mud and the subways were flooded with volcanic ash and mud. Buildings had burned to the ground on the east side of Seattle and the Space Needle was lying in a pile of metal with dead bodies and human bones in the debris.

The buildings stood in midtown with all the windows blown out and the insides burned out; some of the damaged buildings were being knocked down. Buildings near the coast survived untouched by the ash, just mud damage. Most of Seattle could be saved when the mud and ash washed away with the sea.

Ferries were still being used for evacuations. Giant snow-plows arrived to plow the ash and clean the streets and earth mobiles. Robots were used to identify the dead, but the death count will never truly be known. The earth mobile moved across the state of Washington and some towns and cities survived, but most areas across the state burned away and nothing was left but a desert of volcanic ash and mud and burned-out trees.

Robots went up the mountains to take pictures and identify the bones from dead humans and animals, but most people had evacu-ated. All five mountains were still active and Mount Baker, Glacier Peak, and Mount Hood were still getting mild eruptions. Due to a violent undersea earthquake, a massive tsunami roared up the Columbia River through Washington State all the way to Canada, causing catastrophic flooding from the Pacific Ocean by nightfall!

The rescue work stopped before dark. The tsunami helped wash away some of the ash into Puget Sound. The evacuees went to Canada, Idaho, Montana, and the Alberta Province of Canada.

Colleges burned to the ground and the rest of the state was a desert of burned-out ash and a field of mud. The visions of the Virgin Mary hovered above the Cascade Mountains all day long as the military was looking for dead bodies and clearing roads until dusk when they left in helicopters. Then the cool desert winds brought sulfuric thunderstorms, acid rain, and tornadoes, stirring up volcanic ash.

The robots continued to work round the clock, going up the volcanoes and snapping pictures. The NASA crew from New York got the data from the spudweb robots. The evacuation did a good job getting people out, but at least five hundred thousand to a million people were feared dead across Washington State and over the Canadian border.

The next couple of days the heavy rain and thunderstorms continued coming from Glacier Peak and Mount Baker. Erup-tions darkened the skies again stopping rescue efforts. A few days later the heavy rain washed the ash particles out of the sky, allowing the rescue work to continue. The Virgin Mary reappeared over the two erupting mountains—a warning to stay away, but it was clear the state of Washington was destroyed and it was going to take years to rebuild.

The next major tasks were to clear roads and find more bodies, but nothing changed; the final count was made and decided. The military went in to clear roads and knock down disabled structures. After a couple of days of cleaning up, more ash poured out of the volcanoes, triggering bad weather: heavy rain, thunderstorms, large hail, and spinning tornadoes of ash, sulfur, and molten rock covering streets once plowed, again making movement impossible. The only places worth rebuilding were Seattle and the seaports. The rest of the state was a volcanic dead zone desert.

Back at Big Bear Mountain, "Ladies and gentlemen, we have no more options for Washington State. All its volcanoes erupted and it has been ruled a dead zone. Right now we have to concentrate on the state of Oregon and Mount Hood, Three Sisters South here in California, and Alaska, because more volcanoes are ready to erupt. Mount Hood is erupting again. The good news is the five volcanoes in Washington State are quieting down," said Edward Fay.

CHAPTER SIX

THE WEST COAST BLOWJOB!

Portland, Oregon: Mount Hood stopped erupting but it's still active and Three Sisters South in Oregon is threatening. After the great Washington State blowjob, their mountains are finally cooling down, though the mega eruptions left a trail of destruction.

Mount Hood erupted on April 1, 2022, and had the state of Oregon on edge. It is now cooling down and evacuees are coming back to Portland. April 15, 2022, things are getting back to normal and a church service is happening at St. Anthony's Cathedral.

"Good morning, brothers and sisters. I hope you all had a very happy Easter. Welcome to St. Anthony's on this seventeenth day of April, 2022. My name is Father Ruby Feinstein.

"Today we must prepare for the falling angel. The West Coast corner of the United States is about ready to fall into the Pacific Ocean! Mount Rainier erupted, then Mount Adams, and right after that Mount St. Helens erupted twice, killing more than two hundred thousand people because the evacuees in the new military bunkers located inside the mountain all died.

"The eruptions weren't as bad as the 1980 eruption but it killed all those people! The population is much greater forty-two years later and most of the population was living in the Mount St. Helens area because they were told it's the safest place in Washington State.

"Don't kid yourself because nowhere is safe near an erupting volcano. Then Mount Baker, Mount Hood, and Glacier Peak erupted and now Washington State is leveled! Six violent volcanoes erupted over the great Northwest under a dark cloud.

"What's next? More erupting volcanoes! Brothers and sisters, we are in the calm before the storm. Expect record snowstorms, record cold, and catastrophic weather events. Now that the dust is ready to settle these events will begin to happen again. There will be more earthquakes and more volcanoes erupting until the fault line falls into the Pacific Ocean. There will be famine and millions of people are going to die. The world will vanish before our eyes! The end of the world is coming.

"It all started with the coronavirus in 2020. Then the protests and riots, then the destroying of the historic statues in this country, then prayer taken out of schools again, not to mention churches closing in Boston and New York and statues of Jesus Christ taken down in 2021.

"Now hell is beginning to rise from under the ground. First the steam eruptions in New York and a volcano in Vermont erupting, then hell under Washington State, and the devil won! Now, here in Oregon, are we next, then California and Alaska? There will be tsunamis when the fallen angel comes and then it will be over!

"Humanity today is all for themselves; they do not respect God anymore and we all have to suffer because of this evil. It said in the holy bible that these events would happen. When the volcanoes start erupting one after another, that's the beginning phase for the devil to take over.

"The big ones will go first and the earthquakes will open the ground to swallow humanity, then the waves will finish the job! We need to get our heads out of our asses and wake up! Before this is over God will take His people, the people who respect the lord and are true believers in Christ.

"You will survive the devil wraiths; even if the devil takes you, you will be risen. For those who aren't, the devil will take them and they'll burn in hell!" said the priest.

———————

Mount Hood started erupting again; the city of Portland was being evacuated and police drove around blaring over loud-speakers, "May I have your attention please! You must evacuate, Mount Hood is erupting again. Please move south to California to avoid dangerous ash clouds."

People got aboard subway trains, buses, and boats heading south. Airports were packed with people flying south to California and Las Vegas to get out of Oregon. People were running in the streets in downtown Portland watching the ash cloud and volcanic rock coming down the mountain. People stranded on the mountain were driving like maniacs and getting into accidents while trying to get off the erupting volcano. People running down the side of the mountain were being bowled over by snow avalanches then killed by the volcanic eruption and blown off the mountain.

People stuck on Mount Hood were killed by the pyroclastic flow and lava. Their bones were left after the burning ash! A mushroom cloud hung over Portland, dumping hot volcanic ash and rocks on the city and starting fires. Dry lightning added to the fuel, then pouring rain and microburst straight-line winds, large hail, and severe flooding in city streets were burying subways underwater and washing cars away. The sky turned black as night and the heavy rain turned to hot ash and flooding lahars!

Anyone who did not evacuate was dead. The mushroom cloud blew sky high over Mount Hood, helping the rest of the erupting volcanoes darkening the skies over the Great Northwest for months. Then came a late April snowfall caused by the eruptions. The death toll in Washington State, Oregon, and the British Columbia and Alberta provinces of Canada may never be known; the number could be more than a million people!

Back at Big Bear: The NASA volcano crew had a meeting to prepare for more volcanic eruptions. "Ladies and gentlemen, we need to get together and monitor all the Oregon volcanoes very closely because they're all ready to erupt in a domino effect.

"Mount Hood erupted again burying the city of Portland, seaports, and the Columbia River. High levels of magma are rising quickly, threatening the rest of Oregon's big peaks going up in a chain reaction! Mount Jefferson is next, then Three Sisters South, Newbury Volcano, Crater Lake, Mazama Mountain, and Mount McLoughlin.

"Seven motherfuckers are threatening to blow the state of Oregon off the map. The fallout will strike Washington State, Northwest Canada and wake up the Alaskan volcanoes! We are Operation Blowjob, and we have to get busy! First of all we need to fly into Southern Oregon after Mount Hood stops blowing its load then we have to go to fuckin' Alaska! We are getting all the data from Mount Hood and then will be going to set up on Mount McLoughlin, Crater Lake, Mazama Mountain, and Mount Newbury in Oregon before we fly to Alaska to set up there.

"We had sixteen spudweb machines flown into Big Bear

yesterday and I will give instructions on who's going where. We need only one spudweb machine on each volcano and when they're all installed and we are receiving data readings we fly back here to bring more to Alaska.

"Linda Crew and Katrina House, take one spudweb. You're going to the summit of Mount McLoughlin. The helicopter drop-off is halfway up the mountain and the cog rail will take you to the summit. You'll be taken to McLoughlin Place train depot where you will be setting up.

"Nathan Rivers and Paul Numbnutts, you two will be going to Crater Lake to monitor the lake and Mazama Mountain. Your spudweb machine will be set up under the lake on the lakebed floor. Jefferson Steamship Authority will take you there and you will be with a diving crew.

"David Dunkin, you will be going with me to Three Sisters South Volcano facing the Pacific Ocean to avoid the dangerous ash from Mount Hood. We will be flying to Three Sisters South in a small private jet to a small airport and our machine will be set up there.

"Air travel is questionable depending on the ash in the atmosphere and bad weather. We will be using ground transportation when necessary. After all the equipment is set up and we get data reports all six of us will be going to Alaska because there's lots of activity there!" said Edward Fay, head of NASA.

The crew had to make the trip by ground transportation due to bad storms and dangerous ash from Mount Hood and all the other volcanoes that blew their load! The work took much longer than expected. Then David Dunkin was on the national news with the warning about what's to come.

"Good evening, this is NBC News Los Angeles. Seven major volcanoes are threatening to go off in a chain reaction in Oregon. Mount Hood has already erupted, paralyzing Portland and sending up an ash cloud blanketing the northwest corner of the United States from northern California to western Canada and into Alaska.

"Mount Jefferson is threatening to erupt next. Three Sisters South will be after that, followed by Mount Newbury, then Crater Lake, Mazama Mountain, and finally Mount McLaughlin. Magma levels show a severe threat of the greater northwest being blown off the face of the earth if all these volcanoes erupt at the same time! Right now there's action in Mount Jefferson!

"Washington State was completely destroyed from the massive volcano eruptions there. The death toll is still unknown depending on how well the evacuations went. More than two hundred thousand people were killed by the major eruptions of Mount St. Helens and Mount Adams.

"Mount Rainier had a major eruption, destroying the city of Seattle, and Tacoma was wiped out. The Mount Rainier super eruption leveled the Space Needle in Seattle, killing everyone. The Glacier Peak and Mount Baker eruptions were so severe the Puget Sound was buried in ash, stranding boats and killing sea life. Even whales and sharks were burned alive!

"The fallout from ash will darken at least half of the United States and northern Canada and cover the eastern Pacific, causing catastrophic weather events. The Columbia River is covered in flowing ash from the eruptions of Mount Hood, Mount Adams, and Mount St. Helens. Total devastation in Vancouver, Washington, and British Columbia goes all the way to northern Alberta.

"The ash has killed thousands of people in Vancouver, British Columbia, and throughout Canada. The ash clouds are now forming over Anchorage, Alaska, plunging them into darkness and sending the state into a nuclear winter. Several volcanoes are also threatening to erupt in Alaska where NASA will be going next. David Dunkin, NASA New York reporting."

The NASA crew went to Mount Denali, formerly Mount McKinley, and they set up in bunkers at a military base in Denali

National Park where there was an airport. Everything was conveniently there to monitor the volcanoes in Alaska. *The volcanoes are quiet in Alaska but Oregon is getting scary!*

———

May 2022, a brief eruption on Mount Jefferson. Mount Hood calmed down but ash was still trapped in the air, blanketing Portland and Marion County in brown ash snow, still falling. And now Mount Jefferson was erupting.

Police were driving around shouting on loudspeakers, telling everyone to evacuate. It started raining with mud ash falling from the eruption. "May I have your attention, all residents here in Marion must evacuate immediately! Mount Jefferson is erupting."

People were running in the streets, boarding buses and escaping in the subways to safety. The sky turned brown with black clouds hiding the eruption on top of Mount Jefferson. Thunderstorms were developing with terrifying lightning and acid rain, and a thick black fog covered the city of Marion.

Heavy brown muddy rain left a river of mud; then a lahar washed down the mountain. Snow and ice were blasted off the mountain, mixing with heavy rain, hot ash, and a pyroclastic flow. It triggered a severe avalanche lahar, washing people and animals into rivers and lakes, burying them alive!

Hot flying lava rocks burned people alive! Military helicopters flew around the Mount Jefferson eruption out over the Pacific Ocean and around Three Sisters to avoid being caught in the ash.

A violent earthquake triggered a tsunami along the Oregon coast while evacuees were at the beach, waiting for vessels to load them on. The boats took people out to a cruise ship waiting out at sea. Some made it and some did not! When one cruise ship was filled another was waiting in the wings, and more boats arrived to pick up people on the beach. An unexpected nightmare came with no warning: twenty-five-foot waves washed away boats, and people with them!

The ocean rose at the speed of a jet plane and no one had a chance to escape! It was very foggy and nobody saw the waves coming! People were taking their time boarding the vessels, being escorted by sailors. There was no warning that a tsunami was coming. They never knew that there was an earthquake!

All people heard was the roar from Mount Jefferson erupting while watching it unfold from the beach. No tsunami or earthquake sirens went off, and on the beach there was no shaking! People were enjoying the eruption, waiting to be rescued, only to find themselves being pulled out to sea by the giant waves and eaten by sharks. Boats were getting busted up like accordions and piers and docks were smashed up like matchsticks!

One man was yelling for help out at sea while being eaten by a great white shark, trapped in the twenty-five-foot waves. People in Marion City trying to evacuate, running in the mud from the lahars, became stuck in quicksand and died in place. Screams for help were never heard!

Nighttime, Mount Jefferson was still erupting and the vision of the blessed Virgin Mary hovered above! Cruise ships were anchored out at sea waiting for the waves to calm down. Viewers aboard the cruise ships were watching the eruption on top of Mount Jefferson in Oregon and saw the vision of Mary above it.

Finally volcano and tsunami sirens started going off. More waves were coming—the vision of the blessed Virgin Mary was a warning to get out as soon as possible!

The danger of evacuating was obvious. You can't run up the mountain to higher ground and because you'd get burned by falling ash or washed away in a lahar; you can't run to the beach because the waves will wash you out to sea. You can't hide in the subways or underground because of the flooding. But you can get into buildings and climb to higher floors and hope to survive burning ash. There's really no escape.

Portland and Marion City was wiped out by the two erupting volcanoes. The Virgin Mary apparition gave the green light for the cruise ships to pull up their anchors and move on before another tsunami struck!

The evacuation ships pulled out just in time. As soon as the vision above Mount Jefferson disappeared, there was a mega eruption with strong earthquakes and more tsunamis to add to the destruction!

Back in Alaska the New York NASA crew was monitoring Mount Jefferson from the Denali National Park military bunkers.

"Good morning crew, I'm sorry to wake you up at three o'clock in the morning but Mount Jefferson just had a mega eruption. We're getting reports of catastrophic damage in Marion City, Portland, and the seaports, and violent lahars and tsunamis are striking the Columbia River and destroying beaches along Oregon's coastline all the way to northern California. The death toll is unknown! People died from the volcanic eruption, from earthquakes, from flooding, lahars, mud flow, and being washed away in tsunamis.

"The magma level in Mount Jefferson is out of control and Three Sisters South may be next. The lava is heading toward California, erupting one mountain at a time! Washington State and parts of Canada are completely destroyed and the state of Oregon may be next!

"Newbury Volcano is after that, but if Crater Lake and Mount Mazama go off Oregon could split in two, and if it spreads to Mount McLoughlin, we might say goodbye to the West Coast. Right now we need to set up evacuations at Three Sisters South and Newbury Mountain, because they're going to be next!" said Edward Fay.

The cruise ships took the evacuees to southern California, where bunkers and tents were set up in the mountains and valleys burned out by fires in the last five years where homes were never rebuilt. About a million people from Oregon had to be brought by cruise ships and ground transportation because all the airports were closed and there was no air travel because of the ash from the erupting volcanoes.

Military fighter jets were patrolling the skies to warn planes to stay away from the ash. A couple of jets crashed because the ash was clogging the engines. All of a sudden they were falling out of the sky, into the mountains.

Police and the National Guard were riding through, warning everyone to get out over loudspeakers despite an early summer snowstorm high in the mountains.

"Ladies and gentlemen, please evacuate these mountains because Three Sisters South is threatening a major eruption! If you get caught here you will die here!"

Police and the military repeated the warnings. People were stuck in the snow trying to get off the mountains! Most people had evacuated already because Mount Hood and Mount Jefferson were still erupting and the ash was covering the sky, turning daylight into night!

Late May and early June, Three Sisters South erupted then hours later Newbury Volcano erupted! When people left Oregon—only people; they even left their animals!—they evacuated to California, Alaska, and Las Vegas where shelters were set up.

The rules at these shelters were similar to those of the 2020 coronavirus outbreak: wear your God damn mask! People were given masks and respirators to breathe, filtering the falling ash. The lava sheet was heading to Crater Lake and Mount Mazama and then Mount McLaughlin. People were getting out in time and the state of Oregon was a ghost town!

July 2022, there was a massive eruption in Crater Lake. Mount Mazama erupted hours later and was blown apart—now we have a super volcano eruption in Crater Lake and Mount Mazama. Then, in mid-August 2022, Mount McLaughlin blew its load with a major eruption paralleling Oregon. After, all seven volcanoes erupted in a domino effect, sending a massive tsunami across the Pacific Ocean, threatening Alaska, Hawaii, Japan and China, and going across the world.

Evacuation camps were set up in Hawaii. The waves also struck the Arctic regions and Russia. All the casinos in Las Vegas were open to take evacuees. All trips to Las Vegas were cancelled because it was being used for an evacuation camp. All the hotels filled up with evacuees from Washington State and Oregon after twelve volcanoes erupted in less than a year!

When Crater Lake erupted, blowing Mount Mazama out of the lake, Glacier Peak at the other end blew its load again in late August of 2022, triggering an eruption so severe it dried up Crater Lake!

The fallout in northern Canada triggered a blackout! Then it went into the Rocky Mountains and the ash flow crossed the United States all the way out into the Atlantic Ocean. A thick cloud base of volcanic ash was darkening the sky, triggering lots of rain and storms.

The volcanoes also blew clouds of ash across the Pacific Ocean. Violent earthquakes caused tsunamis and killed many people who did not evacuate! News media could not keep up with all these eruptions. Just making sure everyone was following evacuation routes and getting to shelters in time and listening to warnings was too much!

When Three Sisters South erupted everyone was getting out of Oregon and evacuating by ground transportation into California, the Las Vegas casinos; anywhere south to get away from the ash. Then the rest of the volcanoes went off, pretty much blowing Oregon and Washington State and parts of northern Canada off the map!

Coastal areas all around the ring of fire were forced to evacuate because of the oncoming tsunamis! The eruptions were so severe the power grid was out in the northwest corner of the United States and parts of Canada. Only generators at military bunkers and bases were working. All airports were closed and there was only ground transportation away from ash filled areas.

Vancouver, British Columbia, parts of Alberta, Canada, Washington State, and Oregon lost power for at least three months because the Crater Lake super volcano eruption knocked out all the power grids. Then northern California lost power.

November, 2022, a football game was being played by the San Francisco 49ers and the LA Rams and the score was tied at 23 to 23. The teams came to the center of the field in San Francisco for the coin toss for overtime, and the crowd was roaring on a rainy night. During the coin toss the sky lit up and a bolt of lightning struck right between them, knocking football players and officials down to the ground like bowling pins! Two more bright flashes of lightning above, then the thunder went *bang! bang!*

Then the stadium went pitch dark and celebrating fans went from cheering loudly to screaming! Minutes later emergency lights came on so people could leave the stadium and go home. There was an earthquake and the streetlights went out, and all the power was out in downtown San Francisco.

The city went dark, then Oakland, California, went dark. People in the streets in Oakland and San Francisco thought it was an EMP attack, but it wasn't! It was because of all the blowjobs from the northern super volcano eruption in Crater Lake!

Del Norte, California was buried under twenty-five feet of ash from Mount McLoughlin's blowjob! Mount Newbury and Crater Lake finished the job! The town was long evacuated before these fiery Oregon blowjobs!

The NASA crew from New York at Denali National Park military bunkers in Alaska finally got data three and a half months after the Crater Lake super volcano disaster! A week before Thanksgiving, 2022 the ash clouds began to settle from all of Oregon's blowjobs! But all the volcanoes were still active! Spudweb machines started bringing back data after being shut down when the Crater Lake super volcano erupted.

"Ladies and gentlemen, welcome to the Denali National Park Auditorium. My name is Lieutenant Jalen Robertson from the Alaskan National Guard. We have updates on a super volcano eruption at Crater Lake, Oregon. Here's Edward Fay to explain what happened and what to expect next."

"Thank you lieutenant. The state of Oregon was practically blown off the face of the earth when super volcano Crater Lake erupted! Mount Mazama volcano erupted with it! When Mount Jefferson erupted in February the state of Oregon was told to evacuate by the National Guard. I hope they did because when Three Sisters South blew its top people were still there and died on that mountain!

"Then Newbury Volcano erupted, then Mount Mazama in Crater Lake, then Mount McLoughlin, then the Crater Lake super volcano blew! They've been causing mega catastrophic destruction, knocking out power in the entire northwest corner of the United States and parts of Canada for three and a half months.

"The death toll is unknown and we were told that the super eruption at Crater Lake was so severe that the lake dried up! Magma levels are working their way toward southern California and Mount Shasta could be next.

"The ash cloud triggered tsunamis in the Pacific Ocean and darkening skies across the Pacific and the United States. There were no news media or internet and phone service until today and we do not know how bad it really is! My team will be staying put here in Alaska because California is next. Then we have danger here as well because a series of volcanoes is ready to blow here in Alaska.

"Right now Anchorage is in trouble because, though Mount Redoubt last erupted in 2009, thirteen years ago, it's steaming at the summit right now. If this mountain blows we may need to get the first ticket and fly out following the polar bears. We'd need to make our way back to New York because this mountain has the energy to split Alaska in half despite twenty-five-degrees-below-zero cold.

"We do not have accurate webcam data on all the Alaskan volcanoes, but there's a lot of them here and the lava levels are high on every fuckin' one of them. The twelve volcanoes that leveled Washington State and Oregon are filling lava beds with thick molten magma through Alaska, threatening the blowjobs of the century. The next warning: Mount Shasta is next!

"We will not be going back to Big Bear if that mountain blows its load! We're not even safe here! Mount Denali is the biggest volcano in Alaska. We have others threatening here in Alaska. Mount Spur last erupted in 2005 but the last major eruption was in 1992. This volcano is also very dangerous!

"Mount Makushin Volcano last erupted in 1995 and this volcano is due to blow a big load! The Mount Vancouver super volcano is also a threat and it has the capability to blow northeast Alaska and the Calgary, Edmonton, and Saskatchewan provinces of Canada off the map!

"Then we have Mount Sanford Volcano, another giant motherfucker ready to go off! Then Mount Blackburn, another, even bigger giant volcano, and the blowjobs could get worse! Then we have Mount Foraker, another dangerous threat.

"We have Mount St. Elias that's steaming at the top. This mountain is deadly and it's reporting small eruptions right now according to spudweb #18. This mountain is 18,009 feet and if she blows we're in serious trouble!

"Then we have Mount Bona active right now and ready to erupt, another giant motherfucker! Then we have the Aleutian Island Range with thirty-three volcanic little fuckers ready to blow their loads at any time! I'm not done yet!

"We have Mount Iliamna, another molten lava squirter! This mountain is highly active! Then it brings us to Mount Denali where we are. It's not as active as these other motherfuckers but magma levels are rising here too!

"Finally, we have another dangerous volcano here in Alaska. Mount Shishaldin Volcano. Did I cover them all?! We have 3,214 mountains here in Alaska. I'll go through them all if you want me to! Every fuckin' one of them, but I'm just too God damn tired from monitoring them all!" said Edward Fay.

———————

The crew was getting data from so many threatening volcanoes in Alaska. Some of them were ready to erupt, but they were watching Mount Shasta in California and people there were getting ready. Edward Fay and the volcano crew sent warnings to the Mount Shasta region after a big meeting in Alaska. The meeting continued after watching a few films of the disaster from the West Coast Blowjob!

"Ladies and gentlemen, we have a mega disaster here on the West Coast and the Pacific Ocean, where tsunamis ranging from five feet to fifty feet are striking the Western Pacific. Eighty-five-foot waves struck the Hawaiian Islands, killing at least fifty thousand people or more! Japan, parts of China, and the Philippines, to as far away Russia and the Alaskan coastline were struck by tsunamis at the speed of a jet plane, killing thousands of people!

"Who cares what happens in other countries?! We're responsible for what happens here in the United States. There's no guarantee on what can happen with national disasters across the globe; they can happen anywhere! Canada has their own NASA team and we can help them but we have a big mess of our own to take care of before we go there!

"We are Operation Blowjob, responsible for all erupting volcanoes in the United States—anywhere else, who cares?! Hawaii and Alaska, we are responsible! A dozen volcanoes erupted, devastating Washington State, Oregon, and parts of Canada. Right now we have a big issue in California where Mount Shasta is ready to blow, and we have to watch Mount Whitney. The Lessen Peak Volcano readings are at a dangerous level and so are those of the Medicine Lake super volcano. This volcano could devastate a good chunk of California if it blows.

"Medicine Lake is not as active yet; however, we're on the eastern Ring of Fire and the entire west coast is threatening to fall into the Pacific Ocean. Magma levels are rising in the Clear Lake volcanic fields but are not a threat like Mount Shasta, which is ready to blow its top very soon! If Shasta goes off, our work in California is over! We can only monitor the situation from here at Denali.

"Back here in ice-cold Alaska, if Mount Redoubt, Mount Elias, or Mount Foraker goes off we are in trouble. If we get any warnings about any one of these volcanoes threatening to erupt we have to get out of here and go back to New York before the West Coast corner falls into the ocean.

"This mountain, Denali, is the third tallest mountain in the world and the tallest in the United States. Mount Shishaldin, with Mount Redoubt, is at a very dangerous stress level and they could erupt together! One more thing before I close this meeting: If the Yellowstone super volcano goes off you can say goodbye to the United States. The fallout will spread across the globe, crippling the earth with a nuclear winter for more than three years. We will be in the hands of another ice age. It's happened before and it can happen again, all because of earth's magnetic blowjobs! The lieutenant will finish the meeting."

"Thank you Mr. Edward Fay. Ladies and gentlemen, most of the great northwest has been destroyed and we do not know how bad it is. We are finally getting data after almost four months! Here's what to expect: More eruptions with deadly earthquakes; magnetic lightning from rubbing rocks and storms above; toxic rain; high winds, including volcanic tornadoes and volcanic ash; and poison from the eruptions! We need to be prepared. Thank you, I'm Lieutenant Jalen Robertson."

CHAPTER SEVEN

THE MOUNT SHASTA
WARNING

Christmastime at the Inn: People were sitting around the Christmas tree singing carols and keeping nice and warm in front of a big fireplace. Then the ground shook and the Christmas tree was rocking back and forth, ready to fall over. It stayed upright, but people went from singing to screaming. Then there was a bright white flash of lightning, then it flashed blue and green, then the ground shook again, then the lights went out. The shaking was still going, rocking and rolling, but it finally stopped.

The lights came back on but then they went out again for the rest of the night! Only the fire in the fireplace gave light and the guests of the inn put more wood on the fire to keep warm.

It was eighteen below zero outside and the manager covered up all the doors and window frames to keep the cold out. There was no heat due to the power outage, only the fire in the fireplace to keep everyone warm.

The crowd was panicking about the earthquake! "May I have your attention please? Don't panic! We get these all the time in the mountains. California gets earthquakes every day somewhere! Tonight was a little unusual; it's a very cold night and the earthquake triggered ground lightning that may have knocked out the electricity.

"We will be okay. My name is John McKennon the inn manager; if you need anything I will be in the foyer."

The next morning there was another tremor about 7:00 a.m. and the furniture and beds were moving around in the rooms. People ran out into the cold in their housecoats looking out at the mountain peak and the smoke and steam coming out of the top.

"It looks like Mount Shasta's erupting!" a young girl cried.

A man said, "I can't stand here watching it! It's twenty below zero out here, I have to get back inside before I fuckin' freeze to death!"

The tremors stopped and everyone went back inside, away from the cold, in nightgowns and underwear. *Mount Shasta's erupting but it's not ready to blow its load yet.* Clouds covered the view a few minutes later and it started snowing so hard it was a whiteout. Hotel guests near the summit feared the mountain was ready to erupt!

Later in the day the manager at the Inn got emails and calls about the eruption warning. "Mr. John McKennon, this is Mr. Edward Fay from NASA in New York. Mount Shasta is in great danger of a major eruption very soon. You're not in trouble just yet but you did have a mild volcanic eruption. There's no need to evacuate just yet. Our team is called Operation Blowjob, and we are monitoring the mountain. When it's ready for a major eruption we will notify you by email and phone to evacuate, and when we tell you to get out you better get out! The Inn is not far from the summit and if you get an earthquake that's greater than a four, an avalanche will bury your property. I'm just warning you to be prepared when we contact you. Again, if a stronger eruption occurs you need to have an evacuation plan ready."

Edward Fay sent email warnings to all the hotels on Mount

Shasta. The next night power was restored on the mountain after several mild aftershocks. Mechanical rooms were monitoring the earthquakes.

The Lodge at Mount Shasta: Buses arrived, dropping off skiers in a snowstorm, and as people entered the hotel they were greeted in front of a big fireplace.

"Good evening ladies and gentlemen, my name is Mr. Dick Johnson, the manager of the lodge and the Swiss Holiday Lodge Suites. Welcome to the Lodge Resorts Complex. We have a nice warm fire in our eight foot long stone fireplace that stands five feet high. Continental food will be served with red and white wine. Smoking marijuana joints is allowed by the fireplace.

"A piano player will be playing, a DJ will come on for dancing later this evening, and the cash bar opens at 9:00 p.m. It is thirty-three degrees below zero outside with a windchill of fifty-nine degrees below. It is too cold to be outside; the ski lodge is closed because we have a lot of ice.

"It's frozen everywhere! Heat machines can't melt the ice because it's so thick. I'm sorry for the inconvenience. We are having unusual cold due to several erupting volcanoes in Oregon and Washington State. It could be spring or next summer before any melting occurs. I don't know how you people got here in this kind of weather!"

"We came here on buses before the blizzard, Dick," said the group.

The wind was blowing about sixty miles an hour, snow was blowing and drifting for days and the blowing snow was freezing on contact. You couldn't open the doors or windows, everything was frozen in place!

This storm and cold is the worst ever on Mount Shasta. It's going to take a volcanic eruption and a lahar to loosen all the ice; liquid mud flowing down from the small eruption last night froze on contact.

The ice went all the way to the roof then the power went out. Most of the hotels on the mountain had generators and plenty of wood in storage for fireplaces located in tunnels underground. People couldn't sleep in their rooms without a warm fireplace. They all had to bunch together in the lodge in front of the main brick fireplace until the storm let up.

Park rangers and the National Guard couldn't get up the mountain to evacuate the hotels and inns because there was so much ice. Roads going up and down the mountain were closed. Salt trucks went up the mountain putting down sand and salt to get to the summit, but blowing snow was freezing on contact, icing roads over, and it wasn't doing any good. Trucks got stuck up there and some of them slid off the mountain. Some of them died up there, freezing to death!

Military helicopters went up to rescue the hotel guests on the mountain after the storm. Ice crystals mixed with volcanic ash got into the helicopters' engines. A couple of them crashed and burned on the side of the mountain so other choppers had to retreat and get off the mountain before becoming more victims.

Anyone who tries to go up and rescue people on this mountain will die up there because of the cold and ice. Here's a man skiing down the icy mountain having fun in this sixty degree below zero cold; at least he's dressed warm enough! A few seconds later he disappeared! The crazy man died up there!

The manager of the lodge spoke to his guest. "Good morning and Merry Christmas to everyone. It's a nice morning out there and the temperature is nineteen degrees, but it's still not warm enough to melt the ice so we can't evacuate. Look at the outside monitors, the buses are covered in snow and solid ice. The buses are hooked up to electric outlets run by the inn's generators so they will start when we can evacuate, but the problem is we can't get out of here to evacuate if we need to.

"We have heat blowers at the entrance but they're not doing any good melting the thick mountain ice because *more* snow and ice are coming down the mountain, trapping everyone in here. We have no chance of getting out of here until this ice melts. We are half empty in the wood storage department and we still have January, February, and March ahead of us. Winter is just beginning and we have used half of the wood since the end of October. If we don't get out of here by February the wood may be gone and we can freeze to death up here with below zero temperatures.

"We have been notified by the National Guard about the evacuation but they can't get to us. People are dying up here in the mountains trying to help others. Our chance of survival depends on how long we can keep these fireplaces burning and having enough fuel to keep the generators working. This is what we need for survival, heat, and food.

"We have enough food to feed a thousand people for at least six months stored in bunkers. But we have a bigger worry up here on Mount Shasta: if this mountain blows, we're screwed! We already had an eruption a few days ago, one of several we have had on this giant active mountain. We have been warned that a major eruption can happen at any time according to NASA. A volcanologist group will keep all the hotels and resorts informed when the danger is near. If we get an earthquake larger than a four on the Richter scale we need to go into the wood storage bunkers and gather together because we're stuck here!" said manager Dick Johnson at the Lodge Inn on Mount Shasta.

––––––––––

It was Christmas Day 2022 and everyone in the Mount Shasta resorts was stuck there until rescue workers could get to them when the weather improved. Unfortunately, another snowstorm blew in on Christmas night while there were Christmas parties and celebrating in front of the warm fireplaces at the resorts.

8:19 p.m. Christmas night, the mountain rocked a lot with a violent eruption! It was *bang!* and then shaking, and things were falling over and breaking in the Lodge Inn.

"Your attention please ladies and gentlemen, we just had a 6.6 earthquake. Everyone please buckle up and make your way to the underground bunkers for your own safety!" said Dick Johnson. The guests at the lodge went underground in the bunkers and it was freezing down there! The Christmas tree fell and landed in the burning fireplace and a fire started. The main entrance caught fire and burned down from the tremors.

The guests were safe in the cold bunkers. The fire burned its way out by 8:00 a.m. the next morning and the Swiss Holiday Lodge joined the rest of the crew in the icy bunkers. People made their way out of the wood storage shelters but the lobby at the lodge was not there; it had burned to the ground.

The lodge guests were escorted to another hotel and stayed at the Swiss Holiday Lodge until they could be rescued. Finally military earth mobiles with big plows were able to make their way up the mountain to clear the roads so the resort could be evacuated. People could get to their buses safely, and get off the mountain on Boxing Day, December 26, 2022.

The buses left the Lodge Inn and the Swiss Holiday before evening. Military helicopters followed the buses down the mountain and landed at the resorts to evacuate any people left behind. The temperature rose to forty-four degrees, melting the ice and allowing the giant earth plows to drive through ten feet of snow.

It was warm at the bottom of the mountain. It was sixty-seven degrees when the buses arrived and some of the evacuees were taken to area hospitals and treated for hypothermia.

Cold Creek Inn and the Strawberry Inn were not so lucky

because the mountain started erupting again. The Cold Creek and the Strawberry Inn were located in a valley down a ski slope that led to a lake and bridge. The plows and rescue teams had to get off the mountain because lava was coming out of the top even though the other two resorts were in serious danger, not to mention another powerful snowstorm was coming with thunder and lightning!

The cloud base above blocked the view of the eruption, so if a lahar were to come down the mountain, the resorts could be washed away and they'd never see it coming! Tourists were evacuating while a heavy snowstorm was coming down on the mountain. Heavy rain and thunderstorms in the valley were making evacuations there impossible! The mountain was erupting and a lahar was slowly working its way down Mount Shasta, passing through snow and ice and flowing toward the ski slope and down the mountain, threatening the resorts and villages in the valley.

The NASA crew sent warnings to Mount Shasta that a major eruption was coming.

9:45 p.m. December 26, 2022 was a Monday night. Some people had checked out on Christmas Day because of the volcano threat.

"Good evening this is NASA radio reporting. Mount Shasta is erupting and all residents in the Lake Siskiyou region must evacuate immediately due to a severe tsunami lahar warning and a possible major volcanic eruption! Please take this warning seriously, you may have less than five hours to get out! Edward Fay, NASA volcanologist reporting."

All the resorts hotels, inns, and residents got the warning except the inn at Mount Shasta, the Lodge, and the Swiss Lodge which had lost power from the Christmas Day storms, but they were able to evacuate in time before the mountain blew!

The Strawberry Inn: "Ladies and gentlemen, all guests; please leave your rooms and report to the clubhouse lobby located near the pool as soon as possible. We have a mayday emergency!" said the inn manager.

People left their rooms and all the guests walked in the pouring rain, thunder, and lightning to the lobby, running in the rain and the mud to get to the warning meeting. Guests were woken from their beds as warnings on their cell phones, TVs, and computers came on, alerting guests at the Strawberry Inn and at Cold Creek.

"Ladies and gentlemen, my name is Richard Sylvester, the property manager here at the Strawberry Inn and apartments. I'm sorry to wake you up at midnight, but we have a major volcanic eruption warning on top of Mount Shasta and a threat of a lahar. We have to evacuate as soon as possible!

"Go to your cars and leave; get away from the mountain as far as you can and for those who came here by bus, call your bus company. If you cannot evacuate you must get to higher ground! We have a serious problem trying to get out. We have eight inches of rain on the ground and it's still coming down in buckets!

"Our only choice is to get to higher ground and those staying on the first floor will have to sleep in the hallways on the second or third floor to avoid being washed away. We will supply you with blankets and bedding. I don't see any chance of evacuating until this storm lets up."

Richard Sylvester organized the guests at the Strawberry Inn. Nobody is leaving tonight in this weather!

The Cold Creek Inn: 11:43 p.m., sirens sounded in every room, loudspeakers in the rooms and all over the resort reporting. "White night! Ladies and gentlemen please evacuate all rooms and report to the lobby ASAP! This is a mayday emergency warning!"

The warning kept repeating until everyone gathered in the lobby. People were in their pjs and housecoats running in the pouring rain, thunder, and lightning, crowding the lobby where the meeting took place. Just a few people got dressed and grabbed their coats.

"Good evening ladies and gentlemen, I'm Kelsey Kannon, the property manager of the Cold Creek Inn. We have a mayday warning from NASA to evacuate because Mount Shasta is erupting!

"This mountain has been erupting for a week now. It's dark out there except when the lightning is flashing, so I don't see any signs of an eruption right now. However, NASA is warning of a major eruption at Mount Shasta before the night is over and we have less than four hours to get out of here!

"We have no chance of evacuating the Cold Creek Inn at this time; the weather is terrible out there and we need to have some kind of a plan because we also have a threat of a lahar coming. Everyone has to get to higher ground ASAP because we have no chance for an evacuation in this weather.

"I need everyone to go up to the second or third floor in case of flooding. You will need to stay up there for the rest of the night until this storm is over. Our crew will support you with blankets and bedding. Stay up against the walls while sleeping so people can get by you. This meeting is over now get to higher ground right away!"

"Kelsey, suppose I have to go for a shit? Do I knock on someone's door?" asked one man.

"No; just use the restroom in the lobby, then get back upstairs when you're done!"

1:54 a.m. there was a big *roar*! and the Cold Creek Inn resort was shaking and the power went out! The man who said he had to go for a shit yelled, "Everyone get downstairs, we're having an earthquake!"

The building shook so hard that many windows started breaking and everyone went to the flooded ground floor. Some people ran outside at both resorts not knowing what was to come. The roaring earthquake kept getting worse, and there was still thunder, lightning, and downpours all night!

Mount Shasta had a major eruption and lava poured out of the summit's crater. A massive lahar roared down the main ski slope along with a pyroclastic flow racing at the speed of a jet plane, crashing into the lake below, smashing a bridge just after people ran across it and driving it over rocks and broken trees. A trail of debris slammed into Lake Siskiyou, triggering a mega tsunami of lahar mud burying everything in its path. The Cold Creek Inn and the Strawberry Inn were leveled in a matter of minutes and everyone was killed! Flashes of lightning showed a vision of the blessed Virgin Mary before the mega tsunami struck!

CHAPTER EIGHT

THE VOLCANIC
WEATHER AFTERMATH

Wednesday December 28, 2022. Rescue helicopters arrived two days after the lahar and everything was buried in mud. A human leg was stuck in volcanic ash near where a helicopter landed on a hard surface; the rest of the area was buried in mud and volcanic ash!

There was nothing the military rescue team could do; everyone was buried under twenty feet of mud, ash, and rock. They started digging, looking for bodies, and they found a couple ten feet down. The resorts and neighborhood were gone.

The NASA volcano crew was there and Edward Fay said, "Good afternoon, National Guard, US Army, rescue team, and news media. I warned these resorts and neighborhoods and residential areas to evacuate this mountain weeks ago due to the threat of a major eruption on Mount Shasta and possible lahars.

"The first eruption occurred just before Christmas, causing a dangerous core of cold weather, plunging temperatures to as low as fifty degrees below zero. Ash formed ice sheets after a mega snowstorm came down the mountain. That was followed by a violent eruption on Christmas night trapping people on the mountain. Military earth mobiles got far enough up the mountain to rescue them.

"We lost a couple of helicopters trying to rescue people. They crashed into the mountain because ash and ice clogged the engines. The military lost seven soldiers in the helicopter crashes and more people died trying to rescue others on the mountain. Other people died on the mountain, freezing to death or being struck by volcanic debris. One resort was struck by an avalanche. The Strawberry Inn and the Cold Creek Inn decided to wait it out until after Christmas and they got caught in a violent storm and were not able to evacuate in time. I told them to leave ten days ago, about a week before Christmas, and they told me the eruption was not bad enough to affect them so far out in the valley and decided to wait. I told them if we had a major eruption they weren't in a good area because Lake Siskiyou sits right in front of the Cold Creek Inn.

"The mountain had a mega eruption just before 10:00 p.m. on the twenty-sixth. We had a mayday warning of a major eruption coming throughout all of the Mount Shasta region. Four hours later a 6.7 earthquake from the eruption triggered a mega lahar and it came right down the mountain, rolling in a pyroclastic volcanic blast. It carried ice, snow, and rocks bigger than buses, broken redwood trees, molten rock, ash, and mud, striking the lake and triggering a mega tsunami that buried them alive!

"The eruption has caused some serious storms and is now causing fires along the mountain. The mountain is still active but the magma level is dropping and we should not have any more major eruptions here. It's too bad that this happened. I have been warning everyone for weeks that this mountain was going to blow! The ash from all the volcanoes erupting lately is going to cause some serious weather problems," said Edward Fay.

The military and the NASA volcano crew did a walk through the disaster area and the lake was full of debris: logs by the thousands from broken trees, tons of rock that came down the mountain from the eruption, and parts of the bridge torn up like matchsticks!

The resorts, hotels, inns, and residential neighborhoods were buried deep under the mud, unrecognizable! It was still raining, the mountain was still active, and thick clouds were covering the eruption. It wasn't known what else was coming down.

Ash flakes from the eruption torched trees on the side of the mountain. The ski lodge, hotels, and resorts burned to the ground from flowing lava and ash flakes from the pyroclastic flow. The lahars and the pyroclastic burning ash buried everything in the valleys and the lake was half empty from the lahar tsunami. The place was a mess and not an option for any possible rescue crews because everyone was dead!

Helicopters flew low looking for survivors and came up empty-handed. Everyone left the area when another sudden aftershock occurred, strong enough to knock you off your feet! Then the cloud base was so thick helicopters and rescue teams had to get out. News reports could not estimate the dead because there was so much destruction!

"Good evening this is World News Tonight on Fox TV on New Year's Eve. Happy New Year to everyone! It will be here in less than six hours. It was not a good Christmas week for the Mount Shasta Region. About 100 to 150 people are feared dead from three violent eruptions on Mount Shasta, closing all airports in California, including LAX.

"The third eruption triggered a pyroclastic lahar that buried two famous resorts, the Strawberry Inn and the Cold Creek Inn, where several guests who were not able to evacuate because of a violent thunderstorm are feared dead from a mega tsunami. A lahar pushed Lake Siskiyou over the resort and neighborhood, burying towns and cities in the area! Hotels and inns were buried under deep mud from the lahar. This is one of the worst disasters in all of California.

"The Mount Shasta eruptions caused hundreds of square miles of forest fires. Hopefully most people got a chance to evacuate or the death toll may be worse! I hope 2023 will be a better year. Mount Shasta is the fourteenth volcano that has erupted in less than a year! Washington State, Oregon, and parts of northwest Canada have been completely destroyed! Lisa Kumlick reporting on Fox News."

All the New Year's celebrations were cancelled because of the destruction and bad weather on the way! Over in Las Vegas, Nevada, an ash cloud flowed into the valley from the eruptions of Mount Shasta. It formed into a mega rainstorm, dumping tons of rain on the Las Vegas strip. Before the rains came there was a fireworks celebration at midnight on New Year's Eve, only to be cut short as casinos and shelters were getting flooded. The rain came down so hard the slot machines were shorting out, gambling tables were floating in the flooded waters, and lightning bolts were striking the buildings, breaking windows and striking *inside* buildings. All the power went out but generators kicked in at the hotels and casinos.

Evacuees had to go to higher ground to avoid drowning and some people were electrocuted from lightning strikes. The wind was blowing so hard it was breaking windows in the hotels, sucking some people out into the storm to their deaths! The wind, rain, and mud were washing people down the strip. A mega tsunami lahar rushing down Mount Shasta washed into the Las Vegas Strip, leaving a trail of death and destruction. A river of mud came out of nowhere and people outdoors drowned in the path of the storm. People and the evacuees watched the mud flow down the Las Vegas strip for days from the heavy rain from the ash clouds from the erupting volcanoes!

The next day a black cloud crossed into Montana, dumping tons of snow and thundersnow and dropping temperatures to fifty below zero. At the Lancaster Inn where people were staying it was snowing, snowing, and snowing. It wouldn't stop and people were staying there for the New Year's Day weekend. There were ten to fifteen feet of snow and one hundred-mile-per-hour winds burying the resort before the severe cold arrived and froze everything solid, trapping everyone there.

"Good evening ladies and gentlemen welcome to the Lancaster Inn Hotel and Resorts here in Lockaberry, Montana. It's thirty-seven degrees below zero outside and we had a major snowstorm blowing and drifting fifty feet high that may trap us here for a while. Fifty degree below zero temperatures are not unusual here in Montana, but eleven or twelve feet of snow is unheard of! We have blowing and drifts more than fifty feet high and ice flows so severe we could be here until spring. My name is Greg Proofenbaum, the manager of the Lancaster Inn and properties.

"The weather outside is a path of death, nobody can survive in this kind of weather caused by volcanic eruptions. The wind chill is about seventy-five degrees below zero and it can kill a person in less than ten minutes once exposed to skin.

"We have the heat blasting at full force over eighty degrees and we're lucky to be in the forties or fifties inside buildings because of the strong volcanic winds! We have to survive the best way we can in this cold because of all the volcanic eruptions. Do not go outside if you are not dressed for this weather because you may not survive," said the manager, Greg Proofenbaum.

People had to gather together to keep warm and gather in front of warm fireplaces. People going outside trying to evacuate died out there! The resort was buried under snow and ice.

Everyone staying there will probably be stuck there until spring, if they survive.

The Rocky Mountains had record snowfall and record cold! The cold and snowstorms traveled all the way to Texas and the cold covered the United States; even Florida was cold for the rest of the 2023 winter. Heavy rains, thunderstorms, and tornadoes tore through Florida from Pensacola all the way to Key West. There were strange storms in the Gulf of Mexico and storms coming up the East Coast, dumping snow in New England almost every day.

All of Canada was in a deep freeze from coast to coast. All of this weather from the settling volcanic ash from all the West Coast volcanoes, from clouds and cold. Every day, people were wondering if a second ice age was coming! There was so much snow in the Rocky Mountains the polar bears were coming from the arctic, crossing into the Rocky Mountains and down the frozen Mississippi River all the way to Texas. Southern hunters were shooting the bears for food.

Back in Lockaberry, Montana, at the Lancaster Inn: "Good evening, Manager Greg Proofenbaum speaking again in front of a nice warm eight-foot fireplace. This hotel is the same format as the Stanley Hotel in the movie, *The Shining*. In fact it's the same owners. The heavy wood frame structure with brick and slate rock between protects against heavy snow, ice, and strong winds; nothing is going through these walls! The good thing is we're buried in more than ten feet of snow and the insulation snowpack will protect us against the killer cold.

"All the upstairs rooms on the third floor will be closed off and the stairways will be sealed shut. All windows throughout the resort will be taped and wrapped up. The rooms should be warm enough as long as a draft is not getting through air pockets. Turn the heat up full blast and you should be alright.

"When you take a shower or bath, let the hot water run for at least ten minutes because it may take a while to get hot. The heat is up full blast because the temperature is expected to drop to fifty below zero and these fireplaces will always be lit and fed with wood every hour, 24/7. We have plenty of wood in the wood storage in the basement, enough to last for at least six months. We have eleven miles of underground wood storage throughout the resorts here in Lancaster.

"We have enough frozen food to last for years in underground freezer bunkers we stock up all year round. We also have the best deer hunting team in the world. We killed 115,513 deer in the last two years and stored them in freezer bunkers in the mountains.

"It is very warm here in the lobby foyer, eighty-four degrees from the two large fireplaces burning, twenty-four hours a day. We have the heat pumped up at full capacity because the pipes may freeze. If it's fifty below we need to keep the heat on ninety just to keep the pipes from freezing and if we're lucky we'll be safe at forty degrees, the inside temperatures! With the fireplaces burning 24/7 we'll at least keep the resort at room temperature. Now even with all this summer feeling heat, this hotel is frozen shut. Nobody is to go outside until some of this snow melts and temperatures warm up, because being exposed to this kind of cold without proper dress you'll be lucky to last five minutes. Breathing in this kind of cold will choke you to death!

"You must follow my instructions and stay put because you will not survive in this kind of cold. If you leave I have protocol sheets of the instructions I just went over and I want everyone to take one; they are located on the center table here in the resort. The movie in the lounge will be *The Shining*, starting at 8:00 p.m., speaking of the Stanley Hotel. Enjoy your evening," said manager Greg Proofenbaum.

It was a good night and everyone was watching the movie, eating snacks and having a few drinks. At the part about the ghost in Room 237 on the movie, Greg Proofenbaum said, "By the way guests, we have a ghost here too in Room 007, one of our storage rooms in the basement; don't go down there!"

Back in Las Vegas: The entire strip was flowing with mud and it was pouring rain for days. Some heavy rain was coming down with clear water and hail the size of golf balls and some came down like mud with thunderstorms.

Casinos were flooded and more slot machines were shorting out. People at Mandalay Bay were watching the news about the bad weather coming up the Las Vegas Strip. "Oh my God!" said a crowd of people at the casino. The weather wasn't bad there the second time around but that was about to change.

Flights were still coming in and going out of Las Vegas Airport, but it was starting to rain heavily with lightning, and the wind started blowing hard!

People were outside the Mandalay Bay by the pool, eating and drinking near a fire pit, watching the Las Vegas Golden Knights hockey game. Suddenly a strong wind came out of nowhere! A deadly microburst came straight down on a crowd of people, blowing them around like falling bowling pins! The crowd went from a quiet evening to running for cover in seconds! The Las Vegas Golden Knights just scored a goal when the lightning struck the outside TV and set it afire!

People ran back inside, but not before being blown around like papers flying around in the wind. The weather went from a comfortable calm to one hundred-mile-per-hour winds in seconds! One person was killed and several were hurt. Several rescue vehicles, fire trucks, and police cars were at the Mandalay Bay to rescue the injured. The wicker patio people were sitting at when the storm struck was on fire, burning to the ground from several lightning strikes!

People inside the casino at Mandalay Bay were watching the hockey game on an overhead TV while playing the slots. The Golden Knights tied the game at 3-3 with the Pittsburgh Penguins and the people in the casino were cheering like crazy! "With 5:55 to go we have a tie game here at T-Mobile Arena here in Las Vegas!"

Then a sudden news break! "Good evening, we have breaking news on KLVN TV Channel 10. We have a tornado warning for Las Vegas! Doppler radar reported a tornado on the Las Vegas Strip heading right for the Mandalay Bay Resort!" Then the lights went out and people were screaming.

Generator lighting kicked in and casino officials with loud-speakers said, "Everyone get down in a safe position and hold onto something, bad weather is coming!" A violent tornado was coming up the Las Vegas Strip!

Saturday January 7, 2023, Las Vegas was about to get the worst storm ever! While rescue crews were cleaning up from the micro-burst earlier their cell phones were going crazy: a tornado was coming. Before the twister there was a quiet calm and you could see the northern lights. Then rotating clouds, flashes of lightning, and *bang!* just like that!! The tornado hit and it was a big fuckin' thing!

The tornado struck the Mandalay Bay like a bomb, smashing thousands of windows! People in their rooms on the upper floors had to hold on to dear life to avoid being sucked out! The tornado blew the roof off of both buildings. Glass falling on the strip and property hitting some people running for cover caused several injuries and some deaths.

One couple on the thirty-seventh floor were in bed having sex when the storm blew the windows in, striking the couple, cutting them and killing both of them! Seventy-five percent of the win-dows were blown out of the Mandalay Bay Resort and hotels. Glass was blown into the swimming pool cutting the lining, and all the pool water seeped out and flooded the resort and the rest of the pool area was completely destroyed!

The rain was coming down so hard it was blowing sideways, flooding the ground floor and shorting out the slot machines! Guests ran up to higher floors only to be struck by flying glass and get cut! Police and rescues vehicles and fire trucks were coming from everywhere!

The Las Vegas Raiders had a home football playoff game at Allegiant Stadium at the Mandalay Bay Resort and the Baltimore Ravens were winning 48 to 9 with 8:19 to play in the fourth quarter. People were going to the exits when the main video screen read: "Ladies and gentlemen, families and kids! Please take cover immediately! A tornado is coming!" The game was stopped after the warning and the losing crowd went from leaving the stadium to running for cover when the winds started blowing. Then the power went out and the stadium was dark. Seconds later the tornado struck the stadium, smashing seating areas and tearing part of the stadium apart!

Flying glass from the blown-out hotel landed on people, cutting them up like butcher knives! The flying window glass blew through the stadium as the tornado was passing through, leaving a few people dead! The tornado continued and headed toward the T-Mobile Arena where the Las Vegas Golden Knights were playing. It was a 3-3 tie still with the Pittsburgh Penguins and the crowd was roaring away, not aware of what was going on outside! The game was held up with 3:15 to go and there was an announcement.

"Ladies and gentlemen—!" Then the power went out! A second later the roof was being ripped off! People found themselves being picked up and thrown around in the swirling wind! The arena was torn apart by the violent tornado, leaving thousands of fans outside being dragged down the strip in the storm! Black mud rain was pouring down! Then the tornado struck the Las Vegas Airport, smashing planes up like broken toys! Two planes exploded into flames and were tossed into terminals, and hangars were busted up like sheet metal.

People were running in all directions trying to escape this horrible storm. The tornado tore a few terminals apart, killing people, and the airport was completely destroyed! Airplanes and helicopters lay in a burning junkyard of rubble! Then the killer tornado passed into the desert until it hit the mountains and vanished!

The New York-New York Resort, the MGM, the Excalibur and the Pyramid were struck by the tornado before it destroyed the Mandalay Bay. There was an MMA fight going on at the Mandalay Bay Arena when the roof collapsed from the tornado, falling on the crowd and the fighters below.

Treasure Island, the Monte Carlo, and the Paris Hotel were spared from the tornado. The rest of the hotels and casinos on the strip got damaged from the storms. These hotels in the middle of the strip, which luckily escaped most of the damage, were where most of the evacuees from the Oregon and Washington State volcanoes stayed.

People at the Paris Hotel were wondering what was going on with all the fire trucks, police, and rescue vehicles by the hundreds! "Ladies and gentlemen, don't anyone leave the resort. A tornado heavily damaged the Mandalay Bay Hotel and the MGM was hit. New York-New York was heavily damaged and the roof was blown off of the Excalibur and the Pyramid was damaged. Mandalay Bay suffered devastating damage where a few deaths were reported after two tornadoes touched down, destroying the Mandalay Bay resort and casino.

"The Arena caved in where deaths were reported during a mixed martial arts fight. The Allegiant Stadium was hit by the same tornado—or was it a third one?—during the Ravens and the Raiders game and the stadium was heavily damaged. The T-Mobile Stadium was struck during the Golden Knights hockey game where several people were hurt, but it's not known if there were any deaths. The Las Vegas Airport was also leveled and there were deaths reported!

"It is rare that tornadoes strike the Las Vegas Strip; it was the second time since New Year's that we were hit by a tornado. These storms we have been getting lately are being caused by ash from all the volcanic eruptions reaching high into the strato-sphere. They trigger positive magnetic thunderstorms that keep building into a super thunderhead; it travels and picks an area with changing weather to explode in! They usually explode with straight-line winds, a microburst, then large hail and acid rain.

"These thunderstorms can also trigger a massive shockwave, that's what I think happened here tonight from the storms earlier this week. These types of storms can also flipflop with rushing cold air and dump feet of snow with 150 to 200 mile-per-hour winds just like what happened at the Lancaster Inn earlier this week. They're buried under fifteen feet of snow out in Montana and have fifty below temperatures!" said military guards at the Paris resort.

The replica Eiffel Tower was closed off so people couldn't climb it. It was because of the weather and all the commotion going on! "I never heard of a tornado coming up the Las Vegas Strip and doing so much damage!" said one lady.

"It may not be over yet; this storm is still going on and these types of storms return often until all the ash and gases fall down from the sky. When it reaches the stratosphere it's not coming down; it's going to cross the globe. We might get a snowstorm if this storm returns; we're lucky we are on the warm side.

"Fourteen deadly volcanoes erupted destroying Oregon and Washington State, not to mention a good part of Northern Canada. The city of Vancouver in British Columbia, Canada, burned to the ground from the erupting volcanoes and forest fires. The ash traveling from the Washington State and Oregon volcanoes followed the Mount Shasta eruption. We're getting hit with a mega plume of volcanic debris, causing these storms," said the military policemen to the crowd.

Later news reports came out on TVs at the Paris Hotel Resort as guests there watched. All the casinos, hotels, and resorts were on generators because there was no power along the strip.

"Good evening. We have breaking news on KLVN Channel 10 TV. A series of tornadoes touched down on the Las Vegas Strip, causing catastrophic damage and death! The Mirage and Caesar's Palace were struck by the first tornado where there was quite a bit of damage and injuries, but we do not know if there were any deaths.

"The first tornado also did some damage at the Bellagio! A second tornado struck the MGM, New York-New York, the Excalibur, and the Pyramid, leaving a trail of destruction and several injuries! A third tornado struck the Mandalay Bay Resort with catastrophic damage and several deaths were reported. We have fourteen deaths so far in the Mandalay Bay tornado.

"The new Allegiant Stadium was destroyed during a football playoff game between the Baltimore Ravens and the Las Vegas Raiders. Baltimore was winning 48 to 9 when the tornado struck. Thousands of windows were blown out and the roof was blown off of both towers. Minutes later another tornado struck the second tower at Mandalay Bay where several people were killed, and a roof collapsed at the Mandalay Bay Arena where an MMA fight was going on. Deaths were reported there!

"The violent tornado struck the T-Mobile Arena where the Las Vegas Golden Knights hockey game was playing, ripping the roof off. Fans were flying around like butterflies! Another tornado leveled Las Vegas Airport destroying plane hangars and terminals and killing people! We have twenty-three reported deaths and four or five destructive tornadoes that we know of.

"NLVN TV 10 is at the scene and there's bodies lying everywhere and lots of broken glass on the strip! Every window in the second tower was blown out and some people fell to their deaths! The death toll is expected to rise as the Mandalay Bay Resort was completely destroyed! Most evacuees from the Washington State and Oregon volcanoes are staying here. Carmen Truewoo reporting, Channel 10 News."

The next morning: Sunday, January 8, 2023. The Las Vegas Strip looked like Hiroshima after the atomic bomb in World War Two. Several hotels and casinos were damaged. Buildings and stadiums were damaged and the airport was obliterated, smashed up like a junkyard of sheet metal. Airplanes and helicopters were lying on the runway in pieces, terminals were smashed with dead people lying inside!! There was blood everywhere!!

The Mandalay Bay was worst hit; the resort had a river of broken glass with dead bodies buried under it covered in blood! One man was hanging out the twenty-third floor window dangling by his head! Another man lay on the ground with a window pane nearly cutting him in half with blood splattered everywhere!!

Police and resort officials were going over the damage and the dead bodies lying on the strip. A policeman threw up about three times walking through the destruction and over dead bodies! The damage was so bad the National Guard was called in.

Chinook helicopters and whirlybirds were landing, removing the dead bodies, and earth mobiles arrived to start cleaning up the glass. Military road graders and snowplows were used to plow the ash and mud the storms left behind. The rescue vehicles took the injured to area hospitals. The remaining evacuees were bused out into the desert to live in tents.

More storms struck the desert where thousands of people from the Washington State and Oregon volcanoes already were—in fact how many millions of people had now been living in the Nevada desert for months?! The Canadian evacuees stayed there! The Mount Shasta volcanic eruption evacuees were loaded on cruise ships and taken to Hawaii where there were many more volcanoes!

The massive magnetic storm caused by volcanic ash and thirteen deadly volcanic eruptions moved over the Rocky Mountains, dumping hundreds of feet of snow and life-threatening cold! Then it moved into Tornado Alley and picked on Oklahoma where the huge magnetic storm stalled!!

———————

Tuesday January 10, 2023. It was a balmy sixty-four degrees and kids were playing in a schoolyard. At 1:11 p.m. the sky turned pink on a sunny hazy day at Livingston Community Elementary School. Then a vibration was heard, and kids and teachers were coughing and sneezing because the haze was getting thicker and the sky was darkening and the sun was disappearing.

The teachers said, "Everyone get back in the school and close all the windows and doors!" Minutes later the school was on lockdown. Teachers were checking weather reports on their computers and the weather called for a hazy mild day and a cool night with a slight chance of a shower.

The sky was quickly darkening and started turning blood red! The principal came over the intercom. "Attention all students and staff, please follow tornado protocol and report to the storm shelters in the basement!" The principal and office staff went outside the school and they saw this gigantic red thunderhead and heard loud thunder coming out of it. A black fog formed around the red thunderhead and the sky began to darken like night; then came flashes of bright red lightning. The principal and office personnel quickly went inside to the storm shelter where the kids were.

———————

Police were on the highway going into Oklahoma City watching this mega thunderstorm developing. The reddish-pink lightning kept flashing brighter and brighter with big booms of thunder! The officer drove off the highway going into Oklahoma City on the way to the police station. While driving there he radioed to another cop from his police car. "Officer Richie, this is Officer Johnson, over! Do you see what I see up in the sky?!"

"Yes I do; it looks like something coming from outer space showing me lightning from another world!" said Officer Richie.

"We get the worst thunderstorms in the world here in Oklahoma, but I've never seen anything like this; any hurricane or tornado is not as scary as what I see in the sky right now! I don't know what this is; it looks like the end of the world coming!! It's some kind of fiery explosion moving slowly across the sky!" said Officer Johnson.

Then Officer Johnson heard a warning while driving his car into the police station. "The National Weather Service in Norman, Oklahoma has issued a severe thunderstorm warning for Oklahoma City downtown. Doppler radar has reported a huge spaceship-like super cell thunderhead recording deadly lightning, large hail, and strong straight-line winds. A possible tornado can't be ruled out! This is a life-threatening storm and you must take cover immediately! The storm is crossing downtown at this time!"

Officer Richie was on his way to the police station and he saw a bolt of lightning fry a big tree. Suddenly, hailstones bigger than duckpin bowling balls started falling with muddy acid rain, smashing his windshield just as he was getting off the highway. He stopped under an overpass flashing his lights. The front and back windows were smashed on his car!

Officer Richie wasn't watching the storm unfold for long! He had to get out of his car and climb up under the overpass before the wind struck. He was in a safe spot to ride out the storm, but his car washed down the road into a brook from the floods.

The violent storm passed over downtown and unloaded. Huge hail and 150-mile-per-hour straight-line winds and dark brown and black rain came down in buckets! The wind and hard falling hail blew out several city buildings! Windows and roofs were blown off and the city was covered in mud and the air smelled like sulfur! Lightning struck buildings, setting some of them on fire.

Then the storm parked over downtown Oklahoma City, dumping hail and rain for hours, causing catastrophic flooding. It moved northeast of the Mississippi River, changing into a super snowstorm that hit New England, dumping more than five feet of snow before it buried the Canadian Maritimes. The gigantic pink thunderhead dumped record rainfall and hail in the south and record snowfall and cold up north.

After the storm passed, downtown streets were covered in mud and giant hailstones. Windows were blown out in buildings and roofs were ripped off! The lightning in this storm was an odd pink and the thunder was very loud! Most people got to a storm shelter before this killer storm arrived. Of those who didn't, many might have died. The dead had not been found yet; too much damage from flooding to get to the buildings.

Back in Las Vegas, the Weather Channel was there reporting the aftermath of their own storms!

"Good evening, a mega thunderstorm spawned several tornadoes, leaving a trail of death and destruction on the Las Vegas Strip: 237 people dead and more than fifteen billion dollars' worth of damage. The storm struck on January 7. The Las Vegas Raiders and the Vegas Golden Knights games reported deaths and Mandalay Bay is still picking up the pieces where most of the bodies were found.

"People were blown out of buildings and the Mandalay Bay Resort was completely destroyed. The Las Vegas Airport was leveled and many people died there! The same storm moved into the Rocky Mountains dumping record snowfall and record cold, possibly trapping many people.

"This storm was the second mega storm that struck the Las Vegas strip in a week and it's blamed on the volcanic ash from all the volcano eruptions in Washington State and Oregon, plus

Mount Shasta in California. Another storm may threaten Las Vegas next week with snow and record cold temperatures. Julie Judd reporting, the Weather Channel."

———————

January 10, 2023, the Weather Channel was on the news again. "Good evening, mega storms are continuing to move through the United States leaving end-of-the-world like destruction and death! On January 7, the worst storm ever in Las Vegas leveled many casinos on the strip, killing a total of 289 people. The next day this killer storm struck the Rocky Mountains, killing 135 more so far through deadly snowstorms and bitter cold. Several avalanches leveled residential areas, inns, hotels, and resorts in the mountains. Ninety-three inches of snow fell at Denver International Airport and the city is paralyzed! Temperatures in Denver dropped to negative thirty-five degrees.

"On Tuesday January 10, 2023, a strange storm struck Oklahoma City, leaving a trail of destruction and more deaths reported! Several people in Oklahoma reported this unusual reddish-pink super cell thunderstorm with red and pink lightning. Several reports from police and the National Guard feared it was something from outer space such as a giant meteor or earth ending mega disaster about to unfold.

"The storm dumped thirty inches of rain and hail almost the size of footballs and a massive microburst with 150-mile-per-hour winds, destroying buildings, blowing out windows, and tearing off roofs like what happened in Las Vegas. Thirteen people are confirmed dead from this storm, mostly from flooding.

"The damage is unknown at this time and it will be awhile before recovery can start in Oklahoma City. More dead could be found when all the flooding subsides. The National Guard reported acid mud rain and the smell of sulfur, forcing residents to wear masks and respirators. It was an unsafe environment and fiery lightning triggered fires.

"The storm struck western New England, dumping eight feet of snow and dropping temperatures well below zero. The storm is heading toward the Canadian Maritimes, then out toward Iceland. Expect more of these types of storms to continue due to all the volcano eruptions on the West Coast. The Pacific Ocean tides rose five to eight feet above normal due to tsunamis on the West Coast and Alaska. Vancouver City in British Columbia, Canada is partly underwater! Julie Judd, reporting on the Weather Channel."

Newfoundland, Canada, city of St. John. The blue sky turned pink! People walking saw big waves breaking at a beach and went up to higher ground. They went into restaurants and stores because it was mighty cold outside, ten below zero. One couple looking out of their picture window inside their home overlooking the ocean and saw the pink sky turn dark. It started snowing and getting windy as they were watching the big waves rolling in.

Nightfall, the snow was still coming down so they had dinner together, drank wine, and sat in front of the fireplace. "Mindy, we have three feet of snow out there and it's still coming down at a pretty good clip!"

"I see Frank; the weather is calling for three to five feet of snow by morning. It's a big storm we're having." Later the couple went to bed for the night.

People were still out shopping and eating at restaurants and drinking in local bars as they heard the wind and saw the snow falling. Many found themselves trapped in four feet of snow in less than two hours and drifts six to ten feet high. Cars parked outside would be stuck there for a long time. People coming out to the street were in shock!

People at Patrick Fitzgerald's Bar and Grill having fun drinking, eating, and listening to Irish music and forgot what's happening outside are in for a big surprise when the bar closes tonight!

Before the bar closed, one man said to another, "Pat, Mike, we have to get out of here because it's snowing like a bastard outside!"

"Oh my God Carl McMillan, you're right! Look at the fuckin' *snow*! How the hell are we going to drive home in this? Our fuckin' cars are buried!!!!!!!" said Patrick.

"Oh my God!!" said Mike.

"Jackie, we're not going anywhere tonight; look at the snow!! We're fuckin' stuck here!!!!!!!!!!!!"

"Oh my God!!" she cried.

The manager Donald Fitzgerald looked outside and said, "Oh my fuckin' God! Let's get back in the bar fellas, we're not fuckin' going anywhere!!

"Here's the brother Donald who with us tonight; he eats it he beats it he even mistreats it, so here's the motherfucker who's with us tonight, so drink motherfucker drink motherfucker drink!"

"Here's the motherfucker who's with us tonight!!" said the crowd at the bar, singing to the owner!

Everyone at Patrick Fitzgerald's Bar and Grill in Newfoundland was partying all night while being buried in snow and ice, until a tidal wave arrived after the storm, killing everyone!!!!!!!

6:17 a.m. the couple woke up in their home looking out the window and the fuckin' snow had buried them. Then they heard a loud *roar!* The roar was a giant wave, almost a hundred feet high. It buried the island and froze them solid! Everyone was killed within a week, mostly from carbon dioxide poisoning from the snow and frozen ice from the storm!

These volcanoes that erupted on the West Coast are causing

a real fuckin' problem across the globe from wicked whiplash, end-of-the-world storms, killing people at will!

Three months later in late April of 2023, hot weather and Santa Ana storms tore through the Los Angeles areas, setting fires in the mountains, threatening to burn the fuckin' state of California to the ground!!

Planes couldn't keep up, trying to put fires out in the California mountains and valleys. Tidal waves striking at the coast were not helping the fire danger from the eruption of Mount Shasta. People in L.A. and San Diego couldn't evacuate at sea because of the giant fuckin' waves; the Pacific fuckin' Ocean was having an orgasm!!!!! People had to get to higher ground, hiding in the buildings in downtown Los Angeles to survive! Orgies broke out during the evacuations! The bad weather triggered a global end-of-the-world blowjob, killing thousands of people in vicious storms!!

The National Guard and the NASA volcano crew had to come up with a plan to save the fuckin' world from coming to an end!!!!

Denali, Alaska, there was a meeting with Operation Blowjob, the National Guard, and law enforcement. "Good evening, ladies and gentlemen. We have a pretty good count on the dead in the January superstorms and it's close to a million after the snow melted! More than 300 people were killed in the Las Vegas superstorms and hundreds of thousands of people have lost their lives in the Rocky Mountains mega snowstorms and record cold. Over 150 people were killed in the pink mega thunderstorm in Oklahoma City on January 10; the storm killed thousands as it moved up the northeast and left 250 dead when it became the famous pink mega blizzard in Newfoundland, Canada. It also killed hundreds in the North Sea and Iceland.

"These mega storms killed more than five hundred thousand people trapped in resorts and evacuation camps in Montana and up in the Canadian Rockies. Now record heat and drought in southern California! The state is burning out of control and killing hundreds of people! The fires are so severe, threatening to burn California to the ground! All this is being blamed on all the erupting volcanoes and more are threatening to erupt soon, setting off a chain reaction!

"We're in danger right here in Alaska because there's a lot of volcanoes here! All the trees and woodlands in Washington State and Oregon are gone and many buildings and residential areas are wiped out. Parts of Seattle stand, but more buildings may have to be knocked down and the city may be condemned forever. The land is a desert of mud, dirt, and lava fields all the way into northwestern Canada.

"The weather has been catastrophic with cold snow and record cold since November. Now the dust is settling as spring approaches, keeping the snowstorms in Canada and the heat in California. Storms in the mountains and record heat in the southern plains and drought in Hawaii—sheesh! We have been lucky; the sky is starting to clear and the weather is quieting down, but don't be fooled because there's still a lot of dust up there and it can thicken anytime. It will threaten the globe again!

"We will have heat waves, deadly cold, drought, and famine. These storms and volcanic eruptions may one day wipe out the food chain. There is a food shortage going on right now, affecting the evacuations in the Nevada desert bubble and on the Las Vegas Strip. Millions of people from Washington State and Oregon have been cared for the last six or seven months, but food and water are running out.

"Most of these people may be here for the rest of their lives.

We need to be prepared for what's to come. Now we have some bad fires going on in California all the way to Canada and Washington State, while Oregon is a mud desert! These storms will start again and we have to be ready. We have several volcanoes here in Alaska. We are monitoring them closely and a few could go off at any time! Thank you for your time!" said Edward Fay.

———————

May 2023, Florida was next in line for severe weather. A storm was brewing off the coast of Tampa. The sky was black as night over Tampa Bay, moving into downtown where a wedding was going on. The sky went from bright sunshine to black as night. Then the storm unloaded with strong winds and heavy rain, thunder and lightning with bolts hitting the ground. A tornado went through the wedding party, knocking people over like bowling pins. Everyone was running over each other trying to get away from the tornado!

The tornado tore up the wedding reception area! The DJ ran for his life and his equipment was damaged! Big thunderstorms and waterspouts and tornadoes flattened many neighborhoods from Pensacola, Florida all the way to Miami.

Mega forest fires burned and destroyed residential areas in record numbers and lots of people died in the flames! Volcanic ash and lava spitting out of Mount Shasta torched a lot of forest. Heavy rains and snowstorms in the Rockies triggered hundreds of avalanches, killing hundreds of people! Dead people were found in resorts, hotels, and camps from the killer winter storms after snowmelt and several Rocky Mountain resorts were destroyed.

The weather from all the volcano eruptions is leaving end-of-the-world results!!!

CHAPTER NINE

THE EVACUATION
SHELTERS

Las Vegas Strip. The volcano evacuees from Washington State, Oregon, and Mount Shasta were staying at the Las Vegas casino hotels and living in bubble tents with heating or cooling units. Homes were built in the desert to help house millions of people. They were living under martial law set by the National Guard, wearing masks and respirators like for the coronavirus protocol.

People who did not behave were taken to a prison in the mountains. Most people worked with one another and made new friends; it'd been that way for the last six months. Other evacuees were taken on cruise ships to the big island on Hawaii to an evacuation camp there.

Travel was by bus or tram to get people around. Trucks arrived with food to feed people, but over the last six months food and water had been getting scarce! New evacuees from the mountains and those trapped from the big storms were shipped to Las Vegas. They were bused to the Stratosphere Hotel.

"Good afternoon ladies and gentlemen, welcome to the Stratosphere Hotel Casino Resort. My name is Dameon Duke, the manager here at the Stratosphere. The hotel is empty and is only available for the evacuees from storm damage and volcano victims. That's true for all the hotels in Las Vegas. Outsiders can come in and gamble and use the facilities, buy food, but cannot get overnight stays even with casino comps; that's for evacuees only.

"To start off, everyone was given a duffel bag with their belongings. Everyone will get a room where you will stay indefinitely! The rooms for your families are already set up for you. It's not complicated, but we do have martial law here in Las Vegas due to the West Coast volcano disasters. I will go over it with you people later.

"How this works: You get your rooms, up to four people, and eight staying in the suites. The rooms and your food are free and you get three meals a day, but you have to arrive at the same time for your three meals. Continental breakfast is served between 7:00 a.m. and 9:00 a.m. If you arrive late you're out of luck; you have to arrive between those times if you want breakfast.

"Lunchtime is 11:30 a.m. until 2:00 p.m. Dinner buffet style is served from 5:00 p.m. until 7:00 p.m. If you don't eat at those times we have snack rooms throughout the casino floor where you can buy food. If you want to play the slots and tables you may; it's your money. All facilities are open for everyone in the resort. If you need to go shopping or go places you will be given a card to ride the tram. You can get the tram across the street and it's free twenty-four hours a day as long as you show your card.

"We have our own bank, the Stratosphere Bank and Trust. You can open accounts here for convenience or you can go to other banks downtown. It's your choice. You can go to one show a week for free; the shows run seven days a week. Everyone will get a booklet on the privileges you have here and the rules and regulations of the resort.

"Now I want to go over the rules and regulations on things you can do and what you cannot do! Before I go over the rules we have some families bigger than ten people and they will be living in a tent bubble. It's not as bad as you think; you will be living in an apartment set up in an air conditioned tent with heat on cold days. It was 111 degrees today here in Vegas!

"Everyone must be treated with respect; this is a time where everyone must get along. We are at the beginning of the end of the world because of all the volcano eruptions causing violent storms and deadly fires! I see this crowd here is evacuees from the California mega fires! We have more than five million evacuees here in Las Vegas ranging from newborns to 111-year-olds in all nationalities: white, black, brown, red and yellow!

"We must get along with one another. Any racism, you will be removed by military law enforcement. Same for rapes, stealing, or any discomfort from other families! We have cameras everywhere except in hotel rooms or restrooms.

"Everyone will be tested for coronavirus and if you are sick you will be moved into a sick bubble hospital. If you want to bring a prostitute to your room or bubble you may; it's legal in Las Vegas! You can do anything you want; enjoy yourself, just stay out of trouble. Any fights here at the resort, you will be thrown in the ring with the ultimate fighters!

"Other rules: you cannot have animals here at the Stratosphere; if you want a cat just go to the Mirage, they have white tigers there! No cars, no bicycles because we have no room for them. We have buses, trains, and the tram to ride. If you want to fly just go to the airport. You are welcome to be at home here at the Stratosphere. Just don't get yourself into trouble because law enforcement does not play in Vegas!

"Your family will be called alphabetically, and you get your keys to your room and itinerary packets. In your packets you will see face coverings, masks, and a respirator, and you wear them when you go outside because the volcanic dust in the air can choke you. The volcanic dust is still in the atmosphere despite all the storms we had. We have a lot of desert dust here and when it gets stirred up from the wind it's even worse trying to breathe, and it's very dangerous if you're not wearing a face covering. If you forget when you go outside the wind will remind you to put one on in a hurry! That's how bad the outside air is.

"You will see instructions to follow and people to go to if you need to ask questions on rules and regulations and paperwork about your medical records and family history. Good luck and welcome," said Dameon Duke, the manager.

———————

Everything went smoothly; people met lots of friends and there were plenty of jobs and the bubble tents had nice apartments.

The beds and furniture were made from compressed air and they were very comfortable! Each bubble apartment had full bathroom stalls with tanks outside to be emptied when full. Every bubble tent ran on generators or ground electricity from the hotels and resorts. The bubble tents were well-built, able to withstand hurricane-force winds, and the material was strong enough to survive a tornado. It's safer living in these tents than in a home when a hurricane or tornado strikes. No windows, but clean air was pumped in and there was an emergency door to get out in case of a fire.

The bubble tents were also fireproof and had sprinklers throughout. Each apartment was squared off with mail slots in the door. A second door went into a hallway and the apartments were laid out like a hotel. The bubble tents were very long and held more than five hundred thousand people each. A golf cart trolley ran twenty-four hours a day and travelled through the long halls between the apartments to take people where they wanted to go inside the tents.

The material the tents were made of comes from Denver and it got bolted deep in the ground to help people live in them.

Families living in the bubbles were large and could have pets. There were several bubble tents in the deserts holding millions of people, with more living in underground bunkers. The smaller families were living in hotel rooms with no pets; the families with pets lived off the strip in Section 8 housing.

The evacuations at the Stratosphere were well organized in the resort and the bubble tents. But in some places things spiraled out of control.

June 21, 2023, new evacuations were going to Mandalay Bay from the California fires. Some evacuated from the volcanoes were moved from the bubble tents, leading to overcrowding indoors. Fights started erupting before management started giving instructions.

The Mandalay Bay damage from last January's tornadoes was rebuilt back to normal and now the rooms in both towers were filling up, but things were not starting off well with the new evacuees. Two families of four going to one room with two beds doesn't go over well. Management at Mandalay Bay was making costly mistakes. Fights started breaking out everywhere!

Management workers were getting punched and furniture was getting broken and evacuating residents were fighting one another. Casino hosts were getting beaten up and security guards were getting trampled and beaten up and knocked down and punched!

Then the Mandalay Bay resort police arrived, shooting buckshot at the crowd, using pepper spray and tasering people! Then it was an all-out uncontrollable brawl breaking out! Police were overpowered, being punched, kicked, knocked down and stepped on, and there was blood everywhere!! Cops and security guards were beaten to the ground and trampled in their own blood!!!

The Las Vegas city police arrived and the National Guard

was called in to break up this uncontrollable riot at the Mandalay Bay. The crowd threw chairs and lamps and anything they could get their hands on. They threw it through office windows and hotel front windows! They set fire to furniture and threw it outside! The brawl spilled out into the casino with people getting knocked down, making the brawl much bigger! Waitresses were getting knocked down, drinks flying everywhere!

Finally police, the SWAT team, and military personnel poured in to put a stop to this massive Mandalay Bay brawl!!!!!! Fights broke out in the hallways on the floors, making the job for police and military much harder. The SWAT team used teargas to break up the brawls and smoke bombs to make arrests easier. Tasers were used, and gunshots, to cool the brawl down. The riot went on all day and night before it was finally under control.

The National Guard troops went up through the floors to break up the fights and make arrests. More than five hundred people were arrested and taken to jail. The damage was unbelievable! The lobby looked like a tornado hit. People were still gambling in the casino despite a blood-soaked rug. About three hundred police cars, fire trucks, and rescue vehicles arrived to move the injured and take them to area hospitals.

Fire trucks were putting out fires and police were making arrests and taking people to jail. Military armored vehicles arrived to help out. The Mandalay Bay was evacuated! The strip was blocked off going to the Mandalay Bay. One man said to a crowd near the Monte Carlo, "Jesus Christ! Did Mandalay Bay get hit by another tornado?!"

The Mandalay Bay was closed for repairs for a couple of weeks until the damages were fixed. Las Vegas Police were there at the Mandalay Bay talking with officials only half beaten up to find out what happened. The manager was in the hospital with a broken neck and screws in his head; he's lucky to be alive!

The next day, "Hi my name is Keven White from the Las Vegas

Police Department. What happened last night that made evacuees get out of control?"

"Pleased to meet you, Officer White. My name is Gary Golden, the hotel host manager here at the Mandalay Bay. The casino owner Dick Sukoff did not handle the large crowd very well. He was very unorganized, overcrowding rooms and putting two or three families in tight areas. He did not handle the evacuations the right way or get proper instructions to them. He had no idea what he was doing since he became the owner of the resort, just letting people hang around for days instead of instructing them where to go.

"Three families in one room with two beds and one bathroom is not going to go over well! He's a fuckin' airhead! He gave people room keys to rooms already taken. I swear this fuckin' guy has Alzheimer's disease! He was a big political businessman here at the Mandalay Bay before he became manager and he's been here for years. I don't know how he got away with what he does because this fuckin' man is a dummy! This is why things got out of hand here!

"The man got his ass kicked in the brawl and he's in the hospital right now with a broken neck and his head split open. I am surprised he's still alive! He needed to get his head kicked in a few times to knock some fuckin' sense into him! Mr. Sukoff was not very well-liked here. I hate the cocksucker myself! Maybe this ass kicking will straighten him out if he lives!" said Gary Golden, hotel host.

The police got a good laugh and started writing up incident reports and taking damage reports. The hotel was out of control, handling big crowds throughout. The late evening news showed what happened, and people were watching all over the world.

"Good evening, we have breaking news on NBC News on June 22, 2023. A massive brawl broke out at the Mandalay Bay Resort in Las Vegas involving thousands of people because of disputes of wildfire evacuees overcrowding bubble tents and volcano evacuees overbooking hotel rooms. Mandalay Bay officials couldn't handle the melee, a brawl of more than five hundred people damaging furniture and setting fires, leaving a trail of destruction and hundreds of injuries.

"More than three hundred people were arrested and two hundred more ended up in the hospital. Two people were killed in the riots. Hundreds of emergency and military vehicles were called to the scene. The brawl went on for twenty hours before it was under control, leaving millions of dollars of damage. The National Guard will take over the hotel evacuations until things get organized there.

"There have been some bubble tent issues with overcrowding by evacuees because millions of people are homeless due to the West Coast volcano eruptions and California mega fires from the eruption of Mount Shasta just before Christmas.

"It's not the first time there was trouble in Mandalay Bay. On January 7, two tornadoes destroyed the resort. Evacuations overcrowded the bubble tents, where seven people died. Linda Atkins reporting on NBC TV News."

The bubble tents in the desert were more organized because there were hundreds of them, and many newly built homes for people to live in. Plenty of jobs were available.

At the United Pentecostal Assembly Church in Beverly Hills California, on Sunday, July 2, 2023, there was a service about the end of the world because of all the volcano eruptions. "Good morning, welcome brothers and sisters to church. My name is Pastor Dan Cotton, taking over for Pastor Gooding. Today I'm going to talk about the end of the world in the *Book of Revelations*. It's coming soon and we have to be ready. In 2026 there's a threat of a large meteor striking the earth, big enough to end life on earth. But let's not worry about that right now, now we must worry about how we are going to survive the devil.

"All the volcanoes in the northwest corner of the United States erupted, leveling Washington State, Oregon, and northwest Canadian provinces. Nothing left but a pile of dust and stone that has burned from the devil from hell!

"Now Mount Shasta, 601 miles north of Beverly Hills, erupted around Christmastime and is now burning up northern California. Only two places are surviving right now: here in Beverly Hills, and off in San Francisco, with the strong faith of the United Pentecostal Assembly Church. It proves we are God's people, being in this church. Everyone around us is in the devil's path, but we are saved here. Look what happened about a week and a half or two weeks ago in Las Vegas. Look at the brawl at the Mandalay Bay casino and the tornado they had there in January.

"Stadiums were destroyed, the airport was leveled, and the Las Vegas strip was blown down by the storms due to the devil's wrath! Thirteen volcanoes erupted in Washington State, Oregon, and California, killing thousands if not millions because many did not evacuate in time, those chosen by God or the devil.

"Here's what I believe! The ones who could not evacuate in time were taken by God into heaven. Those who remained alive, they're alive until the devil decides what to do with them! Most people evacuated and are now living in makeshift ground houses, bubbles, or tents, whatever you want to call it. It's a temporary living situation and time is running out because food will be gone soon and famine will make people turn on one another just like starving animals in the wild!

"Fights are happening and so are bad things. Too many bad things are happening in the world today! Right now we are in the beginning of the Rapture with all these volcanoes erupting at the same time and evil storms from the volcanoes taking lives in huge numbers. These storms are the wrath of God taking His people before evil in the world gets worse!

"This sermon may not make sense to some people unless you read the *Book of Revelations*. Think about it! I'm not here to scare people away but the words I'm saying during this sermon are a fact! When Mount Rainier erupted, the worst volcano destroying the Space Needle and wiped out downtown Seattle with no warning killing thousands, was God's people being taken into the Rapture before the devil gets them.

"We are living in the devil's time and God will raise the Rapture from hell! All these volcanoes erupting all at once is hell coming out to cover the earth and if they keep erupting the devil will burn the world, killing all life on earth.

"Most people believe that the devil is taking the people being burned to death from the volcanoes but no, it's the Rapture of God taking his people. Those who got away, survived, or evacuated were left for the devil to take later on. These people living in temporary homes, homeless etcetera, better get with God in a hurry before it's too late!

"I have a program on Channel 7 on Sunday nights called, *Prepare for the Afterlife with Pastor Dan Cotton*. I hope the evacuees are listening to my show and they may be saved! Here is what to expect in the future: Washington State and Oregon will rebuild when these volcanoes quiet down, but all thirteen or fourteen of them are still active and will be a threat again.

"Expect more eruptions, fires, deadly storms, famine, and death! It's not going away anytime soon; we are in the Rapture. When God finishes taking His people the devil finishes the rest and that's when the world will end!

"The Rapture began at the start of the twenty-first century with worldwide wars on September 11, 2001, when America was attacked! The coronavirus that killed millions across the globe shutting the earth down in 2020! The Toronto Rapture in 2021 where Asians mysteriously disappeared! It was not the Toronto Raptors basketball team.

"The deadly volcano eruptions in 2022-23, killing millions of people on the West Coast. It's not over people! The Alaskan volcano chain is ready to erupt next and then Yellowstone National Park. If that goes off it just may be the end of everything because it's the biggest and deepest volcano in the world!

"2026 is three years away and a large asteroid is coming. When it strikes it will destroy the world; it will be the time when God comes and takes the rest of His people. Just remember this sermon today. When danger is coming, especially volcano eruptions, evacuate and say your prayers. Read the bible and study the word of God as much as you can and you may be saved! If you do not have a chance to get away and die in the ashes, God will raise you if you believe in Him. If you don't believe in Jesus Christ, the almighty God, the devil will take you! Read the *Book of Revelations,* the section on the Rapture! Amen," said Pastor Dan Cotton.

As the summer progressed, people who heard Pastor Dan Cotton's sermon in the church that day were believers and read the bible at the beach, in parks, along dangerous fire sites, on city streets, in evacuation bubbles and bunker homes, on city streets and in casinos, everywhere. More bubble tents were being built away from volcanoes to hold evacuees.

The desert areas were filling up with living spaces, also helping the homeless, but were run under martial law and controlled by the United States Army and National Guard. All Fourth of July fireworks displays were cancelled on the West Coast except on cruise ships far out at sea. They braved isolated tsunami warnings at all times because some volcanoes erupt under the ocean.

Tensions were starting to build in the bubble tents because food and water were running out as farm areas were disappearing. Animals, including dogs and cats, were getting slaughtered for food, and people were collecting rainwater for drinking and bathing. The use of these temporary bubble tent homes covering up the deserts, the Rocky Mountains, and flatlands and plains in Florida and Canada was taking away land for farming. Greenhouses were set up to keep the food chain from disappearing and the homeless from increasing.

CHAPTER TEN

THE ALASKAN BLOWJOB

Mount Redoubt, 10,917 feet, snowcapped, is ready to erupt. The volcano was already active and the NASA crew at Mount Denali National Park were getting ready for another major eruption on Mount Redoubt. A meeting was held at Denali National Park military bunkers with the Alaska National Guard, park rangers, and law enforcement.

"Good evening, my name is Edward Fay, the head volcanologist of NASA in Houston, Texas. We have another volcano ready for a major eruption. Mount Redoubt is ready to erupt at any time as of today, Saturday, July 15, 2023.

"It has been active and the magma chamber has been at its limit for the last six months. It's a ticking time bomb ready to blow at any time. Lake Clark County has not had orders to evacuate yet and if they do not have a plan soon it might be too late! Ladies and gentlemen, my group: Miss Linda Brew, Mrs. Katrina House, Mr. Nathan Rivers, Mr. Paul Numbnutts, and finally David Dunkin. We are Operation Blowjob! We are here to save the world!

"These volcanoes on the West Coast are getting out of control! We lost several West Coast NASA employees when Mount St. Helens erupted, killing more than 150,000 people. The West

Coast NASA crew were Miss Eleanor Pepperjackcarmmen-
donchampinelli, known as Miss P.; Mr. Steven Jennings; Miss
Gail Porter; Miss Jill Santiago; Mr. Michael Kennedy; Mr. Dick
Colon; Mr. Peter Oakland; Mr. David Vincent; Miss Jessica Vincent; and finally Aden U. Vincent.

"All died from the Mount St. Helens and Mount Adams
eruptions when the military bunker they were in was blown to
pieces! Now we are here to defend the dead and take over the
West Coast NASA operation. We are again Operation Blowjob,
because now we are taking over the load due to the deaths from
the eruptions from Mount St. Helens, the most active cunt in the
United States!

"We have Lieutenant Jalen Robertson here from the eruption
of Mount Shasta in California that destroyed resorts and triggered several forest fires! If volcanoes start erupting on the East
Coast we have to go there too!

"Mount Ascutney in Adamsville, Vermont is still very active
and this volcano can erupt again as well as all the others—too
many to name on the West Coast! Ascutney is part of a super
volcano on the East Coast, threatening to blow the six New
England states off the fuckin' map!!! We have reports of a possible volcano brewing on Block Island, Rhode Island. Right now
we have to worry about Mount Fuckin' Redoubt!!

"We need to have a plan and set up in Lake Clark National
Park and downtown Lake Clark with spudweb data robots
because the mayor has not staged an evacuation in the last few
months. Luckily this eleven thousand-foot sleeping giant has not
blown its load yet! We need to get in there and save their lives
because this volcano has erupted many times before. It's ready
for a major eruption and this town will be gone if we can't get in
there and save it.

"We have our lives in our hands ladies and gentlemen, and
we're the ones who have to monitor Mount Redoubt and we

have to do this now. Number one: I need the town police to force the mayor to hold a town meeting to be ready for a possible evacuation. Number two: We need the National Guard to help with the Lake Clark Police. We will go in placing the spudwebs in the national park at the base of the mountain so we will know how soon this mountain will blow! We don't need to place them up on the summit to see what's happening, we already know that the danger is coming soon.

"Mayor Kriptoff Koon in Lake Clark City is a stubborn bastard and we need to steer him the right way. NASA, National Guard, let's go to work! We're flying into Lake Clark right now! Ladies and gentlemen, law enforcement and military here at the army bunkers in Mount Denali National Park, thank you for attending this important meeting," said Edward Fay, head of NASA's volcanologists.

Helicopters and C-130 airplanes were flying into the Lake Clark Airport and people there were watching and wondering why. The volcano crew went to Lake Clark National Park and military helicopters landed there! The police went to Mayor Kriptoff Koon's office with the NASA leader.

"Mr. Mayor Koon sir, Officer Gordon Blackburn from the Alaska State Police. I have Mr. Edward Fay with me, head of the NASA volcano crew from Houston. He's here to warn you that a volcano is ready to erupt here."

"Officer, I am sick and tired of people telling me that Mount Redoubt is going to erupt. I have been here for ten years and all we had was a mild eruption in 2018, and we do have earthquakes from time to time but nothing worth an evacuation! I understand Washington State and Oregon, parts of California and Vancouver were blown off the earth from fourteen volcanoes or so, and all we're getting is all the bad weather from the eruptions.

"We get bad weather here every day here in Lake Clark and besides, we have more than one hundred volcanoes here in Alaska!

I'm not a bit worried about Mount Redoubt erupting forty-nine miles from here! If fourteen killer volcanoes erupting in Washington, Oregon, and California didn't kill us I'm not worried about Mount Redoubt."

"Mayor, I'm telling you to do something to warn the people because my spudweb data robots are posting warnings that Mount Redoubt is threatening a deadly eruption. If you don't have an evacuation plan and this mountain blows, more than fifty thousand people in this community may die, including the annihilation of Anchorage 113 miles away.

"This is a very powerful volcano and it has a bad history with eruptions. Redoubt has been active for years and nothing very serious has happened other than a few earthquakes and steam vent eruptions, but a major eruption will be very soon. It could go off now killing a lot of people, or it might be two years from now. We don't know, but now we have warnings from spudweb with readings saying this mountain is ready to blow. You make the decision to evacuate this city. If not, we're getting out of here!" said Edward Fay.

"I will inform the police to call on loudspeakers to warn the people, but I'm not evacuating Lake Clark for one volcano because we're surrounded by them!" said Mayor Kriptoff Koon.

"Sir, you have a nice day! We're out of here!" said Edward Fay. The crew left Lake Clark City and went back to Denali National Park after setting up the robots.

Police drove around Lake Clark calling on loudspeakers, "Ladies and gentlemen, the NASA volcano crew has issued an evacuation because Mount Redoubt is threatening a major eruption. Please follow the evacuation route away from the sea." The warnings went on for days but many people were not listening! Some people left the area—very good! Most people rode it out; they heard these warnings all the time and nothing major ever happened!

One day that apocalyptic event will happen, and it may be very soon. The church services say that one day this town will be buried in ash from this powerful volcano.

———

Tuesday, July 18, 2023 at 8:00 p.m. the sun was finally shining brightly. Parts of Alaska have twenty-four hours of daylight during the summer. Sonic booms were heard and lightning was spotted on a clear day out toward Mount Redoubt. A cruise ship, glacier watching, was leaving Lake Clark National Park through Cook Inlet River and heading for Anchorage. Cruise ships were also viewing Pedro Bay, watching ice breaking off huge glaciers. Cruise ships stopped at Port Alsworth, picking up more people and dropping others off.

Glaciers suddenly started breaking off, triggering big waves during the trip to Anchorage. Several sonic booms were heard followed by several earthquakes.

Back in Lake Clark, Mayor Kriptoff Koon was in his office reading a book when he felt the ground shaking a little bit, which stopped. He looked out of his window and didn't notice any damage so he sat down on his fat ass and continued reading his book. Then he heard the sonic booms, then he paused a little, then he went back to reading his book. Then he heard a *roar!* then a powerful earthquake knocked him out of his chair. He hit his head on the ceiling and landed on the floor.

The city hall building was rocking back and forth like a rocking boat! Mayor Koon was being thrown from one side of his office to the other. A light fixture fell and broke over his fuckin' head—maybe it will knock some sense into him! Then the shaking stopped and he now realized he was in big trouble!!!!!!!!!! He got up staggering and he ran out of city hall with a big cut on his head from falling debris.

He saw buildings with windows blown out and roofs caved

in and the road cracked open. Many buildings were so damaged they broke apart and fell into the road's new chasm. The damage was worse than he'd ever seen! The electricity was out, no power, and it was getting dark around 10:30 p.m. Then the shaking started again followed by a loud *roar!* like trumpets blaring, then sonic booms, then a big *bang!* The sound, loud enough to lift debris off the ground, was followed by several flashes of blue lightning from the earthquakes. Mount Redoubt erupted, making a very loud howling noise, and the twilight sky turned orange from its massive explosion. Then there was a pyroclastic flow with a lot of lightning bolts coming out of the top of Mount Redoubt!

Mayor Kriptoff Koon was watching the horror, trying to run to safety. He even saw dead people lying on the ground! Then came a bright flash that followed a mushroom cloud above Mount Redoubt as the mayor was watching in shock! Then he heard a *roar!* and a shockwave came, so strong Mayor Kriptoff Koon was picked up and thrown into a bunch of trees far away. He screamed, "Help!"

The sky clouded up quickly and it started pouring. There was thunder and lightning then the rainwater turned to mud rain. Mayor Koon shimmied down a fifty-foot tree and had an eight-mile walk back to his office. There was no power or cell phone service and he was stuck in his office with leftover food to eat for weeks.

Back at the Cook Inlet glaciers were cracking and breaking off in the river, triggering huge waves and sinking small boats. Cruise ships were rocking and people aboard were screaming. People fell in the icy waters where small boats tipped over, sinking.

People were killed by falling glacier ice as visitors watched in shock from other boats. The falling ice was caused by earthquakes from Mount Redoubt followed by shockwaves. When the volcano erupted it filled the sky with ash and falling, burning rocks. Within minutes, people were dead in the streets and floating in the river. The powerful shockwaves from Redoubt were enough to kill people because, living near the mountain, the pressure from the shockwaves tore the insides out of people and animals, leaving them dead for miles.

Buildings were blowing up into piles of bricks and violent earthquakes swallowed roads, cracking the earth wide open and swallowing everything in their path. Nearby villages and winter resorts were buried before the mountain blew! Then it was the loudest **bang!** Then a mushroom cloud looking like a nuclear bomb went off; then the sky filled with darkness like midnight! The streets were filled with blood and death.

Injured people were walking around like zombies waiting to be rescued! There was no power and there was darkness for days. No emergency vehicles, police, or rescue crews could get through because the damaged earth was cracked open. Only motorcycles and bicycles were able to do any rescue work, and in fear of falling into hell underground.

There were cries for help, only for people to be left for dead! Lightning flashed to show where the dying humans and animals were, then loud thunder followed by airlifting shockwaves shredding the landscape! The eruption of Mount Redoubt was so bad it looked like hell coming to take the world. It was the worst eruption in its long evil history and the damage and shockwaves caught millions of Alaskans off guard. NASA gave several warnings that this mountain was going to have a violent eruption but nobody took it seriously. It was just a sleeping giant, resting in the Chigmit Mountains with the rest of the volcanoes with a nice view and quiet scenery! Surprise! Now death and a trail of destruction!

The NASA volcano crew left long before the shit hit the fan. They came back to Denali National Park days after the eruption, where a meeting took place in the military bunkers with Edward Fay head volcanologist. "Good evening ladies and gentlemen; eight degrees Celsius in late July is a little chilly even here in Alaska. We are Operation Blowjob monitoring all the volcanoes in the United States. About eight days ago we flew into Lake Clark with spudweb data machines and we told the mayor of Lake Clark that Mount Redoubt was going to erupt very soon. We warned them to evacuate the city because if this mountain erupted it was going to be deadly!

"He denied it. He told the police to post warnings but he was not planning a massive evacuation so we did our job and we left. Mount Redoubt erupted, killing thousands of people, and we never heard from the mayor of Lake Clark City again! The magma levels are moving through the Chigmit Mountains at a rapid speed, spreading to several more volcanoes. If they start erupting we better pack up and go back to New York because the whole chain of mountains will cause catastrophic damage to all the Alaskan Islands and serious damage in the Pacific Ocean and other countries.

"That's how the ring of fire operates: a chain of volcanoes all goes off at the same time. Let's hope that's not the case. We have data from all over the world from our robots and they are saying that the Chigmit Mountain Range is in great danger because of the eruption of Mount Redoubt. Even now the mountain is still erupting and the lava is spreading," said Edward Fay.

"Edward, here's what we have now on report from the eruption of Mount Redoubt: A pyroclastic flow destroyed towns and cities, and deadly lahars buried low lying areas around the mountain on both sides under fifty feet of ash and mud. Lantana, Queens, Livingston, and Lake Clark Regency Resort are gone! Homes, businesses, hotels, and ski lodges were wiped out. The entire Lake Clark County has been damaged by a mega shockwave from the volcano. Many people are feared dead and earthquakes opened up the ground, swallowing many properties and buildings. The windows in many buildings were blown out from the shockwaves. There were tidal waves and ships sank in the Cook Inlet. Earthquakes broke off huge glacier chunks and we have many people dead!" said Paul Numbnutts, one of the data operators.

After the meeting, the military flew into Lake Clark City to assess the damage when the storms and the cloudy skies brightened. The area looked like a bomb struck; there were dead bodies everywhere! Buildings collapsed and ships, including oil tankers, ran aground with fires burning everywhere! Floods with dead bodies floating in the water and mud flows.

The National Guard had to go in on foot and kayaks or small boats to find survivors and God damn it! There were none! One man was buried in ash and his butt and two legs were sticking up in the air. A horse with no head and cows and other animals lay dead in the ash. Then law enforcement and military workers went into burned-out and damaged buildings to find survivors and a cop saw Mayor Kriptoff Koons's dead burnt body lying on the floor in city hall. Rats were eating his burnt body and licking up all his blood in his office.

The Cook Inlet River was covered with broken glaciers and sunken ships lying on their sides. There was flooding everywhere and dead bodies of humans and animals floating in the lahar river Everything was broken from the Mount Redoubt earthquakes and shockwaves! The damage was so bad the area was unrecognizable! Helicopters flew over the damage and it looked like the end of the world. News reporters flew helicopters into Lake Clark City to view the damage. Later people watched the news on TV.

"Good evening, we have breaking news on KALS Channel 12. Mount Redoubt erupted on July 18, spreading an ash cloud about a hundred miles wide exploding above the stratosphere.

The eruption sent a shockwave three hundred miles across the Alaskan peninsula through the Chigmit Mountains. Mount Redoubt's eruption was so severe all of Lake Clark County was leveled and thousands of people are feared dead.

"The Mayor of Lake Clark City was told to evacuate the area because of the threatening volcano by the US NASA volcano crew but he chose not to have a massive evacuation. He was found dead in his office at the Lake Clark city hall. A massive microburst shockwave caused catastrophic damage and death in the region. All the building windows in the city were blown out. A massive earthquake opened up the ground, swallowing buildings and making it impossible for rescue crews to get in.

"The National Guard was called in to look for possible survivors on foot. The Cook Inlet suffered the worst earthquake in Alaska's history, a 9.7 which broke apart glaciers by the hundreds, sinking ships and drowning villages from tsunamis. This eruption of Mount Redoubt was the worst disaster ever in Alaska!

"This mountain has a history of violent eruptions and it's still erupting right now. In the 1989 eruption Anchorage was buried under three feet of ash. Property damage and death from this eruption may never be known. Ash is still falling like a mega snowstorm from Mount Redoubt in some areas so expect more damage because this mountain is not done yet! Christy Dallas, reporting on KALS 12 News."

The next day the NASA volcano crew had a meeting among themselves describing the rare shockwaves from the eruption of Mount Redoubt. "Ladies and gentlemen, we have a count of 15,168 people killed in Lake Clark County alone, not to mention the surrounding areas of Mount Redoubt! It wasn't so much the eruption or the earthquakes, but the shockwaves that killed all those people and caused so much damage. It's unusual that shockwaves could cause so much destruction and death because the mountain is so far away. The reason why this happened is because the eruption blew well up into the stratosphere and spread out hundreds of miles, causing a microburst shockwave effect!

"That happened when Mount Rainier erupted, burning down the Space Needle and destroying the city of Seattle, then Glacier Peak also triggered a shockwave to finish the job. Mount Baker had one that destroyed Vancouver, Washington and British Columbia, Canada. The Crater Lake super volcano had a deadly shockwave that wiped out the state of Oregon and triggered massive tsunamis. Mount Shasta also had a shockwave. These volcanoes erupted into the stratosphere causing these shock-waves. The Crater Lake eruption was the worst; it blew Oregon off the fuckin' map!

"What makes this one scary is we have a super volcano threat right here in fuckin' Alaska! Mount Redoubt is one of the most dangerous volcanoes in the world because it's located in the Chigmit Mountain Range with hundreds of volcanoes through-out Alaska. The magma levels are very high in all of these moun-tains and may trigger another super volcano strong enough to blow the Chigmit Mountains off the map.

"If one more volcano erupts we need to pack up and go back to the East Coast because a super volcano will not only blow the Chigmit mountains out into the Pacific, but the state of Alaska may split in two and fall into the ocean. Parts of northern Canada, the Arctic ice, and parts of Russia will be destroyed! The ash will melt all the Arctic ice and the globe will be in serious trouble!

"We need to have a close eye on what's happening because we have the main feeder systems monitoring all the volcanoes here at Mount Denali's military barracks and bunkers. We have plenty of help from other volcanologists across the US. We don't need to leave here and go to Mount Redoubt or any other volcanoes unless there's another Alaskan blowjob! We need to watch these monitors very closely because Mount Redoubt is still erupting and spreading on to others. If one more volcano goes off we have to get out of here!" said Edward Fay, head volcanologist, to his crew.

Later Mount Redoubt had another major eruption and a shockwave, destroying a lot of forests by starting deadly fires! Bears and bigfoot creatures and unidentifiable creatures were found dead along logging highways for hundreds of miles along with moose, fried bald eagles and dead salmon, black bears, polar bears, and grizzly bears. They lay dead in the streets, streams, and in the forests, half-eaten before death from the shockwaves.

Sunday, August 20, 2023 the fear of the great Alaskan blowjob comes true! 11:02 p.m., the Mount Shishaldin volcano erupted and the monitors, bells, and whistles were going off! The crew went to the monitors and Katrina House said, "Edward Mount Shishaldin is erupting, but it's a small eruption."

"Jesus fuckin' Christ! Now Mount Denali is erupting! We're in fuckin' trouble!" The time was 12:02 a.m. on August 21, 2023 when Denali had a mild eruption. At 1:02 a.m. the Iliamna volcano erupted! 2:02 a.m. Mount Aleutian, a small fuckin' volcano, blew its load! 3:02 a.m. Mount Bona, 16,500 feet, blew apart with a pyroclastic flow and a sudden shockwave blew homes and businesses off the fuckin' map! Then at 4:02 a.m. Mount Elias at the 16,000 foot level blew a hole near the summit, exploding ash high into the sky. A pyroclastic flow and a lahar moving six hundred miles an hour was burning up forest, killing animals, and setting hundreds of miles of forest afire!

"Jesus fuckin' Christ, the end of the fuckin' world is coming right now!" said Edward Fay. Then at 5:02 a.m. Mount Foraker blew her load at 17,400 feet with ash, lightning, and a pyroclastic flow and mud lahars, killing people and animals and burning forests!

Then Mount Blackburn went off an hour later with the same results; the 16,390-foot mountain blew apart, splitting in two! By

5:03 a.m. the fuckin' mountain was falling apart! 6:02 a.m. Mount Stafford erupted at the summit, 16,237 feet, blowing villages and resorts off the mountain like throwing trash in the wastebasket! If people didn't evacuate they were dead!

Then at 7:02 a.m. Mount Vancouver erupted at 15,979 feet, leveling parts of Alaska and Canada, leaving a trail of death and destruction with deadly choking ash and gas and thousands dead!

8:02 a.m. Mount Spurr erupted, killing hundreds. 9:02 a.m. Mount Makushin volcano erupted, devastating a Chinese village and killing hundreds, and poisoned a lake with volcanic gas, choking people to death!

10:02 a.m. the Mount Akutan super volcano blew parts of the Chigmit Mountain Range apart, killing thousands of people. Uncountable landscapes were set afire, killing people and animals like you'd kill a fuckin' mosquito! Ash, rock, and ice triggered a massive tsunami in the Cook Inlet out to the fuckin' Pacific Ocean!

Then at 11:02 a.m. Mount Hayes erupted with a moderate eruption, blowing bears off the fuckin' mountain! 12:02 p.m. the Cook Inlet peak exploded, causing more damage to Lake Clark City, setting off fires and killing more fuckin' people! 1:02 p.m. the St. Alliance volcano erupted, spreading ash, lava, and mud lahars to other fuckin' mountains in the Chigmit Mountains!

2:02 p.m. the Padro Bay volcano erupted, making things worse in Lake Clark, Alaska—*the Alaskan blowjob keeps going, leaving more destruction*! Then the Port Ellsworth volcano erupted at 3:02 p.m., blowing holes through the ground and causing earthquakes! 4:02 p.m. Double Glacier One erupted then an hour later the second volcano erupted, a super volcano, finishing the destruction in Lake Clark and burying the city under fifteen feet of ash and mud!

6:02 p.m. Mount Kaun erupted out into the Pacific Ocean! Then Mount Douglas erupted at 7:02 p.m., blowing the Chigmit

Mountain Range apart! 8:02 p.m. Mount Coyal went off, a small volcano, sending fire down to a beach. 9:02 p.m. Mount Gooding blew out of the water, sinking boats! 10:02 p.m. Mount Chigmit blew its load and lava flowed into the Pacific Ocean! Finally Mount Arch at the end of the Chigmit Mountains erupted at 10:59 p.m. and then it stopped. Twenty-two more volcanoes went off after that. *Too many to count going into Russia, Northern Canada, and across the Pacific Ocean!*

––––––––––––––––

The next morning another meeting was held in the Denali military bunkers with the NASA group. "Good morning crew. Forty-three volcanoes erupted in a twenty-four hour period like I predicted, including Mount Denali. Luckily it was a mild eruption compared to the rest of the Chigmit Mountains. When Mount Redoubt erupted the magma chamber flowed through the Chigmit Mountains, spreading hot lava to blow up the rest of the mountains until reaching the Pacific Ocean, setting off undersea volcanoes.

"It's nothing that hasn't happened before, that's why we call it the Ring of Fire! The problem is, how are we going to get out of here?! I have a plan and it's easy. Number one: We're stuck here for the next three weeks until winter weather cools down the ash clouds that right now are choking all of Alaska! We will be boarding the coal running train halfway up Mount Denali on the east side of the mountain. Most of the ash from the erupting volcanoes will flow out into the Pacific Ocean, giving us a chance to get out of here!

"We will board ski buses to get halfway up the mountain, which is about ten thousand feet, to meet the coal running trains that will get us to Canada and up to the Arctic region. Then we board Coast Guard helicopters to get us across the Rocky Mountains and hope to fly back to the East Coast, or go through ground transportation. All the airports in the US and Canada are closed because of all the erupting volcanoes here in Alaska putting so much ash in the atmosphere. If it gets clogged in the engines the planes will crash.

"We need to be wearing masks and respirators all the time to avoid choking to death; definitely when we are in bed sleeping, even here in these bunkers. All the vaults here in the bunkers are sealed shut and we cannot get out of here until the dust settles. All my years in volcanology and I have never seen anything like this. The entire Chigmit Mountain Range all erupting in a chain reaction, blowing the mountains off the map, and all the volcanoes erupting here in Alaska, and being buried under a blanket of ash. We are getting reports that parts of the Pacific Ocean are cooking and snowmelt is turning into boiling mud lahars.

"I hope it's not the end of the world coming because this is very bad!" said Edward Fay. Later the national news was heard on TV across the world.

"Good evening, this is World Network News Cable 1 in Toronto, Ontario, Canada. Alaska has been getting blown away the last few days from erupting volcanoes threatening to blow the state into the Pacific Ocean. Forty-three volcanoes have been erupting across Alaska since August 2, 2023. On August 20 and 21, the Chigmit Mountain Range blew off the map, splitting Alaska in two and killing an estimated three million people and billions of animals! The city of Lake Clark was buried under several feet of ash and mud. The Cook Inlet River dried up, melting all the glaciers and swallowing several cruise ships and boats.

"Most of the disaster was caused by violent shockwaves from all the erupting volcanoes. We will continue with updates on these end-of-the-world volcano eruptions. Corona Virus, reporting on WNN Cable 1."

Around September 15, the volcano crew, dressed in spacesuits, was escorted to a bus on skis and it went up Mount Denali about eight thousand feet to get aboard coal running trains that ran through the mountains into Canada. They traveled in the dark and cold winter weather because the falling snow dropped the ash levels so cleanup could be done. The area was clear despite Mount Denali still erupting twelve thousand feet above them. Lightning was seen at the summit through the heavy falling snow high in the mountains.

From Denali's eastside thru-tunnels in the mountains through the Canadian Rockies, they went up to the Arctic. There, they got on a Coast Guard helicopter that took them to a ski plane to Greenland before boarding a military ship to take them back to New York. They arrived in New York City at the end of September of 2023.

CHAPTER ELEVEN

THE EAST COAST BIG BOOMS IN BLACKSTONE, MASS.

Since May of 2023 people living in Blackstone, Massachusetts were reporting booms; enough to feel like an earthquake but nothing like causing damage or harm. That was about to change because the noises started getting louder and the booms were rattling homes by summer's end. People living there started panicking.

The police had no answers and the military couldn't find the problem. Police were looking at the reports from the massive volcano eruptions in Alaska back in August. They went driving around in town and along the Blackstone River looking for clues on what was causing the sonic booms, and they found nothing.

Saturday October 7, 2023, people were walking and riding bikes along the Blackstone River when a big *boom!* knocked walkers off their feet at about 1:00 p.m. Then people were shopping at Stop & Shop when another *boom!* was heard, knocking things off the shelves. A bottle of orange juice fell and broke on the floor. The store shook and the windows were vibrating, then it stopped. People were screaming, "Earthquake!!!" then started running outside to the parking lot. Later police came to investigate what happened. The time was 2:17 p.m. when the loud boom shook the Stop & Shop.

A wedding was going on at a park when several people reported the booms. The priest had just finished the wedding ceremony, with the new spouses exchanging vows. "Mr. and Mrs. Lucy and Robert Washburn, I now pronounce you husband and wife. Congratulations!" Then the wedding party celebrated and the DJ was playing "Celebration" by Cool & the Gang. Next thing it was *boom!* knocking people to the ground then a second *boom!* knocking people down and off their feet! Then a loud *boom!* then *bang!* shaking the ground and the wedding party went from celebrating to running for cover, crying, "Earthquake!" When it was over the wedding continued. The police arrived to take reports and found nothing.

Later a lady on Main Street called police. "Hi, this is Vivian Mello from 237 Main Street calling. I think we had an earthquake. I have been hearing booms all afternoon but my house is shaking, please help!"

"Vivian, just go outside your home into an open field until the shaking stops because we have been getting several reports of possible earthquakes. We have been getting these strange booms for a long time and today they have been a little stronger. You should be okay!" said the policeman.

Vivian went over to her next-door neighbor to tell her. "Wendy, it's Vivian from next door. Did you feel that earthquake about ten minutes ago?"

"Yes I did. We have been getting these strange noises from time to time, sonic booms and small earthquakes since the end of May. I never heard them here until today, but I did hear many complaints about them. There's been no damage from them, they're just annoying!"

"Wendy, I thought my fuckin' house was going to fall down it was so loud and shaking!"

"It was loud and I felt a vibration and then it was over," said Wendy.

Later Vivian and Wendy watched the late night news at Wendy's home. "Good evening, we have breaking news on WPRI Channel 12 in Providence. Blackstone, Mass., has been reporting several loud booms like mild earthquakes all summer long, but today there were some bigger ones that caused some damage. They knocked several people off their feet at a wedding party and a Stop & Shop where damage was reported. No serious injuries were reported. Police cannot find the reason why these sonic booms are happening.

"Boston College stunned unbeaten Alabama today in college football 31 to 24. WPRI 12 News reporting."

Later Vivian went back to her home and she saw bluish-green lightning rolling along the ground—why wasn't it up in the sky?—and it was raining pretty good. She said to herself, *That's strange, lightning but no thunder!* Then Vivian went in the house and she went to bed.

Little did she know, the lightning she saw was earthquake lightning coming from under the ground. It's called magnetic field lightning and appears before a strong earthquake happens.

3:02 a.m. Vivian woke up to go to the bathroom and felt pressure in her ears, then a loud *boom!* She screamed hysterically! "Aaaaaah!" The shockwave blew out every window in her house and she was picked up and thrown hard against a wall! She dropped to the floor!

The same boom was so loud it knocked Wendy out of bed. All the windows in her house blew in and she was cut up by flying glass from the shockwave. She got up to call 911 on her cell phone and she got no response because all the towers were out and there was no electricity!

She went outside and met Vivian and many other people blown out of their homes by the blast! Police were everywhere and fire trucks and rescue crews were going from house to house looking for injured people. The police and fire station windows blew out and several people were running in the streets looking for help. All of Blackstone was in the dark—even streetlights blew out!—with several windows blown out in neighboring homes. St. Paul's church had no damage; neither did neighboring Rhode Island cities and towns.

"What happened here?!" said Wendy to a policeman.

"I believe we had a strong earthquake!" said the cop. Rescue workers took injured people to the hospital, including Wendy who was soaked with blood. Vivian and several people who were not injured were taken to St. Paul's church and given blankets to keep warm for the rest of the night. The next day the town of Blackstone, Mass., looked like a bomb hit it!

The National Guard from Rhode Island and Massachusetts were called in to find out what was causing these earthquakes! The police spoke to the crowd in the church from the damaged areas.

"Ladies and gentlemen, my name is Officer John Santos from the Cumberland, Rhode Island Police Department. I heard you had a major earthquake here in Blackstone, Mass. I believe these earthquakes are being caused by floodwaters washing out limestone in caves causing these sonic booms, but why one be this strong remains a mystery. This problem has been happening in Connecticut. The Rhode Island and Massachusetts National Guard troops will be here in the morning with a final report so just stay warm until they come; do not go back to your damaged homes," said the Cumberland police officer.

The morning came and priests and nuns brought continental breakfast for the stranded residents of Blackstone. The National

Guard worked through the night until they saw all the damage, then they had an early morning meeting with the police.

"Officers, my name is General Norman Nicholson from the Worcester National Guard Unit #0495. I think you have something here, a lot more than earthquakes according to the town's history of sonic booms. I mean, now you have some serious damage to several homes and businesses including the police station and firehouse. We cannot find the cause and we have no idea on what's going on here! You will need to contact NASA out of New York City to send a volcanologist to investigate."

The police and military personnel relayed the news to the stranded people at St. Paul's church, the same report the military gave to the police. "Ladies and gentlemen, my name is Officer James Madden. You may go back to your homes to clean up. A town meeting will be held at the Blackstone-Millville Regional High School on Tuesday evening, October 10 at 7:00 p.m. with the mayor. If your home is in bad shape we will have shuttles at the police station to take you to a shelter."

Everyone went back home to clean up the broken glass and other damage. Shaw's Lumber trucks arrived to board up the damaged homes. Blackstone looked like a ghost town and the sonic booms continued. Some residents went to a shelter. The police contacted the NASA volcano crew from New York to come and investigate the Blackstone booms. A helicopter landed with a spudweb data robot and placed it in the area where the homes got damaged by the earthquake.

At the town meeting at the high school, the NASA crew reported on the results they found. "Good evening, my name is Mayor Chris Shaw. I also own Shaw's Lumber. Thank you for attending tonight's town meeting on Tuesday, October 10, 2023. The reason why we're here is because of the Saturday night and Sunday morning earthquakes. I have Mr. Edward Fay here to inform us on what happened and yes, it was an earthquake!"

"Good evening, Blackstone, Mass. You did have a strong earthquake here. The booms here have been going on for a while and according to my reports these booms are going to continue. We have a super volcano brewing under Vermont, New Hampshire, and Massachusetts. Mount Ascutney has already erupted and it's still active. The reason why you're getting these sonic booms is because you have steam eruptions underground building pressure, causing these earthquakes. It's like a small volcano underground because gas builds from hot steam air pockets and erupts underground, causing these booms and mild earthquakes. The good news is the strong earthquake might have finally released a lot of the pressure and you might get a break. You will still feel the booms but not as much since the strong earthquake."

"Mr. Fay, do we have a volcano here?" asked Mayor Shaw.

"Not exactly, but you have a steam vent about forty feet underground. Lava may penetrate these steam vents, filling them up with gas that causes these booms. The steam vents are lava tubes," said Edward Fay.

"Could a volcano erupt here?" asked the mayor.

"I doubt it but freak things can happen. Steam pipes erupt all the time in New York City. If a steam vent enters a manhole or sewer under a street it can explode and erupt like a volcano, but steam vents are too far underground to cause a problem here. You will get earthquakes and sonic booms from time to time. Some will be strong and cause a little damage and some of them you probably don't even notice.

"Don't panic ladies and gentlemen, it's only steam air pockets rubbing up against limestone, it's not a volcano. These steam pocket eruptions happens all the time in Connecticut. The vent will find a hole somewhere and release the steam and gases and all of it will be over. A 6.6 earthquake is rare anywhere in Massachusetts; it may never happen again. That's what has been happening here in Blackstone," said Edward Fay.

After the meeting everyone went home. The damaged homes were all boarded up and had their windows replaced a week later. The NASA volcano crew yellow-taped the area where the spudweb machine was placed, monitoring the dangers below-ground. The gas company went around checking for any leaks and they found nothing. People were walking and biking along the Blackstone River when suddenly they saw dead fish and dead animals lying along the river.

The police and the NASA crew arrived with meters to find out why the fish were dying and examine the dead wildlife. Then they tested the water and it was contaminated with some kind of gas.

"Officers, we need to get to the town water supply," said Edward Fay. The police took him there; it was a building overlooking a pond, Harris Pond, where more dead fish lay.

"We have a problem here officers. I can smell sulfur in the water supply storage and in the pond. Volcanic gas is leaking underground and making its way to the surface, so there's a hole somewhere in this pond or in the Blackstone River. I need to contact the rest of the crew to find this leak before something really bad happens here. This explains why a violent earthquake happened; we need to find this leak and shut the water off in the town," said Edward Fay.

FLASHBACK

Before the dead fish and wildlife were spotted, when people turned their faucets on brown water was coming out, even at the police station and firehouse. Everyone was calling the police station wondering what was going on.

A helicopter flew low with a loudspeaker calling for an evacuation order. "Ladies and gentlemen, please evacuate your homes because of a gas leak and go to the shelter located at the Chestnut Hill meetinghouse north of town immediately! This is the National Guard!" The gas leak was never found.

CHAPTER TWELVE

THE MYSTERY
VOLCANOES IN
NEW ENGLAND

Back in Blackstone Mass., people ran in the streets in this small town. Police were driving around everywhere in the pouring rain going door to door, getting people out of their homes to go to the shelter.

The NASA helicopter arrived with equipment to find this hidden volcano. National Guard troops at the shelter spoke to the residents. "Good evening ladies and gentlemen. Welcome to the Chestnut Hill Meeting House. My name is John Thomas from the National Guard Military Police. We have a gas leak here in Blackstone that has not been found yet. The NASA volcano crew believes it could be a hidden volcano somewhere underground. It could be here somewhere, or Cumberland or Lincoln, Rhode Island, or in Connecticut. We don't know.

"NASA said we have a super volcano brewing in central New England but that does not mean we have a volcano here. We may have steam vents and gas fumes from magma deep underground, which would explain the earthquakes and the dead fish and wildlife. Sulfur gas has been reported and contaminated water in homes and businesses, a sign that there is a hidden volcano underground somewhere or a lava tube moving close to the surface.

"Don't go telling everyone that we have a volcano here in Blackstone because it's not a volcano, it's only a threat here. When the water supply is treated you will be able to go back to your homes. The booms and earthquakes that've been happening, you will have to deal with it," said John Thomas, military police.

Halloween night 2023 was a Tuesday evening. About dusk the weather was clear, and it was a cold night on Block Island. It was a ghost town with very few people around and suddenly a fire started in a cove on the west side of the island. Boats started catching fire and a marina burned down. A policeman riding around noticed the fires.

"Car #1 Officer Camron Copperhead to Firehouse. We have a major fire in the Great Salt Pond inlet on both sides. Boats are burning and the main marina is going up in flames. I see what looks like liquid lava coming down Beacon Hill pouring out of a hole into the harbor and spreading along the docks! Several boats are on fire! Please come right away!!"

"Ten-four Officer Copperhead. We're on our way, Fire Truck #1 over!"

The sirens were blaring away at the fire station. "Warning: all firemen, we have a major fire in the Great Salt Pond Inlet! It could be caused by an erupting volcano, everything is burning!" said the fireman in Truck #1.

Other firemen laughed; they thought it was a Halloween joke! Then Fire Truck #1 took off like a bat out of hell and the others followed. When they arrived at the scene it was a mega fire; all the boats and the marina and dock had burned to the ground and lava poured out from Beacon Hill into the water. The firemen went to work putting out fires—there's only three trucks on the island and they need a lot of help!

"Oh my fuckin' God! What the hell is this?! It can't be a volcano! Or is it?! Truck #1 we need fireboats to help out because we're not going to handle this fire with what we have. It's burning everywhere! It's huge!"

Fireboats left Narragansett to help with the mega fire on Block Island. Hotels were being evacuated and guests bused to the ferry back to Narragansett. A lava tube broke a hole through Beacon Hill, pouring liquid lava into the Great Salt Pond Inlet, burning the Block Island marinas, docks, and boats, causing a mega fire! Beacon Hill was now a volcano; there were no earthquakes, no warnings, and it caught everyone by surprise!

The police drove around evacuating the hotels. An emergency ferry left Narragansett to get everyone off the island.

"Ladies and gentlemen, all hotels and residents must evacuate the island due to a major fire and a possible erupting volcano! You must leave immediately!" said the police.

People at the Sullivan House were having a Halloween party when the fire broke out and erupted into a monster. It caused a big panic and people started running uphill to get away from the fire. Buses took them to the ferry. The island was evacuated quickly.

Beacon Hill kept pouring out lava, proving it to be a volcano. Fireboats poured water and foam on the Beacon Hill lava flow and it was not going out. It kept flowing into the water, backing up the boats because the water was bubbling.

The captain of one of the fireboats said, "We have a volcano here on Block Island!"

Later the ferry gathered everyone on the island to get ready to leave. The ferry left the dock around midnight and no one knew it was a fire from a hidden volcano until they heard the news.

"Good evening, we have breaking news on WJAR TV Channel 10 in Providence. A hidden volcano erupted about 5:30 p.m.

on Block Island, setting off a major fire. The island is being evacuated at this time and there are no reports of injuries, but the entire Block Island marina and boats in the Great Salt Pond were destroyed.

"Firemen and fire rescue boats have been spending hours trying to put out the fires and are still there, trying to get the fires under control. Lava has been spotted pouring out of a hole on Beacon Hill on Block Island by the firemen, making it difficult for the fires to be put out. A science team will investigate the area tomorrow to see if it was a volcano. Denny De Jesus reporting on Newswatch 10!"

Newspapers read: "Volcano erupts on Block Island setting marina and boats afire, evacuating the island. A volcano erupted in Vermont; scientists say a super volcano is brewing underground in New England, threatening a mega eruption like the volcanoes out on the West Coast. Warnings for these events to come."

Back at Block Island, police drove around evacuating all the hotels and getting everyone off the island. The ferry left around 1:30 a.m. and took everyone to the mainland; they had to be put up in hotels. The ferry arrived back at Block Island shortly after 3:00 a.m. to pick up more people but the island was empty and the ferry docked there for the rest of the night. Police drove through the island along with fire trucks and a rescue vehicle. Riding by Niles Swamp and Sachem Pond, water was bubbling.

"Car #1, Officer Camron Copperhead to fire and rescue. We have something here. Sachem Pond and the Niles are boiling like a pot on the stove. Let's get back to the ferry at the New Shoreham dock because this island may be ready to blow off the map! We need to contact Mayor Christiana Sweeney aboard the ferry. She was the only bitch aboard ship." The police, fire, and rescue teams boarded the ferry in case Block Island went up like a rocket!!!!

"Mayor Sweeney, did you hear what happened here?" asked the police.

"Yes I did, we have a hidden volcano spewing out of Beacon Hill into the Great Salt Pond, destroying a marina, six boats, and a village campground. I have the NASA volcano crew coming here about 9:00 a.m. Just let the fires burn; there's nobody on the island and if the island catches fire and burns down, or if Beacon Hill blows, step on the gas, captain, and get the fuck out of here!!!!!!!"

"That's not all, mayor! Great Salt Pond, Sachem Pond, and the Niles Swamp are cooking like a hot pan of water on a stove!" said the cop.

Meanwhile the NASA volcano crew got the report from Block Island and was monitoring Beacon Hill's lava flow until morning; it was still coming and setting more fires. The clear skies turned to clouds and heavy rain, cancelling an overnight trip to Block Island. The storms moved over Block Island, dumping heavy rain helping to put the fire out, only Beacon Hill kept pushing lava out of its hole into the pond. The ferry was at the dock ready to depart if the volcano erupted. The heavy rain was a relief but the lightning flashes were not!

8:02 a.m. the sky cleared on Wednesday, November 1, 2023. Helicopters were on the way from New York City, flying over Long Island, and landed on Block Island just before 9:00 a.m., and it was a clear, windy morning. The helicopter landed near the loading dock and a policeman. The mayor met with the crew.

"Good morning, welcome to the Block Island Volcano! My name is Officer Camron Copperhead, the chief of police on this island, and this is Miss Christiana Sweeney, the mayor on Block Island."

"Pleased to meet you both, my name is Edward Fay, the head volcanologist of NASA, Houston. I have Katrina House, Nathan

Rivers, and David Dunkin working with me today to see what happened here last night!"

"Pleased to meet you," they said. The firemen and police drove the crew to Beacon Hill hole as it was still spewing out some thick molten hot lava! Nathan Rivers set up a rotating spudweb data robot that walked up the hill, taking pictures and getting data just like the rovers on fuckin' MARS!

"Mr. Fay, we definitely have a volcano here! The lava chamber is resting in a big bubble basin covering the bottom of this whole island! If it keeps building this island is a ticking time bomb ready to blow at any time, but if the lava chamber empties and keeps flowing out of Beacon Hill's hole into the lake below, it will cool down and Block Island will be saved," said Nathan Rivers.

"Okay, let's get out of here. Leave the robot here and let it do its thing. Do not go down to the lake because it could erupt and you will get seriously burned. Get everyone off the island because everything standing is probably going to burn to the ground, whatever Beacon Hill decides to do! Leave the dock, get off this island, and we will monitor what Beacon Hill is doing in New York. I will let you know when it's safe to return. Before I leave, were there any earthquakes or sonic booms before you noticed the lava flow?" asked Edward Fay.

"No sir; we got a call about a big fire at the Great Salt Pond. When we got there it was a giant inferno and we saw the lava pouring out of a hole at a high rate of speed. We thought it was a volcano right from the get-go when we saw what was happening! Then we started evacuating the island," said the firemen.

"Well let's get out of here before something happens!" said Edward Fay.

The helicopter lifted off and all the firemen, rescue crews, and law enforcement officials boarded the ferry and left the island.

That night the Block Island mayor was sleeping at a Holiday Inn Express in Narragansett and she had a dream that Block

Island blew up. She was blown high into the sky and a molten rock fireball was chasing her and went right between her legs! She woke up screaming hysterically! "Aah!"

The next day another town meeting took place back in Blackstone at the Blackstone-Millville Regional High School. "Good evening, sorry to call everyone here again tonight. Welcome ladies and gentlemen. My name is Chris Shaw. The reason why we are here is because Miss Vivian Mello was struck by debris while walking in Corner Stables Park to go ride a horse. Something mysteriously flew from under the ground striking her in the head, killing her instantly!

"The debris was metal pieces and sticks which struck her at a high rate of speed, according to several witnesses she was with. Things flew from under the ground, lunging at Vivian like the devil coming to get her! We have been getting more booms and earthquakes, causing more mild damage here in Blackstone. I have not told you the real bad news yet. A volcano erupted on Block Island on Halloween night, burning the west side of the island to the ground. A village campground, a boat marina, hotels, and forests burned to the ground and the volcano there is still active.

"Luckily, everyone evacuated in time and there were no injuries. The lakes and ponds on the island were boiling and the island is threatening to blow off the face of the earth, according to NASA. There has been a series of hundreds of volcanoes erupting in the United States alone. Washington State and Oregon were blown off the map and Alaska split in two, killing millions of people! A volcano erupted in Vermont, raising fear the end of the world is coming! Now, a volcano erupting in Rhode Island! We have to deal with what is going on. We are sitting on a ticking time bomb but all we can do is go home and hope for the best.

"NASA is monitoring the gas leak and sulfur deposits and let's hope they find out what's happening. Now a volcano erupting on Block Island raises fear something could happen here. We will have to deal with the booms and earthquakes until NASA finds out what's going on here. Let's go home and say prayers and hope we can be safe. That's all I have to say," said the mayor.

Blackstone residents went home without the answers they wanted. Three days later the lava coming out of the hole on Beacon Hill on Block Island stopped. New Shoreham, Rhode Island was saved.

Mid-November booms and earthquakes, causing damage like in Blackstone, Mass., started happening in Moodus, Connecticut. The place was no stranger to these noises, called the Moodus Noises, but they were getting a lot worse! These noises had been happening in Moodus for a long time.

A family from Texas moved into Moodus, Connecticut in the middle of November of 2023. The family waited at an old house deep in the woods surrounded by trees with a brook flowing in the back. The house was located at 279 North Street and the family met the realtor there.

"Good afternoon, my name is Elsie Chelsy from Earl Davies Realtors. Welcome to Moodus, Connecticut."

"Hi, my name is Allen Hitchcock. This is my wife Linda Hitchcock, my daughter Emma Hitchcock, and my son Eric Hitchcock. We are from Dallas, Texas, home of all the hail, lightning storms, and tornadoes, and we want to move to a quiet place to get away from the severe weather."

"Allen, you may not have much of a deal here. We have volcanoes erupting here in New England. We don't get many tornadoes or hailstorms in Connecticut, but we do get earthquakes and we occasionally get them right here in Moodus because this town is located over a limestone cave. When we get heavy rain or snowmelt and water runs through the caves we get movement more than anywhere else in Connecticut, and you will feel a little shaking or sonic booms from time to time.

"The earthquakes here are not like the ones in California. Our earthquakes never reach a two on the Richter scale; the ones here are less dangerous than the ones out west. A volcano erupted on Block Island, Rhode Island on Halloween night and that's not far from here. Another volcano erupted about a year ago in Vermont and it killed more than two hundred people. Scientists say there's a super volcano brewing under the six New England states.

"A super volcano in Crater Lake erupted last year, wiping Oregon, Washington State, and parts of northern California and northwest Canada off the map! Then fifty volcanoes in Alaska erupted at the same time, splitting Alaska in two, and millions of people died. Worse, scientists say it's not over. If Yellowstone erupts the West Coast may fall into the Pacific Ocean and the rest of the US could be destroyed. The epic super volcano in Yellowstone will be bigger than all the erupting volcanoes on the West Coast. The eruption may cover five thousand miles."

"I heard about that Elsie. If that happens here we may have to go back to Texas," said Allen Hitchcock. The family bought the house and moved in.

———

Thanksgiving Day was a cloudy snowy day. Just after the Hitchcock family finished their Thanksgiving dinner they started hearing the booms on and off through the evening, then shaking. It got worse, then a loud *boom!* that blew their windows out, then a cold gust of strong wind blew things around in their home.

It was a shockwave from underground and blue lightning was seen, the same problem that happened in Blackstone, Mass. Then a second and third booming earthquake knocked them off their feet! They got up and ran out of the house in the rain, snow, and cold, in thunder and lightning! The family went in their car and Allen called the realtor on his cell phone.

"Elsie, it's Allen Hitchcock calling from 279 North Street. Happy Thanksgiving! I thought you told me that earthquakes are not bad here, but all my windows blew out and some of us were cut by glass and knocked off our feet! What the hell is going on here in Moodus?! Is the devil coming??!"

"I'm very sorry, we just had a bad earthquake and there's a lot of damage to homes in Moodus. You will have to go to a shelter. Just stay where you are and the Moodus Police will direct you to a shelter; they will come and get you," said Elsie the realtor.

The Hitchcock family waited in their home. Nineteen minutes later the police came and the cop said, "Go to Moodus Nathan High School, that's where the shelter is. We just had a 7.7 earthquake here. You have the choice to remain here or go to the shelter. Here's the directions on how to get there and there will be a town meeting with the mayor," said the police.

The Hitchcock family followed the directions the police gave them and went to the shelter.

"Good evening, welcome to Nathan Hale-Ray High School. My name is Mr. Earl Davies, the mayor of Moodus, Connecticut. The past few nights we have been getting some bad earthquakes and now we have been getting damage to homes and lost electricity a few times. This problem is getting out of control. On Halloween night a volcano erupted on Block Island and last year a volcano erupted in Vermont. Hundreds of volcanoes have erupted on the West Coast, an end-of-the-world threat just like a woman having an orgasm over and over and over again!!! But not the orgasm we'd like, so to speak!

"A volcano crew from NASA will be here tomorrow to find out what the fuck is going on here in Moodus. Everyone go back home or stay here at the shelter until this crew finds out what is going on here, because it is not normal for this to be happening," said Mayor Earl Davies.

The next day the NASA volcano crew and the Connecticut

National Guard arrived to find out what was happening with these earthquakes! The booms and earthquakes continued. Some were weak and some were stronger than usual!

"We have a pregnancy here in Moodus! It's not a volcano but we have pressure building in the ground. There are sulfur deposits and steam eruptions, which explain the violent earthquakes and sonic booms here in Moodus! But you will have to live with the booms and earthquakes if you want to live in Moodus because it's been happening here for years. We have also been getting volcano eruptions here in New England.

"My name is Edward Fay, the head volcanologist of NASA. I went through a thorough investigation of the Moodus noises, booms, earthquakes, etcetera. You have the ingredients of an active volcano because you have sulfur deposits and steam and gas from pressure underground. It's from a magma chamber deep in the ground, but there is no molten rock; it's just vapor from the pressure. Because you have deep caves and canyons you will continue to have these earthquakes and sonic booms.

"Block Island had a volcanic eruption with no warning on Halloween night with flowing lava. The gas underground travels for miles. Block Island is not too far from central Connecticut. The same problem is happening in Blackstone, Mass. because of Purgatory Chasm, a national park full of caves. Anywhere you have caves, especially deep caves like here in Moodus, you are going to have these earthquakes.

"We have a super volcano warning for all of New England and two volcanoes have already erupted, making earthquakes stronger. But you do not have a volcano here in Moodus because there is no lava. You may have a steam eruption. We get them in New York City all the time but they are not volcanoes. You just have a noisy Moodus!" said Edward Fay.

"Mr. Edward Fay, sir, my name is Mr. Earl Davies, the mayor of Moodus, Connecticut. I have a book here about the Moodus noises, *Ground of the Devil*, written by Richard Rezendes from Brown University. The book is about a meteor that crashed into Moodus. A creature with multiple ways of attacking came from the planet Venus causing all the noises and destruction, spraying fire and burning the town down. It kills any living thing that moves and hides underground when it's threatened! The creature is called the devil from outer space!"

"How interesting Earl, but that's not what we're looking for. We are investigating a possible explosion if these violent earthquakes continue to happen because of the damage here lately and in Blackstone, Mass. I will say again: You do not have a volcano here but you will have to deal with the earthquakes. We will monitor these earthquakes and keep you posted with updates on damages and evacuation. When a violent earthquake happens it's a sign that most of the ground pressure from the caves was released, so these earthquakes should subside soon," said Edward Fay.

———————

A few days later the loud booms and earthquakes continued causing damage in Moodus, but then they stopped and everything went back to normal. Blackstone quieted down. The volcano crew monitored all the earthquakes on the East Coast. Block Island was quiet. The NASA volcano crew was finally home, resting after Thanksgiving in New York City in Room 007 in the sub-basement of the Empire State Building. The crew had to celebrate Thanksgiving dinner on December 1.

Tuesday December 5, 2023, was a cold, raw, rainy day in Manhattan. The NASA crew had a private meeting. "Linda Brew, Katrina House, Nathan Rivers, Paul Numbnutts, David Dunkin, Lieutenant Bowa Bowser of NYPD and Allen Aggingtonconstantinoappopoliss from the New York fire department are with us today. For the last three years we have been going through hell from the coronavirus in 2020, the steam eruptions here in New York City, Blue Hills in Boston, Massachusetts and the eruption of Mount Ascutney in Vermont that killed 289 people in 2021.

"Then we have been on the West Coast to monitor the worst volcanoes in the world for the last two and a half years. More than sixty volcanoes erupted, killing millions of people and leaving more than five hundred million homeless. Washington State, Oregon, the northwest corner of Canada, and parts of California were blown off the map. Alaska, where most of the volcanoes erupted, split in two!

"Anchorage was blown off the map and we don't know where Fairbanks is; it's probably iced by now or buried belowground where the devil is! When Mount Denali erupted, the second tallest mountain in the world, we had to get out of there! We had to get a coal operated train to get us to the Arctic in Canada, in forty below zero temperatures and six feet of snow and four feet of ash, climbing halfway up an erupting volcano to get to safety. We believed that we were going to die.

"We escaped because we were lucky enough to get coal running trains; that's the only transportation in that kind of cold. We made it to a Coast Guard helicopter to get us to a ski plane to Greenland to ship us back to the USA. When we got back here in New York we viewed the lava on the East Coast.

"We've been on the verge of a super volcano warning for all of New England for the last five years, since 2018 when Mount Ascutney in Adamsville, Vermont had warning signs that it was going to erupt—it *did* erupt in 2021. The magma chamber was wide enough to cover Massachusetts, Vermont, and New Hampshire. Mount Ascutney in Vermont was the epicenter of the lava bed and when the volcano erupted, the lava chamber spread, going deeper underground and spreading wider. Operation Blowjob declared the area safe after the violent eruption, then this mountain erupted again a year later.

"The lava chamber is spreading toward the Midwest, weakening the chance of more eruptions on the East Coast, but volcanoes are unpredictable. On the West Coast the magma bed is much bigger, spreading east toward the Rocky Mountains and west out into the Pacific Ocean. The Yellowstone Caldera;s lava field is even bigger and if these faults join together and Yellowstone erupts, you may say goodbye to the USA! Yellowstone is overdue! All we can hope is that this super volcano doesn't go off because it could be the end of the world, just from volcanic ash and violent weather across the globe.

"The other thing is pressure in the ground from the lava vents with no magma. They've been causing violent steam eruptions and are not considered volcanoes, but they can cause the same damage! The biggest surprise is the lava tube fire from Beacon Hill on Block Island, burning the west side of the island to the ground on Halloween night through November 1. Where did that come from?!

"We do have a mild lava flow riding parallel to Long Island, flowing into the Hudson River and threatening New York City! We might be in big trouble here if the lava strikes Manhattan! If it flows up the Hudson to Canada or gets into the Ohio River it may flow to the west, threatening Yellowstone. We don't know exactly what it's going to do.

"Right now the lava stream is heading for Greenwich Village and Freedom Tower; let's hope it doesn't arrive! Now in Moodus, Connecticut there were sonic booms and strong earthquakes that broke several windows and damaged homes but no breaks through the earth or steam eruptions. Pressure underground caused these earthquakes.

"The same thing happened in Blackstone, Massachusetts, but a gas eruption got into the Blackstone River, killing all the fish and wildlife. There were several damaged homes as well with broken windows. They have been getting the sonic booms and earthquakes all summer long. Moodus has been experiencing these booms and mild earthquakes for years. Now ground pressure and a hidden volcano on Block Island raise concerns where trouble is going to strike next.

"In 2021 a steam eruption on top of Blue Hills near Boston, Mass., was classified as a possible volcano because Blue Hills was a dormant volcano. There were several reports of damage and injuries at Curry University and the Canton and Milton areas. A strong earthquake in downtown Boston knocked out power, interrupting a Celtics game, because the TD Bank Garden was damaged.

"We had several steam eruptions here in Manhattan believed to be a hidden volcano under New York City. It was reported as a steam eruption, but with sulfur and gases and damage you'd expect from a volcano! We had some serious damage from the Fifth Avenue and Lexington Avenue steam eruption in 2018. For five years we have not had any more blowjobs in New York and I hope it stays that way!

"But we are not out of danger; look what happened on Block Island, Rhode Island! A volcano eruption, with no warning, no earthquakes! Beacon Hill had an orgasm, next thing you know half of the island burned to the ground with bubbling hot pools in the water, then it was done after a few days! Right now, Block Island is safe to return to but they're closed down until Memorial Day in case the volcano redevelops.

"Moodus, Connecticut and Blackstone, Mass., will continue to get these sonic booms and mild earthquakes because they are over caves underground. Pressure levels went down lowering the threats of strong earthquakes, according to spudweb data, and Block Island is quiet.

"Mount Ascutney in Adamsville, Vermont is still very dangerous and it's still active but stable. We have two areas right now we have to pay attention to. Number one: where this lava flow heading for New York City is going to strike next. Number two: there are two thermal vents just outside of George's Bank and Nantucket; it looks like a pair of tits underwater! Maybe the Titanic struck them instead of an iceberg! Just joking!

"These vents are not active but because of all the action we've been getting in the northeast lately we need to take a look at them to be on the safe side. Mr. Paul Numbnutts and Nathan Rivers, you two will be the divers to investigate these vents. Spudweb is not needed unless they become active.

"We got a call from Sergeant Michael Kock from the Nantucket Coast Guard office reporting mild earthquakes on Nantucket. You two will be flown by the National Guard helicopter to do the work helping them. Otherwise everyone just keep checking the monitors and looking for hotspots," said Edward Fay.

Paul Numbnutts and Nathan Rivers went with dive teams to check under George's Bank and Nantucket, Massachusetts. And they were dead zones. The vents looked like two small volcanoes in the ocean with craters on top of them. Fish were swimming in and out of them.

From December 2023 until July 2024 the volcanoes and steam vents were quiet across the United States from coast to coast. Many volcanoes on the West Coast were still active but not erupting, and Mount Ascutney in Vermont was quiet but still active! *The quiet times are going to change very soon!*

Fourth of July weekend, a packed ferry was leaving Point Judith pier for Block Island. A tour guide aboard the ferry spoke.

"Good afternoon! My name is Jerry Valentino and I'm from Warwick, the Oakland beach area, and I'm your tour guide on the Block Island ferry. It's a hot day for the second of July, 2024. It's ninety-six degrees.

"Our trip will take less than a half hour to dock on Block Island. When we arrive all the cars and trucks will exit the vessel first. All passengers, make your way to your vehicles in the next fifteen minutes.

"Welcome aboard the Block Island ferry, called the *Volcano*. Equipped with a food court, full service bar, and seating inside and outside the vessel, it's run by the Steamship Authority. Look at all the seagulls following the vessel. You know why ladies and gentlemen? They want your food! Be careful eating food outdoors because the seagulls will take it right out of your hands. Especially hotdogs! Seagulls love hotdogs!

"Enjoy the boat ride and we'll be arriving shortly!" said the tour guide. The ferry arrived on Block Island on Monday July 2, 2024. The cars and trucks emptied the vessel first before the passengers. One truck was big, carrying a huge bulldozer on its trailer. The truck had thirty tires; it was huge!

Then the passengers exited the ferry and a cop greeted them, "Welcome to Black Island, ladies and gentlemen!"

"It's Block Island! You dickhead!" one boy said.

"Watch your mouth young man!" said the cop. "Ladies and gentlemen, we will be getting on Bus #1995. We will be going to the Narragansett Inn where we will be staying. Welcome to Block Island, Fourth of July vacationers. We are on Corn Neck Road and turning into Beach Road to take us to the Narragansett Inn.

"Everything is in walking distance; it's a small island. You can rent mopeds or bikes to get around or go on foot. You have restaurants and some bars and plenty of hotels and inns here on Block Island, and beaches all around. The Narragansett Inn overlooks the Great Salt Pond and national parks and a museum.

"The Salt Pond is a volcanic crater believe it or not, but Block

Island is a volcano and it last erupted last year on Halloween night. A plume of molten lava broke through a hole on Beacon Hill not far from here on a boat marina. Several boats caught fire and a village and a campground burned to the ground, and the water boiled in the salt ponds. The smell here is not cool; it smells like sulfur because the effects are still here.

"Great Salt Pond is not recommended for swimming because of the volcanic gases and the water may be contaminated, but to the right are the Mohegan Bluffs and Rhode Island Beach below. This beach is Fred Benson Town Beach, not good for swimming but people are swimming here anyway! To the left is Montauk Lighthouse, and Sachem Pond is polluted with volcanic waste—do not swim there! Mansion Nude Beach to the north on the oceanside is safe for swimming. New Harbor burned down, but since has been rebuilt. Here is the Poor Man's Tavern and down the hill is the Oyster Bar and Grill overlooking Great Salt Pond. Then you have Old Island Pub.

"In New Shoreham, where the ferry docked, are the most popular restaurants, bars, and beaches. You go by the Spring House Hotel, the most expensive place to stay on the island, then the Beach House of Block Island. If you continue to South Beach you will find Ballard's Inn restaurant, plus nightclubs and tiki bars on the beach where the young crowd hangs out. The beach is beautiful but one thing: Great white sharks come to visit from time to time! You have Captain Nick's Irish pub, the Harborside Inn, the Surf, Old Town Inn, and there are several other small restaurants and bars you can go to.

"Welcome to the Narragansett Inn. Overlooking the Salt Pond you have fancy rooms here, and it's quiet. Continental breakfast will be served from 7:00 a.m. to 11:00 a.m. Tomorrow night there will be a fireworks display over the Great Salt Pond and a big fireworks display on the Fourth at Ballard's Inn on South Beach. That concludes our tour and enjoy your stay on the Block Island

Volcano. It's safe here," said Jerry Valentino the tour guide, and he went back to the ferry.

Everyone was on their own and went into downtown New Shoreham to go out to eat, have some beers, enjoy the beaches, and do some exploring. Later in the evening fireworks were going off everywhere from beach parties. Ballard's was going wild with bands playing a good crowd and everyone dancing. Suddenly there was an earthquake that knocked people off their feet; they were falling down across the island. Around 10:00 p.m. there was a big thunderstorm and heavy rain, ending all the fireworks parties.

The people from the tour got trapped in the rain as they were going back to the inn. Shuttles stopped around midnight and people left Ballard's around 1:00 a.m. The storm was still going strong, trapping visitors in the elements: heavy rain, violent lightning, and loud thunder! People were soaked running in the night.

The next day was bright and sunny and another hot day. The tour started the day all over again, visiting different places, but some heard sonic booms which eventually stopped. Everyone went sightseeing, walking and riding bikes and mopeds around the island, spending the day exploring. The hole the lava came out of on Beacon Hill was covered up with big rocks and cemented over, so the tourists didn't know where the eruption came from even if they found it! Then it was party time at the bars.

Ballard's was the most crowded and the beach was packed. Boats out in the water and paragliders and parties everywhere. In the evening it was another night of fireworks going off all over the island and parties all over the beaches. The fireworks left a green cloud in the sky late in the evening that turned the sky green by morning, with the smell of smoke.

The next day was the Fourth of July holiday and it was party time all over again! A nun was sitting in a wicker lounge drinking a glass of orange juice at the Narragansett Inn. She'd had a vision that something bad was going to happen soon. She was talking to a man sitting next to her and the man said, "Happy Fourth of July; it's a beautiful day!"

The nun said, "I can't wait to get out of here! I had a vision that something bad is going to happen here right after the Fourth of July. I had a vision that Block Island is going to blow up starting from the water, and I need to get out of here tomorrow morning before something happens!"

"What do you mean sister?! A volcano maybe?" asked the man.

"I don't know sir but it's something to do with a gas explosion!"

The man thought the nun was acting weird and he said, "You have a nice holiday." And he walked away.

The nun warned several people staying at the Narragansett Inn that Block Island was going to blow off the map soon and other guests thought she was nuts!!!

Sure enough, methane gas started forming in the Great Salt Pond—a clear warning that a volcano was ready to erupt—and started rising to the surface. Some bubbles started coming up to the waterline but nobody was prepared for the warnings from the nun.

Hotel guests thought the Block Island volcano was a hoax, a big joke! Others laughed at the nun's warnings and walked away. People walking by the pond saw the bubbles coming up but they thought nothing about it. People were even swimming in the water despite signs saying "No Swimming." If the water is clear and looks clean enough to swim in, people go swimming anyways!

Between 1:00 p.m. and 3:00 p.m. the temperature reached ninety-five degrees; it was a hot sunny day. From 4:00 p.m. to 6:00 p.m. thunderstorms rolled in with heavy rain, then after 7:00 p.m. the sky cleared and it was a nice evening for fireworks.

Block Island was packed with vacationers, about ten thousand people.

Every bar and restaurant on the island was a full house, eating and drinking and celebrating the Fourth of July! The big show was at Ballard's with bands playing in the club and on the beach. All the tiki bars were filled up with people drinking tropical drinks. There were big parties on all the beaches with plenty of food and barbeques and a pig roast. Plenty of fish and shellfish were served at Ballard's; then a big fireworks show over South Beach was set off from a barge out at sea despite five-foot waves.

The fireworks were fantastic and went on for about an hour. The party at Ballard's was great. Fireworks were going off on the beaches until 1:00 a.m. when local police shut the island down.

Around 2:00 a.m. the island was quiet and the sky was covered with smoke and clouds from all the fireworks displays! Around 4:00 a.m. thunderstorms moved back in over Great Salt Pond, washing all the firework smoke out of the sky into the pond. There, it mixed with the methane gas and sulfur and the heavy rain and lightning, setting the stage for a mega disaster!

People were still out walking around and on the beaches until five o'clock in the morning, watching the storm and the nighttime sky turning green!

"Do you smell that? It smells like rotten eggs!" one man said to a group of people on the beach. Then lightning strikes and loud thunder! The crowds now knew it was time to get inside and go back to the hotels but—too late!—they got caught in a downpour!

At 6:30 a.m. the nun got up and went to the lobby at the Narragansett Inn with a duffel bag. She waited until breakfast was served. Other early risers kept their distance from her. The nun ate a Danish, two donuts, then three muffins: one corn, one blueberry, and one cranberry. She had four eggs, three helpings of bacon, two bagels, five pancakes, two glasses of orange juice, and finally three cups of coffee.

One man said, "Hey you fat bitch! Why don't you eat it all?! There's plenty more there, finish it up!"

The nun was a big woman; she was five foot seven and weighed 429 pounds. Then she went to the hotel clerk and said, "Do you know when the next shuttle is going to the ferry?"

"I'm sorry Sister Woofenhawk, the ferry is not running right now because of the thick fog. Maybe later this afternoon. Did you have enough to eat for breakfast?" asked the clerk.

"Yes I did, I'm stuffed, but I'm out of here before it all hits the fan!!!!" The nun was a big lady but as strong as an ox! She grabbed her bag and she stormed out of the Narragansett Inn. She walked with her heavy bag dragging along the ground to the New Shoreham dock and saw no boats were going out, there was no ferry. Then she tied her duffel bag to her back like a knapsack, jumped in, and swam out to sea, determined to do so until she reached a passing boat. Someone saw her jump and called for help. The police, fire and rescue officials, and steamship authority officials went looking for her and she was nowhere to be found. They called the Coast Guard and boats went out looking for her and found her swimming six miles out at sea, resting on her bag.

She said, "Please take me to the mainland, Point Judith. I tried swimming to Block Island but I don't think I'm going to make it," the nun said to the Coast Guard rescue team.

The Coast Guard took her to the mainland and she got her wish. She was taken by rescue crews to South County Hospital. The rescue workers thought there was something wrong with her; kind of strange a big woman like her was trying to swim to Block Island in seven-foot seas.

"I'm home!!" she said in the hospital.

Back at the Narragansett Inn on Block Island she ate more than half of the continental breakfast before she took off on foot! The guests were pissed when the food ran out!

10:14 a.m. hotel guests were looking out at the water. One man said, "Look at the water, it's bubbling up and it looks like the Grand Rapids! Now the air smells like rotten eggs, and there's green and yellow fog rolling along the water!

"Maybe that fuckin' nun was right! She said something bad was going to happen the day after the Fourth, a gas explosion! It does not look good out there and the air smells terrible! Suppose she's right!?!"

"Eric, is she the fat bitch who ate all the fuckin' food?!"

"That was her!!" he said.

A few minutes later people started choking, passing out and getting sick, and ran back inside! The hotel clerk cried, "Sister Woofenhawk! Please come back and save us!!!!"

The methane gas and sulfur rose up from the pond, choking everyone to death. Suddenly the pond exploded and people went running for their lives as a shockwave blew up buildings with windows breaking, roofs being blown, off and boats blown into the air! People were running toward New Shoreham trying to get away from the disaster, boats landed on them, killing them. Shockwave winds blew people around into the air with building debris, like a mega tornado, and threw them miles out to sea.

The remaining people holding on for cover on the island saw a bright flash followed by a big *boom!* like a nuclear blast and then it was over! Block Island was blown off the map! The blast was like a nuclear explosion and people didn't have much time to think; it was a mushroom cloud like a nuclear bomb went off!

The debris and dead bodies spread out for twenty miles, washing up on shore on the mainland, Point Judith, Narragansett, Newport, the general Rhode Island coastline and along Long Island and Long Island Sound, even into Connecticut. Great white sharks by the hundreds arrived for a mega human buffet in the ocean, feeding on the dead! The blood-filled ocean was turning the sharks on one another!

The shockwave blew out windows on the mainland in Rhode Island, New York, and Connecticut, even killing wildlife in the water.

Back in New York before the eruption, the monitoring machines kept giving warnings about Block Island at the NASA volcano office in the basement of the Empire State Building.

The crew could not figure out what was going wrong until it was too late. They saw a huge mushroom cloud in the ocean and the shockwave made a big *boom!* The blast looked like the Krakatoa eruption in the Philippines! Then came a mushroom cloud like a nuclear explosion!

"Ladies and gentlemen we have a big blast in the ocean; it looks like Block Island was blown off the map! We don't know if it was a volcano or a nuclear explosion! We will have to go in and investigate when the dust settles. If it was a volcano we would know about it already. The data monitors were giving warning signals then *boom!* We need to find out what happened! If it was a nuclear explosion the data machines operated correctly," said Edward Fay.

Every police station, firehouse, and rescue crew came to the rescue from as far away as Fall River, Massachusetts and Tiverton, Rhode Island. Coast Guard boats and helicopters went to the blast site and Block Island was blown off the map. Everyone vacationing there the Fourth of July was killed.

It was Thursday, July 5, 2024, when the blast occurred at 11:02 a.m. Coast Guard and rescue boats were picking up dead bodies in the water between Point Judith and Block Island. Tsunamis seven to ten feet high struck the coastline for a few minutes after the blast!

The news came on all TV and radio stations about the Block Island explosion. "Good afternoon, we have breaking news on WJAR TV Channel 10 in Providence. A major blast struck Block Island a few minutes ago and thousands of people there are feared dead! The blast looked like a nuclear explosion, or it could be a volcano.

"Last year there was a lava flow from Beacon Hill on Block Island that set the island on fire on Halloween night. There were no injuries on that night as everyone evacuated in time. NASA reported a volcano brewing on Block Island that night from the fires and bubbling water. The smell of sulfur and methane gas was reported coming out of the ground and water around Block Island, Great Salt Pond was the epicenter, the most dangerous area where the fires were. Block Island was reported safe for summer vacationers to return.

"NASA will be going there no later than tomorrow to find out what happened. It's not known if it was a terrorist attack or a possible volcano. A tsunami warning has been issued for all Rhode Island beaches with waves that could reach twenty feet high. Janet Price reporting on Newswatch 10."

Windows blew out in Point Judith buildings, restaurants, and hotels. A giant brownish-yellow mushroom cloud appeared, darkening the sky! Narragansett's Scarborough Beach and Narragansett Pier survived the blast, but the beaches were struck by tsunamis. People at Scarborough Beach heard an enormous *boom!* then saw a mushroom cloud darkening the sky after a bright white flash. People screamed, "We've been attacked!"

People raced off the beach, leaving their belongings, getting into their cars and out of there in a hurry! Police drove around Narragansett with loudspeakers. "May I have your attention please, everyone get off the beach! There was an explosion on Block Island and tsunamis are on the way!"

People ran off the beach in a hurry! Around 12:30 p.m., about an hour and a half after the blast, a vision of the blessed Virgin Mary appeared above the blast. Sister Woofenhawk saw it from her hospital room and she opened up her hands saying, "Everyone on Block Island will be going to heaven!"

The police and fire departments blocked off roads getting to the water and people living in those areas had to evacuate in Rhode Island, Connecticut, and New York due to the tsunamis. But the waves didn't cause any damage; just high surf, five to seven feet. The big waves went into Long Island Sound, threatening Long Island and Connecticut residents.

A thirty-foot rouge wave struck the University of Connecticut at Avery Point, flooding the campus. Most people were running for higher ground but some daredevils were riding the wave! The mushroom cloud stayed in the air for three days, triggering thunderstorms and deadly lightning, stopping rescue workers and help from going in ten miles around the blast site.

Newspaper headlines read: "Possible Volcano Blows Block Island off the Map, Killing Thousands!" Police drove around, warning everyone to stay indoors and wear masks and respirators if necessary because of the toxic fallout from the Block Island blast!

Back in the NASA office in New York, "Ladies and gentlemen, the toxic blast from Block Island is going down and we need to go in there by boat. We cannot fly into the danger zone because it's too dangerous; volcanic ash or radioactive toxins could get into the engines of planes or helicopters. We need to dress up in spacesuits and respirators to go in the blast site because of the heat and set up monitoring equipment on the seafloor. We need to find out if Block Island going off was definitely a volcanic blast and we need to find out if there is more volcanic energy under the seafloor.

We will be leaving here at 9:00 a.m. Monday morning boarding Coast Guard Ship #23 out of the Hudson and we will be going to the blast site.

"The blast was so powerful it knocked out the power on the monitors we put in there last year sending out warning waves. We were aware that something was wrong on Block Island but the blast caught us by surprise because there was no magma in the chamber. The pressure levels and gas levels were down so I declared the island safe for summer vacationers to return there!

"Now we need to find out what happened. For the rest of the weekend keep an eye on the blast site and look for other possible dangers," said Edward Fay, head of NASA's volcano crew.

Park rangers and environmental officials monitored residential areas for toxic air warnings and signs were set up. Coastal ports were closed until the toxins went down. The day before the NASA crew went to the Block Island blast site a big rainstorm washed a lot of the toxins out of the air, so it was a clear day when Coast Guard Ship #23 arrived. The NASA dive teams jumped off the ship with monitoring equipment and spudweb data machines.

The blast site looked like a bunch of rocks in the water. Block Island was blown to pieces! The NASA volcano crew set up spudweb robots on the seafloor and got the methane and radiation levels. The area could still be dangerous.

Edward Fay reported to the Coast Guard aboard the ship, "We do have a volcano here! The blast came from a micro methane gas radiation tube from deep under the ground. The methane gas has been in the Block Island waters for years! The buildup of methane gas mixing with other toxins caused this eruption with no warning!"

"Ed, this is Glenn Harper, Coast Guard officer. Can this volcano erupt again?"

"Yes it can, but because the blast was so severe it should be safe now, because most of the gas fumes released its energy. It needs time to rebuild before it erupts again and that may take years. It shouldn't go off again in our lifetime but freak things happen during volcanic eruptions. Just ask about Mount St. Helens; when it erupted in 1980 scientists said that this volcano might never erupt again in our lifetime but it did several times, killing two hundred thousand people the last time it went. The fuckin' mountain split in two and wiped out three-fourths of the state of Washington, along with five or six other volcanoes to finish the job!

"The little energy left from this eruption still could set things off again at any time while we are here. Last year when lava spilled out of Beacon Hill on Block Island and proved it to be a volcano, it cooled down a few days later. I was a believer that it was over and look what happened! There were 3,994 people on that island when that blast occurred! Volcanoes and earthquakes are very unpredictable!" said Edward Fay.

The NASA crew finished their investigation and went back to New York. When the Coast Guard ship was pulling into the Hudson River near the Statue of Liberty, Katrina House saw a shark bite a dead woman's head off and swallow it! Leaving the rest of the body for a second great white shark to finish off! Katrina puked over the edge of the ship!

Later the newspapers and news on TV and radio stations confirmed that Block Island was a volcano! The ship pulled into port and the NASA volcano crew went back to their office by bus. They went back to work looking for lava levels on the volcano data monitors to find out what was coming next. The Rhode Island Coast Guard sent divers into the blast site and they saw black smokers on the seafloor…a sign that another eruption is imminent.

They contacted the NASA volcano crew in New York. Paul Numbnutts discovered something. He said, "Ed, come look at this! Monitor #3."

"Oh my God it looks like more action on the seafloor where Block Island exploded! Holy shit!!" Then Edward Fay got a text message on his phone and his phone went dead! Then he got a call on his phone later.

"Edward Fay sir, this is Tom Sawyer from the Rhode Island National Guard Unit #23. We have more problems at the blast site! Our divers reported some black smokers at the bottom where Great Salt Pond once stood and we fear another eruption could be brewing. There are methane gas and sulfur deposits coming up from bedrock undersea, boiling up from vapor vents."

"Tom! Get out of there right away! We found what was happening and it's very dangerous; get your people out of there immediately!" said Edward Fay in New York. Before it got dark the boats left the area.

The next day Tom had a meeting with his men and the Coast Guard. The NASA volcano crew was watching the Block Island black smokers all night long on the monitors in New York. A spudweb robot at the blast site was sending back data.

Tom Sawyer opened the meeting. "Good morning National Guard troops and US Coast Guard. Welcome to Quonset Point Military Base. I have a probable final death toll from the Block Island methane gas explosion from July 5. The final report from Gina Raimondo, US military agent: We have 3,994 possible fatalities, including the missing.

"According to NASA Operation Blowjob, Block Island was an erupting volcano. The disaster was not from a nuclear explosion as was once thought. Coast Guard Marine divers found black smokers at the blast site yesterday. Now, more eruptions may happen and the area is a danger zone. Black smokers are volcanic steam vents building molten lava under the seabed, pushing erupting gas and methane through the seafloor. Gina Raimondo has a few words."

"Thank you Tom. I want all manholes and sewers checked out in all of Rhode Island in case we have any kind of eruptions on the mainland. We have a minefield in Point Judith and here at Quonset Point that need to be addressed," she said.

CHAPTER THIRTEEN

VOLCANO UNDER NEW YORK CITY PART THREE

Midsummer of 2024 about two weeks after the black smokers were found where Block Island erupted, they erupted again, blowing a geyser high into the air. Then it stopped and the black smokers were quiet. The area was clear and there were no injuries, just a scary geyser.

The volcano crew was watching the black smokers on the data screens while lava was flowing underground west of Long Island and into the Hudson River heading for New York City. The sky over Long Island was a yellowish orange, almost looking like a permanent sunrise or sunset. It was sulfur and volcanic ash from the Block Island blast heading for New York City.

Methane gas flowed out into the Atlantic Ocean following a thin lava stream directly under Long Island and back out into the Atlantic Ocean. It formed an underground whirlpool of lava near the Statue of Liberty then the thick molten lava flowed deep underground under the Hudson River heading to the subways in Manhattan.

"Ladies and gentlemen, look at these monitors. Do you see what's happening? There's a flow of lava deep underground moving like a herd of animals with thin and thick lava flows heading for the Statue of Liberty and into the Hudson River. They're moving at a high rate of speed; I have no idea where they're going to end up.

"I never believed any of the steam blast eruptions over the last several years here in Manhattan were from a volcano despite damage and gas eruptions matching the descriptions of one, because gas line and steam eruptions can cause the same damage.

"The scariest blast was the Fifth Avenue and Lexington Avenue eruption. I declared the blast as a possible volcano but there was no lava found, just gas and steam. But the damage was severe enough to be a threat of a probable volcano. People were killed and buildings destroyed, with sea creatures being blown out of the blast site into city streets. We wound up evacuating all of New York City because of the threat of a volcano. But now I am a believer! We do have something here and I don't know how I'm going to tell the public it's our six NASA volcano crew against millions of New Yorkers.

"I believe this lava flow is part of a super volcano ready to blow the fuckin' northeast off the map. First Mount Ascutney in Vermont, then a blast at Blue Hills in the Boston area, and now a major eruption blowing Block Island off the map on July 5, not to mention the earthquakes and steam blasts and sulfur deposits in Blackstone, Mass., and in Moodus, Connecticut.

"I told them it's not a volcano but now I am thinking different. We do not know what this lava flow is going to do or where it'll go. We cannot put New York City under alert or go to the news because of lava flow data. It might wash away and vanish with the gases and methane going with it.

"However, if we have another steam eruption or some kind of activity we have to put Manhattan on alert. Block Island has been a ticking time bomb for more than a hundred years because the salts and pit ponds there always had a high methane gas level and radiation and sulfur deposits. When a spark comes from the heat from the passing lava it could trigger a volcanic explosion.

"I want all military personnel, NYPD, and the fire department to recheck every manhole, sewer drain, and tunnel throughout Manhattan and all of Long Island looking for activity, especially all the subways and train stations. We need to monitor any possible activity in any hole or below street level in all of New York City and Long Island.

"All seaports need to look for anything unusual! I want water and ground temperatures monitored daily. We have not had any eruptions in Manhattan in six years and I hope it stays that way!" said Edward Fay, head of NASA's volcano crew.

A baseball game was going on in Yankee Stadium between the New York Yankees and the Houston Astros and it was a tie game in the seventh inning. Houston was at bat in a 2-2 game when suddenly an earthquake struck, the lights blinked, and the fans started screaming. Then the ground shook again, the lights went out, and the stadium was in darkness, just like that!

The power went out in the Bronx and stadium officials had to direct the crowd using loudspeakers. All the subway trains stopped running and everyone was in a panic! A few minutes later the train and subway workers came around with flashlights to get all the people off the subway trains and out of the tunnels to street level.

Stadium officials did the same, escorting everyone out of Yankee Stadium into the streets. "Ladies and gentlemen, this is the NYPD on loudspeakers. We just had an earthquake and the power's out in most of Manhattan. No subways are operating so the only transportation is by cab or by bus. Everyone follow the flashlights—there's no need to rush—to avoid being trampled."

The people leaving subways had to go up to the streets and board cabs and buses. One girl said to a cab driver while riding, "What happened? Were we attacked again?!"

"No it was an earthquake! I hope it's not from a volcano like the one on Block Island!" said the cab driver.

"Where's Block Island? Somewhere in the Philippines?!" asked the girl.

"No! It is in Rhode Island!" said the cab driver.

The girl paid her fare then she boarded a bus to Long Island. During the earthquake, the volcano crew was reading the monitors and everything was quiet, then the machines started flashing: "Warning! Earthquake!"

They didn't feel the first one; then when the ground shook again it felt like the office was rocking back and forth in the sub-basement in the Empire State Building. The second aftershock lasted less than ten seconds! The data monitors, computers, and TV screens kept flashing: "Warning! Earthquake!"

Then it stopped and the monitors read: "Epicenter, Yankee Stadium Bronx Station!" Then the crew notified the NYPD, fire department, and rescue crews to go to the scene. Everything was quiet after the earthquake but the area was in darkness. Sirens blared all over Manhattan racing to the Bronx.

FLASHBACK

Just before the earthquake a bank robbery was going on in Greenwich Village and a lot of police officers were there! Then the ground started shaking and rumbling and the buildings were rocking back and forth like bowling pins waiting to fall over. Next thing, all the city lights went out in the buildings and Manhattan was in darkness! Then it stopped and everything went quiet. Even the streetlights were out!

One cop said to another, "Oh my fuckin' God! I think we were attacked again!"

A second cop said, "I believe China may have attacked us with an EMP bomb! They warned the US a few days ago that they were going to attack New York. We do not get earthquakes here!"

A third cop said, "If we were hit by an electromagnetic pulse, our police cars would have stopped running and helicopters above would have fallen out of the sky."

A fourth cop said, "Something happened here! Block Island was blown off the map by an undersea volcano and I hope we're not fuckin' next!"

A fifth cop said, "I have been with the NYPD for the last ten years and I never saw anything like this. I never heard of an earthquake like this in New York City!"

A sixth cop said, "Whatever happened here, it's scarier than 9/11! It felt like Manhattan was going to fall over, rocking back and forth like a baby's crib, and the buildings swayed like rocking bowling pins!"

A seventh cop said, "I thought we were all going to die tonight, this is bad! And it might not be over!"

An eighth cop said, "We have had steam eruptions before in New York City where people have died and buildings were destroyed. We've had a threat of a possible volcano, but to have an earthquake like we did, and watching the buildings move and all the lights go out? Something is going on here and it's not good."

A ninth cop said, "I believe it's the wrath of God and the judgment of the Rapture!"

A tenth cop said, "We can' just be here bullshitting about what happened. We have work to do here and then we have to go into the unknown next."

All of the NYPD was talking among themselves about the freak earthquake plunging all of New York City into darkness! After the robbery was solved the NYPD was off to the Bronx to find out what happened.

Just after the earthquake the NASA volcano crew went up the stairs to the street outside the Empire State Building and saw all of New York City in darkness. They went to Yankee Stadium and Bronx Station looking for what caused this earthquake and they found nothing. The crew was there all night, right until morning, looking for any activity. Checking sewer drains, subways, lifting manhole covers checking for the smell of gas, and there was nothing.

The crew searched Yankee Stadium and found no signs of any activity, then they went back to the monitoring office and had a meeting with the mayor and the NYPD to go over Plan B.

"Good afternoon NYPD, Mayor William De Blasio, and Governor Jerry Cuomo. I am sure we met before. My name is Edward Fay the head volcanologist of NASA in Houston, Texas. My crew: Linda Brew, Katrina House, Nathan Rivers, Paul Numbnutts, and NASA news reporter David Dunkin, also our earthquake monitoring manager. We also have Lieutenant Bowa Bowser and Allen Abbingtonconstantinoappopoliss from the New York Fire Department with us and we have Eric Epicenter from Environmental Steamfitters Inc. here in New York joining us this afternoon.

"It was a sleepless night for all of us because of an earthquake. A 4.5 came out of nowhere rocking Manhattan, nearly knocking buildings over and putting out power all over New York City, and we cannot find the reason why! All our monitors are out until the power comes back on. The earthquake knocked out the main power terminal in Manhattan. Parts of New Jersey also lost power. All three New York airports are down. Computer data is down everywhere here in Manhattan.

"We are Operation Blowjob! And it's not the blowjob you'd like to have. We monitor volcanoes across the United States and about one hundred of them have erupted or threaten some kind of eruption. Most of them were in Alaska. The 4.5 is when the power went out; I don't know how bad the aftershock was when the buildings were rocking. Out west, Washington State, Oregon, parts of northern California, and the northwest corner of Canada were blown off the map! Three-fourths of Alaska is gone! The mainland around Mount Denali remains.

"Fifty to one hundred hills and volcanoes erupted out west, killing millions. At least twenty-five million people on the West Coast are homeless and about fifty million were forced to evacuations! Eventually California will be next and these fuckin' volcanoes are still erupting on the West Coast. The holy bible says that one day the West Coast will fall into the Pacific Ocean because of the weak fault line from earthquakes and several volcano eruptions and that's happening right now!

"We have a super volcano threat here on the East Coast directly under Massachusetts, New Hampshire, and Vermont. The epicenter of the super volcano sits right under Mount Ascutney in Adamsville, Vermont, which erupted twice, killing 289 people despite a massive evacuation! Then Block Island erupted a couple of weeks ago, killing an estimated four thousand people, blowing the island off the map! The eruption was unexpected.

"Halloween night last year a hole burst in Beacon Hill and out comes molten lava burning half the island to the ground. It lasted a day or two then the lava disappeared! Block Island has had a history of methane gas in the water in and around the island for years and sulfur deposits in the soil. That explains the eruption and lava flows. Six months later the island was declared safe for vacationers to return to at the beginning of summer, allowing ferry service and residents to move back there. But everyone on Block Island was warned they were on a volcano, and told about the Halloween 2023 eruption, and that something could happen with little to no warning.

"The July 5 eruption caught our crew by surprise. Then monitors were flashing warnings, 'Block Island explosion,' leaving us no time to react until it was too late! Later we found a stream of lava flowing through Long Island into the Atlantic Ocean, and from there flowing into the Hudson River and forming a whirlpool in front of the Statue of Liberty deep underground. The lava made a thin stream heading for New York City and another one branched off, going toward New Jersey and the White Plains. It stopped under the Tappan Zee Bridge and disappeared!

"The stream heading for New York City disappeared just after passing the Statue of Liberty. We found no methane gas, sulfur, or radiation like that found on Block Island. But this earthquake worries me! Throughout my investigation there was no smell of gas, no threats of a steam blast or volcano threat. The only thing is the threat of a super volcano in New England may have triggered the earthquake!

"I hope everyone could hear me talking through the loudspeaker until the power comes back on because the only way we're going to find out what went wrong is when my monitors are up and running. The good news: the monitors found the epicenter of the first earthquake before the aftershock knocked the power and generators out!" said Edward Fay.

Everyone at the meeting remained until power was restored. The NYPD, fire department, and rescue crews drove around New York City to find several buildings collapsed, broken glass, and flooded streets from a possible tsunami. Parts of Manhattan were a mess. Some areas had so much damage they were unrecognizable!

"Headquarters to Car #17, what's your location?"

"I am in Midtown near 50th Street and Fifth Avenue. There's a lot of destruction here. Jesus fuckin' Goddamn Christ! St. Patrick's Cathedral is gone! Car #17 over!"

"You got to be kidding!" said the officer at headquarters.

———————

Helicopters were flying over Manhattan viewing the damage. The volcano crew was at the NASA office at the Empire State Building waiting for the power to come back on. The power was off for a couple of days.

NYPD and fire and rescue crews were in front of where St. Patrick's Cathedral once stood. It was a pile of bricks with candles still lit inside the rubble. A cross was sticking up in the rubble and a vision of the Virgin Mary appeared above the demolished church for a few minutes, then vanished! Other buildings had broken windows and some collapsed. After the vision disappeared there was a bright white flash then everything was normal.

One cop said to another, "Was that lightning?!"

"No, I think it was the Lord sending a message before the apparition vanished!" said the other cop.

NYPD along with fire and rescue crews drove around day and night looking for survivors and reporting damage to buildings and property. Two days later the fuckin' power was back on, relighting beautiful Manhattan, the part that was not damaged. Gas line fires and watermain breaks throughout New York City were fixed while everyone was waiting for the power to come back on.

The earthquake broke the main power source at the power station, damaging it before workers could get to the power grid two days later. NASA was finally getting data on what caused this powerful earthquake!

"Good morning crew. We have reports from what happened when the earthquakes struck on the earthquake monitors. The earthquake and aftershocks struck the same area, recorded when the first one struck, and the epicenter was under Yankee Stadium and Bronx Station. The first shaking was a 4.5 and the second was a 6.5, strong enough to knock buildings down. We have caves underground and tunnels, not to mention cross rail subways directly under the Bronx Zoo, Yankee Stadium, and the Bronx Station.

"There are six levels of subway trains under the Bronx and Queens boroughs. There's a lot of air pockets underground in those areas and they are no strangers to earthquakes, but not like this one! I doubt it's from a volcano because there are no signs of activity or pressure leading up to a volcano. However, the eruption on Block Island and the threat of a super volcano and the eruption of Mount Ascutney in Vermont have me worried.

"If a volcano erupts in Manhattan like the volcano in Vermont or Block Island we could be in serious trouble! Keep watching the monitors for any activity. I am not putting Manhattan on alert because of a strong earthquake. We're here to monitor volcanic activity," said Edward Fay.

The next day the airports opened in New York and New Jersey and a plane was leaving Paris, France. At Paris Charles De Gaulle airport, a plane was bound for New York City, USA.

"Good morning, this is your aircraft crew. Welcome aboard Flight 900 bound nonstop to New York City, USA. It is 7:30 a.m. local time and the weather is clear. The trip will take about eight hours and thirty minutes and you will arrive in New York City at about 4:00 p.m. our time and 11:00 a.m. in New York. Please listen to the instructions before we depart.

"The aircraft is a 747-400 with three seats on each side and five in the middle. This is a nonsmoking flight. There are two exits on each side of the aircraft and emergency exits are located on each wing. All carryon luggage must be stored in the above compartments—not between the seats—at all times. Seatbelts must be fastened during takeoff until the pilot says you can take them off during flight. You pull the buckle, slide the belt tight, then clamp the buckle.

"In case of an emergency I showed you the exits earlier. For the pull-down mask above you, grab it and place it over your mouth for oxygen. We will be departing shortly. When we are in flight, breakfast, snacks, coffee, and juice will be served. Enjoy Air France Flight 900," said the airline crew, then the same instructions were translated from English to French.

Then the 747 left for New York and it was a smooth flight until it flew over the Hudson River. Volcanic ash from the Block

Island eruption still in the atmosphere was getting into the engines. The pilot on that flight didn't notice right away and he said to the passengers, "Ladies and gentlemen, look out the left side of the aircraft and you can see the Statue of Liberty. We will be landing in Kennedy Airport in about ten minutes. It's eighty-three degrees in New York City."

Suddenly warning signs were going off in the cockpit and the engines were shutting down. The plane was out of control and crashed into the top of the Freedom Tower. It burst into flames and broke into pieces, falling into lower Manhattan. Parts of the broken plane landed in the Hudson River. Dead human bodies landed, smashing into windows in the Freedom Tower.

It was a Saturday morning when the crash happened and people in the streets screamed, "Terrorist attack!" and everyone started running uptown. Parts of the plane landed on rooftops and in the streets, and dead burnt bodies melted on the windows of office buildings!

The NASA volcano crew saw the disaster unfold. The plane was flying into a yellow fog near the Statue of Liberty and suddenly the plane lost control and crashed into the Freedom Tower.

"Oh my God, a plane just hit the Freedom Tower! I don't know if it was another terrorist attack or if the plane was caught in volcanic debris weather. The plane struck the building, bouncing off and breaking into pieces! Holy shit!!!" said Edward Fay.

The NYPD was in a panic watching the disaster unfold. Part of the top of the building was damaged after the plane hit it. The fire department and NYPD were called to repeat 9/11 all over again and military helicopters flew around the crash site as people in the streets ran up toward Harlem in case another building collapsed. NASA send up aircraft to monitor the air where the plane went out of control.

The Coast Guard and National Guard got pieces of the plane to find out what went wrong. Military helicopters reported data back to NASA. Police and firemen went in the Freedom Tower going up 117 fuckin' stories to put out fires and assess the damage, worrying that the fuckin' building was going to collapse like the World Trade Center on 9/11.

There was no damage from the New York City Fire Department or NYPD going through the Freedom Tower but they saw dead bodies from the plane crash melted up against windows. Everyone was killed because the plane broke into pieces. It scattered into the streets of Manhattan, the 9/11 memorial, and the Hudson River. Dead bodies floating in the river were being eaten by seabirds, fish, and sharks.

NASA got a report on the weather over the Hudson River. "Coast Guard Chopper #180 to NASA, over."

"This is Edward Fay, head of NASA volcano crew. Come in please."

"We have discovered volcanic debris from the Block Island eruption over the Statue of Liberty that may have caused this plane to crash. We have volcanic ash, sulfur, and radiation gases in the atmosphere. It's a cloud of thick volcanic ash like a building thunderstorm and we have to fly around it. Coast Guard Chopper #180 over."

"Ten-four #180 we will send boats out there and do a thorough investigation. Edward Fay, head of NASA volcano crew, over."

The military and airport officials got pieces from Flight 900 from Paris, France, black boxes to find out what happened to this plane. Scientists were also called in to investigate the plane crash. The remaining pieces found were taken to a military hangar at the West Point military base. The NASA volcano crew was there.

"Good evening. My name is David J. Yorknew along with Edward Fay, head of NASA's volcano crew from Houston. My job is to investigate plane crashes and sunken ships in the Bermuda Triangle. According to the black boxes, Flight 900 from

Paris to New York was flying through volcanic debris and it shorted out all four engines of the 747-400, killing seventy-one people aboard. Mr. Edward Fay will explain."

"Thank you David. Spudweb and our other volcano monitors have found volcanic debris from the eruption of Block Island, Rhode Island, in the air. We found broken rock ash particles not pyroclastic flow. We found vaporized methane gas, radiation, and sulfur deposits in the area around the Statue of Liberty and rising and sinking into the Hudson River, closing all New York City beaches and the area along Long Island.

"We sent out boats and submarines to find what was out there while wearing respirators. Anyone who attempts to go to the Statue of Liberty at the mouth of the Hudson may die of suffocation. All boats and aircraft are prohibited from going through that area. We will keep monitoring the ash cloud because it's going to flow right up the Hudson River into Manhattan. All airports in New York City and Newark Liberty are closed until this ash cloud vanishes. Any questions?!" asked Edward Fay.

"Hi, my name is John Johnson of the US Air Force. Is it possible that the ash and radiation gases could catch fire when crossing an open flame, such as a candle or even a cigarette, and explode?"

"Yes they can. When the ash cloud arrives everyone must evacuate because you can die breathing it in. Right now I see the ash is evaporating as it's coming up the Hudson River; if that continues to happen that's a good thing," said Edward Fay.

FLASHBACK

When the plane hit the Freedom Tower everyone started running, fearing another terrorist attack, but it was an accident. Manhattan was a ghost town.

News: "Good evening, this is NBC News in New York. There was another tragedy. A 747 from Paris that crashed into the Freedom Tower late Saturday morning was an accident and not a terrorist attack. According to the black boxes, Flight 900 flew through volcanic ash from the eruption from Block Island, causing the crash. Sixty-five passengers and six crew members were killed and the top six floors of the Freedom Tower were damaged.

"The plane broke into pieces and burst into flames, fanning fears of another terrorist attack in New York. NASA says the ash cloud is contaminated with radiation and methane gas. It's coming up the Hudson River and could be dangerous. NBC News reporting."

The NYPD and fire and rescue crews were still going through Manhattan looking for survivors in damaged and collapsed buildings and several streets. The Bronx was shut down. All the subways were closed temporarily.

The following Monday downtown Manhattan was open for business. The ash cloud disappeared, but lava was flowing deep underground directly under Greenwich Village. The volcano crew was watching the lava tube underground. People were going into work as usual on a quiet Monday morning and all the subways were up and running and NYPD was out protecting the public.

Then around 9:00 a.m. a rumbling sound was heard and a slight shaking as usual. With buses and yellow cabs traveling all day, most New Yorkers didn't notice what was really happening. Then a blast through the ground at the 9/11 memorial!

Debris struck buildings, breaking windows, then a second blast and fire came from underground, setting the area on fire. The second blast caused more damage; windows blew through and people were blown into the air. A subway had stopped at the memorial stop when the blast happened. Suddenly the subway station exploded and the train full of passengers was blown through a wall!

Yellow cabs were lined up on Fifth Avenue and a lot of people were walking in the streets, boarding cabs and buses, and going down into the subways. The streets were packed with people when suddenly a manhole cover blew sky high and landed on the windshield of an oncoming bus, killing the driver. The bus ran people over on the sidewalk like bowling pins until it crashed into a storefront window, where it came to a rest after ramming a girl at a cashier's desk, killing her instantly!

Then another blast at 41st Street and Lexington Avenue blowing cars off the road and shattering windows in buildings; then another blast at Fifth Avenue and 58th Street! Then another blast in Central Park. It was an underground volcano erupting, separate blasts threatening to blow Manhattan off the map!

Later the area where the Fifth Avenue steam eruption happened in July of 2018 blew up again, collapsing buildings and sending vehicles and people airborne. It blew out several windows and left a crack in the middle of Fifth Avenue, swallowing cars and buses. Gas line ruptures and fires started explosions everywhere! The NYPD and fire trucks were all over Manhattan.

With a mega explosion in the Bronx, a wall caved in at Yankee Stadium. Bronx Station was blown to smithereens and trains blew up like bombs. Panicking people were in an end-of-the-world footrace toward Harlem. Then a massive eruption in the Hudson River sent a tsunami into lower Manhattan, drowning people in Greenwich Village, and the 9/11 memorial filled up with water.

The explosions in New York City were so severe rescue work couldn't be done—it was either find a way to get out or stay and get killed! The volcano crew went up the stairway in the Empire State Building to the eighty-sixth floor and a rescue helicopter scooped them up one at a time and flew over the damage. A good part of New York City was on fire and more explosions were going off. The Coast Guard helicopter flew them to safety in upstate New York!

The data machines were left on, still sending data that a volcano was now erupting in New York City! Central Park was blown off the map, sending a parade of fires into the city. Parked cars and buses were burning and the monitoring equipment and data machines shorted out when water poured through New York City streets from the Hudson River tsunami! Lower Manhattan, Midtown, and Uptown suffered the blowjob of the century. People were trying to outrun explosions, fires, and floods, running uptown well into the night trying to escape death! The explosions and earthquakes were going on and off all night!

Times Square exploded; a volcanic blast blew up the streets and all the windows blew out and Times Square was on fire in a matter of minutes. A shockwave blew all the windows out in New York City buildings and tore rooftops off. More explosions took place in Harlem, Upper Manhattan, causing gas line ruptures and watermain breaks. Then the erupting explosions attacked Queens, next the Bronx; then came a huge eruption in the middle of Fifth Avenue and a big sinkhole formed. Buildings fell in the giant sinkhole and disappeared, covered with molten rock and lava slowly burning Manhattan to the ground.

Buildings fell like dominoes! The Empire State Building and the Freedom Tower were the only buildings standing, but all the windows were blown out. Some other small buildings survived the NYC volcano but all the windows were blown out everywhere! The ash cloud hung over Midtown; anyone still there trying to get out died there!

Connecticut, Western Massachusetts, and New Jersey were forced to evacuate and find temporary housing in portable tents. Hundreds, thousands, if not millions people, were feared dead from the volcano under New York City! Scientists discovered a giant bed of lava making its way to the surface, threatening to burn New York City to the ground!

The volcano crew went back to Adamsville, Vermont to

monitor Mount Ascutney and it was still active but quiet. The NASA volcano crew had a setup in the basement of the Adamsville, Vermont police station. The team was watching the magma levels in the ground moving under Western Connecticut and Massachusetts under the Green Mountains, and settling under Mount Ascutney in Vermont where it started.

Back in New York City the explosions stopped, leaving a mega disaster. NASA contacted the mayor in New York City.

"Mayor…Mr. William de Blasio, this is Edward Fay, head of NASA's volcano crew, calling to tell you that New York City just had a volcanic eruption disaster! It was a volcano that caused a mega disaster and it's part of a super volcano warning for the East Coast! It is not a terrorist attack! It was a volcano under New York City. Call me or text me at my office in Adamsville, Vermont. Our location in New York was destroyed and my office in Houston was struck by a tornado. I will fill you in with updates on any future disasters in Manhattan."

The news was broadcast to people around the world. People at a bar in Montauk, New York on the tip of Long Island, an area that survived the disaster, watched live on TV. "Good evening, a mega volcano has erupted under New York City. NBC News is here watching it unfold as explosions are still happening everywhere at this hour. Fifth Avenue and Central Park have been blown off the map and several downtown buildings have disappeared. All of Manhattan is destroyed with broken gas lines, watermain breaks, and fires caused by molten lava blown up from under city streets.

"People started running uptown when the eruptions started happening and a tsunami struck. More than one hundred thousand people are feared dead! Over fifty holes erupted from under the streets, and subways were blown up.

"The 9/11 memorial is gone, drowning in a tsunami with fifty-foot waves that crashed into Manhattan streets, killing many people, drowning cars and buses, and flooding subways coming from the Hudson River. Boats were washed into city streets and ships were tipped over by the waves.

"A massive crater was left in the middle of Fifth Avenue about three hundred feet deep, swallowing several buildings and leaving a ring of fire. Many people got out before things got really bad, but if there were a lot of people in those buildings and many couldn't get out in time, the death toll could be as high as a million. Many New Yorkers thought it was a nuclear attack but NASA said the blasts were from an underground volcano.

"A plane from France hit the Freedom Tower, raising fears of 9/11 all over again, but NASA said the plane was caught in an ash cloud. That cloud caused the crash, killing seventy-one passengers and crew members, the plane clipping the top of the Freedom Tower and breaking into pieces! New York City was hit by a mega underground volcano causing total devastation! We will have more updates through the night. NBC News reporting."

September 11, 2024, was a rainy Monday morning and bulldozers and military earth vehicles came into New York City to knock down damaged debris. Several more buildings had to be knocked down and more earthquakes and steam eruptions occurred.

A strong earthquake struck the Bronx Zoo and all the animals broke loose. Many animals burned to death in fires and falling debris from the earthquakes and aftershocks! Lions, tigers, and bears roaming the streets in the burned-out Bronx had to be put down, shot by the National Guard trying to avoid being eaten alive!

Yankee Stadium had to be knocked down; all the subways were damaged and all the animals that escaped from the Bronx Zoo were killed. All of Manhattan was closed off with yellow tape so people couldn't go in without military guards, police, and fire personnel. NYC was completely destroyed!

CHAPTER FOURTEEN

THE BLUE HILLS
VOLCANO TWO

Monday, September 25, 2024, earthquakes and sonic booms started appearing in the Boston area. Milton, Canton, and Curry College also experienced earthquakes, booms, and rocking and rolling for about a week.

Park rangers were checking the mountain. Milton Police arrived and went up Blue Hills to investigate. A helicopter flew over the mountain looking for activity and nothing was happening. The earthquakes and sonic booms were mild, but they got stronger as the week progressed until damage started happening!

The earthquakes and sonic booms started happening in Canton, cracking windows and foundations in homes then suddenly stopped. Alarms started going on, alerting police. After a big *boom!* a woman cleaning her house was knocked off her feet. She ran outside and looked up at Blue Hills, the mountain in view of her home.

She ran down to a corner store, Redford Antiques was the name. She rang the cowbell and she walked in, and she said to the clerk in the store, "Good morning Libby. Did we just have an earthquake?! I was cleaning my house and suddenly I heard a boom like an explosion and the noise knocked me down."

"You're kidding Cindy! I didn't feel anything and I've been here since 6:00 a.m."

"Oh my God I live three blocks from here and the boom sounded like a bomb going off! I went airborne!"

"That's strange Cindy because I didn't feel a thing; that's scary!"

"Libby, did you just feel that! We were moving?!"

"Yes, I felt that and I heard it too! Maybe Blue Hills will be next! Did you hear about what happened in New York and Block Island, the volcano eruptions during the summer?!"

"Yes Libby, I did. That's what's making life very scary; because you don't know where it's going to happen next!" Cindy cried.

More people came into the store talking about the earthquakes. "Libby, my name is Frank and I live here in Canton. We get earthquakes from time to time but nothing like the one this morning. I think something is happening in that mountain out there. About five years ago a steam eruption occurred and the scientists that discovered it said it was a form of volcanic eruption but they couldn't prove it. But they did say that Blue Hills is a volcano and it last erupted in the 1400s.

"A witness from the *Boston Globe* says that there was an eruption in 1998, but it was covered up so as not to panic the community. The 2018 mini eruption caused serious damage to the ski lodge. It triggered a violent avalanche that flattened the resort and ski lodge while earthquakes damaged homes and the Curry College Campus. Students there got hurt. The damage here in Canton was incredible!

"I've felt many earthquakes here, some pretty good ones during that time, and my house got damaged, but the one we had at eight thirty this morning felt like the earth was coming apart. I didn't check if anything got damaged in my house. As soon as I heard the boom and felt the rocking and rolling I had to get out of there!

"New York City and Block Island were blown off the map by what is called a super volcano during the summer and a mountain erupted in Vermont a year or two ago. All the volcanoes on the West Coast, about one hundred of them, wiped out parts of California and Oregon. Washington State and a good part of Alaska and northwest Canada were blown off the map, killing millions.

"I believe we are in the last days of the Rapture and the world is coming to an end or the United States is starting to break apart. The bible says that before Jesus returns, volcanoes will erupt all over the world and the devil will come out of them and take the atheists away, turning the globe into the gates of hell, but God will get His people while these volcanoes are going off!"

"That's enough Frank, you're scaring everybody in my store. Halloween is still five weeks away!" said Libby, the store clerk.

The number of people in the store rose to eight, talking about that morning's strong earthquake. Then another *boom!* and the store shook a little, then it stopped and all the visitors left and went outside. The earthquakes and booms occurred in many areas, including downtown Boston.

———————

Friday September 29, 2024, a football game was being played at Curry College between them and Salve Regina. Salve Regina was leading 33 to 25 with 8:19 remaining and Curry had the ball second down and 8 yards to go at midfield. Suddenly a bright greenish-blue flash of lightning…on a clear night with a full moon showing! It lit up the sky twice! The refs held up the game to check for weather reports. Then play resumed and Curry moved the ball to the Salve 35-yard line with 6:38 left. Then the lights flickered a couple of times and the scoreboard went out.

The refs stopped the game again, checking weather reports and there was nothing. The game resumed and Curry got a first down at the 24-yard line with less than five minutes. The refs were monitoring the time on the field because the scoreboard was out. Then Curry got another first down at the 13-yard line with three and a half minutes to play. Then came third down and a goal at less than two minutes.

A packed house was cheering loudly for Curry then *boom!* the ground shook while the Curry quarterback was throwing a pass. You could hear rocks rolling underground! The crowd ignored what was happening underground as the pass was thrown and Salve Reginia picked it off and ran ninety yards for a touchdown.

After a massive Salve Regina celebration a penalty moved the try for the extra point, making the score 40 to 25, Salve Regina. The packed crowd left the stands in a hurry but Salve kicked off to Curry because the game was not over yet. During the kick the field lights went out and the teams played under the moonlight until the tackle was made. Curry took a knee to finish the game.

The Curry football coaches were talking on the way to the locker room. "This is the second time these motherfuckers beat us at our field during an earthquake!"

The big crowd ran back to their dorms in a panic! Some fans got trampled and were escorted off the dark campus with police flashing their lights! Some kids got hurt and were taken to the hospital.

Later a party was going on at a frat house at Delta Phi Zeta and a strong earthquake struck the Curry campus just before 2:00 a.m. The fraternity house shook, rocking and rolling like a wake-up hangover! The DJ's computer stopped working and the party was over.

Pictures started falling and breaking on the floor and kids were yelling, "Earthquake! Earthquake!" and ran out of the frat house in their underwear; it was a toga party!! The students boarded their fraternity shuttle in their underwear or with rags or towels wrapped around them. Some of them were half naked, wearing robes around them like the Roman days!

The shuttle went to Blue Hills at 4:00 a.m. and all the students went for a hike up the mountain yelling, "Toga! Toga! Toga! Toga!" only to be met by police and National Guard troops and told to leave. The journey was over and the students went back to the Curry campus. When the shuttle got back on campus it started raining and the shuttle got stuck in the mud. The students had to walk the rest of the way yelling, "Toga! Toga! Toga! Toga!"

The police and the National Guard Troops were guarding the mountain because of the earthquakes and sonic booms, not letting people hike. Scientists were at the summit looking for signs of activity. It was shaking and rumbling from time to time but nothing was busting through yet. The mountain was closed off to the public because of the eruption on Block Island and the mega volcano in New York City. The volcano crew got a call in Vermont.

"NASA volcano crew. Good afternoon, Edward Fay speaking."

"Hi this is Steven Brad the head scientist from Yellowstone National Park. I am here on the summit of Blue Hills in the Boston, Massachusetts area, monitoring Blue Hills and fearing that a volcano could erupt here. We are getting a lot of damaging earthquakes and sonic booms so strong that this mountain is moving. During these earthquakes it feels like it's going to crumble!"

"Okay. Steven, get everyone off the mountain and out of the area as soon as you can and we will be there by the end of the day. Get out immediately!" said Edward Fay.

The NASA volcano crew helicopter landed on top of the Blue Hills summit around 5:00 p.m. National Guard troops said about a sign on the chopper, "Operation Blowjob," when the helicopter landed, "What the fuck is this! Are we all going to get blowjobs today!" A crew exited the helicopter and a man came over to the National Guard troops and identified himself.

"Good afternoon men. My name is Edward Fay, the head volcanologist of NASA and we are called Operation Blowjob, a team that investigates volcanoes, and we were called to check out a possible volcano here on Blue Hills. It's not the first time we've been here. We were here in 2011 investigating a possible volcano because of a series of violent earthquakes and a steam eruption that happened here. I did not identify the blast as being from a volcano but the gases and pressure inside the mountain signaled a possible one.

"There were no lava levels that could trigger a volcanic eruption so the decision was denied! But this mountain is indeed a dormant volcano and I did say that one day this volcano was due to go off. According to the recent earthquakes and sonic booms you may have a problem here! Come here, let me show you something.

"This is called a spudweb machine that we have here aboard the helicopter, and we also have spider web robots with legs. According to the data, right now we do have a volcano eruption threat here at Blue Hills because right now lava is flowing deep underground and making its way to the surface.

"There was no lava the last time we were here in 2011. And the result was a volcanic steam eruption because of ground pressure and sulfuric gas. Now there is lava and pressure is building again, forming volcanic gas, due to a super volcano warning for Massachusetts, including Boston and Worcester. New Hampshire also has it, and the epicenter is in Vermont. Mount Ascutney in Adamsville, Vermont, where we came from, erupted two or three years ago, killing about three hundred people.

"Block Island was blown off the map earlier this summer and New York City was annihilated by a series of volcanic eruptions.

The lava bed spread from Vermont under Western Massachusetts and Connecticut and the lava flow settled under Block Island. Not long after, Block Island blew apart, killing nearly four thousand people. The lava quickly flowed into the Hudson River, sparing the Statue of Liberty and New Jersey, but it came right under the 9/11 memorial, blowing that up. Then a major eruption in Central Park blew it off the map and then blew every hole in the ground in Manhattan, swallowing hundreds of tall high-rise buildings, including the Trump Tower. A volcanic blast blew the building out of the ground straight up like a rocket and it landed in the Hudson River! The death toll in New York City is still unknown!

"The lava bed below New England is huge and it's getting bigger and wider. Look at this monitor: we just had an earthquake here in the mountain; it was a 3.2 on the Richter scale and you can hear rocks falling underground. If you look at this monitor you can see the rocks rolling like bowling balls about four miles underground. There is no telling when we are going to have an eruption but according to my data there is a good chance something is going to happen here.

"The earthquakes and sonic booms are going to continue happening here and it's going to get worse unless the molten rock levels go down or vanish. My advice gentlemen: You need to contact local police departments and have a town meeting at a large place. A big ball field, gym, any place that holds a lot of people; tell them that danger is lurking and have an evacuation plan if these earthquakes keep getting worse. You cannot say a volcano is going to erupt until something happens in the mountain. People should be expecting something when earthquakes keep getting stronger, but you tell them there's activity in the ground causing them!" said Edward Fay.

The National Guard was on the mountain twenty-four hours a day making sure people didn't hike or go up the mountain.

Local police had yellow tape all around the bottom, keeping people out. A family of about seven deer was roaming around the summit around midnight—a warning that something was going to happen here!

About a week later the earthquakes and sonic booms stopped for a while but the military and law enforcement were still guarding the mountain in case something happened. The volcano crew bolted another spudweb data machine on the summit to keep tabs on activity before the helicopter flew back to Vermont. Around the middle of October, 2024 the sonic booms and earthquakes were back with their fiercest weapons.

First in Canton, people were sleeping at 3:00 a.m. then *boom!* People were knocked out of their beds! Flashes of blue lightning were coming from cracks in the ground because on Route 138, the road was cracked open. Good thing no cars were coming at that hour, but the earthquake alerted the police and fire departments. Windows were blown out in several homes and screaming people ran into the streets looking for help. One home collapsed and the roof fell in and a pussycat was killed!

Several Canton and Massachusetts State Police cars arrived as the road cracked open. A deer was trapped in the rubble in the middle of the road on Route 138 and the Canton Police had to free the animal, which then ran out of sight like a bat out of hell. Smoke and lightning flashes were coming up from the cracks in the road and in open fields. The earthquakes were still going on. Shockwaves blew windows out in homes.

A couple was in bed at the Holiday Inn in Canton off of 138 having sex. At 3:02 a.m. the earthquake struck and a shockwave blew their naked bodies out of bed and out a window. They had cuts all over them and were taken to a hospital in Boston after they were found suffering on the ground by police. The couple had pieces of glass sticking from their bodies and they were covered in blood from their injuries!

A girl, half naked, ran into a gas station with pieces of glass sticking out of her and she was covered in blood. She passed out when she got inside the gas station store and they called a rescue vehicle to take her to the hospital. She died when she got there.

Several people were taken to the hospital from injuries from the powerful late night earthquakes, and half of them were half-naked men and women. Some of them were covered in blood with cuts all over them! People were running in the streets, crying for help through the night, being knocked around by the continuous aftershocks. One house caved in. The roof collapsed, killing three people!

When police arrive at the cracked open road, one cop said to another, "Jesus Christ, is the devil coming to get us? We have a fuckin' volcano or a violent earthquake in the middle of fuckin' 138! Even flashes of lightning coming out of the fuckin' ground!"

In Milton there were earthquakes, and the road cracked open near the Curry College campus. Police cars, rescue vehicles, and fire trucks were getting caught in the cracked open roads trying to get injured people to the hospital! Windows were blown through in dorm rooms on the Curry College campus and students were forced outside in the pouring rain. Some of them were bare-assed but most were luckily in jammies, and it was an orgy on campus because everyone was forced out of their dorms. The ground was rocking and rolling and moving! Then it stopped.

The damage from last night's earthquakes was severe! The police, fire, and rescue crews were coming out in all communities. Traffic coming up Routes 95, 93, 128, and 138 was at a standstill for hours. Traffic coming into Boston on 95 and 128 was ordered to take a detour or go back. Traffic from all routes going into Boston could not get through. Flights at Logan Airport were cancelled. With all these earthquakes and sonic booms, nothing was happening on top of the Blue Hills summit.

Traffic was jammed everywhere, being rerouted from last

night's earthquakes! The next morning the earthquakes and sonic booms continued to happen, causing more damage! The earthquakes continued all the next day into the evening, making usually level ground very unsteady!

A man was backing out of his driveway into the street during an earthquake. As he was riding up the street, the street cracked open like splitting a hotdog bun, swallowing his car. He managed to climb out of the crack in the street and go back to his house only to see that it had caved in. He ran to his house calling for his wife, "Hilda! Hilda! Hilda!" Then a gas line ruptured and the house caught fire.

Here comes Hilda, out of the house into her husband's arms. "Harry! Harry the end of the world is coming!" she cried. Then the house was blown into pieces! The couple started running for cover to avoid getting hit by debris. They saw their cat flying through the air on fire!

A bus had stopped to pick up people going into Boston on 138 when the earthquake struck. The bus went out of control from the ground shaking and hit a telephone pole! The bus driver went right through the windshield and landed in the road, dead, with his head split open! People on the bus went flying forward like bowling pins being knocked down.

A train was going into Boston on the way to the Canton station when the earth shook and the train derailed and flipped over. The ground cracked open and part of the train landed in the slit in the ground. Several passengers were hurt.

Several police, fire, and rescue crews from all communities nearby went to the damage in Canton and Milton neighborhoods and several homes had broken windows. The traffic on Route 128 going into Boston was at a standstill. The Mass. Pike was closed going into Boston.

People checking in to the Holiday Inn in Randolph said to the clerk, "Did you hear what happened in Canton? They had a bad earthquake and homes were destroyed! A train derailed and roads split open, swallowing cars!"

"Oh my God! Is that why all the sirens are sounding?! We didn't feel anything here!" said the Holiday Inn clerk.

The guests checked in and things were quiet for a while. About three hours later the same clerk at the Holiday Inn was reading the newspaper. Suddenly *boom!!* And the ground shook and the windows rattled. The newspaper fell out of the clerk's hands.

A girl came in the lobby with a suitcase and she said, "Was that an earthquake?"

"Matter of fact, it was! You're checking in," said the clerk.

"I just arrived at Logan Airport coming from Phoenix and it's been a mess out west with all those volcanoes erupting out there!" said the girl.

"Miss, we have a volcano threat right here in the Boston area. Blue Hills is only four miles away from here and New York and Block Island were blown off the map! We have volcanoes here just as bad as out west!" said the clerk.

"I heard!" said the girl. Then she got her keys and checked in. "Where do I find any nightlife around here?" asked the girl.

"We have one of the best dance clubs in all of New England right in back of this hotel in walking distance. The name of the club is Vincent's and they play Top 40 dance music. The place is nice inside, and no cover for women before 9:00 p.m.," said the clerk.

"Thank you," said the girl, and she went to her room. About an hour later the girl was in the shower washing her hair when she felt a vibration. Suddenly she felt the ground moving under her and she started screaming, and she was knocked out of the shower, crashing through the shower door onto the bathroom floor. The lights blinked on and off then everything went dark. She had to find her way to her clothes, get dressed, and get out of the room, going down a stairway in the dark to street level because fire alarms sounded.

"What happened?!" she said.

"We just had an earthquake! Stay put and don't go inside the hotel. Don't go walking around because there's no power because power lines are down!" said a Holiday Inn official.

Police were everywhere and the earthquakes continued on and off all evening, leaving everyone in the dark. Emergency vehicles had to be careful riding through cities and towns in the dark because of life-threatening earthquakes expanding cracks and sinkholes in the ground!

The mountain started rumbling and now the earthquakes were affecting Milton and Curry College right up to the Randolph area. The Blue Hills region was threatening a volcanic eruption.

The night was dark coming down 128 from Boston. There were lights in downtown Boston and on 128; neither was affected much by the earthquakes. But Route 93 South was in the dark and detoured off by police.

Later during the wee hours of the night around 4:00 a.m. rumblings started happening on the Curry College campus, waking up students. Then the rumbling turned into sonic booms, rattling windows. Another powerful aftershock broke windows in the dorm rooms and a couple of buildings collapsed. Milton Police were racing to earthquake calls from Curry College and were stopped short because the road on 138 cracked open. You could barely see the crack in the road, even with the bright head-lights on the police cars, what with the foggy mid-October night.

"Holy shit! What happened here?! We almost fell into the gates of hell!" a cop said to his partner. There was no way the police were getting into the Curry College Campus unless they went on foot because the road was not there anymore! The policemen got out of their cars and walked over to the sinkhole crack in the middle of the missing 138.

"Headquarters, this is Officer Ken Hopkins in Car #12. I am near the Curry College entrance with Officer Randy Kellmore my partner and there's three more police cars on the scene. We're trying to get into the campus, but there's no road. It split into from the earthquake. We almost fell into it!"

"Okay stay where you are and try to go in on foot. If necessary we'll send helicopters in there if people are hurt. Captain Poli Cappa, Milton Police Headquarters, over."

Helicopters flew over the Blue Hills area—Milton, Canton, Randolph, and Quincy—with military orders.

"May I have your attention; all residents must stay in their homes due to strong earthquakes, sinkholes, and no electricity! This is a life and death situation; there's live wires down and openings in the ground. This is an extreme emergency! Check local news reports. This is a warning from the National Guard." They were calling out the warnings all night on loudspeakers from helicopters flying over. Fire and rescue made it into the Curry College Campus and some kids were cut with glass and taken to hospitals, but no other serious injuries or death.

Screaming kids cried, "The end of the world is coming!" Some buildings were destroyed and homes and businesses were damaged in Milton and Canton. There were broken windows in homes in Quincy and Randolph. The Holiday Inn in Randolph suffered broken windows and downed power lines.

The next day at sunrise, people were watching the news on TV in the Boston area about the violent earthquakes.

Encore Boston Harbor Casino: "Good morning, we have breaking news on WBZ Channel 4 News in Boston. An 8.4 earthquake struck Canton and Milton neighborhoods, damaging fifty-four homes with everything from collapsed roofs to broken windows and chimneys. Roads were opening up and swallowing vehicles. At least two people have died. A bus struck a sinkhole and upon hitting a telephone pole, the bus driver was killed. Another man was found dead in his damaged home. Several people were injured from several strong aftershocks.

Those and openings in the ground knocked out power to several communities.

"The Curry College campus suffered severe damage with broken windows and damage to buildings and students were hurt. The 8.4 earthquake was centered directly under Blue Hills. According to Operation BJ a volcano could be brewing in Blue Hills, causing these earthquakes.

"The Massachusetts National Guard ordered people to stay put because of darkness and unsafe areas. Randolph and Quincy also had some damage and power outages. Portable tents will be set up on the Curry College campus for homeless people to go to temporarily.

"A meeting will be held at Gillette Stadium on Friday evening October 26, at 7:00 p.m. Shuttles and buses will leave from the Curry College campus to Gillette Stadium. If it rains or there's other bad weather the meeting will be moved to the TD Bank Garden on Sunday, October 28, at 3:00 p.m. The meeting will be held with NASA's Operation BJ about an evacuation if necessary. WBZ 4 Extreme News Report in Boston."

The next day an announcement came across the casino. "Ladies and gentlemen, all hotel rooms must vacate by noon today because of earthquake victims! Arthur Angell Aries, host manager." Hotels in downtown Boston had to house earthquake victims until the portable tent homes were set up, ready for possible evacuation.

The manager said to another casino host at Encore, "Did I hear right? I need to vacate all the hotel rooms because of a volcano? Where's this volcano!?" asked Arthur Angell Aries.

"Blue Hills!" said the host.

"You got to be kidding!" said Triple A!

There was a meeting planned at Gillette on Friday, October 26. People were lined up waiting for the shuttles and buses at

Curry College to go to the meeting, but they never came because of thunderstorms in Foxboro. The meeting was moved to Sunday afternoon at 3:00 p.m. at the TD Bank Garden in Boston.

"Good afternoon ladies and gentlemen, welcome to Boston, Massachusetts. My name is Edward Fay, the head volcanologist of NASA, and I have Brad Stevens with me—I'm sorry, Steven Brad, a head scientist from Yellowstone National Park. I don't mean to scare the public here in the Boston community but we have a super volcano warning for all of New England and New York. You are aware that Block Island and parts of New York City were blown off the map, and Mount Ascutney in Adamsville, Vermont erupted twice and the town was annihilated.

"Now there's a huge lava field sitting under Blue Hills ready to blow the mountain apart. The problem is: When? It comes and goes! I declared Block Island safe after lava appeared out of the ground, setting half the island on fire on Halloween night about a year ago. The lava had left the area and I said it was safe to return in the summer and then a hidden eruption caught our team by surprise. Almost four thousand people dead because the island was blown off the map.

"Then the lava went in the Hudson River, attacking New York City. Then it disappeared, but I held my ground that New York City was in danger and look what happened! The death toll is unknown! Volcanoes are unpredictable; you never know when they're going to erupt. I suggest everyone be prepared. All the bad earthquakes here are a sign that Blue Hills may erupt!

"I can't call for an evacuation even if I think this mountain is going to erupt because it might not, but until something happens you go back home until told otherwise by your local authority. All I'm saying is we have a super volcano warning, an end-of-the-world threat! The question is: Who's going to be next?! My machines read a dangerous level of lava making its way to the summit. Hopefully it will go back down, sometimes it may not.

That's all I have to say. The floor is open for questions," said Edward Fay.

"Ed, suppose this mountain erupts. What will happen?" said someone in the crowd.

"It's hard to say, it depends where the wind is blowing. Most of the time, the wind blows across Boston from the north. If that's the case Canton, Milton, and Route 95 South heading toward Providence, Rhode Island will get the asshole—I mean the ash flow! If the wind is blowing off the ocean then Boston and Cape Cod better watch out! If there is no wind the fallout will cover all of the Blue Hills region, including downtown Boston.

"If we get a major eruption like what happened with Block Island and New York City, everyone is in trouble! Look what happened in New York! Boston will disappear if we get an eruption like the one there. This mountain is small—it's classified as a hill—but it is a dormant volcano. Because of the large lava field underground it doesn't matter if it's a small hill or as high as Mount Everest; the mountain is going to blow apart if we have a super volcano and we are heading in that direction," said Edward Fay.

The NASA crew showed films on the giant scoreboard at the TD Bank Garden about all the erupting volcanoes across the United States. Edward Fay said, "We are Operation Blowjob. And we're here to protect the public."

Everyone got a good laugh at his speech. After the meeting, the buses and shuttles took everyone back to Curry College. Some residents had to stay there in portable tents until their homes were fixed. Roads and side streets were fixed and repaved and power lines were restored within a week. Homes that got damaged were fixed and the area recuperated. Most people in temporary housing were able to leave the tents and go home. The Curry College campus was repaired, except a couple of buildings had to be knocked down.

———————

November 2, 2024 the Boston Celtics were playing the Atlanta Hawks in a tie game, 115 to 115, with a minute and fifteen seconds left, and suddenly the ground shook and the lights blinked on and off. A packed crowd at the TD Bank Garden went from cheering because the Celtics was bringing the ball up the court to screaming from the building shaking! The game was stopped immediately and then the lights went out for good! The Garden officials had to escort the crowd out with flashlights.

People were traveling over the Tobin Bridge into downtown Boston and the bridge was swaying back and forth. The road was going up and down like waves in the water when downtown Boston went dark. It was pouring rain when the earthquake struck and drivers were hysterical, driving through Boston in the dark. The streetlights were out and all the lights went out in the city; all you could see was headlights in the pouring rain.

People were gambling at Encore when the earthquake struck. One person hit a jackpot for ten thousand dollars when suddenly, shaking rocking and rolling, and then the lights flickered and everything went dark. Mary Little stayed put at the machine she won on—she's not leaving until she gets her jackpot winnings! A host came over to her with a jackpot sign to put on the slot machine with several flashing lights, then darkness.

People were screaming and messages came on their cell phones, smart phones, personalized electronic devices: a 7.6 earthquake struck Boston. The manager Arthur Angell Aires tried to control the crowd with a loudspeaker. "May I have your attention please, we just had a 7.6 earthquake and the electricity is out in all of Boston. Anyone staying here at Encore please follow generator lighting to a safe area of the casino and wait for the shaking to stop. You must exit the casino to avoid flying debris."

Mary Little said, "I'm not going anywhere until I get my ten thousand dollars!"

"Well lady, you're going to have to wait until the power comes back on to get your money; that could take days or weeks!" said a casino host. She was given a free room and the casino said she would get her money to shut her the fuck up!

Around midnight everyone was able to get out of the TD Bank Garden with help from flashlights from arena officials and generator lights. Then they checked for damages and the game was allowed to finish under floodlights at 1:00 a.m. and the Celtics won 120 to 119.

Then an aftershock struck at 2:00 a.m. The earthquake struck downtown Boston again. Then at 3:02 a.m. a bridge collapsed in downtown. At 4:02 a.m. a series of tsunamis were going down the Charles River. At 5:02 a.m. it started raining again, then thunder and lightning. At 6:02 a.m. a train derailed going into Boston, crashing into a ditch in Canton. At 7:02 a.m. gas lines ruptured in downtown Boston. At 8:02 a.m. another aftershock struck downtown Boston. 9:02 a.m., military workers at the summit of Blue Hills heard rocks rolling underground. The mountain was vibrating but it all stopped a minute later. 10:02 a.m., power was restored in downtown Boston.

Traffic coming into Boston was at a standstill! 11:02 a.m. the rain clouds broke and the sky cleared over Blue Hills. At 12:02 p.m. a vision of the blessed Virgin Mary appeared on top of Blue Hills!

It was Saturday afternoon November 3, 2024. A huge crowd gathered to watch the vision. Several Curry College student families and friends had a bird's-eye view of the Virgin Mary, watching from the athletic fields on campus. The vision disappeared an hour later at 1:02 p.m. Then at 2:02 p.m. the sky clouded up again. At 3:02 p.m. it started raining. 4:02 p.m., there was a small eruption on top of Blue Hills!

"Oh my God, Blue Hills just erupted!" Curry College students were yelling! The blast was a fiery orange, then black smoke, then it stopped. Minutes later sirens were heard from police cars and fire trucks racing toward the mountain. No one was on the mountain when it erupted.

Military helicopters taking off from aircraft carriers parked in Boston Harbor flew to the mountain, taking pictures of the smoky summit before clouds covered it over. Police got several calls from residents: "Blue Hills just erupted!"

5:02 p.m. it started thundering and raining. The lightning started flashing at 6:02 p.m. At 7:02 p.m. there was a mild earthquake! At 8:02 p.m. the ground shook again and was vibrating, then stopped a minute later. At 9:02 p.m. the sky cleared and the stars and a halfmoon was out in the night sky.

Military helicopters made a return trip to the Blue Hills summit and nothing was happening. The time was 10:02 p.m. The military helicopters contacted Edward Fay of NASA about the eruption at 10:11 p.m.

"Good evening, this is the Massachusetts Air National Guard Chopper #6 calling for Mr. Edward Fay, head of NASA volcanology, over."

"Good evening Chopper #6, Mr. Edward Fay, over."

"Edward this is Lieutenant Davidson, Massachusetts National Guard. We had an eruption on top of Blue Hills about 4:00 p.m. this afternoon. Are you aware of it?"

"No, we were monitoring the West Coast. Mount Ascutney here and hotspots in New York City and the black smokers below where Block Island once stood all are still active, but I will check the monitors there. Give me a minute and I will pull it up and see what we have!

"I do see that there was a fiery gas eruption at Blue Hills in Milton, Massachusetts at 4:02 p.m. Magma levels have calmed down for now, but you may continue to get these eruptions on and off for a while. I don't see a major eruption happening but it could! You will continue to have earthquakes and sonic booms.

"If you start getting earthquakes like before chances are good that this mountain is going to have a volcanic eruption. The magma levels are slightly elevated, a little above average. The mountain may calm down for a while but with higher levels things could get worse."

"Edward, two things. One: Can this mountain blow apart? Two: What do I tell the public?"

"Lieutenant Davidson, to answer question number one: The mountain is dangerous and could blow apart because it's the same lava field forming the super volcano under New England that erupted Mount Ascutney in Vermont, Block Island, and New York City. If magma levels keep rising it could not only blow Blue Hills apart, but could have enough energy to blow the city of Boston off the map! Look what happened to Block Island! Gone!! Most of New York City was leveled!!!

"Your second question: There is nothing you can do until this mountain is a deadly threat, but you can tell the people that you have an active volcano in Blue Hills and it can be dangerous. People will have the option to evacuate voluntarily. But don't tell the people that this volcano is going to erupt because it's possible that it may not. If you tell the public that this volcano is going to erupt and it doesn't you will be in a lot of trouble! This mountain has had several steam eruptions in the past and has been known to be an earthquake prone area for years. There has been damage to property before in those areas. The thing that scares me from today's eruption is that it was a fiery gas explosion with blast debris; that shows that you have had a volcanic eruption! Edward Fay, head of NASA volcanology, over!"

"Thank you, sir. Lieutenant Davidson, Chopper #6 Massachusetts National Guard, over!"

The helicopters flew away from Blue Hills and went back to

Boston. 11:02 p.m. sonic booms were heard but they went away a minute later. At 12:02 a.m. a strong wind blew down the mountain flattening a few trees, and a passing car was blown into a ditch! Then a blue rotating cloud with flashes of lightning appeared on top of the Blue Hills summit at 1:02 a.m.; then it went away.

One hour later there was a big *boom!* and a huge shockwave. Everybody felt it as it roared down the mountain. People complained their ears were popping and they were suffering from migraine headaches and passing out! The fuckin' shockwave was over a minute later and people started feeling better. The time was 2:02 a.m.!

People were running in the streets wondering what the hell was going on! Curry students paraded on the campus and ran into the streets. Police and fire engines were called out all night long because of all the alienlike complaints. Then at 3:02 a.m. there was a bright flash of lightning and a big *bang!* Then it was snowing like a bastard! It stopped a minute later. Then horns and trumpets were heard—so loud in the middle of the fuckin' night!!!! A vision of the blessed Virgin Mary appeared at the summit of Blue Hills, almost as bright as the sun, drawing a big crowd out of their dorms and homes after 3:00 a.m. to view the mother of God. The vision appeared for an hour before finally fading away just after 4:00 a.m.

The horns and trumpets were heard again but not as loud, then it was over. The rest of the night was quiet. The weather was clear and seasonable for a few days, giving the Blue Hills region time to recuperate and the mountain was quiet, still being guarded by police and the military.

Sunday, November 11, 2024, Veterans Day, Canton and Milton were preparing for a big Veterans Day parade with floats and balloons. It was a sunny fifty-degree day. But before the parade a mass was heard at St. Mary's Catholic Church in Canton, Massachusetts.

"Good morning brothers and sisters and happy Veterans Day to our military. Welcome to St. Mary's church this morning. My name is Father Gary Goldfab. Today's sermon is about the end days of the Revelation. The bible says the end days will arrive around the year 2000 and last seven to twenty years, or twenty years after the twenty. That brings us to the year 2020, four years ago when the coronavirus killed millions across the globe and a golfer hit a hole in one when the ball skipped on the water three times, 265 feet up on the green, and rolled into the cup. It was the most incredible moment in sports history. It happened by an act of God.

"Early that morning a thunderstorm almost cancelled the golf match and after the rains the formation of the clouds looked like Jesus Christ coming down from heaven to save the world. Hundreds witnessed it and it was all over the news, it and the impossible golf match. If the vision or cloud formation was for real that day, it was telling the crowd 'this is what God can do and now I come to get my people before it's too late!'

"The last six weeks of 2020 was the time for the devil to come and finish the job! The coronavirus returned with a vengeance and it was the beginning of the devil's days. In 2021 we were told that a super volcano may reshape the six New England States and rise with the devil! DEATH!!!!

"A volcano erupted in Vermont, killing about three hundred people. We had warnings that Blue Hills might be next. The 'last' eruption was in 2011, a gas geyser, then we had another on November 3. This year a fiery volcanic eruption, and we're still in danger here in Blue Hills. In 2017 scientists found that a super volcano was brewing underneath Vermont, parts of Western Massachusetts, and New Hampshire. Scientists also said the West Coast was ready to break off and fall into the Pacific Ocean by 2025.

"In 2022 and 2023 more than eighty volcanoes erupted almost all at the same time and Washington State, Oregon, about three-fourths of Alaska, parts of northern California, and the northwest corner of Canada, were blown off the map! Most of those volcanoes are still active and Seattle, where I am from, is no longer there!

"Since the summer, the devil has been coming after us! A volcano blew Block Island, Rhode Island, off the map and two violent mega eruptions blew up New York City. About four thousand were killed when Block Island disappeared and the death toll is unknown in NYC!! The earthquakes and damage here and last week's eruption are signs that it's the beginning of the end.

"Before last week's eruption a vision of the Virgin Mary appeared at the top of Blue Hills, after several warnings at two minutes after every hour. Everybody was standing around watching as earthquakes and storms continued. People were still staying put! It's a sign: get out now while you have a chance! The vision came back after the Virgin's twenty-four-hour message ending with a thundersnow. Her final message telling the public to get out before it's too late!

"A week later we still have a packed church this morning. The Virgin Mary visions are an act of God telling everyone to leave before the devil comes to get his remains! After this sermon, I'm out of here before it all hits the fan! Father Gary Goldfab, thank you."

After the powerful sermon everyone left the church and went to the Veterans Day Parade in Canton. The priest just told everybody to get ready to leave before the devil comes! Fuck that! They were going to the parade!

The NASA volcano crew flew in from Vermont in a helicopter to monitor the volcano. Edward Fay called the mayor to hold a town meeting because this mountain was ready to blow at any time!

The meeting was held on the Curry College campus the day after the Veterans Day Parade. That went well, but the next day, Monday, November 12, 2024, the meeting was back to reality! The volcano crew was there with the military, and the mayors of Milton and Canton, and the dean of students at Curry College, Eddy Headheart.

"Good evening, welcome to the Curry College Eleanor Mayereoff Katz Gymnasium this evening. My name is Edward Fay, head of NASA volcanology along with Big Ed, the dean of students; Annie Kokeye, the mayor of Milton, Mass.; Carly Candy, the mayor of Canton, Mass.; and Steven Brad, the head scientist of Yellowstone National Park. We have a serious problem here in Blue Hills, a volcano threatening a possible eruption. The question is: when?

"We have had signs from earthquakes to a small eruption, but a major eruption is unpredictable! We saw the vision of the Lord, a sign that this volcano may be ready to erupt, and we must be prepared. You may leave the area voluntarily or you may stay; that's up to you! If this volcano erupts it's going to be bad! The problem is when! It may go off anytime or it might go dormant. We don't know! I can't evacuate a town because of a volcano threat when nothing more than an earthquake occurred!

"Until this volcano erupts we can't say 'get out now,' not while nothing happens. If you want to evacuate that's your choice! We don't know when this mountain is going to erupt but we do know that it's dangerous and it's a threat.

"Block Island and most of New York City were blown off the map from three underground volcanoes. Today remains a concern from the warnings in Blue Hills. Ladies and gentlemen, use your own judgement. The dean of students would like to have a word. Thank you," said Edward Fay.

"Good evening all students and Milton and Canton residents. My name is Eddy Headheart, the dean of students here at Curry

College. Starting tomorrow the Curry campus will be going to off-campus learning just like we did four years ago during the coronavirus pandemic, the same protocol! If you can, leave campus and go home; if not, there will be no classes or activities on campus. Do your work in your dorm rooms because this volcano threat is too dangerous for anyone to be roaming around. The libraries will be closed. The only building that will be open here on campus is the food hall. We had too much damage here because of earthquakes and the less students we have on campus the better it will be. We already had a volcanic eruption on Blue Hills."

"Thank you Eddy. My name is Annie Kokeye, the mayor of Milton, Massachusetts, the town where this Blue Hills volcano is located. Until the earthquakes start up again or a volcanic eruption I am not evacuating this town. Go and plan your day just like yesterday's Veterans Day parade; that went over well. However, you must find a way to get out of here; if we get anymore earthquakes or if this mountain blows you better start running! We are in danger but right now nothing is happening. If you need to evacuate and get out of here you may but I'm not going to have a massive evacuation! Anyone hiking: the mountain is out of bounds. The mayor of Canton would like to give her message."

"Thank you Annie. I have to disagree with the mayor of Milton because we have some serious damage from so many earthquakes, including roads opening up and more than forty homes damaged. Most of Canton left their homes after last week's eruption on Blue Hills but we still have residents here, and after repairs some are making their way back home. Let me tell you something: If this mountain blows it might be too late to do anything. I told everyone three weeks ago to get out and right now I will say it again! Get out if you want to live!!!!!!!!!" said Mayor Carly C. Candy.

"Thank you mayor. My name is Steven Brad, the head scientist of Yellowstone National Park. This mountain is dangerous and unpredictable! You don't know what it's going to do. You had an eruption and earthquakes here, but the good news is that you have a small mountain. There is a history of steam eruptions here, but now you've got a fiery eruption for the first time since the 1400s. Now you have a dangerous mountain.

"In Yellowstone we have steam eruptions and geysers every day and earthquakes like here, but we get bigger eruptions and some fiery explosions in hot springs or in mud holes. Then we get a series of earthquakes; then it slows down then picks up again in Yellowstone. It's everyday life out there, but you have a small area here and this mountain is at level eight and it could have a major eruption.

"The three volcanoes that erupted under New York City and Block Island reached the top level: ten! You have an eight here, a dangerous mountain. Mr. Edward Fay, head of NASA volcanology will finish this meeting."

"Thank you Steven. Like I said before, use your own judgement. The last report: magma levels are rebuilding, threatening a possible major eruption or a strong earthquake! Even if the mountain is quiet right now—there's nothing up there but a little steam coming out a small crater from last week's eruption—hear me out, you are in danger here!"

Then a strong earthquake happened, shaking the gym on the Curry College campus during Edward Fay's second speech. It caused a big panic and people started running for the exits just like in the movie *Dante's Peak*.

"Ladies and gentlemen, exit slowly to avoid serious injuries and make your way to the portable tents outside!" said Edward Fay.

Sirens were heard and police and fire trucks were everywhere! Ceiling tiles started falling in the gym and the lights flickered. The power went out and meeting officials and police officers used flashlights to see where they were going, getting people out of the gym safely. Light fixtures fell with wires hanging down and some people got hit in the head. Rescue crews arrived to remove the injured. Most people got out in time. The violent earthquake lasted a minute then stopped. People were stranded, prevented from going to their homes for the rest of the night. The NASA crew, riding the helicopter, went up to the summit on Blue Hills. Nothing was happening so the chopper flew to Boston.

The Boston Bruins were playing and they'd just scored a goal when the earthquake happened! The crowd was going crazy when the TD Bank Garden shook, rocking and rolling, the lights flickered then it went dark. People started screaming; then the generator lights came on and the earthquake stopped. The TD Bank Garden was evacuated.

At Tiffany's Restaurant in downtown Boston, people were eating and some were at the bar drinking. There are not many people in that restaurant on a Monday night. Unexpectedly the earthquake struck and people found themselves flying in the air with their dinners and drinks. Bottles flew off the shelves, smashing all over the place, and windows broke! Patrons were screaming in the restaurant.

"A bomb went off!!"

"No, it was an earthquake!" said the manager.

Traffic crossing on the Tobin Bridge coming into Boston was stopped at a tollbooth when the earthquake struck. The bridge vibrated and shook, swaying back and forth as people got out of their cars, running toward the tollbooth to get to safety, fearing the bridge was going to collapse. Then the earthquake stopped and one car at a time crossed the bridge. People went back to their cars one at a time to cross over. Then the bridge was closed for the rest of the night. There was no tsunami.

People walking downtown when the earthquake struck saw the buildings looked like they were ready to fall down, rocking back and forth and rising up and down. The city skyline went dark as screaming people went running for their lives! The earthquake was over a minute later and some city lights came back on and everything was normal. The electric companies were out all night restoring power from the earthquake.

The next day, the rude awakening. About 9:00 a.m. it was a normal cloudy, cold morning with people boarding trains and subways going to work, and people leaving their homes driving out on the highway. Until 9:11 a.m. that Tuesday, November 13, 2024!

Loud trumpets and horns were heard in the neighborhoods, bringing people out of their homes! Then *boom!* Mount Blue Hills erupted and ash and rocks were pouring down the mountain. People at a coffee shop at the bottom of the mountain had a bird's-eye view of the eruption.

"Oh my God! Blue Hills just erupted!" some lady cried.

A mushroom cloud appeared above the mountain and lightning bolts were coming out of the sides. It made a thunderous roar. People were running in the streets, screaming!

The people in the coffee shop ran out in the street to see the horror above, shouting, "Oh my God!"

A meeting was going on in the observatory of the Prudential Building when suddenly a *boom!* was heard and people rushed to look out the window. "Oh my God! A big explosion outside!" some man yelled.

"Jesus Christ! Blue Hills just erupted!"

Everybody in the room looked out the window and saw what looked like a nuclear explosion with lightning bolts flying out of it!

The phrase was all: "Oh my God!"

Announcements warned everyone: "May I have your attention please, everyone must evacuate the building to street level. Blue Hills had a volcanic eruption!" The Hancock Building and several high-rises got the same warning.

The subways closed and people had to take buses to get out of

Boston. All train services were cancelled and downtown Boston shut down by the end of the day. Shuttles had to take people home because the commuter trains were cancelled too.

Blue Hills was not done blowing its load! It erupted again just like earlier but this time it was tossing debris around. A man had just finished cleaning his roof and was watching the eruption, talking on his cell phone, when suddenly a fireball rock crashed through a window, setting his house on fire in seconds!

He started screaming and he dropped his cell phone. Another volcanic missile landed on his roof, setting off a big fire. He had to jump off his roof and he couldn't retrieve his cell phone because his whole house was ablaze! Then a third volcanic missile struck the house next door, setting it afire, then another one struck the roof and a lady ran out of her burning house in her housecoat.

Both homes burned to the ground in minutes! Then a *third* house caught fire when it burned down, the owner said, "We're at the end of the fuckin' world!"

Blue Hills blew apart and the fuckin' mountain split wide open! The noise was so loud it broke the windows in every home near the mountain from a whiplash shockwave; even breaking windows in skyscrapers in downtown Boston. The blast was loud enough to break your eardrums, sounding like loud trumpets and horns! Lava and molten rock missiles set the entire Blue Hills region on fire and countless homes burned to the ground!

Then came another eruption setting off a pyroclastic flow, lava pouring out of the mountain, into streets and neighborhoods. Fire trucks were set up on the Curry College campus, spraying water to protect the campus from burning down. People were running like bats out of hell as fast as they could through the campus to get away from the violent eruptions. The lava flow set neighborhoods on fire all the way to downtown Boston, and this fuckin' volcano was still blowing its load as it kept erupting! Routes 138, 128, and 93 were covered with molten rock. People running away from the eruption started choking on the ash coming down from the pyroclastic flow.

Blue Hills split in two with hot lava bubbling in the middle, shooting boulders of molten rock into the highways and residential neighborhoods, setting fires. Fire trucks from all communities came to fight the fires and planes flew over the mountain, dumping water on the pyroclastic flow to put a damper on this volcano.

The eruption spilled into the Charles River, cooling it down a little before it stuck downtown Boston. The lava flowed into the MIT campus, setting fires, and the Boston fire department had a mess to clean up! Some Boston neighborhoods were under attack. A fireball missile struck a school in Roxbury, setting it on fire, and nearby homes caught fire!

The Dorchester section of Boston got the worst of the Blue Hills attack. Most of Dorchester was covered in the pyroclastic flow after fire rock missiles struck apartment buildings, setting them afire.

People watched volcanic meteors falling in large numbers, striking buildings in the streets, setting Dorchester ablaze. People were lying in the streets, struck by the meteors or choking on the volcanic ash. Dorchester and some Boston neighborhoods were blackened by the pyroclastic flow and burning ash. People that didn't evacuate after the first evacuation in these Boston neighborhoods were likely dead. Dorchester was burning to the ground! More volcanic meteors flying from Blue Hills struck the Boston Gas Tank, bouncing off the LNT tank, but there were no explosions.

Military planes and helicopters flew over the busted-in-half Blue Hills, spraying water and foam to cool this fuckin' volcano down! The fires burned for days before the National Guard could move in, despite a major snowstorm; even *that* couldn't put all these fuckin' fires out!

Shockwaves from the eruptions blew out several windows in downtown buildings in Boston. The rest of the city and the north end survived when it was all over. The Curry College campus survived thanks to the fire department and military water-dropping help. But several windows were blown out in campus building and some buildings were damaged. The November 13 eruptions went on all day from morning until evening, leaving apocalyptic destruction and fire everywhere!

People watched the 6:00 p.m. news in Rhode Island at Chelo's Restaurant at the airport. "Good evening, we have breaking news on WJAR TV 10! A volcano erupted in the Boston area today leaving a trail of destruction. Blue Hills erupted several times today burning up Boston neighborhoods. Several explosions buried homes, businesses, and roads, closing several highways. Boston and several residential areas suffered broken windows and damaged homes. People who did not evacuate in time are feared dead! The eruptions were as bad as the Block Island volcano and the volcano eruptions in New York City. We will have updates through the evening about the Blue Hills volcano eruption. Mary Martha reporting on Newswatch 10!"

The next day: Wednesday, November 14, 2024. The entire Blue Hills region was covered in ash, airport foam, snow, and water. On top of that it was raining hard! All the lava rock hardened, covering Routes 138, 128, and I-93, trapping all traffic going into Boston. Ultimately, Route 95 North was spared from the ash. All routes in Canton and Milton towns were destroyed and new roads had to be built around the dried-up lava. Military earth mobiles came in to plow the ash and push it back up the mountain, but that plan didn't work. Then they tried using dynamite to blow up the hills of piled up lava in the streets and the result made matters worse! So, law enforcement and military had to go to Plan B and work around the dried-up lava.

While that was going on, the Boston Area was turned over to

the National Guard, police, and fire and rescue crews looking for the dead! Gigantic military dump trucks with huge rocks managed to crawl over dried-up lava to get to the blast site to fill it in. The volcano crew arrived to monitor any future eruptions and the mountain—what was left of it—was quiet. All Canton and Milton neighborhoods were either burned to the ground or covered in ash. Some roads with soft ash had it removed by bulldozers.

Everything was shifted to Dorchester and the National Guard went in there on foot. All the buildings were burned out, all the windows blown out, and dead people lay in ash and dried up lava. Bobcats, raccoons, foxes, seagulls, and crows were feeding on the dead! Also dead animals, cats, dogs, etcetera, lay in the ruins!

The area looked like it'd been through the Nagasaki and Hiroshima atomic bomb attacks from World War Two! Loose ash was shoveled away to remove some of the dead. Burned-out buildings started collapsing. Some of them were getting knocked down. Workers were breaking out broken glass and repairing windows in downtown Boston.

Only 11,989 windows had to be replaced in the John Hancock Building and a little over two million across the city! Damaged homes in Canton and Milton areas were knocked down. Looters inside were shot by police and National Guard troops, either killed or taken into custody!

The Curry College campus was the only place that survived. It only had broken windows and some buildings were damaged. Everyone there evacuated in time before the mega eruptions.

———————

Saturday December 1, 2024 the volcano crew held a meeting in a makeshift tent that could hold a lot of people. Military and law enforcement from both Canton and Milton and local Boston Police attended the meeting on the Curry College campus at 2:00 p.m.

"Good afternoon ladies and gentlemen; forget about today's high school football super bowls today at Gillette because we have a bigger issue here. Milton and Canton residents will not be celebrating Christmas at home this year because of the Blue Hills volcano eruptions blowing this area off the map! Dorchester is gone! The area burned to the ground and most of the buildings and streets were leveled! This volcano was a six; the highest level is an eight! Because Blue Hills was a small volcano Boston wasn't blown off the map, but the earthquakes and pyroclastic eruption blew out millions of windows and some buildings were damaged in downtown Boston. Bridges shook but they are okay.

"The city is closed until cleanup is done and that might not be until spring. Everyone here in this meeting staying in portable tents will have to find places to live because all of the Blue Hills region has been destroyed, including Quincy, Randolph, Avon, and some Boston neighborhoods. There is no transportation, no trains or subways going to these areas. The only way you can get out of here is one road leaving the Curry campus.

"Route 138 in Milton and going into Canton is buried in volcanic rock! If you live in Canton or Milton you're not going home; there's no roads going to your home if it's still there. If it is, you're going on foot! The volcano here is finally dead, there's nothing left of it!

"The magma is heading west toward the Green Mountains in Western Mass., then traveling north into Vermont where it started from. We are Operation Blowjob and we're leaving here for Great Barrington, Mass., our next threat, then we're going to Florida because they're getting blowjobs with geysers and sinkholes swallowing homes! The death toll from this volcano is unknown. Thirty-eight deaths have been confirmed but there's probably a lot more. Thank you," said Edward Fay, head of NASA volcanology.

CHAPTER FIFTEEN

BLOWJOBS IN FLORIDA

From mid-November and now in December of 2024, geysers, ground explosions and sinkholes have been a problem, mostly manhole covers and ground cave-ins due to heavy rain, but they're getting bigger like volcanic eruptions. Blast eruptions out in the ocean raise concerns because of all the volcanoes erupting all over the United States, and now we have these blowjobs happening in Florida.

NASA flew down from the Blue Hills region in Massachusetts to check out what was going on in Florida.

Sunday, December 9, 2024, Tampa, Florida, 9:00 a.m., stadium officials were getting ready for the Tampa Bay Buccaneers and the New England Patriots football game at the Bucs' stadium. The stadium officials just finished getting the field ready for the 1:00 p.m. game. Minutes later *baa boom!,* a big explosion in the middle of the field, leaving a crater about thirty feet deep. Dirt and rocks went flying everywhere!

Then water came up, flooding the hole and the field then flooded out to street level. About ten minutes later boats were making their way into Tampa Bay Port with Buccaneers fans cheering when a geyser exploded in the water under a bridge, tipping boats over. Everyone landed in the water! A few minutes later another geyser blew high in the sky, blowing dolphins out of the water. People had to swim back to the boats, turn them right side up, and make it back to shore. Some people clung on dolphins' fins and rode to safety.

A third geyser erupted in Tampa Bay near the port and boats were rocking back and forth and got water in them; two of them sank. Then manhole covers were blowing out in the streets in downtown Tampa, geysers bursting out of them. A car was coming down a city street when one of those manhole covers blew and struck the car, going through the windshield and killing a couple who just got married! They were on their way to the game. The game was cancelled because of the eruptions and floods.

Downtown Tampa was flooded from the geyser eruptions. Police, fire trucks, and rescue crews were racing to the downtown area and the seaport. Military helicopters flew above and saw the damage and flooding. People driving on Route 75 on their way to the game had bells, whistles, streamers, and Buccaneers signs, Some were riding on the freeway with motorcycles. Then a news report on the radio:

"Good morning, we have breaking news on WFLZ. Possible volcanoes are erupting in downtown Tampa at this time. A major eruption exploded right in the middle of the Tampa Bay Buccaneers stadium, flooding the building. Geysers erupted in Tampa Bay, sinking boats and flooding boating docks. Several manhole geysers exploded in downtown, striking buildings and a car. It is not known yet if anyone was killed or how much damage there was. Witnesses and stadium officials reported a volcanic-like eruption inside the stadium blowing out dirt, rocks, and water, flooding the stadium. If you're on your way to the game right now it has been cancelled! Lisa Peanut reporting on 93 WFLZ."

Traffic on I-75 was very disappointed about the news on the

radio and all the cars on the way to the game and tailgate parties had to turn around and go home. All getting off at the same exit, jamming up more traffic on and off exit ramps. All the Tampa ground eruptions and those out at sea stopped over a period of fifteen minutes.

The police called NASA at Cape Canaveral, and NASA in Florida transferred the message to Houston, and Houston contacted Edward Fay in Massachusetts to go to Florida to investigate the eruptions. The NASA helicopter landed in the evening outside the Buccaneers' stadium and went inside to the flooded crater and started hooking up equipment. The entire six-person crew, including Edward Fay, was there.

"Holy shit! What happened here?" Edward Fay said to a stadium official!

"We had just finished preparing the field, ready for today's game. Suddenly, we heard a loud noise and dirt and rocks flew all over the stadium. A big hole appeared in the middle of the football field and it filled up with water and flooded the stadium. Then I heard there were more eruptions in Tampa Bay, sinking boats, and more eruptions downtown. Nothing like this has happened here in Florida before. My name is James Buck, one of the stadium managers."

"Edward Fay, head of NASA volcanology in Houston. It's a pleasure to meet you. It sounds like you have a methane gas explosion, not a volcano because there are no volcanoes in Florida, but we will check it out. This is my crew: Linda Brew and Katrina House, eruption monitors; Nathan Rivers, he investigates volcanoes and activity; Paul Numbnutts looks for cracks and earthquake activity; and he's David Dunkin, volcano news media," said Edward Fay.

"Pleased to meet you James!" they said.

"We currently have a strong methane explosion here. Methane gas is found in volcanoes and causes them to erupt! But we do not have a volcano here. Florida and the East Coast have been getting record rainfall since the 2020 record-setting hurricane season. 2023 was another bad year for hurricanes and these storms stir up the methane gas in the Atlantic Ocean around the Bermuda Triangle, so it settles on the east coast of Florida and gets into the Florida water system and seeps underground. The state of Florida is built over an underground lake and that's where the methane gas settles. It does not have the open ocean to let it breathe so pressure builds in the ground. All it takes is a spark and you have a volcano-like explosion because rocks crash into one another in the flowing water in underground caves. That activity causes explosions and sinkholes here in Florida.

"The last four years volcanoes have been erupting all over the United States. Parts of New York City and part of the Boston area were blown off the map, joining Oregon, Washington State, parts of Alaska, and the northwest corner of Canada. On the West Coast even parts of northern California and islands were blowing up and the death toll still is unknown.

"Block Island of Rhode Island disappeared in the ocean, killing about four thousand people just this past summer. Finally Mount Ascutney in Vermont erupted a couple of times, killing about three hundred people. Now we have a super volcano warning threatening to blow New England off the map.

"Glacier Peak Volcano in Oregon was a super volcano when it erupted, killing about a million people. It reshaped the land and swallowed the lake below! Blue Hills in Boston blew half of Beantown off the map. Now we're getting reports that Yellowstone National Park is ready to erupt and if it does we might be saying bye-bye to the US!

"This is why we're here: to find out why these explosions are happening! We are Operation Blowjob and we investigate underground explosions and volcanic activity. Linda and Katrina, you ladies will be going to the Tampa Bay area and boating docks to investigate the erupting geysers in the water. You will be going there with the Florida National Guard and law enforcement. Nathan, Paul, David, and I will be going into downtown Tampa to find out what's going on there, followed by the military and Tampa Police.

"Mr. James Buck, we will be setting up a spudweb machine inside this hole to find out if we are in danger. All the volcano eruptions across the US raise concerns about what's happening here. I will find out what's happening soon," said Edward Fay.

Paul Numbnutts and Nathan Rivers hooked up the spudweb robot inside the Buccaneers Stadium crater. A few minutes later there was a report and it was a methane gas eruption.

"Mr. Buck, there's your answer. It was a rare methane gas explosion. Get everyone out of here because you may get more explosions! Methane gas is deadly!" said Edward Fay.

The NASA crew investigated the other geysers and it was all related to methane gas eruptions! The next day newspapers read: "Methane gas eruptions cause several explosions in Tampa, sinking boats and blowing up Buccaneers Stadium, cancelling the game with the New England Patriots. The game will be played tomorrow night in Foxboro, Mass. Three people have been killed by flying sewer drain covers striking cars."

Monday night football in Foxboro, Massachusetts during a snowstorm, Tampa Bay won 35 to 28. The next day, Tuesday December 11, 2024, back in Florida, work from hell on earth was keeping the NASA volcano busy.

11:02 p.m. a hole blasted through the floor in a mall in Pensacola, Florida and police and fire trucks arrived at the scene and saw a crater and mud splattered all over the walls. Rocks broke store window glass and the mall was flooded with fish flopping around on the floor!

"Jesus fuckin' Christ! Did we have a fuckin' volcano erupt in this mall?!" a cop said to a fireman.

Everyone was in shock! 12:02 a.m. on Wednesday, December 12, 2024, a security guard heard a crackling sound in a booth at an apartment complex in Jacksonville, Florida just before midnight. The booth he stayed in was connected to a gate to let cars in and out of the apartment complex. A car drove in at midnight and the gate opened and closed. The security guard looked at his watch and the time was 12:02 a.m. Then a sinkhole occurred!

The security booth collapsed into the sudden sinkhole! Dirt covered the collapsed security booth and the guard was killed! The sinkhole triggered an alarm and the police and fire department arrived. The officer and booth were buried!

1:02 a.m. a parking lot collapsed at the Tallahassee Police Station, swallowing about twenty cars. Police walking around in the station heard a *crash!* and alarms were going. Officers were going out to their cars when suddenly the ground gave way and all the cars fell in a big sinkhole!

Some cars caught fire and all the policemen ran out of the station and watch the horror. The fire department and rescue crews arrived and other police from different communities came to help.

"Something is happening here in Florida! We are sinking! There was a possible undersea volcano in Tampa and sinkholes are everywhere in Florida. The world's falling apart with all these volcanoes erupting lately." Officers were talking with one another watching their cars go bye-bye! The sinkhole filled up with water and all the police cars sank.

At 2:02 a.m. another sinkhole took out Route 95 from Jacksonville to Daytona Beach. Suddenly there was a blast and the highway disappeared. A tanker truck stopped just before the highway gave way and washed out into the ocean. The driver got out of the truck to direct traffic to turn back then his truck disappeared, washed away! The driver ran toward the traffic, stopping the cars. "The highway ahead is washed away; turn back!" he told other drivers.

3:02 a.m. a freak wave struck a hotel in Daytona Beach, breaking windows and setting off alarms. Hotel furniture was washed out into the street and their Christmas tree was washed away as well! The police and fire department arrived. A blast in the ocean triggered the freak wave.

A fishing boat was going out of a harbor at Cocoa Beach just before 4:00 a.m. during a thunderstorm. Two minutes later the boat sank and everyone aboard was in the water! The boat sank so fast—and in methane gas bubbles!—all the fishermen had to grab their lifejackets and jump in the water. The time was 4:02 a.m.

They were in shark infested waters, but dolphins were jumping around them. The victims called for a mayday; they needed to be rescued. Later a Coast Guard helicopter came out to rescue the eight people in the water in the heavy rain, thunder and lightning, and big waves; it was the perfect storm. They all survived, being protected by the circling, jumping dolphins.

Manhole geysers started erupting, blowing sewer drain covers in the streets, setting off alarms in downtown Orlando and hitting buildings and parked cars. The time was 5:02 a.m. Wednesday morning when Orlando was waking up! A sewer drain cover flying through the air struck an oncoming bus, going right through the windshield, just missing the bus driver. The bus ran over a rushing geyser and it flipped over on its side; the bus driver had to swim out of the gushing water to safety. Windows were smashed and cars damaged!

A custodian was cleaning in Disney World before the park opened when the ground burst open and water mud and rocks were coming out. It was another methane blast and the time was 6:02 a.m.. The custodian ran to get his supervisor and he said, "Roger! Roger! A volcano opened up in the ground outside!"

7:02 a.m. there was another blast in Epcot Center with dirt, rocks, and water spewing up like a geyser! Then another blast at

University Studios with rocks, dirt, and water, and the time was 8:02 a.m. for that one

Another ground eruption blast happened at Orlando International Airport on the runway, knocking a small plane in a ditch as it was ready to take off! People on the plane screamed, "AHH! A volcano is erupting!" The plane was back on track after the eruption and it took off on schedule. The blast was another methane blast. The volcano crew was monitoring all the explosions across Florida from Tampa and all of them were methane gas water explosions. The time of the airport blast was at 9:02 a.m.

A realtor was showing a house in Lakeland, Florida to a football coach for the Lakeland Horses. He said, "Are you Amy Tappin from Bruce Realtors?"

"Yes sir. Welcome to Lakeland. What's the Lakeland Horses? Are you a coach or player?" asked Amy.

"I'm a coach. The Horses is a semi-pro football team. By the way, my name is Scott Angell."

"Pleased to meet you. Come in and I'll show you the house. You have a two-car garage and a long driveway. The front door enters the living room and you have a dining room kitchen combination. Straight ahead are the sliding glass doors that go out to the pool and closed-in screen patio that keeps the alligators out. Left from the living room is the master bedroom with a small bath, and a door that goes out to the pool deck. Behind the kitchen you have a closet and laundry with a door going into the garage, and you have two more bedrooms and a bath. Here's the lease, just sign here and you can start moving in," said Amy the realtor.

"Amy, what's that cracking noise I hear in this house?" asked Scott.

"It might be the tree branches hitting the roof because it's windy outside and a storm is coming."

"Okay, I have to go to a football game here in town. The Horses are playing in the semi-pro Super Bowl against the Leeham Armadillos."

"Good luck Scott, I hope you guys win!" said Amy, and the realtor left. Scott got in his car and drove off just before 10:00 a.m.

While he was pulling out of his driveway he looked at the house and he said to himself, "Tree branches hitting the roof; there's no trees near my house." Then he drove off. A few minutes after he left the house it collapsed in a sinkhole; the time was 10:02 a.m.

People were going to the beach in Miami and they saw a blast out in the water at 11:02 a.m. The geyser-like eruption lasted about a minute.

There were so many explosions the volcano crew had to go out separately all over Florida to find out why these eruptions were happening. An hour later an explosion at the Magic Kingdom blew Mickey Mouse off of the ground! Dear old Mickey flew high into the sky and landed on the ground, smashing into a million pieces! The time was 12:02 p.m. during that blast! The kids started crying because Mickey Mouse was blown to pieces!

1:02 p.m., another blast at Fort Myers Beach. A big hole blasted through the sand. Dirt, rocks, water, and a dead shark blew out of the hole, leaving a crater in the middle of the beach. The dead shark landed on someone's tent and everyone ran off the beach like bats out of hell!

2:02 p.m., a carnival was going on near Disney World and there was a big explosion in the ground like a fuckin' volcano! "Ladies and gentlemen, boys and girls, welcome to the Osceola Grounds Carnival!" Then *boom!* People, rides, and animals went flying in the air and a few people died from injuries from debris crashing on them!

3:02 p.m. there was another blast inside a Miami hotel! People went flying! The hotel floor exploded like a volcano with rocks, sand, mud, and seawater killing a few people.

Another blast happened an hour later in Miami when a main street blew open on a busy highway, blowing cars off the road in a giant geyser. These methane gas eruptions were getting worse and worse! This blast happened at 4:02 p.m.

The man that bought the house in Lakeland arrived home and he saw police cars surrounded the area. He saw a big hole in the ground and his house was gone! The man cried, "Oh my GOD! My house is gone; I just bought this house this morning! What happened here officers, did we have a volcanic eruption?!"

"I don't know mister but there have been reports of several sinkholes and earthquakes across Florida since yesterday," said the police.

A church blew apart and disappeared from another blast sinkhole in West Palm Beach and the time was 5:02 p.m. Viewers were shocked and ran for cover!

Another blast in downtown Orlando blew a hole in the street and dirt, rocks, mud, and dead fish flew out from the blast, breaking windows in nearby buildings. The blast happened at 6:02 p.m.

The devil from underground continued to haunt Florida at two minutes after every hour for twenty-four hours with its blowjobs. The danger was not over.

Coral Gables, Florida is the rich section near Miami. At exactly 7:02 p.m. an explosion blew up an apartment complex, killing about ten people. People were eating dinner and some were taking a dip in the pool then *boom!* people and debris were flying through the air and everything went dark! Police were everywhere and news reporters couldn't get ahold of the disaster from all the blowjobs happening in Florida! The blast was like a volcano—another methane attack!

A cruise ship was coming into Miami's harbor when suddenly there was a big blast out in the water and the ship rocked back and forth, nearly flipping over. The blast, a yellow geyser, blew high into the night sky, sending fifteen-foot waves to shore and several people on the cruise ship were hurt. The time of the blast was at 8:02 p.m.

A Christmas party was going on at Boardwalk Park near Fort Lauderdale Beach. It was a nice night and fireworks were going off. People were enjoying the good times and watching the news on TV at the same time Florida was getting attacked! Then a lightning bolt struck the water and it triggered another mega methane gas explosion! It was a blue color; then came a bright yellow flash then a loud *bang!* The explosion was like a volcano going off, sending a fifteen-foot wave toward the beach! The blast happened at 9:02 p.m. Thousands of people attending the big party ran like bats out of hell, trampling over others to get away from the water. The boardwalk was washed away!

Another blast ruined a Christmas party in Key West, where a methane eruption blew an island with a big Christmas tree off the map, sending big waves toward shore and people running for their lives! The time of the blast was 10:02 p.m.

At 11:02 p.m. the whole state of Florida felt a mild earthquake! The lights blinked on and off and back on; then it was over! People at a Christmas party in downtown Tampa watched the eleven o'clock news on TV.

"Good evening, we have breaking news on WFLZ TV Channel 9. There were several volcanic-like eruptions and geysers going off across all of Florida since yesterday afternoon. Here in Tampa, Florida they blew up Buccaneers Stadium, cancelling their game with the New England Patriots. The game was moved to Foxboro and Tampa Bay won.

"Several more geysers erupted in Tampa Bay sinking boats, and geysers blew out sewer drains in downtown Tampa where three people died from flying debris. At two minutes after every hour there's been a volcanic-like blast in different locations, starting at a Pensacola mall and working all the way to Key West.

"There were several explosions in Miami and hundreds of people are feared dead! In Coral Gables an apartment complex was blown up, killing at least ten people. Many more volcanic-like eruptions took place across all of Florida.

"We have more breaking news! We just had an earthquake at 11:02 p.m.; it's not known if there was any damage. The NASA volcano crew from Houston is here investigating possible volcanic eruptions because they are happening all over the world. Nothing like these explosions across Florida has ever happened before, and for the explosions to happen at two minutes after the hour for twenty-four hours raises concerns that it could be terrorism, especially since Christmas is coming!

"According to NASA all thirty-plus eruptions and geysers were related to methane gas explosions, not a volcano. Since each happened at two minutes after every hour and was followed by an earthquake, NASA, law enforcement, and the National Guard will continue to investigate if Florida is being attacked. Mary Martha, WFLZ TV 9 News."

People living in Florida were in a panic, fearing the end of the world was coming! When the earthquake rattled Tampa for a minute people started leaving the party and went home.

The next day was Tuesday, December 13, and the NASA crew had to split up to find out why so many explosions were happening. A few days later the crew got together, gathering up information. It was all the same: methane gas eruptions and geysers.

Saturday December 17, 2024, a meeting was held at the Orlando Arena at 2:00 p.m. NASA was there. So were the Florida State Police and sheriffs and the National Guard, fire and rescue crews and law enforcement, doctors and lawyers.

"Good afternoon ladies and gentlemen. Welcome to the Orlando Arena and happy holidays to everyone! My name is Edward Fay, the head volcanologist of NASA in Houston, Texas.

My five-man crew here—I should say five men and women—Linda Brew, Katrina House, Paul Numbnutts, Nathan Rivers and David Dunkin. Our crew is called, Operation Blowjob! We are called that name because we monitor all volcanoes across the United States on land and sea. We monitor all blast sites coming from the ground and seafloor. We know where all volcanoes are located and when they are going to go off!

"In the last week and a half we had thirty-seven methane gas explosions from Pensacola, Florida all the way to Key West. They were all methane gas ground blasts; eruptions, explosions, geysers, or blowjobs, whatever you call it! Any blast that comes out of the ground our team calls them blowjobs!

"We have an issue here in Florida and it's a methane problem. Methane gas does come from volcanoes. However, you do not have volcanoes here in Florida. Methane gas comes from pressure from underground that caused explosions and sinkholes. It's been going on for years here and I think why there's been so many in a short period of a time; there's so much pressure in the ground from all the volcanoes erupting on the East and West Coast!

"In the last five years there have been a lot of storms in the Bermuda Triangle stirring up all the methane gas from the bottom of the ocean and pushing it under Florida. It seeps into the freshwater lakes and caves beneath the state and settles there, creating the bubbling substance that causes sinkholes.

"Florida is the fuckin' sinkhole capitol of the world! Methane gas deposits live here in Florida. Once in a while there's a blast or a geyser. They have happened here before, but what alarms me is the blowjobs all over the state—all this, caused by too much ground pressure! These eruptions have killed 447 people in the last two weeks and that's scary!

"The other thing, that they seem to occur at two minutes after every hour, raises concerns that maybe terrorism is going on here. We don't know but something strange is going on and we have to live with it until we find who is attacking Florida!

"Some blasts erupted like volcanoes and some were water geysers sinking boats and some were sinkholes, but none of them appeared to be a volcanic eruption because there was no lava or measurable magma levels. It is not impossible that a volcano could be brewing underground, but according to our records there is no volcano anywhere in Florida.

"About the terrorist threat, the National Guard and law enforcement have not found any terrorism across Florida. Having disasters regularly at two minutes after every hour is the reason why there is a big panic going on. All transportation is stopped coming into Florida because of the explosions, but going out is okay. There is no need to evacuate, but if things get really bad you have to use your own judgment.

"The explosions have been quiet since December 13. Our monitoring equipment has not been getting any activity but we will be here for at least another week in case action picks up. The two minutes after every hour thing happened on the West Coast when a series of volcanoes erupted in Alaska, one at a time for twenty-four hours. Visions of the Virgin Mary appeared and I believe it's an act of God. That could be the case here too. There was a report of a Virgin Mary vision in Tampa last week; someone spotted the vision driving on the highway and it was reported on the news.

"Before we open the floor for questions, the worst explosions occurred in Miami where a lot of people died. Fort Lauderdale had a bad explosion. Tampa got hit hard! There were eruptions here in Orlando, a few of them. Micky Mouse got his fuckin' head blown off and he was blasted into the air! Tampa Bay Buccaneers stadium had a big hole in their football field. The floor is now open for questions," said Edward Fay.

"Sir, I have a question about the explosions at two minutes

after every hour and the vision of the Virgin Mary. I'm a pastor at Grandview Baptist Church. And you cannot see the Lord; it's an act from the devil!"

"Sir, if you believe that, that's fine. No one knows for sure but it does mean some kind of a warning," said Edward Fay.

"Edward, some of these eruptions like the one in Tampa Bay stadium were like a volcano, blowing rocks dirt, mud, dead fish and seawater. How can that not be a volcano from underground?" asked someone in the crowd.

"I just told you earlier in the meeting: because there was no lava or a magma chamber. No doubt it was as dangerous as a volcano but it's not a volcano, it was a methane gas explosion."

"Edward, I have a second question. How come these eruptions killed so many people if it's not a volcano?"

"I just gave you the answer why—because there's no fire—in the first question," he said.

After the meeting, the National Guard went to the damaged areas, staying until all the craters and sinkholes were fixed. Craters on beaches were getting fixed and some homes had to be destroyed from sinkhole and explosion damage. The dead were laid to rest. Newspaper headlines read: "Methane Explosions in Several Locations Were Not Erupting Volcanoes According to NASA."

People making arrangements to come into Florida for Christmas were denied because all flights were cancelled. Flights and transportation were still okay to leave Florida. NASA went to all the blast sites to monitor possible activity but everything was quiet. Ports coming into Florida were closed but boats and ships were okay to leave Florida.

The homeless and apartment buildings that were destroyed were placed on cruise ships. The NASA volcano crew went to a military barracks in Orlando to set up equipment, waiting for something to happen. Nothing did. The volcano crew talked about all the volcanoes that erupted in the US. Before leaving Florida they were getting ready for their next destination.

"Okay everyone, before we go back to our hotel, go in the pool, and have our Christmas party we have been getting updates on high magma levels in Yellowstone National Park, where we will be going next. Next thing: let's set up our data gathering for what's going on in Yellowstone and the state of Utah. Nice meeting you Florida, hope there are no more blowjobs here," said Edward Fay.

Then the NASA crew left Orlando military barracks for Yellowstone National Park. Later there were three more eruptions in Miami, which all stopped, but the sinkholes and disappearing homes continued across Florida!

CHAPTER SIXTEEN

GROUND OF THE DEVIL: THE GATES FROM HELL

The NASA volcano crew arrived by helicopter at a military base in Yellowstone National Park. Scientists met the crew when the chopper landed on Christmas week.

"Welcome, Operation Blowjob, to Fort Yellowstone military base. You remember me from Blue Hills in Boston; Steven Brad, the head scientist here in Yellowstone. Come inside the barracks where you will be staying while working in Yellowstone National Park. Before we go out on a tour we will have a brief meeting about what's going on here. Dinner will follow at the main lodge with a big fireplace! It's eight degrees out here and it's windy and very cold. Check in and we'll all meet in front of the lodge fireplace at 4:30 p.m." Then Steven Brad walked away.

"Operation Blowjob! What a name for the fine crew you have here. My name is Michael Montana, the hotel manager of the Met Café Lodge. You will be staying in luxury rooms with two queen beds, wall-to-wall carpeting with a fifty-inch flat-screen TV, and a warm gas fireplace. You also get bureau tables, fancy lamps, a bath with a Jacuzzi, and a nice view of the airport. You can watch airplanes and helicopters landing and taking off all day! It gets kind of noisy once in a while when the jets get going. It's not that bad but we are staying on a military air base and you will hear them!

"I will hand out the keys to your rooms. There's plenty of room to set up your equipment and be here for your meeting at four thirty. In the morning we have a full continental breakfast before you go out to work, meetings, tours, etcetera. My name is Michael Montana and welcome to Yellowstone National Park."

"My name is Mr. Edward Fay, the head volcanologist of NASA from Houston. And this is my crew of five: Linda Brew, Katrina House, Nathan Rivers, Paul Numbnutts, and David Dunkin."

"Pleased to meet you, Michael," said the crew. Edward Fay and David Dunkin stayed in one room and Katrina House and Linda Brew stayed in a room across the hall from them. Paul Numbnutts and Nathan Rivers stayed in another room next to the others, setting up monitoring equipment, complete with computers and TV screens, getting data on the Yellowstone super volcano caldera.

Nathan Rivers said to Edward Fay on the way to the meeting, "Ed, this volcano is ready to erupt and I fuckin' hope it doesn't happen while we're here!"

"I saw it on the monitors in my room too! We'll find out what's going on at the meeting."

———————

4:30 p.m. meeting: "Good afternoon...er...twilight! Welcome Operation Blowjob from Houston, Texas to the Fort Yellowstone Met Café Lodge military meeting about the latest updates on the Yellowstone super volcano. My name is Vincent Victoria Volcano, the head volcanologist in Yellowstone National Park. It's not a volcano it's my real name; just call me Triple V."

"Pleased to meet you, Vincent. My name is Edward Fay, the head volcanologist of NASA, Houston. This is my crew. My roommate, David Dunkin, is my earthquake data news reporter. Nathan Rivers and Paul Numbnutts are volcano monitoring workers, using spudweb robots that go inside volcanoes, monitor earthquakes, and tell when volcanoes are ready to erupt. And the ladies: Linda Brew and Katrina House; they monitor oncoming trouble, reading monitoring screens and computers. We have been all over the United States working with over two hundred erupting volcanoes and ground geysers. We're coming from Tampa, Florida working with methane gas explosions there."

"Pleased to meet you and Merry Christmas!" said Edward Fay and the crew.

"Yellowstone is a super volcano ready to blow at any time! We have been getting warnings for years, though the last time this super volcano really erupted was in 1350 BC. However, we had a small eruption on January 29, 2014; it was nothing major. The only thing saving Yellowstone is that we have forty-three erupting geysers and mud pools, giving the caldera breathing room.

"The caldera under the lake is fifty-nine miles wide. It looks like a woman's vagina with a gigantic clit! Oh! I'm sorry I forgot you have women here, excuse my French! The caldera was thirty-five to forty-five miles wide and now it's fifty-nine miles wide. The magma levels are barely a few feet underground and are expanding. Dig a hole about three feet deep and you can cook a pig in twelve hours. If you dig eleven feet you will strike moving volcanic bedrock," said Triple V.

"Vincent, I was looking at my monitor in my room and it looks like the lava chamber is just below ground level. That's a lot of molten rock below," said Nathan Rivers.

"I see that. It's much higher than normal and the geysers are getting pretty active. Some wildlife is getting hurt," said Triple V.

"Vincent, we have spudweb machines that will walk right into the volcano and we also have spider leg robots. They go into the crater, take pictures, and monitor activity," said Edward Fay.

"We use drones because the hot springs and geyser eruptions will melt the equipment you have. Animals diving into these hot springs disappear and the acid eats them away like a pack of piranhas! What I need you people to do is keep up with updates and warnings while we do the evacuations and closing."

"Vincent, if Yellowstone erupts, how bad would it affect the United States?" asked Katrina House.

"Three-quarters of the United States would be blown off the map! The West Coast would fall into the ocean and the fallout would choke the rest of the country in ash and block out the sun for about three years. We'd be living in a nuclear winter; the ash could cover the globe and famine would kill billions of people if that happens. There'd be no vegetation, water would be contaminated, and food would possibly not exist here in the US. A lot of people would die, like how the dinosaurs were killed more than sixty-five million years ago. We hope that doesn't happen but we are under a super volcano warning right now!

"Dinner and drinks will be coming out soon so just relax in front of the warm fire and tomorrow we will have a helicopter tour then a ground tour through Yellowstone National Park. Enjoy your dinner," said Triple V, Vincent Victoria Volcano.

Dinnertime, and there was steak, chicken, lobster, crabs, oven-baked potatoes, salad, string beans, red and white wine, beer, and Jack Daniels whiskey. Then the crew watched movies and played cards in front of the fireplace, then bedtime.

The next day they got up for breakfast. Muffins, pancakes, eggs, sausages, hash browns, hash pot, orange juice, and coffee. Then the crew went on a helicopter tour.

The military chopper lifted off and Triple V spoke. "Welcome aboard US National Guard Chopper #1350. Ladies and gentlemen, look out the left of the chopper and there's Old Faithful blowing her load right now! Now we are flying over the Rocky Mountains north toward Wyoming with a shitload of snow on the mountaintops! We will be flying into the mountain range between Wyoming, Idaho, and Montana looking for possible volcanic activity!"

"Now we're flying over Yellowstone Lake in Wyoming, now the Grand Canyon of Yellowstone where we have some earthquake activity, but no blowjobs here! Look to the right and there's Yellowstone Falls. Now back in Yellowstone National Park take a look below at the Steamboat Geyser. Finally, we're flying over the Upper Geyser Basin; you can see bears below looking to go for a hot dip!

"One more flyover before we close our military air tour. Look out the right of the chopper and you can see the Morning Glory Pool hot springs and a group of deer, birds, and zebras attempting to take a drink. It looks inviting but the water in the pool is 636 degrees. All the animals are standing around waiting for the first one to screw up and melt away!

"There's Old Faithful again, and that's the end of our tour. The helicopter will land at the Fort Yellowstone landing strip and you will board a bus to go through the park and visit all our little blowjobs and mud pots and see all the wildlife here at Yellowstone. Later we'll meet at the lodge before dinner, before we go to Plan B. Thank you very much and Merry Christmas!" said Vincent Victoria Volcano.

The helicopter landed and the NASA crew went on the ground tour through Yellowstone National Park. They boarded the bus from the helicopter. "Welcome, Operation Blowjob, aboard Met Military Tours Bus #1. My name is General Michael Hypperrenoldslaughiapindania, your tour guide through the park.

"As we leave the base we enter the wildlife zone. As we ride out of the base you can see wild bison walking through the snow then we will be going to Yellowstone Lake to monitor earthquake and lava flow zones. Look to the right and you can see bison, buffalo, and thousands of Canadian geese circling around the Grand

Geyser hot spring. Look to the left and you'll see the boardwalk where people walk through the park taking pictures of all the animals, mud holes, and geysers. Look far to the right and you can see bears! Grizzly bears! Look to the left and right and you see mud holes and bubbling hot springs with Christmas trees decorated with lights and cardinals flying in and out of the branches.

"We're now going up a hill and if you look to the left there's a frozen pond with bald eagles flying around; there's a lot of them out there. Look to the left now and you'll see more bison and a couple of bears; then straight ahead is Yellowstone Lake. Look to the right and you can see deer in the valley and moose on the hill. Downhill we get into the volcanic section of the park. If you look over the lake you'll see the Rocky Mountains all covered in snow. All these mountains and the lake are all part of the Yellowstone Caldera. Now we are going to see some mini volcanoes, spitting geysers. Look to the left and that's the Grand Prismatic Spring. We can get out here and take pictures.

"Don't get too close to it because it will burn you until you melt. This geyser has violent eruptions so keep your distance. We have fifteen minutes to view the geysers and mud holes. Watch your step or you will be a goner. We have wild turkeys and coyotes here.

"Here we have Mammoth Hot Springs and baboons swimming in them. Keep away. There is a snack bar and fast food restaurant to the right called the Nook Lodge. We have a one-hour stop here for you to get something to eat and take pictures of the mini volcanoes.

"Welcome aboard after getting your bellies filled. Next we will be visiting the Grand Canyon of Yellowstone and Yellowstone Falls. Be aware of mountain lions, black and grey wolves, and snow leopards. We will be here for thirty minutes, enjoy and keep your distance from wild animals. We have grizzly bears here too!

"Next we have the Mud Volcano Trail and Old Faithful as we're riding through. We can't get out here because this area is very active lately with a lot of leaking hot springs and dangerous bubbling mud holes. People walking around in this area will fall into the gates of hell. Eleven people and thousands of animals died here last week!"

Then the ground shook so violently it was rocking side to side and Old Faithful was really blowing its load, spraying hundreds of feet into the air, trapping a flying hawk. The bus felt like it was going to fall over into the mud holes and everyone on the tour was screaming.

The tour guide continued, "Jesus Christ! Did you feel that?! We need to get the hell out of here fast! Our next stop is the Steamboat Geyser with Christmas trees lit up around it. Let's get out here for about fifteen minutes to take pictures, get some snacks and have a quick pee break, then get back on the bus to continue our tour."

"I have to go for a wicked shit!" said Nathan Rivers.

"Me too!" said Katrina House.

Afterward the tour guide continued, "Next we have the Upper Geyser Basin. A brief stop here. We have plenty of beautiful lit Christmas trees here around the squirting geysers. Next we have the Morning Glory Pool hot springs, mud holes, and mini volcanoes. Here we will be getting dinner at the Morning Glory all-day breakfast buffet. We will be here for an hour and a half and there's a Christmas bazaar and festival. It looks like a summer picnic but the temperature is nineteen below zero so bundle up!

"Enjoy because there's a lot to see. Warm up near the hot springs and sing Christmas carols with the crowd in the freezing cold. Our tour ends here," said Michael Hypperrenoldslaughi-apindania, the tour guide.

CHAPTER SEVENTEEN

GROUND OF THE DEVIL: THE GATES FROM HELL PART TWO

The tour was over and the crew went back to the Fort Yellow-stone Met Cafe' Hotel to monitor the caldera at Yellowstone National Park. "We just had a 7.6 earthquake today at the Volcano National Trail and Old Faithful. It was the biggest earthquake since the last time Yellowstone erupted! That's not good news; that's why we're here. The magma chamber is higher than it has ever been and while I'm not surprised that Yellowstone did not go off yet, I kid you not, I think it's going to blow very soon! All of us could have died on that bus if we fell into those bubbling mud pits; it would have been all over," said Edward Fay to the crew.

Later he had a meeting with Triple V showing him the monitors. "Vincent, this looks bad. The lava bed is ready to take over Yellowstone Lake; it has broken through. Methane gas levels are high. We're getting these small earthquakes every day at Old Faithful and the geysers are getting out of control, and you're telling me that we don't have good equipment. We better get our spudwebs and spider legs and get them into the lake, and plant one or two on the most active area. Our machines will give you a good idea when Yellowstone is expected to blow! I will get my crew to install them first thing in the morning. Today is December twenty-third and I don't want to be burning in hell for Christmas!" said Edward Fay.

With the first warning that Yellowstone was about to erupt, several buses, snowmobiles, trains and air travel sent evacuees to the Rocky Mountains military bunkers. They bunkers held thousands of people and were called, "The Denver Nuclear Fallout Shelter."

The next day was the day before Christmas and there was a big snowstorm. After breakfast the crew went out in snowmobiles to a waiting helicopter to bring the spudweb and spider leg machines. They went out by the lake to bolt them down then went to Old Faithful with Vincent Victoria Volcano.

"Vincent, this is how spudweb works. It's the same machine used on the movie *Dante's Peak*. This is a spider legs robot and it will walk along the boardwalk, getting pictures and data. It has not gone for its walk yet and it's already sending data and taking pictures. This machine may stay here for hours then when it's done it will walk to another area, and if it walks itself into trouble falling into one of these mud holes or in water it will still do its job. This machine can withstand temperatures up to three thousand degrees.

"We went through this at our meeting and now you will see how it works. Its yellow lights are flashing, that means the spider legs robot is retrieving data and when it's done it will walk to another area. If you look to the left hand corner on the screen the machine is telling you when this volcano is ready to erupt, and it's telling us right now that Yellowstone's ready to erupt within three to five days. You need to give Yellowstone National Park an evacuation plan because the time for a major eruption is less than a week away!

"NASA volcanology is not a Mickey Mouse company. We're the best in the world and you better take us seriously because these machines don't lie; they cost fifty thousand bucks apiece and every time the red lights came on volcanoes were erupting. Look at spider legs go, walking through twenty-five inches of snow with no problem, and it will move to another hot area, taking pictures and gathering data.

"These are the same robots NASA uses on Mars. We know what we're doing, that's why we're here. Your drones will help but they're not going to give you exact data like these machines. Spider legs has stopped and the light went off. As soon as Old Faithful erupts it will trigger a mild earthquake, and the yellow lights will start flashing again and it will start getting more data," said Edward Fay.

"Ed, suppose the red lights comes on?" asked Triple V.

"Say your prayers for the resurrection because you have thirty minutes or less to get out or you will be going to hell. The machine will give you a warning an hour before the red light comes on through a talk box."

"Ed, what if the yellow lights and green lights are flashing?" asked Triple V.

"The green is a warning that the magma level is rising and starts before an earthquake happens. There's your answer! Old Faithful is erupting! You have less than five days to close this park and get the fuck out before it's too late! Don't hang around because spud-web is predicting a major eruption!" said Edward Fay.

After several questions, the NASA crew flew back to the hotel and loaded the equipment from their rooms and flew back to Vermont.

"Edward, what are you doing with the spider machines?" asked Triple V.

"Leave them where they are because we need to get data before danger happens. Close the park and get out!"

Police and the National Guard started evacuating Yellowstone National Park and closing it down. People were incredibly still in the park, viewing the animals and the geysers in a snowstorm! Police and park rangers were driving around in snowmobiles, calling on loudspeakers to evacuate the park.

"Ladies and gentlemen, please evacuate the park! Yellowstone is ready to erupt! Thank you and Merry Christmas!"

People listened and the park was a ghost town for miles. By 6:00 p.m. Christmas Eve, earthquakes started happening and the ground was opening up and swallowing animals! The animals had to fend for themselves. Fires started coming out of the cracks, melting the snow, which flowed into a hot spring pool. Then explosions started happening. Residents that lived near the park started feeling some strong earthquakes and got some surprises on top of that, beginning on Christmas Day.

1350 Lennard Drive in Utah, a family was coming over for dinner and the ground shook then stopped. They greeted, "Merry Christmas! Was that an earthquake?"

"It sure felt like it Mary." Then a mountain lion came crashing through a window, striking the Christmas tree! It ran around the house and jumped up on the table, eating the turkey and the food and a couple of human legs as it bit. The family ran out of the house screaming hysterically until a man grabbed a shotgun to kill the mountain lion.

The animals were running for their lives out of Yellowstone National Park, up into the hills and mountains. Another family was having Christmas dinner and a bear broke into their home through a window, knocking the Christmas tree down and attacking screaming people! The big grizzly ate their food, breaking the table and crushing chairs! It ate all the food in the house before it was shot with a shotgun!

A quiet family was celebrating Christmas when suddenly *boom!* and the picture window smashed through, knocking over the Christmas tree. A bison was crashing this Christmas get-to-gether and it ate their food before it was shot dead with a rifle!

Other families suffered more attacks from animals running out of the park. A goat came crashing through a window at another house as it was tossed into the air from an earthquake. A bear broke into a nursing home, chasing a bunch of old ladies around before it got trapped in an elevator. Screaming ladies ran out of the nursing home out into the snow. Some of them were half naked!

Another grizzly bear broke into a hospital and doctors and nurses were throwing things at it. The bear busted through a wall and broke some windows. It ran out in the snow with a human leg in its mouth and police shot the animal dead! A man was killed in the hospital when the bear bit his leg off! A hawk crashed into a window at the same hospital then it was flying through the halls as all the patients started screaming. A doctor threw a piece of ham out for the bird to eat and a second doctor bashed the hawk's head in with a metal crutch!

A man was on a snowmobile leaving the park and a bear knocked him off and ate him! The snowmobile hit a tree and burst into flames, scaring the bear off with the man still in its mouth! The bear took the man into the woods for a meal! The molten rock started bubbling aboveground and flowing into the lake. Any animals still in the park were soon dead.

Fiery lava started erupting out of Old Faithful, triggering a mega explosion launching powerful earthquakes and firestorms. It went on all day Christmas Day and into the night. chasing animals into residential areas. Military helicopters were flying over Yellowstone National Park and saw there was lava flowing aboveground everywhere! The entire lake was glowing and the helicopters quickly exited the area.

December 26, 2024, Yellowstone was melting away and strong earthquakes in Utah, Idaho, Wyoming, and Montana were sending people out of their homes into the streets in the freezing cold and deep snow. The ground started opening up, swallowing cars, homes, and businesses into death! Blue and green lightning was coming out of the ground cracked open from the earthquakes, blowing snow high into the air!

Military helicopters flew toward the East Coast until they ran out of gas and had to refuel at another military base. The helicopters sent data to the NASA crew in Vermont.

"Fort Yellowstone Chopper #1 to NASA volcano crew, Edward Fay come in please!"

"This is Edward Fay in Adamsville, Vermont, over!"

"Edward this is Vincent Victoria Volcano speaking. We did a flyover of Yellowstone on Christmas Day and the whole park is on fire. You were right, Yellowstone is ready to blow!"

"Vincent get your crew and everyone out of there and go as far away as you can, because when Yellowstone finally blows it may cover two-thirds of the United States with burning ash. Your best bet: fly out toward the Carolinas or south toward Florida."

Triple V took Edward Fay's advice, flying out of Fort Yellowstone in a private jet. All the planes and helicopters flew out of the military base and landed at other airports on the East Coast and on aircraft carriers out in the Atlantic Ocean.

Nighttime on December 26 and into the next day there were uncontrollable earthquakes and violent geyser explosions! People watched the evening news the day after Christmas all over the US.

"Good evening, we have breaking news on FOX Tonight. Seismologists, scientists, and NASA warn that the Yellowstone super volcano is ready to erupt sometime between Christmas and New Year's. The park was evacuated a couple days ago and scientists say this eruption could be catastrophic! Elaine Ezerins, FOX News Tonight from Vermont."

December 27, 2024, at 1:11 p.m. Yellowstone erupts! Two hours later another eruption; then five hours later a mega eruption! Twenty minutes later the entire lake disappeared in a blast that was unimaginable! Then Yellowstone was blown off the map! This super volcano was the worst one ever on earth, even worse than Krakatoa!

The Yellowstone Caldera exploded like a mega nuclear bomb but two hundred times greater! It was a huge mushroom cloud with lava, fire, rocks, dirt, and water blown more than fifty thousand feet into the stratosphere that will darken the sky for years! The following states were told to evacuate: Wyoming, Idaho, Montana, and Utah. They suffered severe damage and the death toll may never be known!

Ash and pyroclastic flows and lightning storms raced across the United States at a high rate of speed! Nobody knew what to expect but they did know something really bad was happening. The blast was more than three hundred miles wide and the mushroom cloud was two-thirds the size of the United States. The eruption of the Yellowstone Caldera was not done yet; it was still erupting, setting fires thousands of miles away from fallout. News reports said an asteroid struck the Yellowstone Lake at 1:11 p.m. that day, spotted on Weather Doppler Radar. Every state in the US plus Canada and Mexico felt earthquakes during Yellowstone's eruptions.

Back in Adamsville, Vermont, the NASA crew was watching the eruptions on the monitoring screens. Edward Fay was watching the lake eruption unfold and he saw a meteor strike the lake then all the screens went dark. The video returned a few minutes later showing more eruptions.

"Hey crew, did you see this?! A meteor just struck the Yellowstone Lake causing a violent volcanic eruption! There have been several reports of asteroid strikes in Yellowstone for the last three months that may have been threatening this volcano, but it's the first time I saw this happening in broad daylight. I just saw a bright fireball come through the clouds striking the lake then we lost all our data. Now you see nothing but clouds of ash and pyroclastic flow with bolts of lightning striking and fast moving ash rising very high into the upper atmosphere without end! The eruption is still rising and spreading, moving fast! This is bad!" said Edward Fay.

"I saw it; there were two asteroids striking, one after another, both striking the lake then it was *boom!*" said Nathan Rivers.

Edward Fay rewound the video but lost it somehow.

"Nathan, see if you can find the video, I can't find it!"

Nathan and Edward Fay went through all the data and could not find the asteroid strikes.

"Everyone please get together. The Yellowstone super volcano has been threatening eruptions for the last ten years because the magma level crusting the break was triggering stronger erupting geysers, opening up hot springs, killing thousands of animals, and thinning the park for miles every year! According to our data we predicted that Yellowstone was going to erupt by December 28, and it erupted today because of the high lava levels burning in the lake. I was told another asteroid struck Yellowstone on Christmas Day; now I know the asteroid strike was causing all the violent earthquakes. The whole mess sent all the animals running out of the park on a rampage, attacking neighborhoods and breaking into homes, eating Christmas dinners and people!

"I don't know how bad this is going to be but I think a lot of people are going to die. This eruption could cripple all of the United States; we are burning in hell from all these volcano eruptions! Weather patterns are going to get nasty! All it takes is an asteroid strike to blow up Yellowstone! They have been getting bombarded since September. Let's concentrate on our data and find out what we are going to do. We may end up hiding in military bunkers because of violent weather and ash fallout!" said Edward Fay.

Evening news: "Good evening, we have breaking news on KLAX TV Channel 5, Los Angeles. The Yellowstone National Park super volcano erupted just after one o'clock this afternoon, sending ash ten to twenty miles up into the stratosphere. The blast covered about three hundred miles, leaving a path burning to hell! Witnesses and weather radar reported meteor strikes that may have caused Yellowstone to erupt. This is a worldwide panic situation! Yellowstone has been getting reports for the last ten to fifteen years that this super volcano was ready to erupt at any time, according to seismologist Steven Brad from Yellowstone.

"The California National Guard will guide people to evacuation shelters because the weather and ash fallout may get out of control! Please stay indoors; tape windows and seal any open spaces in your homes to avoid beathing in the ash, and do not run air conditioners. Rachel Tippton, KLAX 5 News from LAX Airport."

Yellowstone was still erupting, threatening to split the United States in half. Christmas week and after New Year's the danger of bad weather and ash fallout was about to unfold. The Yellowstone eruptions blew up from "HELL UNDER THE UNITED STATES!" All the way to St. Peter's Gate in the stratosphere, only to be pushed down back to hell. When they land on the earth the devil takes over!

Military planes and helicopters flew between the California mountains, putting down foam to catch some of the ash from Yellowstone. Lightning was seen in the Rocky Mountains and the dark brown mushroom ash cloud could be seen hundreds of miles away. It stood out despite the grey-blue and green sky and violent thunderstorms!

A dust cloud with choking ash, pyroclastic flow, and burning tree limbs raced east at the speed of a jet plane. It burned out the Great Plains, striking cities and burning buildings and killing millions of people! The giant ash cloud went all the way to the Atlantic Ocean!

Screaming people had nowhere to go but underground. Most people chose to go in storm shelters only to get buried alive! Lightning storms, several tornadoes, and deadly straight-line winds flattened everything in their path! The Rocky Mountains were buried in acid snow, choking people to death.

Northern New England and Florida were spared most of Yellowstone's damage. Yellowstone National Park was blown off the map from the continuing violent super eruption, beginning to split the United States in two! What good did it do, military aircraft dumping foam in the mountains? California was ready to fall into the Pacific!

Earthquakes started cracking open the earth, swallowing everything into hell under the United States! The violent Yellowstone super volcano leveled Los Angeles as earthquakes toppled buildings like dominoes and city streets opened up, swallowing them. Fire came up from gas line explosions to finish the job. People and animal skeletons lay all over in L.A.! The Rocky Mountains cracked open, causing more blowjob volcanoes to erupt, all being pulled into the Yellowstone super eruption. The West Coast fell into the Pacific Ocean when the San Andreas Fault gave way from a huge molten rock push from Yellowstone.

Everything from the Rocky Mountains, from Mexico all the way to fuckin' Canada: *gone*! Then a massive tsunami about ten thousand feet high washed over the Rocky Mountains, flooding the plains, burying everything in its path! Cities and residential areas drowned! Tornadoes about five to ten miles wide with over six hundred-mile-per-hour winds reaching from the ground to the beginning of space were being pushed out from this mega Yellowstone super eruption! They did unimaginable damage, digging craters in the ground from the eruption site all the way to the Atlantic Ocean in a straight line.

Lightning bolts about five feet wide coming from the top of the eruption near space were driving craters through the ground about one hundred feet, opening up the earth a little wider so more earthquakes can happen. The lightning bolts fried everything in their path. Positive red lightning from space above Yellowstone's super eruption was so severe it triggered an EMP attack in a two thousand mile radius across the United States. It interrupted the grid across all the United States, Canada, and Mexico for days!

There was no electricity, no lights! Anything that ran with electricity was out, plunging the United States into permanent darkness! The sky was black as midnight day and night, only bright lightning flashes and striking bolts were seen. If you didn't have a generator you were fucked! The EMP affected areas triggered by the positive red lightning bolts had no electricity indefinitely!

No cars could run, no TV, computers were completely in darkness. The wind was just as bad as the Yellowstone super blowjob coming straight down from the eruption at the speed of a jet plane!

A man was standing over Yellowstone's crater with a fishing pole—he's going fishing in a hot spring! How the hell he got there after all this...then he fell in the crater and he was gone! *IT WAS A GHOST!*

The ash cloud covered the Atlantic Ocean all the way to Europe. It continued around the globe, thickening. The world was about to experience a nuclear winter!

———

February 2025. Yellowstone finally stopped blowing its fuckin' load! Nobody knew; the West Coast had disappeared and the earthquakes continued until the United States split in two! More tidal waves, ten thousand feet high or better, flooded all of the United States. Believe it or not people were surfing them—can you believe it?! But they were ghosts!

The only states that survived were Vermont, New Hampshire, Maine, and Florida! Cape Cod broke off from the Massachusetts mainland, taking Rhode Island with it! Connecticut and Massachusetts burned in the ashes then drowned in the floods.

The Yellowstone super volcano killed three-fourths of the world's population by the year 2030. Those who survived were waiting for a rocket trip to Mars hoping for a better life! The NASA volcano crew had to fly back out to investigate the Yellowstone super blowjob to find out why it was a global killer! When the chopper reached the blast site, ash got caught in the engine and the helicopter crashed into hell under the United States, killing everyone aboard!

THE END

ABOUT THE AUTHOR

Richard Rezendes worked at Brown University and the East Greenwich, Rhose Island school department before retiring at age of sixty-two. He likes sports, football, basketball, and baseball, in that order. He is a bowler tenpins and currently holds a 220 average. His dream was to one day publish a book, and he has since published four—*Ground of the Devil, The Revelation of Emma Grace, A Haunting in Mattapoisett,* and *Hell Under the United States.*

www.ingramcontent.com/pod-product-compliance
Lightning Source LLC
Chambersburg PA
CBHW050925030726
47503CB00007BB/2464